W9-BDL-428

Victoria
Christopher
Murray

truth be told

A NOVEL

A TOUCHSTONE BOOK
PUBLISHED BY SIMON & SCHUSTER
New York   London   Toronto   Sydney

TOUCHSTONE
Rockefeller Center
1230 Avenue of the Americas
New York, NY 10020

TOUCHSTONE and colophon are registered trademarks of Simon & Schuster, Inc.

Designed by Jan Pisciotta

Manufactured in the United States of America

ISBN 0-7394-4394-1

During the final stages of writing this book, my husband, Ray Allen Murray, passed away suddenly. It was only God's grace that sent me back to the computer to complete this novel. And as the Lord always does, He sent angels to help me work through the darkest hours of my life.

So to those whom God sent, I dedicate this book:

Cecile Christopher, my sister, who from the moment she heard the news took hold of my hand and never let go. The younger sibling became the wiser one as she sat with me, and for months took care of my every need.

Dr. Beverly "BAM" Crawford, my pastor, who helped me to stand, reminding me that the way through all of this was to lean on God. Her love, prayers, and hour-long telephone Bible studies allowed me to take my first steps.

Ruth and Elvis Murray, Ta'shara Murray Riedel and Allen Riedel, Veronica and Joseph Austin, Tracy and Walter Downs, Rick and Marie Pogue, Kimberla and Will Roby, Patricia Haley and Jeffrey Glass, Portia Cannon, Eric Jerome Dickey, Lolita Files, E. Lynn Harris, Kay Smith-Holt, Dee Sanford, my friends and family who formed a united alliance, a protective hedge. Each helped me to take small steps toward a future that I did not want to face. My friends reminded me what I had forgotten—that I had much more of a life to live, and that's what Ray would have wanted.

Special thank-yous to my sorors of Delta Sigma Theta Long Beach Alumnae chapter, Brandi Jones, president. There are no words to express how much I appreciate your love, support, concern, prayers, and friendship. I love all of you.

Also I must thank the hundreds of friends and readers who sent cards, letters, thoughts, and prayers. You all helped me through.

All of you have my love and complete gratitude. It is only because of you that today I smile and am able to appreciate the wonderful life that God has given me.

Chapter 1

"You're going to be the first female mayor of Los Angeles!"

Thunderous applause exploded inside the Biltmore's Colonnade Room.

"You forgot the first black female mayor," a woman bellowed above the noise.

Grace Monroe smiled into the crowd of rainbow faces. She motioned with her hands to quiet her supporters. "Thank you, but my focus is not on the mayor's office. I want to serve the people of the Eighteenth District—you, who with your confidence and countless dedicated hours have elected me today as your councilwoman."

A roar reverberated through the room. Grace glanced over her shoulder. Behind her, Conner beamed. Next to him stood their daughters, whose smiles matched the ones in the crowd. Jayde, her fifteen year old, raised her thumb in the air.

Grace turned toward her constituents as the cheers faded. Her smile disappeared. She scanned the quieting crowd for unfamiliar eyes. She shook her head to dislodge those thoughts. Out of more than two hundred people in the room, she knew fewer than fifty. Eager faces stared back at her, and she cleared her throat.

"I will fulfill my campaign promises—the most important being that our children receive the education they deserve. We're going to begin with morals and ethics." Minutes passed before she was able to continue through the applause. "We will address the questions that are important to you. We will provide solutions to the challenges of drugs and teenage pregnancy." Another eruption of applause. "I thank you for your commitment, but remember, this is the beginning. We must work hard to make the Eighteenth District of Los Angeles a model community, an example for the nation." She paused for just a moment. "God bless you."

Silver globes, reminiscent of the disco decade, glittered from the high ceilings as strobes swept rainbow meteors across the room. Bass tones blasted, and then Jeffrey Osborne's baritone serenaded the crowd, turning Grace's feelings into song.

We're going all the way.

Grace swayed to the music as her family joined her at the podium. Conner entwined his fingers in his wife's and raised her hand in the air in victory. "I am so proud of you. Congratulations, Councilwoman." His lips grazed her ear.

She shined with pride as he kissed her cheek, and the crowd cheered their approval. She could feel her daughters on her other side.

Amber giggled. "Mommy, the music is so loud."

Grace laughed, stooped, and hugged her seven year old. Then she pulled Jayde into her arms.

"Congratulations, Mom," Jayde grinned.

Grace smiled, relieved that her teenager was in the mood for the celebration.

"Well done, dear." Grace turned at the sound of her mother's voice. Lily had squeezed between her grandchildren to stand at her daughter's side. Grace hugged her mother.

Lily patted her daughter's back as they embraced. "I'm proud of you." As Grace pulled away, her mother whispered, "The only thing missing is your sister. . . ." Grace shrugged from her mother's arms, her smile gone.

Before a tick clicked on the clock, Conner stepped between the two women and put his arm around his wife. "The cameras, honey," he said through lips that hardly moved. He motioned toward the crowd with his dimpled chin.

Grace returned to center stage, her practiced smile in place. She waved, then took Conner's hand and moved toward the curtains behind them. Lily and the girls followed. Before she was two steps backstage, Zoë, her campaign manager and now chief of staff, ran toward her with headphones covering her braids and a clipboard in her hand.

"Grace, Channel 2 wants the first interview. We should give it to them because their polls supported us, and they were the fairest in reviewing our platform." She took one glance at the clipboard, then added, "Next, we'll go to Channel. . . ."

Grace held up her hand. "Zoë, take a breath."

Zoë stared speechless for a moment, then smiled. "Have I congratulated you?" She squinted, as if trying to remember.

"No, you haven't." Grace hugged her. "And I haven't thanked you." She squeezed Zoë's hand. "Tell Channel 2 that I'll be right there." Zoë nodded and rushed away. Grace shook her head, knowing that in five minutes, she'd be back with three more interviews arranged.

"Girl, girl, girl!" Devry clapped, and Grace laughed at her sister-in-law. "You did it!"

Grace hugged Devry, then stepped back when she felt the gentle swell of her sister-in-law's belly between them. "Don't want to hurt the baby."

Devry laughed. "Girl, Baby Monroe is having a blast. Just like the rest of us." She took Grace's hand. "I'm so proud of you."

"It's still unbelievable," Grace said. Then her eyes wandered over Devry's shoulder into the face of Conner—only the man didn't have her husband's eyes. Chandler's were a tint lighter than Conner's dark brown ones. As she hugged her brother-in-law, she thought for the thousandth time that the doctors had been mistaken—they couldn't be fraternal twins.

The family's circle was infiltrated by others, from campaign workers to church members, all offering their congratulations. As she stood in the crowd's midst, Grace stepped away in her mind. With the music blaring at levels that would make an audiologist cringe, Grace felt as if she was in the middle of a Times Square New Year's celebration. She smiled. It was a new year—a new beginning for a community that she loved and another new start for her. God just continued giving her new blessings.

Grace joined the crowd again and continued hugging and kissing her well-wishers until her cheeks ached from the smile she'd worn since all three networks declared her the victor.

"Honey, we should get out there," Conner said. "There're a lot of people to meet and greet."

She nodded and turned to Jayde and Amber. "Give me a hug, ladies. Are you sure you have everything?"

Amber nodded and embraced her mother. "Yes, Mommy."

When Grace turned to Jayde, her older daughter stood with her arms crossed. "I don't know why I have to go to Nana's. There are other kids here," she said, peeking through the stage's curtains.

Grace stroked Jayde's cheek. "You have school tomorrow, and that's all that counts." She kissed her, then stepped back as Conner kissed their daughters good-bye.

Grace turned to her mother. "Thanks, Mom."

"There's nothing I like more than having my grandbabies with me."

Conner motioned to Frank Austin, Grace's driver, that Lily and the girls were ready. He waited until they were out of view and then, with pandemonium still surrounding them, pulled Grace into his arms. "Well, Miss Councilwoman," he began, and kissed her nose. "It's time for my personal congratulations." He paused, becoming serious. "I wish we could leave now for our own celebration."

Her eyes glittered. She pulled away and faked a yawn. "It's been a long day." She looked at her watch. "Let's sneak out in five minutes."

"What would Channel 2 say?" He laughed. "But the quicker we make our appearance, the quicker we'll be able to escape." He put his arm around her waist. "Come on, Councilwoman Monroe, the people want you." He took her hand. "Just remember that your husband wants you more."

As Zoë led them into the waiting crowd, neither noticed the woman whose eyes watched them and whose steps matched theirs as she moved along the room's perimeter.

Grace leaned against the Suburban and laughed at Conner, whose arms were spread wide.

"I'm not kidding," he said. "I'm going to carry you over the threshold."

"You didn't have anything to drink, and you don't do drugs, so this must be mad cow disease."

He pursed his lips as if he was annoyed, but he couldn't hide his smile. "I've done this before."

"Fifteen years ago. You were younger, and I weighed . . . less." She paused when she saw the laughter in his eyes. "Are you making fun of me?"

He held up his hands. "Never, because you are more beautiful today than the day we married." He held his arms open to her again.

She shrugged. "Okay."

He lifted her, then grunted.

"I told you." She laughed as he struggled. A moment later, she squealed as he raised her high, letting her rest on his shoulder.

"Ssshhh. The neighbors," Conner huffed.

They laughed as he staggered into the house, wobbling through the long hallway, then letting her slip from his arms right under the living room arch, the special place where they had renewed their wedding vows ten years before.

"I can't believe you did that." She laughed and smoothed her red Tadashi suit over her waist.

"And I can't believe that you had doubts about winning this election." The smile left his face. "Grace, the city is blessed to have you . . . and so am I."

Her eyes burned with warmth. It was more than his words that made her want to cry. In his eyes, she saw their history. In his tone, she heard him say, "I forgive you," all over again.

She stroked his face, then brushed her lips against his.

He kissed her and, with his tongue, erased every memory of the election until their thoughts were of themselves alone. He took her hand, pulling her into the living room. He used the dimmer to lower the lights to their softest glow before he led her to the couch.

He kissed her again, then turned away, moving to the entertainment center that covered one wall. With the press of one button music, filled the room.

My love, there's only you in my life, the only thing that's right. . . .

Grace's eyes followed Conner as he walked across the room and turned off the lights. The room was illuminated only by the outside streetlights that filtered through the sheer curtains hanging at the living room's tripanel bay window.

Conner stretched his hand forward, lifting her from the couch. They leaned together, two lines in poem, swaying to Lionel Richie's serenade.

Grace laid her head against Conner's chest, closed her eyes, and sank into the words that she and Conner had first danced to at their wedding.

Two hearts. Two hearts that beat as one.

Grace was sure the song had been written for them.

Our lives have just begun.

As the music continued, Conner lifted her chin and pressed his mouth against hers, gently pushing her back until her legs pressed against the couch. They continued their horizontal dance until they heard the three beeps of the alarm indicating that a door had been opened.

Startled, Conner and Grace slipped from their embrace and jumped from the couch. The chandelier in the foyer brightened the entire front of the house.

"Mommy, why are the lights off?" Amber asked.

Grace smoothed her skirt as she rushed toward the foyer, while Conner turned off the music.

"What are you doing here?" Grace asked, glancing from her mother to her daughters.

Jayde yawned. "Amber wanted to come home."

"You did too," Amber asserted. Then she leaned against Grace.

Grace looked at her mother. "Mom, it's almost midnight."

"I know, honey, but when Amber started crying, I thought it best to bring them here. I didn't think you'd be home. I was going to put them to bed and wait for you."

Grace opened her mouth, then shook her head. "Come on," she said to her daughters. "Let me get you to bed. You have school in the morning." She looked at her mother.

Conner said, "I'll take care of the girls."

"I told you we should have stayed with you," Jayde smirked, as she trotted up the winding staircase.

Grace was silent until her husband disappeared with their daughters. "Mom, they should be in bed."

"I'm sorry." Lily moved toward the kitchen. "I thought this was better than having Amber cry all night. She's so spoiled."

Grace followed her mother. "It must have been the excitement. Amber hasn't done that in a long time. Anyway, do you want to stay here instead of driving back home?"

Lily shook her head and ran her hand through her closely cropped white-gray afro as she sat at the kitchen table. "No, I just want a quick cup of coffee." When Grace stood still, with her arms folded, staring at her mother, Lily added, "Decaf, of course."

With a sigh, and a shrug, Grace set the coffee maker, then pulled a mug from the cabinet, setting it heavily on the counter.

"I said I was sorry," Lily exclaimed, then paused, twisting her lips into a lopsided grin. "And I'm sorry that we interrupted you and Conner. Looks like you weren't expecting anyone."

Grace smiled and sat with her mother. Her fingers danced on the table to the rhythm of Lionel still singing in her head.

"You have a good husband."

Grace's smile widened.

"Not every man would stand by his wife. . . ."

Grace's fingers stopped. "Mom!"

Lily held up her hands. "I'm just speaking the truth."

"And you speak it every chance you get."

"I want you to remember."

"With you, there's no chance of forgetting." Grace paused. "Mom, my mistakes were long ago forgiven and forgotten. I know I have a wonderful husband, and now Conner knows that he has a terrific wife." Another moment passed. "Can we change the subject?"

Lily shrugged, giving herself just enough time to gasp new air. "When was the last time you called your sister?"

"Argh!" Grace stood, walked to the counter and opened the cabinet above the sink. The blue plastic cups were stacked, waiting for her to fill one with coffee, drop in a plastic stirrer, and send her mother on her way.

"I guess the subject of your sister is off-limits too," Lily huffed.

Grace raised her glance toward the ceiling. "Help me, Lord," she whispered, before facing her mother with the coffee pot in one hand and the mug in the other. She walked toward the table, feeling the heat rise through the pot's cover.

Lily held up her hand, stopping Grace. "Not too much. I don't want to stay long."

Grace had a myriad of retorts but said nothing. She poured the coffee, filling the mug less than a third full—just enough for a few sips. They sat in silence as Lily blew on the liquid and then swallowed the coffee in just a bit more than a gulp. When she finished, she stared at her daughter.

Grace tried not to sigh as she refilled her mother's cup. When she finished pouring, she said, "No, Mom. I haven't spoken to Mabel."

"Your sister's name is Starlight now."

Grace groaned inside and hoped her silence would keep her from being pulled into this conversation. But silence didn't stop Lily. "I wish you two would settle your differences. The only thing that matters is that you're sisters."

"Mom, we'll never agree, so can we not talk about this?"

Lily shook her head, and tsked. "You should have included your sister tonight. Don't be judgmental, Grace. Conner forgave you."

Grace's eyes thinned to slits. The ticking of the pear-shaped clock above the sink that Conner helped Jayde make in a fifth-grade science project punctuated the seconds of their silence. She finally cut through the quiet. "Mom, I don't have to forgive Mabel. She didn't do anything to me. I just don't like how she takes advantage of women." She stood from the table. "Second, I am blessed that my husband has forgiven me. But that's between Conner and me only."

Lily glared at her daughter.

Grace leaned against the counter and folded her arms. "Are you finished?"

Lily looked down at her mug still filled with coffee. She returned her glance to Grace. "I've had just about enough." She stood and marched through the hallway back to the foyer. At the front door, she whipped around. "I forgot my . . ."

Grace handed the oversized Coach bag to her mother.

Lily slung the purse over her shoulder, then lowered her eyes.

"Mom, are you going to be okay? Conner can follow you home."

She waved her hand. "I don't want to be any more trouble. . . ."

"I know you want Mabel . . ." Grace paused at Lily's disapproving glance. "You want Starlight and me to be close, but we're not. You have to accept that."

Lily shook her head. "Family is the most important thing."

She looked into Grace's eyes. "And now that you're both successful, you should stop this stupid competition."

She wanted to tell Lily there was no competition, but she said nothing.

Lily continued, "Make peace."

That will never happen, Grace thought. But as she looked at her mother's mournful eyes, she said, "Maybe one day, Mom."

Sadness slumped Lily's shoulders, making her five-foot-two frame even more petite.

Grace softened and pulled her mother into her arms. Lily felt like a porcelain doll that would crack under the slightest pressure. It always amazed Grace that such a small woman had birthed two daughters, who with their five-foot-eight and -nine frames were Amazons compared to their mother.

The strain of her daughters' estranged relationship weighed heavy on Lily; Grace could see that. And since her second husband's death over two years before, it seemed even more important for Lily to bring her daughters together.

"Mom, I'll give Mabel . . . Starlight a call." Grace wasn't sure if she was speaking the truth, but when Lily smiled, she was glad she'd spoken.

Lily planted a soft kiss on her daughter's cheek.

Grace opened the front door, and together they stepped onto the brick walkway into the coolness of the April night. Lily slipped inside her Toyota Camry and, through the closed window, wiggled her fingers, waving good-bye, saying thank-you. Grace stood in place until her mother's car vanished into the night.

Grace returned inside, slumped against the door, and wondered how the sweetness of the day had shifted to the sourness she now felt.

"I heard some of that."

She raised her glance to the second-floor landing and smiled when Conner stretched his arms, beckoning her. Weariness pressed her down as she climbed the stairs. Conner held her for several moments before he switched off the light, darkening the house's interior.

They took two steps when Grace stopped. "Let me check on the girls."

Conner took her hand before she could turn away. "Already done." He pulled her into their bedroom. "It's time for you and me." He lowered his lips to hers, pressing her against the closed door. "Where were we?"

Grace shut her eyes, trying to fall into the feeling, but she couldn't find the place where she'd been before the girls burst in. It took only a minute for Conner to lean away. Her eyes apologized, but he brought his finger to her lips, telling her there was nothing to be sorry about. Then he took her hand and moved to their hand-carved canopy bed. As she sat on the edge, he removed her pumps, then massaged her feet before he stood and slid her jacket from her shoulders. He lowered his lips to her neck as he unbuttoned her satin blouse.

Grace moaned, dropping her head back so that she could receive her husband's warm lips. In less than a minute, Conner had his wife naked above the waist, but when she reached for his belt, he pushed her hands away. He laid her on the bed, rolled her onto her stomach, and slipped her skirt from her hips.

She closed her eyes and moaned even before his fingers began to push and pull against her skin. Her gasps were deep under his touch, and she melted under his fingers. Moments later, she drifted asleep.

Grace wasn't sure how long Conner worked, providing her pleasure, but she didn't awaken until he turned off the light and slid onto the cool sheets next to her.

Conner pulled her against him. She stretched, pushing her back against his chest.

"I love loving you," he whispered.

"Hmmm," was all she could manage, weak from the release Conner's fingers had afforded her.

He squeezed his arms around her. "I would do anything for you, Grace."

She was almost asleep again when he spoke, but she heard him. She snuggled deeper into his arms, secure in knowing his words were the absolute truth.

Chapter 2

"Mommy, what am I wearing to school?"

Grace opened her eyes, then shut them as the sun squeezed through the bottom of the window shade. Behind her, she heard Conner's soft snore. She pushed herself from the bed and reached for her navy silk robe draped over the chaise.

"Mommy!"

She wrapped the robe's belt around her waist. Her eyes were still heavy when she opened the door. Both Jayde and Amber stood in front of her—Jayde fully dressed in jeans (with more holes in them than in a slice of swiss cheese), a white T-shirt, and navy blazer, with headphones to the CD player that was clipped to her waist around her neck.

But Amber stood in the chill hallway covered only by her underwear. "Mommy, Jayde won't help me."

"She didn't want to put on what I told her to." Jayde shook her head. "It's a no-brainer, stupid," she said to her sister. "You're supposed to wear what you would've if we had stayed with Nana."

Grace said, "Jayde, don't call your sister stupid."

Amber stuck her tongue out at Jayde. "See, you're the one who's stupid."

Grace pulled Amber down the hall. "What did I tell you about walking around without your bathrobe?"

"I'm sorry, Mommy."

When she stood outside Amber's bedroom door, Grace said, "Jayde, thank you for getting your sister up. And change those pants. I don't want you wearing them to school."

Jayde rushed to Amber's bedroom door. "Mom, I love these. Everyone's wearing them."

"And you think that's going to change my mind?" Grace raised one eyebrow, indicating the end of the conversation. "And make sure you eat before you leave."

Jayde pouted. "I'm not hungry."

Grace sighed. She had read countless books offering advice on surviving the teenage years. But she could write volumes that would shock the experts. And what wore her down was the thought that by the time she made it through Jayde's teen battlefield, her sweet Amber would be poised to wage a new war.

"Jayde," Grace said with all the patience she could gather. "Eat something." She combed through the bag she'd packed for Amber yesterday.

"Mom, I called Brittany, and her mother is driving us to school," Jayde whined, "so I have to be ready." When Grace turned around, Jayde lowered her head, then sulked down the hall. "Why do I have to eat when there are people starving in Africa?"

"Remember to change your jeans," Grace yelled, just before she heard Jayde's bedroom door slam.

"Mommy, who's going to take me to school?" Amber asked, as Grace helped her push her arms through the white blouse.

"I'll have to, since we canceled the school bus."

Amber's eyes watered with sadness. "I'm sorry, Mommy. I wanted to come home last night because I was worried about you."

Grace stopped buttoning her daughter's shirt. "Why, sweetie?"

"I didn't want all of those people to bother you."

Grace pulled Amber into her arms. "Honey, no one is going to bother me . . . or you." She loosened her embrace. "I'm going to make sure that we're always safe."

Amber's downturned lips slipped into a smile. "I'm still sorry that you have to take me to school."

"Why don't I take you?"

Grace's and Amber's glances lifted at the same time.

Amber ran to her father. "Yeah, Daddy. You take me, and Mommy can go back to bed."

"That's what I was thinking." Conner grinned and leaned over, kissing Grace's cheek. "I'll get rid of this child and return before you have time to dream about what we're going to do."

Amber cocked her head at her father's words, and Grace knew a question was coming. When her daughter remained silent, Grace asked, "What about the office?"

"I told them I wouldn't be in. Today, it's just you and me and the bed."

She shook her head. "You're incorrigible."

"Mommy, what does that mean?"

"Ask your father," Grace said, trying to hold her laughter. When Conner shrugged his shoulders, Grace said, "Amber, let's finish getting ready for school." She held up the denim skirt.

"Give me a few minutes." Conner kissed Grace before he turned from the room.

Grace helped Amber into her skirt, then in the kitchen, filled a bowl with Cocoa Puffs.

Jayde slinked in, her headphones covering her ears. She moaned as she dropped a slice of raisin bread into the toaster and stuffed a banana into her packed book bag.

"Do you have money for lunch?" Grace asked, raising her voice to be heard over Jayde's music.

Jayde lowered her headphones. "Yes," she said, tossing her micro-braids over her shoulder. The wrinkles in her forehead disappeared. "But I can always use more." She grinned as she grabbed her toast.

"Good try." Grace kissed Jayde. "Have a great day."

"You too, Mom," Jayde said cheerfully, the discussion of money changing her attitude.

Grace shook her head as Jayde finished her toast in just a few bites, then rushed through the front door. She clicked on the TV on the counter before she sat the cereal bowl in front of Amber. "Be careful, sweetie." Grace covered her daughter with an over-sized napkin. "Your father will be down in a bit."

Amber's eyes were already plastered to *Tom and Jerry* as Grace ran up the stairs.

In the bedroom, Conner sat on the bed, slipping into his sweatpants. He smiled. "Do you want to pray now?"

She nodded, and he took her hand as they knelt at their bed-side.

"Dear Heavenly Father," Conner began, "we come to you with praise and thanksgiving, raising before you the gifts you have blessed us with . . . our children. Lord, give unto Jayde and Amber perfect hearts to keep thy commandments, thy testimonies and thy statutes, and to do all these things, in Jesus's name."

"Amen," they said together.

It was a simple prayer that they prayed daily, patterning their words after David's prayer in 2 Chronicles for his son Solomon.

Grace slid under the bed covers, and Conner grinned as he pulled a pair of socks from the dresser. He leaned toward her, but before their lips could meet, the phone rang. They sighed, and Grace reached for the phone on the nightstand.

"Hi, Marilyn." Grace's shoulders sagged as she looked at Conner. He mouthed no, and shook his head.

"Congratulations, Grace," Marilyn said. "We're all so excited here."

Grace breathed, relieved. At least Conner's assistant wasn't calling for him. "Thanks." Grace's glance followed Conner as he moved toward the closet, her gaze focused on his naked torso.

"Well, Marilyn, thanks for calling," she said eager to dismiss the woman.

"Is Conner there?"

Grace's smile faded. "Yes." Her simple answer was meant to deter Marilyn.

But Marilyn continued. "May I speak with him? It's important."

Grace wanted to hang up as Conner pulled his sweatshirt over his head, then walked to the dresser for his watch. Once he took this call, it would become a war of wills—whether to stay with his wife or service his clients. In this place, at this time, she wouldn't win. He was as committed to his work as she was to hers.

"Grace," Marilyn said again.

"Hold on a second." Grace put her hand over the receiver. "Marilyn said it's important."

Grace tossed the cordless phone toward Conner with more force than she expected. The phone's tip smashed into a silver-framed photo of the four Monroes. The picture seemed to float as it descended toward the floor and hit the carpet, splattering glass slivers across the room.

"My goodness." Grace jumped from the bed.

Conner picked up the phone, then stepped with caution over the glass. He sat on the bed as Grace moved toward the fallen family photograph. "I'll clean it up," he said.

Grace picked up the photo and stared at the picture taken a year before, when she'd declared her candidacy. Conner was standing with his arms around her, with the girls in front. Exhilaration covered their faces, though she knew her children didn't understand the enormity of her decision.

Before she decided to run for office, Grace had considered the effect it might have on her family. They were a strong unit, bound together even more by their tragedies. But they'd danced through their storms, and now their future was clear of any clouds.

The campaign had been clean, thank God, though Grace had held her breath. But her opponent, Samuel Douglas, had played only two cards—her inexperience and her religious conviction.

"My opponent has served only on the school board. No one with so little experience can serve a community like the Eighteenth District. Also, Ms. Monroe has made it very clear where she stands in terms of her Christian beliefs. We cannot allow politics to mix with religion. We are a mixture of black and white, Christians, Jews, Muslims, Protestants, and Catholics. We live in a great country that calls for the separation of church and state."

That was the worst of it. And she'd held onto her convictions throughout the campaign.

"I am not saying that everyone has to share my beliefs," Grace had said at her campaign rallies. "What I am saying is that I am a woman of God who will seek to do what is right for everyone. No matter what your beliefs are, you must see that there is a negative correlation between the increase of violence among our children and the absence of prayer in the schools. Children are wielding guns instead of praying for friends, family, and country. There is a breakdown in the family and an increase of sexually active teenagers. The question we must ask is, What has to be done to change this? I'm talking about morals, and honor, and a belief in something besides the sex on television, the anarchy in music, and the violence in movies."

It had been a risky platform, but one she believed in. She didn't want to be councilwoman if she couldn't bring her faith with her. The electorate had agreed, though it had been a tough race. She'd won with fifty-five percent of the vote.

As her eyes remained glued to the photograph, she said a silent prayer of gratitude. God had certainly bestowed blessings on them.

Grace looked over her shoulder, but the smile that accompanied her thoughts turned upside down. She recognized the crease in Conner's forehead.

"You have no idea who this woman is?" she heard Conner ask. The lines in his face deepened.

Grace moved to sit next to him. She took his hand. *Go ahead,* she mouthed.

"Okay, Marilyn," he said. "I'll be there in about an hour." He hung up and turned to Grace. "I promise I'll be back before you can say, 'Thank God for my husband.' "

She nodded.

"I wouldn't go in at all, but a woman has been calling the office saying she has an emergency only I can handle."

"Who is it?"

He shrugged. "I don't know, but . . ." He stopped as Grace

stood and slipped her robe from her shoulders. The silk fluttered to the floor, settling around her ankles.

Conner's glance roamed over his wife's nakedness. "I can't believe I'm letting this woman take me away from you."

Grace put her arms around his neck and pressed against his torso. "Don't be fooled, honey. I'm letting you go to the office. If I wanted, there'd be no way for you to leave."

"You got that right," he said, pulling her closer.

He aimed for her lips, but the sudden knock on their door stopped them from kissing. "Daddy, I'm ready," Amber sang.

"It's a conspiracy to keep us apart." She chuckled and grabbed her robe.

He shook his head. "They'll never win."

"Daddy!"

"Honey, I'm going to take you to school," Grace yelled through the door. "Give me a minute."

She turned toward her closet, but Conner pulled her back. "Do you think we can get Lily to take the girls tonight?"

She laughed. "Not a chance." She paused and fluttered her eyes. "But if you hurry back, we'll have lots of time. Amber's going to Nicole's house after school, and Jayde has tennis practice. So it will be you and me and whatever your mind can conceive."

"Promises, promises."

She nodded. "You just keep whatever you had in mind on your mind, and I'll take care of the rest."

She sashayed toward the closet.

Conner shook his head. "Whatever this woman wants better be important." He paused. "Let's meet back here at two."

"If you can wait that long," she purred over her shoulder. He laughed, then went down the hall. Grace smiled as she jumped into a sweat suit and listened to Conner's off-key serenade as he pulled the vacuum into the bedroom.

"You'll always be, my endless love."

Conner was still singing when she stepped from the closet. The vacuum whirred, sucking glass from the carpet. Grace kissed him, then stood at the door watching for a moment. Even through his sweatshirt, she could see his back muscles flexing as he pushed the cleaning machine.

I cannot wait to get back here, she thought, before she stepped into the hallway and closed the door behind her.

Chapter 3

Starlight took another sip of coffee, her eyes plastered to the newspaper. She squinted as the sun's light cast a glare over the article. The brightness of this penthouse was one of the reasons she'd chosen it. This was the first morning she'd had time to relax in the breakfast nook. She looked toward the windows. Even though she didn't want to cover the glass, she'd have to find something to soften the light.

She returned to the paper. *Monroe is the first candidate to win on a totally Christian platform. . . .*

"Still reading about your sister?"

She forced herself to look up. "Did you get me all the newspapers?"

Lexington, her assistant, nodded. "Every one." He settled across from her. "Still think . . . big mistake not going to the celebration last night. Grace would've been surprised."

Starlight smoothed the paper onto the table. "Surprise doesn't describe what my sister would have felt if I'd walked into that ballroom." Her glance returned to the newspaper.

Lexington lifted the coffee pot from the table and filled his cup. He took a sip and grimaced. "Awful . . . it's cold."

"Carletta," Starlight called.

A moment later, a stocky woman appeared cradling a pile of purple towels. "Yes, Ms. Starlight?"

"The coffee is cold," she said without looking up.

Carletta laid the towels on the couch and ambled through the maze of moving boxes that filled the room. She grabbed the pot, then disappeared into the kitchen.

Lexington picked up one of the papers Starlight had discarded. "Can't believe Grace did it. Didn't think she had a chance."

"Why?" Starlight asked, still not raising her head. "Every poll said she was ahead."

"Polls said she was in a dead heat."

Starlight looked up. "Same thing. If an incumbent can't beat you in the polls, he certainly can't win at the polls."

Lexington waved his hand in the air. "Never believe the polls; believe only facts. The Eighteenth District is one of the few predominantly white communities left in the city."

"And that means?"

"White people don't vote for us."

She shook her head. "Maybe in your mind. But it's not about color. Grace is part of that Christian coalition, and with all that's going on in this world, that's all that matters to white folks." Starlight stood and walked to the gold-trimmed french balcony doors. From her thirtieth-floor window, she could barely see the traffic below on Ocean Boulevard, but across the street, she had a one-point-two-million-dollar view of the Pacific Ocean.

"It makes me laugh sometimes," Starlight began, though there was no humor in her tone. "My sister judges me so harshly, but really, we do the same thing. We say the same thing. Our goals are the same. But she doesn't see it." Starlight sighed.

"What Grace thinks certainly doesn't bother you."

Starlight turned to her assistant—her armor bearer was what she called him. She liked that term from the first time she heard a pastor refer to someone that way. At that time, she didn't know what it meant, but she knew one day she'd have one. Two years from that date, she had her armor bearer, in the person of Lexington Jackson, and they'd been together for seven years now—actually longer, if she counted the year they spent with Dr. Carr, her mentor.

Although her look had evolved over the years, Lexington's had not. The first time she saw him, he was wearing a navy blue pinstripe suit with a white shirt that had been so starch stiff, she wondered how he moved. Today, his suit was still navy, though absent of the pinstripes. But his shirt could have been the same one he wore the day they'd met.

"Starlight?" he said interrupting her memories. "Your sister doesn't bother you?"

"She doesn't bother me," she affirmed. "I am so over her." Her purple silk robe fluttered at her ankles as she returned to the table.

"Good. 'Cause look at it like this," he continued. "She's playing political footsies while you have a personal banker."

Her eyes narrowed. No matter how many times she told him, he didn't get it. The dollars she earned were great—beyond anything anyone would have imagined for her. But it was what came with the money that made her love this life. She couldn't walk down the street without someone calling out to her, requesting an autograph, or begging to say hello. And she lived for the times when she pulled out her credit card. People fawned when they saw her name. *Starlight.* There was no last name. One day she'd be as famous as those other single monikers: Oprah, Rosie, Whoopi.

Carletta returned with the coffee pot. "Do you want anything else?" Her accent made her words sound more Spanish than English.

Starlight motioned to Lexington. When he shook his head, she said, "That will be all."

Carletta bowed, then rushed to the couch, picked up the towels, and vanished into the hallway.

"I hope she works out," Starlight said. "I hate that I lost Maria."

Lexington said, "She'll be fine. Just a little nervous. She knows she landed the best job in the housekeeping industry. But why do you have her in a uniform?" He laughed as if he'd told a joke

She ignored his question and poured coffee into her cup.

He glanced at his watch. "Need to set a time for a run-through. Gotta practice for tonight."

Starlight closed her eyes. There wasn't a number high enough for the times she'd spoken in the last year. From women's organizations to community centers to corporations across the country and internationally. She'd even appeared on *Good Morning America* and *Dateline*. She'd been everywhere—except a church.

But tonight, she'd be speaking at Greater Faith Chapel, one of the city's super-churches. The main sanctuary held eighty-five hundred, and yesterday Lexington told her that the tickets were sold out. Now they were selling seats for the overflow section.

I'm speaking at a church, she thought to herself. Grace should accept me now. She opened her eyes. "I don't need practice. I want to relax. Maybe I'll go out to lunch."

Lexington leaned back in his chair and clasped his hands behind his head. "What's bothering you? Tell me."

She stared at him. He was her confidant—or so he thought.

He believed they shared everything. That's what she wanted him to think. She said, "There's nothing to tell."

"Doesn't make sense," he said.

She cringed. Sometimes his fragmented style annoyed her.

Lexington continued, "Should be ecstatic today." He covered her hand with his and stroked her fingers. "This is our first church," he whispered. "If we do this right, all kinds of doors will open for us."

She slid her hand away. *Our, we, us?* "I just want to relax," she repeated. She stood, piling all the newspapers into her arms even though she'd read every article. "Meet me back here at six."

He blinked. "I . . . thought I'd hang out with you."

"No need."

"I could help you . . . release some of your tension."

Starlight knew Lexington's smile was meant to be seductive. Instead, he was a twenty-eight year old, wearing an eighty-two-year-old man's leer. For an instant, she thought she might lose her breakfast. "You should leave."

He sat up straighter, his smile gone. "Where should I go?"

She raised her eyebrows, daring him to ask the question again. "Do you remember where you live?" She left him at the table and rushed to her bedroom.

Sitting in the middle of her king-sized bed, she heard Lexington and Carletta exchange mumbles before the front door opened, then closed. Starlight sank back into the eight down-filled pillows. She didn't have any reason to be mad at Lexington. He was the closest person in her life. Maybe that was the problem.

She picked up the *Los Angeles Times* and looked at the picture of Grace waving to reporters after she stepped from the voting booth. Conner was by her side, as he always was, smiling, looking disgustingly doting. The headline read, "Getting to the God Part." It was amazing—her sister had turned a small neighborhood election into front-page news just talking about God.

"And she has the nerve to criticize me?"

Starlight tossed the paper aside. She gazed around the room. This was the only space that looked as if she'd lived in the Santa Monica penthouse for more than two days. In her head, she calculated the cost of her designer furniture and antiques. From the Queen Anne–styled bed to the custom-made chairs, she could have easily spent over thirty thousand dollars in this room alone, though she didn't know since a decorator had chosen everything.

She leaned back and molded one of the purple satin pillows to fit under her neck. She now lay in the lap of opulence, but there was no one who would have bet a nickel on her a few years ago when she worked as a beautician, or when she sold insurance, or when she took classes to become a masseuse. She had taken every sales position available, hawking everything from Amway to Avon.

But ten years after her high school graduation, she still hadn't found her way—until she met Nathan Carr. She had been sitting in the dentist's office, staring at the Victoria's Secret ad in *Cosmopolitan*. She shook her head, marveling at how women could spend fifty dollars on a bra when she didn't even have four dollars to buy another small tube of Orajel. She certainly didn't have the money to pay for this dentist visit, but her gums ached so much that she was willing to write another bad check.

"Must be a good article." She hadn't noticed the gentleman who sat next to her. She looked up, forced a smile, then turned her attention back to the magazine.

"I didn't mean to disturb you," he apologized.

She sighed. "I'm sorry. I'm just not in a good frame of mind."

"Really?" He smiled. "That's my specialty."

She frowned.

"I help people frame their minds."

She wasn't sure what made her put down the magazine. "How do you do that?"

He pulled a card from his jacket. She read the words on the white linen paper: Dr. Nathan Carr, Carr Enterprises, Inspirational Speaker-Author.

"Maybe you've heard of me," he said, drawing her attention back.

She shook her head. "What do you do specifically?"

"I help people find their life's calling," he said through his permanent smile.

He sounded like her pastor, who preached about being called in life. "How do you do that?"

"I teach how to tap into your inner being. To find that power inside so that you can go places you never dreamed."

She had chuckled. "I don't know, Dr. Carr. I've had so many living nightmares, I'm afraid to dream."

"Really? What do you do?"

She grimaced. "I'm in between jobs."

"Ah . . . actually, you're just between successes."

She laughed.

"See, it all depends on how you frame thoughts in your mind."

"So that's why my thoughts are going every which way."

"What do you mean?"

"Right now, I can't even afford a frame."

This time, Dr. Carr laughed. "Well, that might change. What's your name?"

She took his outstretched hand. "Mabel Morgan."

Their conversation continued until she was called in for her appointment. She waited another hour for Dr. Carr to come out of his. She agreed to walk with him around the corner to Denny's, where he treated her to a chicken-fried steak lunch. Then she followed him in her car to Zahra's Books 'N Things, where he impressed her with their collection of his books.

"This was my first book," he said, handing her a thin paperback—*Honor Thyself.* "And this is my latest." This time, it was a two hundred page hardback—*Unleash Your Hidden Gifts.*

She stared at the shelves that contained twelve of his books.

A woman walked up to them. "Dr. Carr? Oh, my God! It is you!"

Mabel had watched as Dr. Carr spoke to the woman, who gushed that she had all of his books and had attended every seminar she could.

"I even went to your three-day conference in Palm Springs. But I missed you at the Forum last month." The woman lowered her voice. "I didn't have the one hundred and seventy-five dollars. But my friends said the place was sold out."

Mabel's eyes widened. One hundred and seventy-five dollars . . . a sold-out Forum. Mabel hadn't graduated at the top of her class, but she didn't need a statistics degree to calculate the numbers. As Dr. Carr continued chatting, Mabel stepped back and considered him with fresh eyes. Now she noticed his suit— tailored. Her glance moved to his polished Italian shoes. The deep burgundy leather matched his suit. She shook her head. It wasn't like her to miss the signs. Yes, she had followed his platinum BMW 740i as they drove to the bookstore, but this was Los Angeles. He could have been sleeping in his car.

Before, she'd seen just the gray that sprinkled his thinning hair, the weathered skin on his hands, and the fact that he would see five-feet five-inches only if he stood on his toes. He was seventy—sixty, at least, and looking as if he'd see ninety in just a few years. But now, he was Denzel with Wesley's body. Nathan Carr was a man with money.

"Well, thank you for your kind words." He shook the woman's hand and turned back to Mabel. "Are you ready?"

She nodded, wondering if it was his soft voice, gentle manner, or the dollar signs that now appeared in his eyes that made her want to follow him.

As they stood at her car, he said, "Mabel, give me a call tomorrow. Our timing just happens to be right. I'm looking for an assistant, and you might fit the position."

It had taken all that was within her to stop herself from throwing her arms around that man in the middle of the Ralph's Foods parking lot. But as she drove home, she began to wonder what Dr. Carr really wanted. After all, how could he offer her a job without knowing anything about her?

Well, whatever he wanted, it didn't matter. She had checks that would hit her bank today and bounce all the way to New Jersey. If he wanted sex, fine. She'd done that before and for much less than a regular paycheck.

But when she met Dr. Carr two days later, she realized only business was on his mind. Although she'd worn her tightest red wrap dress (one size too small, to flaunt her assets), all he looked at were her eyes.

"I see something in you, Mabel, that makes me want to help you become the best you can be. And I always listen to the spirit. I'm going to take you to the top."

The next weeks moved at space shuttle speed. Dr. Carr's office was in his home, in the Wilshire district. That had surprised Mabel—she'd expected a sprawling expanse in Beverly Hills. Within days, she learned one factor of his success: "It's not how much you make, it's how much you keep," he said.

For the next year, she watched. She became his right hand, doing everything from running errands, to attending his seminars and selling his books in the back of the room, to typing and editing his manuscripts. But it was the trips to the bank that she loved. Dr. Carr's personal banker cleared his calendar whenever she walked in. And it was not just the banker who rolled out the royal carpet. From the publisher to the attendees at Dr. Carr's events, everyone wanted to do her bidding. Mabel knew it was so they could get close to Dr. Carr, but that didn't matter. The way the Carr entourage was treated amazed and pleased her.

The Carr retinue was small—just Mabel and a man, Lexington Jackson, whom Dr. Carr called his valet. Besides the two of them, he used outside contractors for everything from typing to sales at the seminars. It lowered expenses and kept his dealings private.

Working for Dr. Carr was the first time Mabel stayed with one employer for more than nine months. But almost eighteen months into her career, it ended. The nation was shocked when Nathan Carr collapsed on stage at his Living Your Best Life seminar.

Mabel mourned with the rest of Dr. Carr's disciples, though her distress came from having to face the question: What am I going to do now? Her despair changed to hope as she sat in the wooden pew in the third row of Unity Baptist Church at Dr. Carr's funeral. As speaker after speaker exalted praises to the man who changed their life, Mabel realized she could do the same thing. She had the knowledge, she had some experience, and she had what she believed to be the sole copy of an unfinished Dr.

Carr manuscript. She would use his outline, fill in the blanks, and complete the book.

For weeks after the funeral, Mabel laid low, watching and waiting to see if any of Dr. Carr's family came forth. When three months had passed, she exhaled. But she knew she couldn't do it alone. That was when she approached Lexington. He wasn't her first choice, but Dr. Carr had taught her that it was important to have someone watching your back—and your front. If Lexington was good enough for the doctor, maybe he would work for her.

She planned her presentation and called Lexington.

"Great idea!" he exclaimed as if she had answered his prayer too.

When she thought about it, she had. Lexington was just twenty-one years old and had worked for Dr. Carr from the moment he had graduated from high school. Where was he going to go?

Six months later, she emerged as Starlight. Dr. Carr's publisher, New Vision Publications, rushed her first book to the market. Starlight suspected her editor, Susan, was aware that Dr. Carr had written much of the book, but she asked no questions. New Vision was eager to continue to capitalize on Dr. Carr's market. It didn't take long to build a following: she was promoted as Dr. Nathan Carr's protégée, the one designated to sustain the self-esteem flame for African Americans.

Now, seven years later, she had taken her business to levels beyond even what Dr. Carr could have imagined.

Starlight stood and stepped onto the terrace. The April morning breeze swept across the balcony, and she tightened her robe. There's only one way to describe this, she thought as she looked onto the beach. I have come a long way.

She saw it best in her mother's eyes. Gone was the look of hopelessness that Lily had carried for having given birth to a child she thought would never amount to anything. Now Lily wore a gleam when she looked at her elder daughter or when she stepped inside her two-bedroom Ladera Heights condo and remembered that it was Starlight who lapped her in luxury. Starlight wanted to give her mother everything—to repay Lily for standing with her through her years of searching and to keep Lily as proud of her as she was of Grace.

Starlight shook her head. With Grace's latest accomplishment, she didn't know where she'd end up on the familial food chain. "This is silly." She stepped back into her bedroom. "We're not kids vying for Mama's affections."

But even as she spoke, she didn't feel foolish. She was in a competition—one that had been rigged from the beginning from when she'd grown up with her mother, her sister, Grace, and Neil, Grace's father. It was more than she could take when she was six and realized that her last name was different from everyone else in the house. She'd cried nightly tears after Neil told her, "You're not my daughter, Mabel, but I love you as if you were."

His words weren't good enough. The baby, Grace, had a father. All she had was an unanswered question when she asked, "Where is my daddy?"

For Starlight, that was where the race began. But even then, Grace was just inches from the finish, while she felt as if she was well behind the starting gate. From Grace's top grades to her discussions (when she was only eight) of which college she would attend, Grace was the shining light in the Hobbs family. Mabel's sole hope was to wear the banner of the bad seed. At least that garnered attention.

But everything had changed. Mabel had emerged as the star,

and she had at last caught up with her sister on the track of life. There was no way that she was going to lose ground.

Starlight moved to the eighteenth-century desk that she'd purchased with her first royalty check. She turned on the light and looked at her notes. It wasn't quite noon, but she was going to spend the afternoon preparing. After tonight, she'd be far ahead in the race.

Chapter 4

The moment Conner opened the door, the applause began. He sauntered into the office, his smile wide.

Kym, the receptionist, was the first to hug him. "Congratulations." The others followed—assistants, law clerks, and attorneys alike.

Conner strolled past the cubicles and outer offices, nodding his head, smiling as if he had won the election. When he got to his office, Marilyn stood, smiling.

"Why the fuss?" Conner chuckled.

"We're happy because we know the man who's married to the new councilwoman," Marilyn gushed.

Conner sat behind his desk. He tapped the tips of his fingers together and looked at the photo of Grace, Jayde, and Amber that sat in the center of his desk.

"We didn't expect you today." Chandler leaned against the door post. "Was sure you'd be home celebrating."

"I'm here for just a minute. I want to get home real quick."

Chandler chuckled and settled in a chair across from his twin. "So did you guys have a big night?"

Conner thought back to the plans that had been deterred, but the night had still been special to him. "Yeah, but I still want to get out of here. Grace won't be having too many early nights."

Chandler nodded. "Why did you come in?"

"Marilyn told me that I got a call."

"Man, you should have passed that to me."

Conner leaned forward onto his desk. His smile faded. "A woman's been calling saying she has an emergency, but that I was the only one who could help."

Chandler matched his brother's posture. "Who is it?"

Conner shrugged. "I don't know. That's why I'm here. I want to take her call and then . . ." He leaned back in his chair and his smile returned. "I'm going home."

Chandler stood. "Well, you're the one who has the day off. Let me get back to work."

"How're things with the Empire suit?"

"We're going to file the papers on Monday. This is going to be a long battle."

Conner nodded. "Don't worry. I'll be back in the morning."

"Bro, I'm not worried. Fourteen years is no accident. I know you're not about to let me down." Chandler playfully saluted his brother before he walked through the door.

Once alone, Conner swiveled in his chair and faced the wall behind his desk—his wall of fame, he called it. His eyes scanned his degrees from Stanford and Yale and photos of Chandler and him with the mayor and other city dignitaries. But there was nothing on the wall that made him prouder than what his wife had accomplished.

When Grace told him that she wanted to run for the council seat, he'd been surprised, then ecstatic. It was different than when she told him she wanted to get involved with community affairs. At that time, all those years ago, he knew she was searching for anything that would keep her busy and away from Drew, her high school boyfriend.

There was still a little ache in his heart when he allowed that name to enter his thoughts. Drew had been a force in their marriage since the beginning. Most men would have walked away, and even he was surprised that he had remained through the heartache and humiliation. But he loved Grace and was determined to stand.

There was a quick knock on the door before Marilyn walked in. "That woman is on the phone."

Good, he thought. *I'll take this, make an appointment, and get home to my wife.* He lifted the phone and waited for Marilyn to close the door. "This is Conner Monroe." His professional voice was deep, a tone above James Earl Jones's.

"Conner . . ."

He frowned. Although he couldn't readily identify the familiar voice, his heart pounded. "This is Conner Monroe," he repeated.

"This is Pilar Cruise."

Her introduction made him bounce back in his chair. "Pilar," he said, recovering. "How are you?" His professionalism was all that allowed him to ask that question rather than the ones that galloped through his mind. *What do you want? Why all the mystery?*

"I'm fine."

In the silence that followed, he calculated how many years had passed since he'd seen her. Twelve . . . no, thirteen, although it wasn't clear. He couldn't even draw a mental picture. All he remembered was her long blue-black hair.

Conner coughed. "I understand you've been calling."

"Yes."

Why? he screamed inside. "You have a legal problem?"

More seconds of silence before she said, "Yes . . . and something more."

Dread began to invade his body. He cleared his throat. "I have time tomorrow."

"No."

He didn't know why that single word swelled the lump in his throat.

Pilar continued, "I'm not going to be in town. . . ."

"You don't live in Los Angeles?"

"Not anymore."

He shifted in his seat.

"I came from New York to see you."

He knew for sure—this was trouble. No one flew three thousand miles to see an attorney. He took a deep breath. "Okay." He opened his calendar, though he knew it was clear. "How soon can you get here?"

"Not there." Her demand was quick.

He nodded, as if he understood.

She asked, "Can we do lunch?" She paused. "Encounters, if it's still there."

"Fine," he said, although he wasn't fine at all. "I can meet you in an hour."

He could hear her exhale. "Good."

He was filled with the urge to get away. "I'll see you then." He hung up without waiting for her response. Conner stared at the phone as if it was a poisonous snake. The knock on the door broke his gaze.

Marilyn stepped inside, then stopped with she saw his expression. "Is everything all right?"

He swallowed the lump that had been lodged since Pilar had said her name. "Sure."

Marilyn frowned. "Was that call a problem?"

"No," he said quickly. "It turned out to be an old friend . . . acquaintance. Do you remember Pilar Cruise?"

She frowned. Then her eyes brightened with recognition. "Your assistant, the one I replaced." She exhaled, as if she'd been holding her breath. "Well, it makes sense that she would call you if she had a legal problem."

Her statement made him want to respond as if she'd asked a question. "I'm probably the only attorney she knows." He stood. "I'm going to meet her now."

"Are you going straight home after that?"

Grace's face flashed through his mind. Ten minutes ago, his answer would have been a resounding affirmative. "I think so," he said, lowering his gaze.

Marilyn stared at him for a long moment before she walked out of the office.

He looked at his watch, surprised that only five minutes had passed since he'd hung up. This was going to be the longest sixty minutes he ever lived.

"This April election delivered a surprise when Grace Monroe defeated the incumbent, Samuel Douglas, for the council position in the Eighteenth District. Ms. Monroe is a former member of the Beachside School Board. Monroe, part of the religious right, surprised pundits winning on a Christian platform . . ."

Grace clicked off the car radio. Where did reporters get their information? She wasn't part of any religious right. First, she wasn't religious, although she'd tell anyone who'd listen that she was a Christian, serious in her love for Jesus.

Her ringing cell phone turned her frown into a smile. "Hey, Devry."

"Hey, girl. I called the office, and your people said you were missing."

"I took the day off. I needed to recover—away from the cameras and other probing eyes. Plus, Conner and I plan to celebrate, since things got mixed up when my mother brought the girls home last night. . . ."

"They weren't supposed to come back until today."

"Exactly."

"Oh." Devry laughed.

"Anyway, we thought we'd have all day, but Conner got called into the office."

"So now that your husband is buried under his law books, what're you going to do?"

"I don't have anything set," she said, turning onto Pacific Coast Highway. "Conner's plan is to escape at two."

"Yeah, right," Devry said. "I can't imagine Conner making it home in the middle of the day."

"Don't be a pessimist."

"Can't help it. My husband works with yours. Chandler always promises to come home early, but he's yet to make it."

"Well, you weren't there this morning when I almost had my husband quoting scripture from the Song of Solomon." They laughed together. "Nothing will keep Conner away from me today," Grace said.

"Okay, I'm convinced. But can we get together for a quick lunch before then?"

"Business or pleasure?"

"A bit of both, dear. It's always a pleasure to be in your company." Devry chuckled. "But I have a proposal, and since I'm related to the new councilwoman, I should be first in the hand-out line. I won't keep you long. You'll be home in time for your afternoon sexcapade."

Grace laughed. "Okay, where should we meet?" She swung into the curve of her driveway and turned the ignition off.

"Encounters," Devry suggested. "They love you. We might get a free lunch."

"Encounters is fine, but I'm paying. I don't want anyone from Sara Spears's group accusing me of getting any free lunches."

"Have you heard anything from those crazies?"

Grace shook her head, thinking how much of a blessing that was. Sara Spears was the self-appointed leader of the ACC—the Anti-Christian Coalition. She was a proud atheist who claimed that she wasn't against Christians, just against Christians holding offices where they could force their beliefs on the public. In the past, Sara and the ACC would have dragged Grace's candidacy through mounds of mud. But Grace had been spared since the ACC's focus was on getting two of its candidates elected to the city council. Grace knew her reprieve wouldn't last long.

"I wouldn't call Sara Spears crazy," Grace said, finally responding. "Not that Harvard-educated fox."

"Well, don't think about her. Just think about how your marvelous sister-in-law is going to present you with something that will make even the ACC shut their mouths. I'll see you a little after noon, Councilwoman."

Grace clicked off the phone and jumped from the car. As she trotted to her door, she heard Devry's words—"see you . . . Councilwoman." It was still hard to believe. She dropped her keys on the foyer's table, then ran up the stairs. She disrobed as soon as she entered the bedroom, throwing her clothes onto the bed before she went into the bathroom. For a moment, she eyed the tub. The Jacuzzi's jets beckoned her, tempting her to call Devry and cancel. Instead, she turned on the shower.

She posed in front of the mirror as she waited for the water to warm. She'd heard an Oprah guest once say that if you could look at yourself naked, you could do anything. She did that every morning. Some days were easier than others. Today was a good day.

Not bad, she thought, for a woman approaching forty, who had carried and then pushed two children from her body. And Amber had been a difficult birth. At that time, she'd thought about having every tube inside her tied. She'd decided against it, because although Conner never admitted it, she knew he still hoped for a son. But as the years passed and their days grew happier with their girls, they'd agreed there was no need—and no room—for another child.

And now that Devry was pregnant, the family hope was that she'd give birth to a son to carry the Monroe name.

She twisted, staring at her reflection in the mirror. "What would Sara Spears think of me now?" She laughed, feeling as if she was drowning in a sea of blessedness.

She stepped into the shower and allowed herself to think about all that God had done. Even when she'd turned her back on Him, He'd taken care of her. Carried her through everything from law school, to motherhood, through an adulterous marriage that He salvaged when He revealed Himself to her and Conner. Grace sighed as the dual shower heads sent pulsating water beads against her skin. She turned the knob, increasing the pressure, and once again scolded herself for making the date with Devry.

She wanted this time alone to bask—not just in the awesomeness of winning an election that she didn't dare dream about. But to also revel in the wonderment of just how far her life had come.

"Thank you, Lord."

It had been a wandering road, with potholes that should have swallowed her. But her life was divided into two parts—what she called pre-Lord and post-Lord. Some would say that she'd been lucky during her pre-Lord days. When she'd traveled across the country to attend Hampton University, then on to Yale Law School, where she fell in love with an ambitious classmate. People would say that she was lucky after becoming pregnant at the end of her second year and being with a man who was committed to her—enough to marry her just four months before their baby, Jayde, was born.

But it seemed then that her luck had run out. She still wondered what she was trying to do during that time. Why she was trying to destroy everything good in her life? Why she couldn't stay away from Drew? But even though she behaved as if she had made a deal with the devil, God had other plans.

It was her sins that had led her to the Lord. And it couldn't have been more appropriate that Devry and Chandler played a role in leading Grace and Conner to Christ. The two had been inviting Grace and Conner to church for more years than Grace could count, but she and Conner had believed that Sundays were best spent in bed recharging for the coming week.

It wasn't that she didn't believe in God. Her earliest memories were of being awakened on Sunday mornings and she and Mabel being forced to go to church with neighbors while her parents slept. But there was little that she could speak about on God from those days. She knew God was a Higher Being who controlled everything from his estate in the sky. She knew that God was mad at just about everything. There was nothing humans could do to please Him. And she knew that she would never make it to the nirvana that was promised to those who lived a holy life. So it was easy to turn away from a God she couldn't please.

But it was the hell that she was living in this life that sent Grace searching for salvation. And it was Devry who took her hand, helping her find peace, on the day that Conner found out about her affair with Drew—for the second time.

"I'm afraid I'm going to really lose Conner this time," Grace had sobbed.

"Well, you may."

Grace was shocked at Devry's words. In the past, her friend had comforted her, always reassuring that all was going to be fine.

Devry continued, softening her voice. "Grace, something's wrong. If this was the first time, I'd say you'd made a mistake, that you were just lonely. But how many chances do you think a man will give you? Many men would have left after the first time."

Devry's truth twisted like a wasp's sting. "What am I going to do?"

Devry had moved to the couch and sat next to Grace. She lifted Grace's chin and stared into her eyes. "Come with me to my Women's Recovery Group at church."

"What is that going to do?" Grace wailed.

"It's going to give you a chance to talk. It's going to give you a chance to listen. There are many who have been through the same thing. And you'll meet Pastor Ford. Not only does she understand, but she'll counsel you."

"You want me to talk about my problems to a stranger?"

Devry had looked at her as if she'd asked a stupid question. "The judge in divorce court is going to be a stranger too, Grace. And he's going to be all up in your business."

It took everything inside of her for Grace to go to that meeting. But although she didn't open her mouth, she had walked away enlightened. She felt as if she was at an AA meeting for cheaters. As Pastor Ford directed the women through the discussion with an understanding that made Grace suspect that she had once been in the same place, the participants talked about what they'd been willing to throw away—family, careers, money—all to be with a man who was giving them something they didn't think they were getting at home.

As tragic as they were, those weren't the stories that moved her. It was the small group of women who attended because they were trying to understand their husband's infidelity. Their tales of misery rammed a hole through her heart. Is this how Conner feels? she had wondered? She didn't want to believe that she had caused him that kind of pain.

Grace had returned to the next meeting, then another, and another, while Conner slept in the guest bedroom. The first words they exchanged came three weeks from the day that Conner had found her in the motel with Drew.

She'd spoken first. "Conner, I love you. And I finally understand what's going on with me. I know I've hurt you, and I know I don't have a right to ask, but will you come with me to counseling? I want to save our marriage, and I think Pastor Ford can help us."

He had stared at her with dark, blank eyes, and she shuddered inside. But the victories she'd heard about in those meetings gave her courage. "I will do anything to make this up to you. I pray that you'll forgive me."

His stare continued until he turned and walked away without saying anything.

She had slumped into the kitchen chair and laid her head down on the table. An hour passed before she moved, first checking on three-year-old Jayde who, blessedly, was oblivious to the ongoing saga in her home. Then Grace went into the bedroom, sliding under the covers without changing from the leggings and T-shirt that she wore. As she lifted her hand to turn out the light, the bedroom door opened.

Conner stood with his arms crossed. He looked so good in his black T-shirt and boot-legged jeans. All she wanted to do was run into his arms. But she stayed, locking her eyes with his, though inside she prayed for his words.

"I'll go to counseling," he said. Then he disappeared.

Even when she no longer heard his footsteps, she remained fixed in her space, not wanting to jar his words from the atmosphere.

Her heart was heavy now as she remembered that time. It was over twelve years ago, but the emotions she recalled were as fresh as yesterday.

Grace turned off the water and stepped from the shower. She pulled a towel from the heated rack, shook the shower cap from her head, and ran her hand through her short curls. When she looked in the mirror, Grace couldn't tell if the water that damp-ened her face was from the steam that still filled the room or from tears that filled her eyes. If they were tears, they were ones of joy. After months of counseling with Pastor Ford and finally giving themselves to the Lord, Conner and Grace had reconnected in ways that she had never dreamed possible. It was as if God was glue that couldn't be purchased but was more powerful than any-thing found in the best of stores.

She looked in the mirror and smiled. Yes, she had much to be thankful for, but right now, she had to get ready for lunch.

Chapter 5

"Congratulations, Ms. Monroe. I guess that should be Council-woman Monroe."

Grace chuckled and handed the keys to the valet. "How are you, Stanley?"

He smiled. "I'm fine, knowing that voting works."

She laughed.

Inside the restaurant, the congratulations continued, until Grace wanted to beg for mercy. She exhaled when Devry rushed in just minutes behind her.

"Sorry. I got stuck on the phone," Devry gasped.

They hugged before Grace motioned to the hostess. "I asked for a table near the back, so we wouldn't be disturbed," she whispered over her shoulder to Devry.

They followed the hostess, zigzagging through the table maze filled with the lunch crowd. As they moved toward the restaurant's center, Grace's steps slowed.

Devry's glance followed Grace's. They stood for a moment, staring at the man and a woman, hovered close, deep in conversation.

Grace stepped toward the table. "Conner?"

His head rose slowly. A thin layer of water covered his eyes, as if he was having difficulty focusing. Their gaze froze on each other until Conner jumped from his chair, pushing himself from the table. He collided with the man sitting behind him. "Excuse me," he said, though his eyes never left his wife. "Honey." Conner kissed Grace. "What are you doing here?"

Her eyes asked the same question. "I thought you were going to the office."

"I . . . was," he stammered. "But, this . . . something came up."

Devry said, "Grace, I'm going to our table. See you later, Conner."

Neither noticed Devry's exit as Grace stared at her husband. Her eyes made a slow descent to Conner's lunch partner. "Hello, Pilar." Grace didn't know why she trembled.

Pilar smiled. "It's been a long time, Grace."

She nodded, and then turned back to Conner. When he offered no explanation, she gave him one. "Devry and I are having lunch."

It was Conner who broke their eye-lock, his eyelids becoming too heavy to hold her gaze. When he finally looked at her a few seconds later, he kissed her again. "I'll see you at home . . . later."

She was dismissed.

"At two, right?" She felt the need to remind him. When Conner nodded, she smiled her good-bye to Pilar. She moved toward the table where Devry was sitting, though she didn't know how she made it without turning back. She didn't breathe until she sat.

"Girl, I am famished." Devry's head was buried in the menu. "It's the baby's fault."

Grace's gaze drifted across the room. All she could see was the stiffness of Conner's back.

"I think I'll have the crab cakes." Devry frowned when she looked up. "What's wrong?"

It took a moment for Grace to stop staring at her husband. "I'm surprised to see Conner. He didn't even want to go into the office and now . . ."

"Who's that with him?"

"Pilar Cruise. She used to work for Conner."

"Oh, yeah." Devry almost sang the words. "When they first opened the firm, right?" Grace nodded. "Is he handling a case for her?"

"I don't know." Grace picked up her menu, and studied every item, though she ate at Encounters at least four times a month. "I'll have the barbecue pasta." She put down the menu and smiled at Devry. "So what did you want to talk to me about?" she asked with cheer she didn't feel.

"I have an idea for a true abstinence and drug-free program and you're the council member who can help me get it implemented."

"Are you thinking about what we tried in the schools?"

Devry nodded. "But I want to raise the stakes. Instead of adults lecturing kids, we need to have children talking to children."

Grace nodded and kept her eyes planted on Devry with all her might.

Devry continued, "Teenagers who have dropped out to have a baby can be paid to speak at assemblies. Students who are in twelve-step programs can visit classrooms." Devry took a portfolio from her briefcase. "I've made a few notes . . ."

Grace's glance wandered back toward Conner against her will. He and Pilar held their stance, heads so close together that Grace knew neither of them was aware of the sights or sounds of the Wednesday lunch crowd.

"Grace!" Her head snapped back to Devry. "You're not listening."

"Yes, I am."

"Then why didn't you say anything when I said you should dance down Crenshaw Boulevard naked at noon."

Grace smiled. "Because that's a good idea."

Devry laughed, but only for a moment. She covered her sister-in-law's hand. "You're not bothered by Conner meeting with Pilar, are you?"

She shook her head. "No, but their meeting looks serious, and Conner never mentioned this."

Devry leaned forward. "You're not thinking they're involved?"

Grace sat back. "Of course not. That's my style, not Conner's."

"That's not your style anymore."

As Devry spoke, Grace watched Conner get up. Then Pilar stood, and they rushed away from Grace's view.

"So what's bothering you?" Devry asked. "I don't want to sit here and not know what's going on."

Me neither, Grace wanted to say. But she smiled. "They're gone, so I won't be distracted anymore," Grace said just as a waitress came to their table. But even as they gave their orders and Devry presented her proposal, Grace couldn't focus. All her mind's eye could see was Conner with Pilar. A few hours before, she had been reveling in how wonderful their lives were. Now she had a feeling deep in her center that the wonder of their lives could be in danger.

Grace rushed into the house and began unbuttoning her blouse as she raced up the stairs. Although she was finally able to concentrate on Devry's proposal, she'd been bombarded with the image of Conner and Pilar as she drove home. She didn't know why their meeting had upset her so. Maybe because it felt as if it were shrouded in mystery.

"Stop it, Grace. It's just your imagination," she scolded herself.

She was not going to allow those thoughts to interfere with this special time she and Conner had planned. She glanced at the clock as she stepped into the bedroom. In fifteen minutes, her husband would waltz through the front door and make her forget all thoughts of Pilar Cruise.

She wiggled into the fire-red teddy and robe Conner had bought for her last week when the polls for the first time had showed that she was ahead in the race. They'd planned this celebration then.

Fourteen minutes later, Grace sauntered into the living room. She wanted to be waiting at the door when Conner entered. She wasn't going to waste even a minute.

She sat in the chair by the window, picked up an *Essence* magazine, and flipped through the pages. A half-hour later, she peeked through the curtains, wondering if Conner had run into traffic.

She was speed-walking from wall to wall by the time the clock in the foyer chimed three times. "Where are you, Conner?"

She picked up the phone and dialed the office. "Hi, Marilyn. Is Conner there?"

"No, Grace. He said he was going to spend the day with you. You'd better hurry home." Marilyn giggled. "I'm sure he's waiting for you."

I am home! Grace wanted to scream. *I've been waiting for him for an hour.* But instead of saying anything else, she hung up and dialed Conner's cell.

"Honey, I'm just checking to make sure everything is all right," she said when his voice mail came on.

She returned to the chair where just an hour before she'd been filled with the promise of an afternoon that she wouldn't soon forget. But instead, her heart pounded. "Nothing's wrong, Grace," she said aloud. "He just got held up a bit. He'll be here." But she was not convinced by her own words.

In the next hour, she called his cell phone every few minutes but stopped leaving messages. When the clock in the foyer chimed five times, she returned to their bedroom. The girls would be home soon, something she couldn't say about Conner.

Just as she slipped the teddy from her shoulders, she heard the three beeps from the opened front door. She held her breath, but a second later, she heard, "Mom, I'm home."

"Okay, honey. I'll be down in a moment."

"Mom, I need to tell you about a group thing we want to do on Saturday."

Grace knew that Jayde was standing at the foot of the stairs yelling. No matter how many times she'd been told that it was more civilized to use the intercom, she preferred her vocal cords.

Grace pressed the intercom button on the wall for the foyer/kitchen. "I'll be right down, Jayde, and we can discuss it."

A moment later the front door opened again.

"Hi, Mommy."

"She's upstairs," Grace heard Jayde yell to Amber.

"Mommy!" Amber's voice grew closer.

A moment later, Amber knocked. Grace slipped into her robe a second before she opened the door.

"Hi, Mommy." Amber smiled, then frowned. "Are you sick?"

"No, honey. I was changing my clothes."

Amber's smile returned. "Can I go with Nicole to the museum on Saturday?"

"I don't know. We'll see."

"But, Mommy, Nicole's mother is waiting. . . ."

"Amber, let me get dressed. Then we'll talk about it. You can call Nicole later."

"All right," Amber mumbled and turned away.

Grace jumped into her jeans, then tucked a white T-shirt into her pants, all the time praying that she would hear Conner's car enter the garage. This wasn't the first time plans changed because of work. Their schedules were hectic, so this wasn't different. But it *felt* very different to Grace.

She brushed her hair, glanced in the mirror, and then went to her children. Both Amber and Jayde rushed to her.

"Mom, I need . . ."

"Mommy, I want . . ."

Grace held up her hands. "One at a time. Amber, what do you want?"

"Why does she always go first?" Jayde pouted. "I never get anything around here."

"Jayde, I am not in the mood."

"But I was home first and . . ."

Grace held her hands to her head. "Jayde, go to your room," she yelled.

Jayde's eyes widened. "I didn't do anything."

"I said . . ." Her expression completed her sentence.

Jayde picked up her backpack and CD player and stomped up the stairs.

Grace took a deep breath and walked into the kitchen. She opened the refrigerator and took out a package of chicken wings. "Now, Amber, what do you want?" Amber stood in the doorway with her hands clasped behind her back. She pressed her lips together and looked away from her mother. Grace sighed. "Come here," she said in a softer voice, and sat at the dinette table.

Amber followed her mother's command.

"You wanted something." Grace took Amber's hand.

Amber nodded, but kept her eyes lowered. "Can I go to the museum with Nicole on Saturday?" she whispered. "Her mom said it was okay and that you could come too."

"I think it'll be fine, but let's check with your dad."

"Okay," Amber agreed weakly.

Grace lifted her daughter's chin with her fingers. "I want to make sure that your father didn't make any weekend plans. He could have something fabulous planned, and I wouldn't want you to miss it."

"What are we going to do?" Amber asked, now meeting her mother's gaze.

Grace smiled and shrugged. "I don't know. Let's just check and see, okay?"

Amber hugged Grace. "Okay, Daddy is the best." She kissed Grace's cheek. "And you are too, Mommy."

Grace laughed. "Go upstairs and change for dinner."

Amber ran toward the stairs, then turned back to the kitchen. "Mommy, do you want me to tell Jayde that you're sorry?"

Grace pressed her palm against Amber's cheek. "Thank you, but I should do that."

Grace waited until she no longer heard Amber's footsteps before she looked at the clock. It was almost six. A plethora of scenarios paraded through her mind, none of which stopped her heart from sinking. She shook her head, ridding the images from her mind, and then stood and trotted up the stairs. She knocked on Jayde's door and opened it. "Can I come in?"

Jayde continued shifting the electronic solitaire cards across the computer screen.

Grace sat on the edge of the bed. "I'm sorry. I shouldn't have yelled at you."

Jayde clicked the mouse again, moving the ten of spades beneath the jack of hearts.

Grace continued, speaking to her daughter's back. "I know you'll forgive me because you've had bad days."

Jayde faced her mother. "Why are you having a bad day?" She sounded astonished. "You just won an election." She sat next to Grace.

Grace took her daughter's hand. "I should be happy, huh?"

Jayde nodded. "You were happy yesterday, but today you seem mad."

Grace shook her head. "I'm not mad, sweetie." She paused as the image of Conner and Pilar flashed behind her eyes.

Jayde smiled. "I understand, Mom. You have a lot of people depending on you."

She nodded. "But none are as important as you and Amber . . . and your father." She kissed her forehead. "Dinner will be ready in thirty minutes."

"Okay." Jayde wrapped her arms around her mother. "I love you, Mommy."

Grace closed her eyes and held onto Jayde. She couldn't think of anything that she needed more at that moment. It seemed that Jayde knew everything without knowing anything. Grace kissed Jayde, then rushed from the room, not wanting her daughter to see tears that she thought might come.

Forty minutes later, she called the girls to a dinner of grilled chicken and cucumber salad. As they sat at the kitchen table and chatted about school and what they were going to do over spring break, Grace strained to press thoughts of her missing husband aside. After they cleaned up, Grace helped Amber with homework, while Jayde searched on-line for information on Zora Neale Hurston for an English report. The time almost felt normal, except for the way Grace looked at her watch every ten minutes and glanced through the window for oncoming car headlights in the time in between.

It was eight-thirty when Grace tucked Amber into bed. Amber pulled her children's Bible from under her pillow and handed it to Grace.

"Do you know what you want to read?"

Amber nodded. "About the Hebrew children. We're studying them in Sunday school."

Grace sat on the edge of the bed. With one side of her brain, she read scriptures from the Book of Daniel, while with the other she tried to figure out where her husband could be. She was grateful when she was able to turn off Amber's light, then kiss Jayde good night with an admonition not to stay up past ten.

When Grace stepped into their bedroom, the space felt empty, so she settled into the office that she and Conner shared across the hall. She pulled her Bible from the book shelf and stretched out on the couch. She leaned back into the leather, trying to find a comfortable place, but she couldn't find any comfort tonight. Still, she was determined to read. She turned through the pages of Isaiah to the fifty-fourth chapter. She'd missed the last two Women's Fellowship meetings, but Devry told her what they were studying. Her eyes roamed the scriptures until she stopped at the last verse. This had always been one of her favorite scriptures:

No weapon that is formed against thee shall prosper; and every tongue that shall rise against thee in judgment thou shalt condemn.

Tonight, the scripture made her heart pound. The words

replayed in her mind as if they were a warning. She stood, leaving the Bible open on the couch. Downstairs, she set the alarm, closed the windows, and then checked on her daughters. Inside her bedroom, she changed into an oversized Hampton University T-shirt and climbed into bed.

No weapon that is formed against thee shall prosper.

Grace couldn't count the number of times she'd stood on those words. But as she lay back in the bed, she had the feeling that she was going to need to stand on that scripture more than she ever had before.

Conner stared at the twin towers across the Avenue of the Americas. Los Angeles hadn't recovered from the energy crisis, yet the high-rise buildings were glistening as bright as Fifth Avenue at Christmas. He shook his head. His mind was filled with thoughts of Los Angeles's crisis when his own loomed ahead. Disaster had waltzed right into the middle of his life, right into the soul of his marriage. A low moan escaped from deep inside him when he thought about what this could mean to Grace's career.

But this tragedy went beyond him and Grace. There were his children. The tears almost flowed when Conner thought about his girls.

He squeezed his eyes together, wishing he could force Pilar and her words back to yesterday. But what would change? He massaged his closed eyes with his thumbs, but no matter how hard he pressed, he couldn't erase the images planted in his mind. He should have listened to his inner voice. Even as he drove to Encounters, his mind screamed, "Turn back!" The warning had tolled louder with each passing mile.

"What is wrong with me?" he had asked himself as he drove to the restaurant. There was nothing to fear. He was meeting Pilar, an old friend, acquaintance, employee—he wasn't sure what to call her. Whatever she was, she couldn't cause him harm. He held that thought until he slowed his car and saw Pilar standing stiffly straight at the restaurant's entrance. Then he knew there was much to fear.

He didn't use the valet and instead parked his car at the far end of the lot. The entire time he lumbered toward her his heart pounded like a jackhammer.

Pilar's smile was warm enough as he approached. They stood, without words, in front of each other. It was an awkward stance, neither knowing what to do.

Pilar leaned toward him. He wrapped his arms around her. They barely touched.

"How've you been, Conner?"

He stepped back, swallowed, and nodded. "Great. And you?"

"Just fine."

Conner opened the restaurant's door, allowing Pilar to move in front of him. He frowned as she dragged inside, her steps taking effort. The hostess led them to a table near the front.

"Not here," he said, even though Pilar had pulled out her chair. He lowered his voice. "I'd prefer one of those." He pointed toward the tables lined against the paneled wall.

Pilar nodded as if she understood, and they followed the hostess. They waited until they were alone before they spoke.

Pilar smiled. "It is good to see you."

He returned her smile but not her words. Conner opened his menu, and Pilar followed. Restless seconds suspended between them as they pretended to study the food choices.

Over the top of his card, Conner assessed Pilar. He had been surprised when she said she had moved to New York, and seeing her now made him wonder why she'd left the city she once said would be the only place she'd called home. With her departure from L.A., she'd left much of herself behind. She was no longer the quintessential California girl.

At the door, he'd noticed the way her mustard brown pantsuit hung on her much thinner frame. Gone was her smooth olive complexion, which had been a mix of her ethnicity and long summer days at Venice beach. Now she looked as if her blotchy-red skin never saw sun. Her blue-black hair, which once swayed past her waist, had been traded for a short cut that bluntly ended above her ears.

But, it was her eyes that were most different. He remembered how they glittered and how he often caught himself staring just to see her irises dance. Now her eyes looked dark, almost blank, as if there was no longer any music to dance to. He wanted to ask if she were well, but it was difficult to press words through his throat.

Pilar put down her menu, and Conner returned his eyes to his card. He could feel the strong glare of her glance. Still, he waited a moment before he put down the menu. "I was surprised to get your call."

"It's been a long time."

He glanced around the restaurant, then rested his arms on the table. "I was as surprised as when I walked into my office that morning and found your resignation."

She lowered her eyes. "It was the best thing."

He nodded, though he was sure she didn't know how true her words were. It had all changed for the better the day she left. That

made him think of Grace. "My wife was elected to a council position last night." He wanted her to know how good his life was.

"I was there," she said, and paused when he fell against the
back of his chair. "At the hotel." Her words came quicker as anger
filled his face. "I stayed in the back. No one saw me. I needed to
see you . . . and Grace together."

He frowned. He was filled with questions, but instinct kept
him silent.

Pilar said, "I have to tell you what this is about."

He nodded and pressed his lips together, thankful that she
wasn't going to make him suffer through minutes of chatter.

Pilar's water glass shook in her hand as she took a short sip.
Then she slid her chair closer to the table. Her glance darted from
him to the other tables.

His heart returned to its frantic beat.

"Conner," she started. "I don't know how else to say this . . ."

Suddenly, he didn't want to hear. "Pilar, do you want to order
before we talk?" He hoped his voice didn't shake the way he trembled inside.

She shook her head. "I've come a long way. There were many
times when I almost turned back, but you have to know."

I don't want to know, he screamed inside. His heart pounded
harder. He wanted to ask how she liked New York.

"Conner, I have a son."

He squinted, focusing on her lips. Okay, he wanted to say. Congratulations, *sustantivo,* felicitations; in any language, it added up
to, "What does this have to do with me?"

"Your son."

Her words hit him like a boxer's uppercut. He shook his head, feeling the need to regain his balance even though he was sitting. Then he looked at her, his eyes speaking for him.

"Are you ready to order?"

His head weighed one hundred pounds as he struggled to raise his glance to the waitress. *Why are you interrupting us?* he wanted to ask. *Do you know what this woman just said to me?* He shook his head. "No, we don't want to order. We're not hungry."

The waitress raised her eyebrows. "So you're going to sit here, at the busiest time of the day, at my station, and not order anything?" Her neck swayed with each syllable.

Pilar said, "I'll have the barbecue chicken salad." She handed her menu to the waitress and smiled at Conner.

He glared at her. How could she eat after sputtering such lies? His eyes bore into Pilar. "I'll have the soup," he said not breaking his gaze.

The waitress looked around as if she wanted someone else to hear this madness. "What kind of soup?"

His eyes were still on Pilar. "It doesn't matter."

The waitress shrugged her shoulders, then walked away. Conner and Pilar stared at each other, a battle of wills. It was Pilar who looked away first.

"What did you say?" His question sprang through clenched teeth.

A thin layer of water covered Pilar's eyes. "We have a son, Conner."

He leaned forward. "How can that be?" he whispered.

Her eyes widened. "Conner, we were together for a few months."

"We were not together."

"Five, six, seven times . . ."

"We were not together."

Pilar grimaced from the pain of his words. "I know you never considered it a relationship. . . ."

"I was married." Conner paused. "I am married."

"That's why I left." Her words were soft and sad.

"You knew this when you left?"

She shook her head. "I found out a few weeks later."

He covered his face with his hands. When he looked up, he wondered why Pilar wasn't smiling—telling him this was a joke or a mistake. It didn't matter which to him.

"Conner, I'm sorry."

He glared at her, understanding at last the purpose of this meeting. It was a shakedown, a demand for money. She knew how well they were doing. "How do you know the child is mine?" He spat the words across the table as if she were a hostile witness.

Her entire body shook. With her eyes still on him, she lifted her purse from the floor and took out her wallet. Her eyes were glassier than they had been just a minute before as she slid a picture across the table.

Conner folded his hands inches away from the photo and stared at the caramel-colored boy sitting on a stool with his elbow resting on his leg. He swallowed the lump that threatened to block air from reaching his lungs. The boy had the same bushy eyebrows, high cheeks, and cleft in his chin. He carried his DNA.

He looked up at Pilar, then returned his glance to the picture. Pilar's sole contribution had been the black of his eyes.

His fingers edged toward the photo, but he allowed just the tips to touch it. "What's his name?" He almost choked on his question.

"Solomon." Her voice was low.

The waitress put a plate in front of Pilar, but before she could place the soup on the table, Conner said, "Take it back." He stared at Pilar.

Both Pilar and the waitress frowned. "What?" the waitress asked.

His eyes roamed back to the picture. Then he looked again at Pilar. "I'll pay, but I don't want it."

Tears sprang into Pilar's eyes.

"It's your money," the waitress sang. She looked at Pilar. "Do you want your salad?"

Pilar nodded, and the waitress walked away.

Conner was drawn back to the photo. "How old is he?"

Pilar tried to smile through tears that threatened to fall. "Twelve."

Inside, Conner counted. He closed his eyes, ready to make a denial, but the truth burned his heart. How could this happen?

Now, as he sat in his office, that question continued to haunt him. He was the father of a child by a woman who was not his wife. He couldn't think of a greater offense. Nothing could be worse—except for what Pilar wanted him to do. He closed his eyes and remembered the rest of their conversation.

"Why are you coming to me now?" he had asked.

"You should know you have a son." She spoke as if she were scolding him, then added, "It's called responsibility, and I need your help with Solomon. You need to do the right thing."

"Wait a minute," he had said through clenched teeth. "Don't tell me . . ."

She hadn't let him finish. "Conner, you have to take Solomon." His eyes had widened, but before he could object, she added, "I have AIDS. I'm dying."

A moment passed before he whispered, "You're HIV positive?"

She had raised her eyebrows. "That's not what I said. I have full-blown AIDS." She paused. "You're probably wondering how."

Conner bit his lip.

"I'm a growing statistic. Women who have unprotected sex." Pilar chuckled, but without humor. "I don't sleep around. But I did it enough not to know who was responsible." She shook her head. "Not that it matters. All I thought about when I was given my death sentence was Solomon."

Conner blinked. "Is he . . ."

"No," she answered before he could ask. "He's fine. Though they don't know for sure, it seems I became infected after he was born."

Conner exhaled.

"You seem relieved," she had said. "Although you're probably clean, you should still get tested." Pilar paused. "You don't want to expose your wife."

The muscle in his jaw jumped. "I don't have sex outside my marriage." He was sure Pilar almost laughed. He looked away for a moment, then met Pilar's glance. "I'm sorry . . . about what you're going through. Still, if something were to happen to you, wouldn't it be better for Solomon to be around people he knows? Others who love him?"

Even now, he remembered the anger that flashed in her eyes. "I'm praying that you will love Solomon because without you, he will have no one." Her voice trembled so much he thought she would cry. "The Cruises of Connecticut disowned me when I returned home with Solomon. He wasn't even nine months, but when my parents saw him, my mother asked if the father was a Negro." Pilar shook her head as if trying to dislodge the memory.

"I told them it didn't matter. This was their grandson. Still, they shunned me like I had leprosy."

Conner had not been surprised by Pilar's words. From what she'd told him years before, her Cuban parents had fled Castro's country when they were twenty and worked their way from the tip of Florida to the countryside of Connecticut. Her mother cleaned houses along the way, while her father landscaped many of those same estates.

By the time they arrived in the Constitution State five years after settling on American soil, they had metamorphosed from the Cruzes of Havana to the Cruises of Greenwich, absent of their native accents, with a plan to take advantage of America's riches.

Leonard (changed from Leonardo) Cruise landed a job at Zytec Corporation, the nation's largest pharmaceutical company. His passage from mailroom to boardroom took thirteen years. As upstanding citizens of Greenwich, Ellen (formerly Elena) sat on committees with women who would once have hired her to clean their homes. It was a rebellious Pilar who used her middle name instead of her first name, Angela, who left home at eighteen to pursue an acting career. It didn't hurt that she was leaving a family who held disdain for their second born because she refused to leave her Cuban heritage behind.

Pilar had continued, "When my parents looked at me and my child as if we were the refugees, I remembered why I moved away. I was so thankful that Solomon couldn't understand." She had faced Conner. "Our son has only you."

Almost nine hours had passed since Pilar had uttered those words—simple words that now complicated his life. He was the father of a child by a woman he never loved, never wanted. All those years ago, Pilar was just a convenience. She had allowed him to march through the challenges of his marriage with his head up. There weren't many he allowed into his life, but the few who knew about Grace's infidelity always said that he was so strong. Repeatedly, he'd heard how a lesser man would have left his wife. He had embraced those uplifting words, standing as the martyr who held his family together.

But no one knew the truth—that he had tried to wash away the image of another man bedding his wife with his own indiscretion. It had never worked. He loved Grace and ended it with Pilar.

He never felt as if he'd escaped his infidelity. The memory haunted him like a recurring cancer flaring up at odd moments, like when he was holding his wife or playing tennis with his daughters. He had to work at keeping the memory in remission.

But he had kept the secret. Even when Grace had spoken honestly about her affair, he'd remained silent. Even when they became members of the church and, later, leaders of the Marriage Enrichment Fellowship, he'd kept the truth hidden. He had many justifications for his sin of omission: he had already confessed his sin to God, he didn't want to hurt Grace, they'd suffered too much, his affair had been retaliation only, not meant to cause any harm. Conner chuckled bitterly at that last thought. What Pilar told him went beyond harm. It brought his secret to light.

For there is nothing covered, that shall not be revealed; neither hid, that shall not be known. The truth of God's words, he thought, as Luke 12:2 passed through his mind.

His eyes moved to the phone, and the ache in his heart became stronger. He was surprised that Grace hadn't called, though he imagined there were countless messages on his cell phone. He picked up the message sheets that Marilyn had left for him. Just one from Grace: three-fifteen—long after they were supposed to meet. Conner had wanted to call Grace the moment he left Pilar, but what would he have said? "Hi, honey, I can't come home right now."

In an instant, Grace would have known that something wasn't right. And how was he supposed to respond when she questioned him? He feared that he would blurt out everything. Another part of him feared that he would not.

He picked up the phone, but before he dialed, he dropped the receiver back. He slipped into his jacket, then picked up his brief-case. A phone call wouldn't do. He had to see his wife.

The red digital numbers on the clock screamed at Grace: 9:57. This was not late for Conner. Many nights he hadn't come home until almost midnight.

But he always called.

She pushed back the comforter, got out of the bed, and walked to the window. The sky's blackness was interrupted by the full moon's brightness. When she was seven, her father told her that a full moon was a new moon, representing a new cycle of life. That fascinated her, and for years, she'd run to the window every night, eager to view new life. Her search for the full moon contin-ued until she received that call in her first year in college.

"Grace, dear," her mother had sobbed. "Your dad . . . Neil had a heart attack."

She had slumped on her bed in Kelsey Hall, understanding the words in her head but having no comprehension in her heart. When she glanced up, it was through tear-filled eyes that she saw the full moon. She stared at the earth's satellite until she said good-bye to her mother. Then she stood and closed the curtains.

Now she looked at the moon a moment longer before she closed the drapes and returned to bed. Less than a second later, she heard the creaking squeak of the garage door. She jumped up, then sank back under the covers. To Grace, the minutes felt like hours as she waited, but when she heard Conner in the hallway, she glanced at the clock again: 10:04.

He walked into the room with his eyes lowered, but then he looked up and their stares held each other. He forced a slight smile. "You're still up."

"I was worried."

"I'm sorry."

With heavy steps, he moved to her and allowed his lips to meet hers. It was a perfunctory kiss, and when he pulled back, the sadness in his eyes belied his smile.

Grace's glance followed Conner as he moved across the room. "So," she called out when he stepped into his closet. "I was here this afternoon." She waited for him to answer her unasked question.

Seconds of silence passed before he said, "I got caught up."

She jerked a bit at his explanation. "You weren't at the office. Marilyn thought you were here."

Again silence. Then, "I went back to the office . . . afterward."

After what? she wanted to ask.

He stepped from the closet, dressed in black checkered pajama bottoms. "I'm sorry I missed our date."

She couldn't tell if it was sadness or sincerity that veiled his eyes. She forced herself to smile. "That's okay. Whatever came up must have been important." Her statement was a question, but he responded with just a nod before he pulled back the covers on his side of the bed.

He closed his eyes the moment he touched the pillow, and Grace wondered if he were praying. She'd sat frozen since he'd come into the room, but now she rolled onto her stomach.

"Conner, do you want to talk about it?"

His eyes opened, and he shook his head. Then he pulled her against his chest. "I just want to hold you."

She wrapped her arms around him, feeling the hammering of his heart. *What's wrong, Conner?* she pleaded inside. It was nothing more than a case, she rationalized. Conner's and Chandler's reputation brought the opportunity to litigate countless class action suits since they'd won the thirty-million-dollar settlement against the Apex Corporation for faulty hip implants that thousands had received. That case had brought professional and financial success, as well as overwhelming pressure to continue to deliver. She couldn't count the number of times Conner had come home like this. Sometimes it took him days to talk.

She held him tighter and soon felt the calm of his sleep breathing. Still, she didn't move. She needed to feel his arms, holding her as if he would never let go. Grace closed her eyes, but knew she would not rest. It wasn't that the lights were still on or that her leg had stiffened under the weight of Conner's leg over hers. It was the ache that kept sleep away. The ache that began deep and rose to her heart's center, and told her there was a reason that the full moon had come to visit her tonight.

Chapter 6

Starlight was sure that there were at least ten stacks of cash and credit card slips on the conference table in her home office. Lexington sat with the piles, steadily recording. He hadn't looked up in an hour, but his smile widened with each tick of the clock.

"Have to admit, Starlight. Brilliant."

She folded her arms across her chest. With a pencil behind his ear, a pencil in his hand, and the grin on his face, he looked like Uncle Billy from *It's a Wonderful Life*.

When she didn't respond, he looked up. "What's wrong?"

She lowered her eyes. A second later, she could feel him moving. *Probably hates leaving that money,* she thought.

The couch's violet leather squished as he sat. Their shoulders almost touched when he took her hand. "Thought you'd be happy," he whispered. "So much money in just three hours."

There it was again—the money was all he saw. She turned away, not hiding her disgust.

He sighed, and Starlight wanted to kick herself. She knew he was thinking this was one of those high-maintenance-chick moments that required him to talk, soothe, and carry her through some crisis that neither could identify.

She walked to the windowed wall. This view was the same as

the one from her bedroom. But the ocean that settled her during the day couldn't be seen at midnight. The night sky converged with the ebony water, making it impossible to discern the ending of the sea and the beginning of the heavens. The glow of the full moon hanging in the center of her view was the sole source of light, and the vision made her smile.

Through the glass, she watched Lexington's reflection. His face was covered with confusion, but his concern was short-lived. With a shrug, he returned to the cash and credit slips and calculators and receipts and ledgers.

She sighed. Lexington thought she should be dancing in the streets. He hadn't given the final count, but she could imagine the numbers. Between their percentage from the tickets and the sales of her books and CDs, they had easily cleared one hundred thousand dollars. And as Lexington said, it hadn't taken three hours.

Speaking at Greater Faith Chapel was a major coup. Before she finished, those church women dashed to the back, eager for a piece of Starlight. She'd signed books, tapes, and CDs until her hands cramped.

At first, she'd been concerned about her church appearance. Although she'd been speaking at sold-out venues for years, she'd never been at a house of worship. In fact, many of those do-good-holier-than-God pastors put her down, knocking her principles from their pulpits. She'd read about their attacks in Christian newspapers. On one occasion, Lily told her of the words of a pastor who was unaware that Starlight's mother was a visitor in his church.

Lily had repeated the pastor's words: "The Word of God warned of Starlight and others—false prophets appearing during the end times, professing enlightenment, and having some direct channel to some higher being. I'll tell you where their direct line leads—straight to hell. As 1 Timothy 4:1 and 2 says, these people are here to lead you astray. As Christians, we must be grounded and stand with the truth. We cannot fall prey to false doctrines and teachings that are disguised in messages of self-esteem."

The pastor had continued to quote scripture, associating her with the evil one:

"Just read 1 John 4:1: *Beloved, believe not every spirit, but try the spirits whether they are of God: because many false prophets are gone out into the world.* Starlight is one of whom the Lord speaks."

She laughed about it in public. "You know you must be doing something right when people persecute you."

But she grieved about it in private. "Mom, why do people hate me when I'm only trying to help?"

The worst condemnation came from her sister. Grace had broken off almost all contact as Starlight became more successful.

But today was the beginning of redemption. Pastors were beginning to realize that she was a motivator, helping women to recognize their inner strength. It made her want to kick her heels; Christians were waking up.

Tonight, she proved that her message and the church could coexist. Before she'd uttered her first words, she'd received a standing ovation. When she spoke, she had to pause often because of the applause that stretched her normal fifty-minute speech to ninety minutes.

"We all know there is a God," she had said. "But the greater God resides in you." Those words brought her second ovation.

"We have to rely on our power within. The higher being has given it to all of us." The applause was deafening.

"It doesn't matter if you worship Jehovah, Allah, Buddha, or God. This is about the One. And, you are one with the spirit." She'd had to walk over those words with alacrity when murmurs filled the sanctuary. "Of course, there is only one God, but what I'm talking about is the spirit within you." The applause returned, and she sighed with relief, making a mental note. She needed to pass her words by a Christian—maybe her mother.

She hadn't changed her presentation much. She always talked about a higher being, a he/she supernatural spirit, because that appealed to all of her followers. All she had to change tonight was sprinkling God throughout her speech.

"The church is where all the money is."

This time, she had to smile at Lexington's words. Nothing would change his thoughts. And it was his monetary focus that afforded her an ocean-front penthouse, credit cards to every Rodeo Drive boutique, a full-time housekeeper and a driver, and a staff of twelve in her Beverly Hills office.

He stood when she smiled. "That's my girl." He swaggered toward her and stroked her cheek. "You did great tonight."

Her smile widened.

"Wanna know how great?"

"I've been waiting for you to tell me."

"Almost thirty-three thousand from the books and tapes. I could kill New Vision. We only had fifteen hundred books. Could have doubled those sales." He turned back to the table. "About fifty women registered for the Sisters of the Sun conference."

"Didn't we already have forty?"

His grin met her frown. "I think we can get two hundred and fifty there."

"I thought we were sticking with one hundred attendees."

He shook his head. "The response is too great. At five hundred dollars a pop, why not maximize?"

"But it's our first conference."

"Don't worry. I'll work this. All you'll have to do is show up." He stuffed a stack of cash into a bank bag. "I've figured that we could clear two hundred fifty thousand for the day. And it'll be good practice for the Revival in June."

She nodded.

"Greater Faith is transferring the ticket money to our account. I expect it's well over one hundred thousand."

She smiled. Now the talk about money didn't seem so bad. "Make sure you go over Greater Faith's records," she said.

He looked at her as if she was speaking in tongues. "You think I'm going to trust a pastor?"

They laughed together.

"Why didn't you do the love line?" Lexington asked. "Pastor Carey suggested it. Would've been a lot more money."

"I wanted to be careful this first time. The news will travel, and I want everything Pastor Carey says to be good."

He gave a slow nod. "Makes sense." He walked toward her. "I have an idea."

Don't you always? she wanted to say. But she smiled, her signal for him to continue.

"Next time, don't just talk about God. Talk about Jesus. Christians are so emotional. If you work them up about Jesus, then when we do the love line and get their gifts . . ." He stopped, but she knew inside he was singing, "cha-ching."

"Churches are more profitable," Lexington continued, as if he'd given this much thought. "We don't have to pay for the venue, and Christians are a giving breed. They feel guilty if they don't support whomever their pastor has brought in. We can really work this word of God into quite a profitable business."

She bit her lip and looked away.

"Could come a time when we could make a million at one huge church event."

When she turned back, she was sure the pupils in his eyes reflected dollar signs. "Do you think that's possible?"

"The Revival in June will give us a good start." He laughed. "This is better than being a rock star."

She couldn't help it—she laughed with him.

He pulled her into his arms. "Glad to see you happy."

She hugged him, then pulled away. "It's late. I'm going to bed." His eyes became glassy. "Alone."

His smile disappeared. "I was hoping to stay. It's been a while."

She stared for a long moment. "Maybe tomorrow." She gave him a light kiss. "Lock up when you leave." She walked down the hall to her bedroom. When she undressed and slipped into bed, she still hadn't heard Lexington leave. It would be like him to work through the night.

She snuggled under the royal purple duvet and closed her eyes. There was no way Grace or anyone else could deny her contributions now.

Chapter 7

Grace's mouth stretched wide in a yawn.

"Must've been some celebration you and Conner had last night," Zoë teased as she entered the office.

Grace lowered her eyes to the report on her desk.

Zoë slipped a computer printout in front of Grace. "Here's the city budget. I'll give you a full report next week."

Grace didn't lift her head until Zoë left. She tried to suppress another yawn, but her mouth stretched wide with exhaustion. She hadn't rested last night. Even when her eyes had closed after four this morning, it was a fitful sleep. And she'd gotten out of bed before seven. As she helped Amber dress and solved Jayde's morning challenges, her mind's eye was on her bedroom door. She prayed that Conner was still asleep, so they could talk once the girls left. But after Amber climbed into the school van and she stepped back into the house, Conner stood at the foot of the stairs, fully dressed.

"Early appointment?" she asked, trying to keep the other questions out of her tone.

He nodded. "I don't think I'll be late tonight, but if I am, I'll call."

She hadn't missed the way his eyes averted hers. Or the slight touch of their lips when they kissed good-bye. Or that he hadn't mentioned their morning prayer.

As she thought back on Conner's actions this morning, the same chill that surged through her as she watched him walk away made her shiver again. She shook away the feeling and lifted the city council manual from her desk. There was no way she was going to expend more energy on what was on Conner's mind. He would tell her soon enough. Whatever it was didn't affect her anyway.

She flipped through the two hundred page manual, scanning committee descriptions—everything from Accessible Freeway Improvements to Widening Diversity Programs. There was little on public schools. Education was the responsibility of the school board. But from her past position, she knew the school board needed support.

This was going to be her legacy: improving the city's schools. Getting higher pay for teachers, implementing special programs to improve test scores, and executing the kinds of programs Devry was talking about. Her toughest battle was going to be for what Grace felt strongest about: holding public hearings and then developing a city initiative to be presented to the governor to return prayer to schools.

Yes, she thought, as she pulled out a notepad. If morals became as important as mathematics, the children would be blessed. She frowned as that thought passed through her mind. Schools weren't the only place that needed God's blessings. Right now, she could use a few in her own home.

She closed her eyes and prayed.

*　　*　　*

It was more than the conference room's heat that made Conner twist. He couldn't keep his eyes off the boy across from him. Every few minutes, the boy would feel Conner's stare. He'd smile, and Conner would look away.

"So, Mr. Monroe, can you help us?"

Conner looked at his brother. This was his consultation, but he was more than relieved when Chandler took the lead. He hadn't asked Chandler to do that; he didn't have to. Just the blessing of being a twin.

"Well, Mr. Jacoby," Chandler began, "from what you've told us, we want to pursue your case." Chandler looked toward the opposite end of the conference table, and Conner nodded.

"I thank you for Stefan," Mrs. Jacoby sobbed, dabbing a tissue under her eyes to dry her endless stream of tears that began when her husband related their son's story. She was a slight woman who seemed sicker than her son.

Conner's eyes drifted to the boy again. He couldn't get a good look, not with the way the noon sun cast its long shadow along the conference table. The black bandanna that covered Stefan's head glowed under the light. He was twelve years old, according to Mr. Jacoby, and if Conner didn't know, he would assume that the boy was suffering from cancer and its treatments—radiation, chemotherapy—something that would have caused the loss of hair. Even his brow was bald.

But it was drugs that ravaged this boy. Drugs developed by a national pharmaceutical company and administered by a doctor. V.Q. was a medical breakthrough, designed to reduce the symptoms of asthma. But when Stefan became violently sick after seven treatments, the Jacobys were told the doctors had made a mistake. That was the extent of the explanation.

Conner suspected that V.Q. had been approved—but for adults. He'd bet his researchers would find similar cases across the country.

It took a moment for Conner to realize that Stefan was staring at him. This time Conner didn't look away. He stared into the boy's eyes.

A moment later, Conner pushed away from the table, startling everyone. "Are we done?"

Chandler frowned. "Well . . . ," he paused. When the Jacobys nodded, Chandler said, "We're finished."

"It was nice meeting you." Conner couldn't press any more through his lips. He rushed into the hall. Behind him, he heard Marilyn's steps, as hurried as his. But he closed his office door before she could catch him.

With heavy legs, he moved to his desk. There was no way he could stay in that conference room. Not with his secret planted in front of him.

He had to tell Grace.

Last night, his nerve had melted with his heart when he saw his wife's face lined with worry. Even now, he knew Grace's thoughts were with him, wondering what case had him so riled that he'd missed their afternoon tryst without explanation.

There was a light knock on his door, and Chandler walked in. He sank into one of the chairs and their eyes held for a minute.

"What's going on?"

Conner knew what the lines in Chandler's forehead meant. There was no use lying.

Conner shrugged. "Just a lot on my mind."

"Something at home?"

His heart's ache sharpened. He had to tell someone. Conner stared into his twin's eyes, trying to convey without words all that he held inside. After a prolonged moment, he said, "Can't talk about it right now."

More silent moments. Then Chandler nodded. He stood and leaned across the desk. "I'm here when you're ready."

"You always have been."

"It's like that with us."

Conner remained still until Chandler left. Then he swung his chair around and faced the window. The sun was making its journey from east to west, dimming the light in his space. "I have to tell Grace," he whispered.

"Did you say something?"

He spun around. "I didn't hear you come in."

Marilyn said, "I'm sorry. You have a call."

His heart knocked against his chest. He waited until he was alone before he picked up the phone. "Conner Monroe."

"It's Pilar. I've been waiting for you to call me."

He'd told her he'd call this morning. "I need more time."

There was silence before Pilar said, "You didn't tell Grace." He knew her statement was a question, but he didn't feel compelled to respond. "I need to get home, Conner. To my son. With what's happening . . ." She left her sentence unfinished, leaving them with their own thoughts of why this had to come to light now.

Pilar said, "You're Solomon's father."

He pursed his lips. "That hasn't been established." He heard her hurt through her silence. He apologized by saying, "I will talk to Grace."

"When?"

"When I think the time is right."

"We don't have time. You have to do this, Conner, or I will . . ."

His back straightened, stiffened. "Don't threaten me," he uttered, the lawyer's fight in his voice.

"That's not what I'm doing," she said softly. "I'm thinking about our son."

He closed his eyes.

"I will call you tomorrow," she said. The next second, he heard the dial tone, and he let the phone fall from his hands.

For minutes he sat, hearing her words in his head: "You're Solomon's father." He wanted her to take those words back and go away, never to return to this side of the country. But he couldn't dismiss Pilar. Not with everything that she'd told him.

He had to talk. Tell someone. Picking up the phone, he practiced the words he would say to his pastor. But before he punched the last digit for Pastor Ford's office, he hung up. Although he could almost hear the comforting words from her mouth, he could definitely see the disappointment in her eyes.

With a deep sigh, he stood, inhaled, and then walked down the hall to Chandler's office.

The door opened before Conner knocked. Chandler stood on the other side, as if he knew the exact moment his brother would come. He stepped aside, allowing Conner to come in.

"I need to talk to you."

"I know." Chandler moved to one of the chairs in front of his desk, and Conner joined him.

Quiet sat between them. Words floated in Conner's head, but

he couldn't grasp any to form a coherent thought. "I love Grace," he said finally.

Chandler's eyes widened a bit at Conner's statement. "I know that." He paused. "Grace knows that."

Conner pushed a stream of air through his lips. "I hope she remembers."

"It would be difficult for her to forget." Chandler paused. "And Grace loves you too."

Conner knew his brother's words were meant to comfort, but that truth sharpened his pain. How could he tell the woman he loved, the woman who loved him, this news?

"Grace and I have been through a lot."

Chandler leaned forward and rested his hand on his brother's shoulder. "Your history makes you strong. That and the Lord."

Conner closed his eyes. He had to say it. "I have a son. Another child."

He felt Chandler's hand tighten, then slip from his shoulder. This time, there were no words of solace from his brother. Just silence. A quiet that intensified his grief.

Conner stood and walked to the window. With his back to his brother, his words poured from him. He repeated the conversation he'd had with Pilar. "She said this happened twelve years ago," he finished. "My son . . . the boy that Pilar is claiming is mine . . . his name is Solomon."

He waited for Chandler to speak, but when silence filled the room, he took a breath and turned, focusing on the space over Chandler's shoulders. He couldn't meet his brother's glance. He didn't want to see his eyes.

"Well . . . ," Chandler began.

It was the steadiness in that syllable that gave Conner the

courage to look at him. Chandler hadn't moved, but now his elbows rested on the arms of the chair. He tapped the tips of his fingers together in a slow, steady motion. Conner recognized the pose—his brother was in lawyer mode.

"So what does this mean? What did you tell her?"

Conner raised his eyebrows. These weren't the questions he expected, but they were ones he could handle. It was easier this way. Turn this disaster into business. There would be plenty of time to handle it on a personal level.

Conner rushed to sit next to his brother. "I haven't told her anything . . . not really. I don't know what I'm going to do."

"Good. You can take your time."

"That's not exactly true. I don't have a lot of time."

Chandler's fingers froze in mid-air. The silence didn't hide his question.

"Pilar has AIDS. She doesn't know how much time she has."

"Wow." A few moments of silence passed before Chandler said, "I'm sorry for Pilar, but this doesn't change how you should proceed. Pilar has relatives. Someone else could take her son."

There was no humor in Conner's chuckle. "That's what I said, but apparently none of Pilar's relatives want anything to do with a black boy. She says if I don't take him, he'll be alone."

Chandler took a deep breath. "Okay, so this is more complicated than I thought, but still we need to do the right thing."

"That's what scares me," Conner said. "Suppose the right thing destroys my family?"

"I take it you haven't said anything to Grace."

Conner shook his head. "I can't even imagine saying these words to her. It's going to break her heart."

"She's strong, though. You can help her to understand."

"But how can I help her understand that I hid my relationship with Pilar? While she confessed what went on with her and Drew, I kept quiet." Conner stood and leaned over the desk. "I feel as if I've been lying to my wife for years. It's like I'm a fake."

Conner waited for his brother to tell him that's exactly who he was. But when Chandler stood and placed his hand on Conner's shoulder, all he felt was his twin's strength.

"I admit this is going to be tough. But we'll figure it out—through time and prayer." Chandler paused. "I'll do whatever you need me to do, but bro', there is one thing you have to do."

Conner closed his eyes and nodded. His brother didn't need to say anything more. Conner knew what Chandler meant. He had to tell Grace. He would do it tonight.

Grace gazed out onto the courtyard. Even though she had three months before she officially took office, she planned to use the time to read through the countless city proposals and referendums. But today she'd spent hours rereading papers, unable to keep her mind from drifting.

"Maybe I should just go home."

"What?"

She swiveled her chair around. "Just talking to myself."

Zoë smiled. "A lot of that going around," she kidded. "I wanted to go over tomorrow's council meeting. You'll be certified, along with the other new members at nine. Then the mayor's reception begins at eleven. By the time we do lunch and the requisite schmoozing, we'll be out by four." She paused and looked at her watch. "Need me for anything else?"

Grace shook her head. "No. Go on home."

"Want to walk out together?"

"No, I want to clear my desk. I won't be much longer, and Frank is waiting. He'll drive me home."

"Okay. I'll meet you at city hall in the morning."

Grace heard the front door close, but a moment later it opened again.

"Zoë?"

"No, Grace."

Grace stood. Before she could get to the door, Starlight appeared in front of her.

"Surprise." Starlight smiled, but her tone was stiff.

Grace tried to smile. "How're you . . . Starlight?"

"I'm good." She paused, looked around the office, then returned her gaze to Grace. "I came to congratulate you."

"Thanks." Grace hesitated. "Do you want to sit down?"

"Sure."

The office was heavy with silence as both shifted to find a comfortable place in their seats.

"I hope you don't mind my dropping by."

Grace shook her head.

"Mom said Tuesday night was wonderful." Starlight paused. "She's proud of you."

Grace took a slight breath and nodded. Silence filled their space again before Grace asked, "How have you been?"

"Good. I'm doing seminars, writing another book. I spoke at Greater Faith Chapel last night."

Grace's eyes widened. Pastor Carey was one of the city's most influential and respected clergymen. Although he wasn't part of her district, she'd received a lot of campaign support from him, especially about returning prayer to school. Why would Pastor Carey allow Starlight to speak at his church?

"Mom didn't tell you," Starlight said through Grace's thoughts.

Grace shook her head. "No, but . . ." Her voice trailed off.

Starlight tilted her head. "You still have a hard time accepting me, don't you?"

Grace looked straight into Starlight's eyes. "I accept you, Mabel. I just don't agree with what you do."

Starlight's smile disappeared. "We do the same thing, Grace."

No we don't, Mabel, she thought. *You hustle people for money in the name of God.* But Grace held that thought inside since she had spoken those words to her sister many times in the past. Instead she said, "Let's not talk about this."

Starlight's eyes narrowed. "I'm committed to helping people, just like you are," she said, wanting to convince her sister. "You wouldn't believe the mail I get about how I've changed women's lives."

Grace pressed her lips together, remembering the look in her mother's eyes when she told her that she and Starlight would never get together. And they wouldn't if she allowed this conversation to weave its way to its obvious conclusion.

"So you're still judging me."

"No I'm not, Mabel . . . Starlight."

Starlight looked away and wrapped the strap of her purse tighter around her arm. "I thought I'd come by . . ."

"And I'm glad you did," Grace said quickly.

Starlight glanced up, her eyes hooded with hope. "We're both doing well, Grace. That's our common ground."

We have nothing in common, Grace thought, though she kept her smile in place.

Grace stood. Starlight followed.

"Maybe one day we can meet for lunch," Starlight said.

Grace hesitated. "Maybe you can come by . . . one Sunday after church." She waited for her last words to settle. "The girls would love to see you."

Starlight grinned. "How're my nieces?"

"Fine. Jayde is talking about college, and Amber, well, she just wants Jayde's room when she goes away." Grace chuckled.

Starlight laughed. "I miss them. But I stay away."

Grace nodded.

Though they were just inches apart, it took a minute for Grace to reach through the space and take Starlight's hand. "Call me. We'll plan something."

Starlight leaned forward. Their hug was more the wooden embrace of strangers. But for the sisters, it was closer than they'd been in years. And in that moment, it felt good to both of them.

Starlight grinned when she pulled away. "I'll call."

Grace watched her sister walk to the door. Starlight was right. It was time to find common ground, even if just for twenty minutes once a month.

Conner took another sip of his chardonnay. He peeked through the curtains. *This is what the waiting was like for Grace last night,* he thought.

He looked at the clock. Almost seven.

When he had walked into his home two hours ago, his faith was strong. Chandler's encouragement had sustained him. But the passing minutes chipped at his confidence.

Conner stiffened when approaching car lights illuminated the darkened living room. He lifted his glass to his lips, relishing the last of the wine. He rested the glass on the table, then clasped his hands together.

It had been planned, but now he wasn't sure. Should he have on music? Should he sit on the couch? Should he be standing, waiting? Should he turn on more lights?

The opening door didn't give Conner a chance to answer any of his questions.

"Hi, sweetheart." He stood under the living room arch. Her smile made his heart pound harder.

"Hey." She kissed him. "When I saw only the foyer light, I thought you'd taken the girls out."

"I'm here," he said, because he couldn't think of any other words. The smile that he forced to his lips didn't stop the pressure building inside his head.

Her smile widened. "Where're the girls?"

"They're staying with Lily tonight."

"Really?" She wrapped her arms around Conner's neck. "So you must have plans for us." She paused. "I'm glad, because I was worried about you."

He swallowed.

"But it seems you're just fine." Grace chuckled.

Conner did not share her laugh. He turned away and walked to the table, filling his glass with more wine. "How was your day?" The question came from his lips, but it was the question in his mind that had his attention. How was he supposed to do this?

"Okay." She sat on the couch, but kept her eyes on her husband. "Starlight stopped by."

It took both of his hands to steady the shaking glass. He sat next to Grace. "Really?"

Grace said, "We had a decent chat, but . . ." She paused. "I still know who she is. Starlight's a liar. She's a fake."

He nodded because he couldn't speak.

"She uses half truths to get women to follow her. If I felt that her message really helped," Grace continued, "or even if she believed what she was saying, I could be more accepting. But it's all about money for her." She sighed. "She's spiritually poisoning people. She doesn't care about anyone but herself."

With one swallow, Conner finished the rest of his wine.

"I can't even imagine what she does behind closed doors," Grace continued, shaking her head. "The worse part for me is that Mabel knows she's misleading people." Grace sighed. "I don't want to be judgmental, but it's hard when I know my sister knows what she's doing. She's a liar."

Conner stood and walked to the window.

"I don't want to talk about Starlight anymore." Grace paused. "Honey, how was your day?"

He could hear the frown in her voice. He stood still, even when he heard her footsteps behind him. When she placed her hand on his shoulder, he was sure he'd stop breathing.

"Conner, what's wrong?"

He licked his dry lips, then faced his wife. In his mind, he heard her words again, "Starlight is a liar. She's a fake." That's what he felt like.

Conner shook his head. "I just have a lot on my mind."

"Is it a case?"

He nodded instead of speaking the lie out loud.

"Is it something that I can help with?"

He shook his head. "I think I'm going to go up to the office for a while. I've got a bit of work to do." With two steps, he fled from the living room.

"Conner."

When she called his name, his pace increased. Taking the stairs two at a time, he didn't stop until he was behind the closed door of their office. He breathed deeply, trying to calm the beating in his chest. He prayed that Grace wouldn't follow him.

When minutes passed, he took heavy steps to his desk and held his head in his hands. There was no way he could do this. No way he'd ever be able to utter the words that would permanently break his family. He'd have to find another way. He'd have to handle Pilar without Grace ever finding out.

Chapter 8

"Mommy, I think Daddy is mad at me."

Grace lifted her eyes from the newspaper. She reached across the kitchen table and covered Amber's hand. "Honey, that's not true. Why do you think that?"

Amber pushed her spoon against the pink, turquoise, and purple circles in her cereal bowl. "He won't talk to me."

"Your dad just has a lot on his mind, sweetie." She paused. "He's been working on a hard case at work."

Amber tilted her head to the side. "Like when Jayde was getting ready to play that tennis game?"

"That's right, sweetie. Remember how much Jayde wanted to win the championship?"

Amber nodded. "I thought she was mad at me, but she said she was just concentrating."

"That's what your father's doing. He'll be finished with this case soon, and everything will be back to normal. You'll see." Grace forced a wide smile and grabbed Amber's bowl. "Sweetie, go upstairs and put on your jeans. We'll take a ride over to Nana's house, okay?"

Amber's grin was back. "Okay, Mommy," she said before she ran from the kitchen.

Grace placed the bowl in the sink, pushed her weight against the counter, and stared out the window. The Saturday sun dazzled against the backyard gazebo. But the morning's warmth was so different from the heat rising in their home. Outside, the sun brought promises of another glorious April day. Inside, there was only the promise of the emotional silence that had invaded their space. For more than a week, the weight Conner carried hovered over them, threatening to crash down. There were times when she could almost feel the words that Conner wanted to share. But he remained silent, shutting her out. Although it took more willpower than she was aware she had, she'd stopped questioning, knowing that he would have to come to her eventually or that whatever was troubling him would pass.

But now their children were being affected. She was able to placate Amber, but Jayde wouldn't be so easy.

"What's wrong, Conner?" Grace whispered the question that she'd asked at least a million times in the last week.

Grace rinsed Amber's bowl, then placed it in the dishwasher. She marched up the stairs and stood outside the office. She closed her eyes, took a deep breath, and then stepped inside.

Conner was sitting at the desk, staring at the wall.

"I need to talk to you." When he looked up, the weariness in his eyes was what she felt in her bones. She leaned against the edge of the desk, hoping to find the question that would give her answers. "Sweetheart, what's wrong?" They were the only words that came to her mind.

Conner looked away and closed the folder on the desk. "Grace, I don't know why you keep asking me that. I told you . . ."

"You haven't told me anything," she said before he could finish, unable to keep the frustration from her tone.

"It's work."

"What about work?"

"Grace, I don't know why you're giving me a hard time. I've had difficult cases before."

"But nothing that made Amber think you were mad at her."

He paused, then took her hand. "Grace . . ."

The weariness that she saw in him before shifted to sadness, and in that second Grace wanted to flee. She was filled with fear.

After a moment, Conner looked away, letting her hand slip from his at the same time. "I don't know why Amber would think I'm mad."

Grace sighed. "Conner, you're different. You've been leaving early, coming home late. You didn't have dinner with us all week, and I can't think of the last time that's happened." She softened her voice. "You didn't even go to church last Sunday." She paused. "Whatever it is, I want to help. But I can't if you won't let me in."

He kept his stance, as if he was stuck in place. His silence was his armor. After long minutes passed, Grace raised herself from the desk and left the room. She leaned against her bedroom door, closed her eyes, and pressed back her tears. She knew for sure now that it wasn't a case holding her husband hostage. There was something much more.

The image of Pilar and Conner in the restaurant popped into her mind, and she snapped opened her eyes. Did this have something to do with her? Was Conner having an affair?

"No," she said, shaking her head. "That's not possible."

"Mommy, are you ready?"

She hadn't even heard Amber in the hall. "Give me a minute, sweetheart. Watch TV in your room, and I'll get you when I'm ready."

"Okay, Mommy."

Grace watched Amber skip to her room. Just a while ago, Amber was concerned, but her assurances had made Amber feel better. Grace sighed. That's what she wanted—the heart of a child.

But what she needed were answers. And if she couldn't get them from Conner, she'd have to find another way to uncover what he was hiding.

Even though it was Saturday night, lights from inside the Century City office buildings still shone brightly. Conner turned from the window. He glanced at his watch, although he knew the time. It was only five minutes since the last time he'd looked—just a bit after eight. Time was slowly passing. It was still too early to go home. Grace would be there, waiting with her questions. Questions that he couldn't respond to because he didn't have the answers himself.

He returned to the desk and flipped through the notepad. Beyond work, he'd never been much of a writer, but for the past days, he'd put his troubled thoughts onto these pages. There was a boy in New York, a child who could be his son. On the other side of his life's ledger were his wife and the two children whom he'd loved before they took their first breaths.

Conner stared at his notes as if his glare could transform the words. But nothing that was before him was going to change.

The beeping of his cell phone startled him. He hadn't expected Grace to call. Days ago, she'd stopped trying to track him down. He glanced at the Caller ID and frowned.

"Yes, Pilar," he said, his words and tone lacking any pleasantries.

"I haven't heard from you in a few days."

"I've needed some time to sort this through."

"I don't have time."

"I know that, Pilar. But this is not easy."

"Have you told Grace?"

His silence was his response.

"I need to see you," she said.

"There's no need for that."

"Tomorrow."

He leaned forward in his chair. "You're in L.A.?" Questions swirled through his mind like a deadly tornado. What was Pilar doing here? Was she going to try to see Grace?

"Yes, I'm in L.A. I need to talk to you."

"We can do that over the phone." He paused, then added, "It's better over the phone." He closed his eyes as he imagined meeting with Pilar and Grace seeing them again.

"This will be the last time, but I have to see you." She hesitated. "You owe me this much, Conner."

He wanted to be angered by her words, but she was right. He did owe her one more meeting. He needed to tell her face-to-face what he'd just decided. That he would do everything he could for Solomon. That he would pay any amount of money to make sure he was well taken care of. That he would make sure all was well with him, even after she was gone. He would do it all—except be his father.

He'd help her make other plans, find another home where Solomon would be safe and loved. But not with his family. Not with the Monroes.

"We can meet tomorrow," he said. "After church. I'll call you in the morning to let you know where."

"Fine." A second later he heard the empty air of the phone.

He leaned back in the chair. Maybe it was good that Pilar had come back. Her call had helped him decide. Now he could move forward, handle this without Grace ever knowing. His secret would remain. The truth would never be told.

As he picked up his briefcase and stuffed his cell phone into his pocket, he tried to push aside the voice in his head. The one that said that the truth always came to light. But maybe this one time it didn't have to.

Chapter 9

"I have to make a quick stop," Conner said as he pulled the car to a halt in their driveway. He could see the protest in Grace's eyes. "But I'll be right back," he added. When Grace stared at him a moment longer, he said, "I promise."

Grace nodded and moved toward her door. But before she could get out of the car, Conner reached for her, leaning over the console of the Suburban. He held her tight, wanting the embrace to resemble the thousands that they'd shared before Pilar had come to Los Angeles. When she pulled back, Conner traced the edge of her face with his fingertips, and a smile filled her face.

Conner smiled too. This was coming to an end. By the time he returned home, his life would be the way it should be.

"See you in a little while, Daddy," Amber said before she ran into the house after Jayde.

He squeezed Grace's hand. "Give me an hour."

Her smile widened. "The girls and I will get dinner ready." She paused. "Maybe we can catch a movie tonight. Mom asked if the girls could stay over since tomorrow begins their spring break."

He nodded. "Let's do that," he said before he kissed her cheek.

Conner smiled as he pulled away from his home and directed his car toward the meeting place with Pilar. But as he got closer to

Kenneth Hahn Park, his grin faded as he thought about the words he'd say. He would explain that he'd take this journey with her, but there was no need to disrupt his life and no need to disturb Solomon any more than they had to. After all, he was losing his mother. He didn't need the added emotion of finding out about his father. Surely, there was someone to whom Pilar could give custody, especially since he was willing to take care of Solomon financially. He hadn't worked out all the details, especially not how he was going to provide money for Solomon without Grace finding out. But those were minor details that would be solved once Pilar agreed.

Conner swerved into the park and then rushed up the hill to where he'd told Pilar to meet him—away from the main thoroughfare. At the top of the hill he paused, until he spotted her sitting on a bench. His steps slowed as he approached her. He searched for signs of how she would accept his words. But it didn't matter. This was his plan; she'd have to agree.

He sat next to her, feeling the hard wooden planks of the bench through this suit.

"Hello."

She nodded, keeping her eyes straight ahead. He followed her glance and saw four boys tossing a football. He wondered what she was thinking. Wondered if she was imagining her son's life in the years without her. He would assure her that Solomon would have a good life.

"Thank you for meeting me," she spoke finally. "I needed to move this along. We have to start making plans."

"I agree. I want you to know that I will do everything I can to take care of Solomon."

For the first time she looked at him. She smiled. "Thank you."

He looked down. The words had been in his mind since they'd spoken last night. He'd hardly been able to sleep. He'd prepared what he'd say as he would a summation. But now that Pilar sat next to him, this was tougher than any courtroom situation he'd ever been in.

"I will do everything I can. . . ." He stopped. He didn't need to look at her to know that her smile had faded as she waited for his next words. "I'm sure there is someone who would be better for Solomon."

"I told you, there is no one else."

"I'm really thinking about Solomon."

Pilar turned away and raised her hand above her head. Conner frowned and followed her glance. In an instant, one of the boys broke from the group and raced toward their bench. With each of the young man's steps, Conner's heart stabbed his chest. Approaching him was the image in the picture that Pilar had given him. The boy with the bushy eyebrows, the high cheekbones, the cleft in his chin. The boy who left no doubt. The boy who was his son.

"Mom, did you need me?" the boy said to Pilar.

She smoothed her hand against his head. "No, I just wanted to make sure that you weren't overdoing it. You know there's a three-hour time difference between home and L.A."

"Oh, Mom." The boy grinned as if he were used to this protectiveness. "I'm fine." His grin went away. "Are you sure you're okay?"

She nodded.

The bench was Conner's prison. He felt as if shackles bound his feet, his hands, his head. Only his eyes were able to move as he followed every movement, each gesture, trying to ingest twelve years of information about the boy. His mind raced, yet he captured a single thought: I love my son's smile.

His son turned to him. "Hello." Solomon tilted his head. "Do you know my mom?"

Before Conner could respond, Pilar said, "Solomon, you'd better go back to your game. We'll be leaving soon."

"Okay, Mom." He stared at Conner for a moment longer, then ran back to the group.

Conner tried to swallow, but his lips were pinched together. Pilar allowed the silence and the sight of her son to settle before them.

Finally he said, "That was Solomon." His voice was soft, as if he couldn't believe what he'd just seen. "Why didn't you tell me he was here?"

"Would that have made a difference?"

Conner didn't respond. He didn't know.

"It's time for us to make plans, Conner. I have to make sure my son is taken care of when . . . I'm no longer here." She stood and swayed slightly. Conner reached for her, helping her to steady her stance. "We'll be leaving for New York in the morning. I have a doctor's appointment, and I don't want Solomon to miss too many days of school." She began to walk away, but just steps later, she glanced over her shoulder. "You just laid your eyes on your son, Conner. I'll be waiting to hear from you."

Conner stayed as Pilar trudged across the grass to where Solomon tossed the football to one of the other boys. Then she placed her hand on his shoulder, and they walked away. He stared, still unable to move. He wanted to run after them. He wanted just another minute, even just a second . . . with his son.

Just before Pilar and Solomon disappeared over the curve of the hill, the boy turned around and waved. He could have been waving to the boys he'd just played with, but Conner was sure the gesture was for him.

He closed his eyes and pressed the tears back. Every thought, every plan, all the preparations dissipated inside of him. There would be no hidden checks or hushed meetings. There would be no secrets at all. He had to claim his son.

Conner's hand trembled as he pressed the remote for the garage door. It's good that it's Sunday, he thought for the thousandth time. At least this morning, he and Grace had prayed together, worshipped together. And by the time they got home, they had hoped together. Although they still had not talked, Conner knew that Grace had the same wishes he had—that their lives would return to normal.

But that was hours earlier.

He didn't know how much time had passed since he'd left Pilar, but he knew that it had been too long for Grace. He was sure she and the girls had long ago had dinner.

When he stepped to the door, he closed his eyes. "Dear Lord," he began. "I'm finally doing the right thing. Please help me to find the right words." He'd said that prayer in variations all afternoon.

Inside, he moved slowly through the darkened hallway, but at the kitchen door, he stopped. Grace sat at the table with her arms crossed, her frown planted as if it had been in place for hours. The curry from the shrimp she'd cooked still fragranced the air. Conner tried to gulp the lump in his throat. His wife had prepared his favorite dish.

"Grace . . ."

She held up her hand and stood. "Conner, I am not going through this anymore. You've disappointed me and the girls for the last time, and . . ."

This time he stopped her. "I know. We need to talk."

She backed away slightly as if surprised by his words. "Okay."

He looked around. "Where're the girls?"

"With Mom. They're spending the night."

He took a breath, and then reached for her hand. The chains that he'd felt in the park returned as he led them to the living room. But it was the noose he felt around his neck that frightened him the most.

"Is a case bothering you?" she asked as they sat.

He knew that was her thought, that was her hope. He stroked her face with his fingertips and wished that God could take them away from this place. Finally, he took her hand and moved closer. Their knees touched. "I'm so sorry, sweetheart." The apology was a good beginning.

"About what?"

He lowered his eyes. "There's something I have to tell you, but I don't know how." His tongue grazed his lips again.

Grace took both of his hands into hers. "You can tell me anything."

The water welling in his eyes blurred his vision. "I love you."

"I love you too, Conner." Her voice trembled.

He hoped she'd say those words again when he was finished. "I found out something. I don't understand . . . I don't know how . . . I don't know what . . . ," he jabbered.

Grace held his hands tighter.

"Pilar . . ."

She pulled away.

He looked down at his hands, alone now. "She told me something you have to know."

It was time to say it. He stood and looked at the fireplace. Even though it was spring, he wished he had started a fire. Anything to warm the sudden chill that filled the room.

When he turned back to Grace, her face was already filled with pain. He was torturing them both. He looked at her hands, wanting to take them into his, wanting to hold her as he twisted her world inside out.

He returned to the couch. "Pilar has a child." He paused to make sure that he was still breathing. "A son." He coughed, hoping in that second he'd discover courage. "He's mine." The two syllables stopped his heart.

An eternity passed in the seconds that ticked from the grandfather clock.

Though every nerve inside him screamed to touch her, he was afraid. Instead, he rested his elbows on his thighs and clasped his hands under his chin. But the shaking that quaked through his body continued.

"What are you talking about?"

Conner stared at Grace. Her question was casual, as if she were talking to one of her aides, asking them to repeat something she didn't quite understand.

"Grace, I'm so sorry."

Her face was stiff with seriousness. "What are you talking about?"

He blinked. Did she want him to repeat what he'd said? He didn't have enough inside of him to utter those words to her again.

"You are the father of Pilar's child," she said for him.

He nodded and trembled more.

"That can't be." She shook her head. "In order to father a child, Conner, you would have to sleep with that person." She stood, and her voice rose with her. "You would have to have sex, intercourse, intimacy." She turned to him with fire in her eyes. "Tell Pilar she's a liar."

"It's true, Grace," he said softly.

She held up her hands. "It's not true, because, Conner, I know how much you love me. I know how much you love God. I know how much you love our children. I know that with all we've been through, you would never do this now."

He jumped from the couch. "Oh, no, Grace. This didn't just happen. Her son . . . my son . . . he's twelve years old."

"He's older than Amber?" she whispered.

Conner swallowed and nodded.

He could tell by her eyes that her mind was calculating, asking, and answering questions.

"Please, Grace, sit down. I want to explain."

Her eyes filled with water. "You've told me everything I need to know. You have a son with another woman." She bit her lip, trading that pain for the words she'd just uttered. "There is nothing more to explain." Grace turned abruptly.

Conner grabbed her arm, stopping her. Her eyes moved from his hand to his eyes. Then she jerked from his grasp and ran up the stairs.

Grace opened her eyes; it took a moment for her to adjust to the darkness. It wasn't that she'd been asleep. Unconsciousness was too easy.

She didn't know how much time had passed—it could have been four minutes or four hours. It was an empty canvas of time with a battle between empty thoughts and ones that warred in her mind.

She rolled to Conner's side of the bed, stroked his pillow, and whispered his name. She wished that he would come, lie beside her, and assure her that her ears had deceived her. But she knew he spoke the truth. Only truth could push those words through his lips.

She wiped invisible tears from her face. She was surprised. She hadn't cried. Her calm felt eerie. As if the news hadn't yet traveled to her brain.

"Pilar has a child . . . a son . . . he's mine."

She jumped from the bed, rushed to the door, and stood listening before she stepped into the hallway. The house was dark, except for the gentle glow of bronze from the night lights in the hallway. Her eyes adjusted, and the years in the house allowed her to take the familiar steps to the stairs. At the bottom of the staircase, she paused when silence and darkness were all that met her. She moved to the living room.

Conner stood the moment she came under the archway. She folded her arms and blinked back tears that now filled her eyes. "Tell me everything."

In the dark, she could see his shadow nod. "I want to." He walked to her, but with just a small slip, she evaded his arms.

Conner turned on the light.

He moved toward her, but when he got to the couch, his eyes darted between where she sat and where he'd been. He lowered himself away from her. "I don't know where to begin."

His words made her tears flow as her mind took her back to a time when she'd sat in the same place, uttering the same words: "I don't know where to begin." It was a statement of betrayal and a sign that more would follow—apologies and explanations. She wondered if his heart had ached then as much as hers did now.

"The first thing I want you to know is that I am so sorry."

She stayed stiff in her place, not giving him a reprieve.

Conner began, "It was a long time ago, Grace. It was right after I found out about you and Drew."

Her head jerked back at her ex-lover's name. "You're saying this is my fault?"

He shook his head. "I just want to explain." He lowered his eyes. "It seemed like Drew was going to be part of our lives forever. I was trying to understand what he gave you that I couldn't. I was hurting."

"And she was there."

He nodded. "I tried to fool myself into thinking that I felt better, but I didn't." His words came quicker. "It didn't last, Grace, because I knew that I wanted you, and I prayed that you wanted me. Pilar left, and we began counseling. I never thought about her again."

She let his words hang in the air for a moment. "I can't believe this, Conner."

"I know. I am so sorry."

"That's not what I'm talking about." She stopped. "During our counseling, during our healing, you let me believe it was me. That I was the cause of our problems."

"I never said that. We were both responsible."

"But I believed that I was the root of every trouble we had." Her voice trembled.

"I never wanted you to think that."

"I've carried this burden for years."

"You shouldn't have. I told you, Grace, I forgave you a long time ago."

She glared at him. She could see the moisture covering his eyes. "That's the problem, Conner. Because you forgave me, but you never gave me the chance to forgive you."

She stood and left the room.

Chapter 10

Grace blinked, until her eyes focused. Where am I? she wondered. Then she remembered. Conner's confession—the pain of his words. It had all driven her to a fitful night on the couch in their office.

Last night, she'd retreated to their bedroom, but the moment Conner joined her in bed, she had rolled away and stomped from the room. She'd seen every hour pass from the clock on the desk. From midnight to four, she'd laid awake, praying that Conner would come and comfort her. She wanted to talk, to understand. But the fusion of pride, anger, hurt, which twisted her insides like a pretzel, kept her away from him. Finally, she'd fallen into a restless sleep that was crammed with images of Conner and Pilar, and their son.

She pushed herself from the couch and moaned at the stiffness in her legs. As she massaged her thighs, she listened to the quiet of the house, absent the normal morning sounds. It was a blessing that the girls had been away. But now she needed to hear their voices.

She picked up the phone and dialed her mother's number. "Hi, Mom," she said after a groggy Lily said hello.

"Honey, what's wrong?"

Grace tried to grin, hoping that would keep the tears from her voice. "Nothing. I just called to check on the girls."

"It's so early."

Grace glanced at the clock and almost cursed. It wasn't even six. "I'm sorry. I have an early meeting."

"The girls are fine. Still asleep." She paused. "Grace, what's wrong?"

Her mother sounded alert now. Grace could imagine her sitting up, her head tied in one of the hot-purple silk wraps Starlight had given her. Her eyes thinned and filled with concern, trying to figure out what she heard in her daughter's voice.

"Mom, I'm fine. Listen, I'll call you later. Maybe the girls can spend another night with you."

"That would be fine with me."

"Thanks. I'll call later." She hung up before Lily could ask another question. She exhaled. That was over. Now she had to get past Conner.

She opened the door and listened for sounds from their bedroom. When she heard nothing, she tiptoed to the bathroom the girls shared, pulling a towel from the linen closet on the way. Inside the shower, the heat of the water soothed the fatigue that seeped through her bones. But nothing blocked the questions that fired through her mind.

She wanted to stay in the shower, away from the world. But soon Conner would awaken and come looking for her. This morning, she did not want to be found.

She crept into their bedroom and stood at the door until she was sure he was still asleep. Inside her closet, she slipped quickly into jeans and a matching jacket. She grabbed her briefcase and rushed down the stairs. In the kitchen, she paused. She needed coffee, but the aroma would be a ringing alarm for Conner. Instead, she got into her car. It wasn't even seven o'clock.

A few minutes later, she pulled into the Starbucks parking lot. After ordering a venti espresso, she returned to her car. She sipped the drink, shrinking a bit at the taste.

What am I supposed to do? she wondered. She wanted to answer that question, but too many other thoughts swirled inside her. What would Conner's revelation mean for her and her family? Did Conner want a relationship with the boy? What did Pilar want? And how could they be sure that she was telling the truth?

It was all too much.

Grace turned on the ignition. She'd drown in these thoughts if she let them continue. They'd invaded too much of her space already. Within ten minutes, she was at the office, and by the time Zoë walked in at nine, Grace had buried herself in work.

"What are you doing here?" Zoë asked.

Grace kept her eyes on the computer screen as her fingers danced across the keyboard. "I wanted to get an early start on my education proposal for the mayor," she said. She stopped and pulled three pages from the printer. "And I just finished the application for the school prayer hearings."

Zoë looked at her watch. "Grace, you were due at city hall at nine. The committee review meeting is this morning."

"I forgot," Grace exclaimed. "I can't miss that. I'll go right now." She wondered why Zoë frowned when she stood. Then Grace remembered and looked down at her jeans. "I can't go like this." She sighed. "I can't believe I'm going to miss this. I want to be on the Education Committee, and this isn't going to look good."

"Just go the way you are." When Grace began to shake her head,

Zoë continued, "Look, you're new, you're bringing different ideas to city hall. Why not go like a young, hip representative?"

Grace laughed. "Because I'm not young and hip."

"That's a minor technicality." Zoë put her hand on her hips. "What would you prefer? To show up dressed like that or not go at all? It's not as if you're making a presentation. You're just going to listen to the mayor, schmooze a little, and make sure that you're assigned to that Education Committee."

Grace looked at Zoë, then looked down at her jeans again. "Okay. Give me a minute to freshen up."

Zoë raised her thumb in the air. "I'll call Frank so you won't have to deal with the traffic."

Grace waited until Zoë closed the door before she sank into her chair. How could she have forgotten about this meeting? She'd been looking forward to it since it was announced at the reception last week. She pressed the heels of her hands against her eyes. For a few hours, she'd been able to escape the thoughts of home. But it was all still there, right at the front of her mind.

Grace stood, grabbed her briefcase, and headed toward the door. She couldn't spend her day drowning in Conner's revelation. Not now, since she was sure her husband's admission would be dominating their lives for many days to come.

Chandler high-fived Conner the moment they stepped into the elevator. "Man, you were on fire."

Conner smiled. His presentation to Crosby Enterprises had been one of his best. The final preparation this morning had been a welcome respite, keeping his mind buried in business.

"What got into you?"

"You know me. The best way to handle challenges is to give it to God, then jump into work."

Chandler's smile disappeared. "I was waiting for you to bring it up."

Conner knew Chandler would never mention Pilar first. Not until he told Chandler that he was ready to talk—either aloud or by transmitted thought. Newspapers reported it, and talk show hosts spoke of it, but he lived it. Chandler knew him as if he was inside his mind.

"Any new developments?" Chandler asked as they stepped from the elevator.

The building's security guard lowered his eyes, then did a double-take, realizing he was seeing twins. He nodded as the brothers passed.

"Quite a few." Conner handed his parking ticket to the valet, and Chandler did the same.

Chandler waited until they were standing alone. "You told Grace?"

"Most of it. Last night."

"How'd it go?"

Conner glanced at his brother sideways. "Imagine the worse scenario, then multiply it by infinity. She didn't scream, she didn't cry. She just looked at me as if she'd stepped in something." He stopped, remembering the way Grace had stared straight through his bones. He shivered and wondered for the first time what he hadn't dared. Would Grace leave him?

"She's in shock, that's all," Chandler reassured, as if he was answering the silent question Conner had just asked himself.

"But there's more." He paused. "I saw Solomon."

"What? When?"

Conner told Chandler about the meeting in the park. "Pilar never introduced me, but, Chandler, it was amazing seeing him. Being that close to him."

"I can't even imagine."

"And," Conner paused and tried not to smile, "he looks just like us."

Chandler nodded slightly. "So what are you going to do?"

"I don't have it all worked out yet. I need to talk to Grace. But I'm going to do the right thing."

Chandler patted his brother on his shoulder. "Let me know what you want me to do."

Conner's Suburban came first. He tossed his briefcase onto the passenger seat and turned to his brother. "Going back to the office?"

Chandler shook his head. "Devry and I have a doctor's appointment." He grinned, then turned sober.

Conner knew what Chandler was thinking. There was a chance both were going to be new fathers.

"Hey, Conner," Chandler said, as he opened his Mercedes door. "Just know, bro, this is going to work out. The Lord will see to that."

Conner handed the valet a ten-dollar bill and signaled for him to keep the change. He fastened his seat belt, attached his cell phone to the in-car speaker, and pulled away from the curb. Chandler's words played in his head, and he prayed that his brother was right: it would work out. He just had to keep believing . . . he had to keep believing in himself and Grace.

*   *   *

Grace pressed the Talk button on her cell phone without looking up from the report on her lap.

"Sweetheart, it's me."

Grace tightened at his voice.

"What is it, Conner?"

"We need to talk."

"Not now."

"Are you in a meeting?"

"No, I'm in the car." She pressed the button on the side panel, closing the privacy window. "I just left city hall. I almost missed a very important meeting this morning." She didn't add the most important words that she wanted to say: because of you.

"I'm sorry. Is everything okay?"

She paused. "No, Conner. Nothing's okay, and I doubt if anything will ever be okay again."

"I promise, Grace, we'll be fine."

"How can you make that promise?"

"Because I know how you feel and . . ."

"No, you don't."

He exhaled. "You're right. But remember, this is as much a surprise for me as it's been for you." When she remained silent, he said, "We really need to talk more."

She pressed her lips together, imagining what he wanted to discuss. How he would tell her that he wanted a relationship with his son. That thought brought her repressed tears to the front. Her husband had a son. Pilar had given him that gift—the one thing she had not been able to do.

"Grace . . ."

She said, "Conner, this is your problem."

A thin breath of air escaped through his lips. "I wish it were like that, Grace. I wish I could handle this and not get you or the girls involved."

Her heart stood still. "My daughters are not involved. Don't you dare say anything to them."

"I won't, not until we're both ready. But this affects our whole family." He paused, searching for his next words. "I can't walk away from this, Grace. I tried to, but I can't. That isn't in my makeup. That's not the man you married."

The man I married wouldn't have me in this place! she shouted inside. She blinked to keep the tears from falling. "What do you want from me?"

"I want you with me, Grace. We can get through this. We have danced through our storms . . ." He stopped.

She held her hand over her heart, remembering when he'd first uttered those words. They were part of his pledge when they renewed their vows. Through the years, he repeated them, reminding her they could conquer any challenge.

He continued, "And because Pilar won't go away."

Her face tightened as he brought her back to her point of pain. "Solomon won't go away either."

She covered her mouth, holding back her gasp when he said his son's name.

Solomon.

She hadn't asked. She didn't want a name for the faceless image that had filled her mind in the last hours.

"Grace, if there was anything I could do to take this away, I would."

"I'll see you at home." She clicked off her phone and leaned back in her seat. How was she supposed to handle this? How was she supposed to keep her family together? How was she supposed to protect her daughters?

She wiped a tear from the corner of her eye. Conner was right. This had to be handled, but it didn't have to be disruptive. Conner didn't sound as if he wanted a relationship with the child, though the thought made her heart sink. She wished the boy could know his father, but she couldn't feel bad when she had her own girls to think about.

But he's a child.

She crushed that screaming thought. She couldn't care about anyone who could rip her family apart.

But he's a child—your husband's son.

Grace shook her head. This sin had to stay buried deep in their family closet.

But he's a child—one of God's own.

They would provide financial support, but her care could go no further.

A calm comfort came with this new determination. Her family would get through this. They would lean on the Lord, as they always did. Their prayers would guide them. She thought about what Pastor Ford always said—how standing on God's word brought peace.

"Learn to quote God's word back to Him," Pastor Ford had said dozens of times. "Know scripture—not to memorize for the sake of knowing, but memorizing for the sake of life. God's words will protect and lead you through any human thunderstorms."

Grace leaned back, settling in the softness of the seat, and closed her eyes as Frank inched the car forward on the 10 Freeway. There was no better time to put into practice what Pastor Ford taught.

I will call upon the Lord who is worthy to be praised: so shall I be saved from my enemies.

Her eyes popped open as Psalm 18:3 passed through her mind. Why would she think about enemies? She shook her head. No, she wouldn't think about the end of that scripture. She'd focus on the beginning. She would call on the Lord, again and again, until this all went away.

Chapter 11

The long beep of the fax machine alerted Starlight. She pulled the last page from the machine, then put them all in order. Though she had read each page as it was transmitted, she settled onto the couch and pulled her feet underneath her.

She felt as if she were having an out-of-body experience as she read the contract. She knew it by heart; she'd negotiated for weeks, letting Forge Publishing feel the unspoken threat—that there were other publishers eager to please her.

It worked. Forge had offered Starlight a blockbuster deal, all without an agent. She chuckled. No one could have brokered a better deal, and she didn't have to pay the agent's fifteen percent.

Two books, three million dollars, with escalators that could take the total to almost four million. Five hundred thousand for just signing. For thirty minutes, she relished every word on each page.

Finally, she stood and laid the contract on the desk. She stared at the first page, at the line that showed the amount of the agreement. She counted the zeros and laughed.

Lily Hobbs-Richards's daughters had done well. Grace had always excelled. Even with her troubles, she emerged shining brighter than the stars. But Starlight knew there was no star in the universe more radiant than hers right now.

"Miss Starlight, what would you like for dinner?"

Starlight whipped around. "You startled me."

Carletta lowered her eyes and almost bowed. "I'm sorry."

Starlight held up her hands. "I'm not hungry." Then she said, "I do want something. Run and get me . . . Thai. You know that restaurant on Olympic?"

Carletta frowned, and Starlight imagined what her housekeeper was thinking: *That was so far away.* Starlight smiled. That was the point.

She pulled bills from her wallet, and then walked to where Carletta waited in the hallway—following the instructions given on her first day—never to enter Starlight's office. She handed the woman three twenty-dollar bills.

"What would you like?"

Starlight waved her hand. "Anything."

"Do you have a menu? I can call."

"No," Starlight snapped. "Order it when you get there. I want it warm when you bring it back." Starlight held her breath as she listened to Carletta go to her room for a sweater, then leave.

In the Friday evening traffic, it would take the housekeeper at least twenty minutes to get to the restaurant, twenty minutes to wait for the food, and another twenty minutes to return. If luck was on her side, Carletta's 1981 Mitsubishi might have a little trouble too.

Now she'd be able to savor the sensation of success without Carletta lurking. Starlight placed the contract inside a folder, then dropped it into the file cabinet. She locked the case and returned the key to her pocket. No one had access to her most personal papers.

As she moved from the office to the living room, her bare feet made light imprints in the custom-dyed lavender carpet that perfectly matched the walls, creating a continuous sea of soft purple. Tranquility shrouded her when she stepped into this space, with its hues of royalty and ocean views that still made her gasp. The oversized room had been created when she knocked out an adjoining wall, making the area massive. Though the room could hold a football field, its sparseness was surprising. Two custom-designed twelve-foot couches (one shade deeper than the carpet) sat in the middle facing each other, but most of the seating was designated to overstuffed velvet pillows. She wanted people to sit on the floor, supporting her philosophy that the closer you were to the earth, the closer you were to self.

Starlight dragged one of the pillows to the window. Then she sank into its softness. Even on the floor, she could see the ocean through the balcony's glass casing. She sighed. But her sigh wasn't one of joy. There was no one to share her success with. That thought often brought her to tears.

Starlight reflected on the time she spent with Grace last week. Though they wouldn't yet win any Sister of the Year awards, it was as warm as Grace had been in years. Maybe they would call a truce, and Starlight could once again be an aunt. She wanted to share this with her family. Especially Jayde. Though she loved Amber, she didn't know her. Amber was an infant when Mabel became Starlight, a false prophet in Grace's eyes. It was then that she was unofficially banned from the Monroes' life.

But she had a feeling that life was going to change. Now she would have family and fame.

The click of the door's lock made Starlight rise. How could Carletta have returned so soon? She should have sent her farther south.

"Starlight."

"I'm in the Grande Room," she yelled.

A moment later, Lexington appeared, his face filled with a smile. "You look happy." He hugged her, then grazed her cheeks with his lips.

As he stepped away, she pulled him close and kissed him, nudging her tongue between his lips. He leaned back, surprise incised in every line on his face. Starlight returned her lips to his, and pressed her body against him. Moments later, she took his hand and led him from the room.

"Where's Carletta?" His voice was husky.

"She went to get food."

"You're hungry?"

At her bedroom door, Starlight answered his question with another kiss. The feast from the East would have to wait. She hungered for something else now. She needed to celebrate her wonderful life.

Chapter 12

The moment Grace opened the door, the aroma greeted her with the gentleness of a lover's hug. She stepped inside and paused at the bottom of the stairs.

"Daddy, can I have another taste?"

"You just tasted it, Amber." Jayde's annoyed tone floated into the hallway.

"Daddy, tell Jayde to mind her business."

Grace almost smiled as she listened to the sounds of her family, but reality would not allow her joy. She turned from the noises of normalcy and climbed the stairs, not wanting to disrupt.

She was glad when she heard Conner's voice mail message saying he was picking up the girls. Although it hadn't been planned, Jayde and Amber had spent the entire week with Lily. So many times Grace had wanted to bring her daughters home, needing to feel what was usual. But when Jayde had called and asked if they could spend extra days, Grace knew it was a blessing from God, although she suspected that Amber had been bribed with ice cream and Jayde was just pleased that her grandmother was free to drive her from activity to activity during this school-free week.

It had worked for them all. Even she and Conner had been able to hang onto the edges of peace.

On Tuesday, when she said, "I don't want to talk about this right now, Conner," he'd left her alone in the office.

"Give me some more time, Conner," was what she said on Wednesday.

Last night, she'd jumped into bed the moment she heard the garage door open and pretended to be asleep when Conner came into the bedroom.

But Grace knew that this reprieve was coming to an end. She'd have to face Conner soon. Face him and discussions about his son.

She didn't make a sound as she closed her bedroom door. She couldn't wait to hug her daughters, but she needed some time before she greeted them. Before she faced them knowing that their father wasn't their's alone. She shrugged her jacket from her shoulders and smiled when she heard a knock on the door.

"Come in." She wondered which child had discovered that she was home. She froze when Conner entered.

"I thought I heard you." He hesitated, brushed his lips across her cheek, then stuffed his hands into his jeans. "I cooked." His smile was unsure.

"Thank you," she said. Then, "Excuse me," as she stepped by, careful not to touch him as she went to her closet. In the dark, she hung her jacket, but remained inside the chamber.

"Honey, are you coming down?" Conner stood outside the closet, watching her.

"Give me a few minutes."

She could feel his gaze before he turned away.

When she was alone, Grace slumped onto the bed and leaned against the headboard. She pulled her knees to her chest, letting her chin rest on her legs. She was sure she had made peace with this. But every time she saw Conner, she saw Pilar in her mind's eye.

"I can't do this." She pounded her fist against the mattress and almost jumped when she looked up and saw Conner standing in the doorway.

His eyes were a mirror to her heart, reflecting her sadness.

Grace stood. "I'm coming now." She wiped her face, tugged at her shirt, and walked toward the door. She paused, waiting for Conner to step aside. When he stayed in place, she brushed past him.

With just the tips of his fingers, he reached for her arm. "We can do this, Grace," he whispered. "Together."

She pulled from his grasp with more force than she expected and swept through the hall. At the bottom of the stairs, she took a breath before stepping into the kitchen. "Hello, ladies." On the outside, she smiled as she kissed Amber, then Jayde. "I missed you guys. How are my girls?"

"Fine, Mommy. I missed you too." Amber lifted the paper in front of her. "Do you want to see what I worked on at Nana's?

"Sure." Grace scanned the numbers that Amber had scrawled.

"Mommy, listen to this." Amber took a deep breath. "One times one is one . . . one times two is two . . . one times three is . . ."

"Do I have to hear this again?" Jayde whined.

Grace ignored her oldest daughter. "Amber, this is good."

"That's what I told her," Conner said as he entered the room.

Grace kept her eyes on her children. "Jayde, what did you do at your grandmother's house?"

"I hung out with Brittany most of the time, and I worked a little on my paper that's due when I go back to school on Monday. But we don't even get a break. Mr. Berg already assigned our next project." She sighed as if she carried a burden equal to the world's weight.

"What's next?" Grace asked.

"We have to write about Christian heroes—one living and one dead—and then compare their lives." Jayde smiled, the load now somehow lifted. "The living one is easy. That's you, Dad."

Grace felt Conner's smile even before he came to the table and kissed the top of Jayde's head.

"Thank you, honey."

"You're my hero, too, Daddy," Amber chirped.

Conner chuckled, Jayde rolled her eyes, and Grace was sure that she'd be ill.

"I'll help you finish your paper," Grace said, returning their attention to Jayde.

"You don't have to, Mom. I'm really done. I just want to go over it to make sure I'll get an A."

Conner put his arm around Jayde's shoulders. "Can my beautiful, straight A daughter set the dining room table?"

Jayde frowned. "Why are we eating in there? It's not Sunday."

Conner looked at Grace. "I thought we should have a family dinner tonight."

"But it's only spaghetti, and there's no TV in there," Jayde said.

Conner's glance didn't leave his wife. "That's why we're eating in the dining room." He paused when Grace looked at him. "We're going to sit and talk together."

"Why can't we do that in here?" Jayde pouted.

"Jayde, set the table, please," Conner said.

Grace broke their stare and turned to Amber. "I'll take these papers so they don't get messed up. Go wash up, okay?"

Amber ran from the kitchen, and Jayde, still sulking, filled her arms with plates.

When they were alone, Grace watched Conner as he pulled a tray of garlic bread from the oven. She folded her arms. "Is there anything you want me to do?"

He dropped the tray onto the counter. Then he lifted her chin with two fingers. "I want you to remember that I love you."

She looked at him for a moment, then turned into the dining room.

Minutes later, the clatter of silverware clanging against the plates filled the room. Grace sliced the bread before they sat and bowed their heads.

"Heavenly Father, we thank you for this food, but most important, we thank and praise you for this family. Thank you for keeping us and for the blessings that you've given us. We are grateful, Lord, for your grace and mercy. And for your hand in every part of our lives. We know that we can do nothing without you. As you said in your word, *for with God all things are possible.*" He paused. "So, Lord, we know that whatever fires come our way, we will not be burned. Thank you for protecting us. In Jesus's name, Amen."

"Wow," Jayde said. "That wasn't grace; that was a prayer."

"What's wrong with that?" Conner twirled the pasta around his fork.

"Prayers are for bedtime," Amber piped in.

Conner looked across the table at Grace. "Prayers are for whenever you need them."

Grace lowered her eyes and took a small bite of bread. She was relieved when Amber began chatting about the upcoming class trip to the L.A. Zoo and she was able to retreat into her thoughts. Jayde and Amber didn't notice her silence, although every few minutes, she felt Conner's gaze.

She looked at her husband with their children, and her heart ached. There was another life, existing parallel to theirs, that could rip their world apart. She lowered her head as tears threatened.

"In history, Mrs. Jaffe said we're going to develop our family trees."

Grace's head snapped up.

Jayde continued, "She wants us to do it using the Internet. Will you help me, Daddy?"

Conner nodded, then looked at Grace.

"I could probably use the one I did in the second grade," Jayde said.

Grace stood.

"I would only have to add you." Jayde laughed and pointed to her sister. "We didn't even know about you then."

Grace lifted her plate and turned toward the kitchen.

"Finished, honey?"

Her glare was strong when she whipped around. They all froze under her stare. "Yes, Conner," she said, though her lips didn't seem to move. "I'm totally finished."

In the kitchen, Grace leaned against the counter, taking deep breaths to control the bile rising inside. Gently, she placed her plate on the table, even though she wanted to return to the dining room and throw every dish she had at Conner's head.

She sat and listened to her family's chatter.

"I'll help you, Jayde," Conner said. "And Amber can help too. I want you both to know everything about your family."

Her anger seethed, pushing her to the edge of a rampage.

"Daddy, I want my own family tree," Amber said.

"Okay. We'll do one for you and one for Jayde and one for . . ."

Grace held her breath.

". . . your mother and me."

Grace stood and ran up the stairs, needing to escape this lunacy before she released the fluid inside that she had worked so hard to keep down.

Grace cracked open the bedroom door, and Conner looked up.

"Are the girls settled in?"

She nodded. "Jayde's reading." Grace glanced at the floor, then turned back to the door.

"Grace, wait. Please don't leave." His words came quick. "I know you're hurt, and I'm sorry. But we can work through this." He paused. "Just like we did before."

His words made her grip the doorknob. "You're not comparing . . ."

"No." He sighed. "I just want to move forward."

She heard his weariness and, against her will, faced him. He wanted to move forward. She wanted to go back to where they'd been before Pilar had twisted their lives with this news.

She moved from the door to her side of the bed. "I don't know what to do."

"I don't have any answers either," he said from the other side of the bed. "But we have to try."

"Maybe we should talk to Pastor Ford." There was hope in her voice.

He nodded. "That would be good." With his eyes still focused on her, he moved around the bed, removing the barrier between them. When he stood by her side, he took her hand. "There is something else that I have to tell you."

She lowered herself onto the bed.

Conner knelt beside her. "I love you, Grace."

Grace tried to swallow the hardness in her throat. She had a feeling that only pain followed those words. But she held onto his hand, sure that nothing could be worse than what she already knew.

"I don't know how to tell you this." He sounded sadder than when he'd first delivered this news.

"How can there be more, Conner?" she asked, though she could feel it—more grief just moments away.

He closed his eyes, as if searching inside for the words he needed.

"Pilar had no intentions of telling me about Solomon."

Grace focused on breathing.

"She came to me when she found out . . . Pilar . . . has AIDS. She doesn't . . . the doctors don't give her much time."

At first, his words pinned her to the bed. A moment later, she jumped up. "What does that mean?" The question shook from her. She knew his most important words had not been said.

Conner half-closed his eyes. "She has less than a year. . . ."

Grace shook her head. "No, Conner."

"I wish there was something else I could do."

The emotions that she'd held exploded like bombs in a mine-field. "Conner, I have tried to understand."

"I know." He held up his hands as if that would hold back her flaring anger.

"I thought I could grit my way through, even though fathering this child is a thousand times worse than anything I've ever done," she yelled.

He looked toward their closed bedroom door. "You can't keep score, Grace," he whispered, hoping that if he lowered his voice, she would do the same.

But his efforts spurred her on. "I think I can. How can you tell me that you want to bring this child into our home?" she asked, stating what he had not yet said.

"Grace, we don't have a choice. The boy is losing his mother." He paused. "And I'm his father. We have to step in."

"We?" She paused long enough for her eyes to pierce his soul. "I don't think so, Conner."

His eyes narrowed. "What do you want to happen to the boy?"

"Let me ask you something. What would you have done if I'd brought home Drew's baby? What if I had asked you to raise Drew's child?"

Conner's lips trembled.

She waited a moment before she said, "That's what I thought."

"Grace, I can't turn my back."

"So what do you expect me to do?" She held up her hand before he could answer. "I guess the first thing is to get an AIDS test." She glared at him, and then her tears flowed like water gushing from an exploding hydrant. "How could you do this to us?"

He rushed to her, wanting to give her the comfort that he also needed. She pushed him away with a force that startled him.

"I would do anything for you, Grace. But I can't abandon Solomon."

The whites of her eyes were crimson. "What about *our* children?" Grace asked, one decibel below a scream.

The knock on their door stopped them, and Grace turned

away when Jayde entered. Through the reflection in the window, she could see her daughter's eyes darting between her and Conner.

"Mom, I need you to sign the permission slip for the Sacramento trip with my government class next month."

"I'll sign it tomorrow." She spoke without facing her daughter.

"I'll sign, sweetheart." Conner took the form. As he signed, Grace could feel Jayde's stare.

When he handed her the sheet, Jayde took it and moved toward the door. Before she stepped into the hallway, she stopped. "Are you all right, Mommy?" she asked walking toward Grace.

Grace wiped her face and turned. "Yes, sweetie." She hugged her. "Go to bed." She held her hand over her heart as Jayde moved with slow steps from the room. She couldn't imagine what this was going to do to their children.

"Grace," Conner whispered her name the moment Jayde closed the door. "I don't know what else to say. Solomon needs me. Pilar needs me."

The grace of God kept her silent.

"Pilar needs us," he corrected, feeling her fury.

Grace stared at him for a moment longer. Then she rolled her eyes and walked from the room.

Grace pulled the comforter and pillow from the linen closet, then went into the office. It wasn't until she closed the door that the sobs she'd held escaped. She covered her mouth with her hand, trying to push the cries back inside. It worked until she lay down.

Pilar. Solomon. AIDS. Those words floated in the air. How was she supposed to get up in the morning and live as if life were normal?

The knock on the door startled her. She was sure Conner would leave her alone.

"Mommy?"

Grace sat up. "Yes, Jayde."

When she opened the door, the soft light in the hallway glowed behind her, leaving only a silhouette of Jayde in the doorway. "Mom, what's wrong?"

"Nothing, sweetie." It took every muscle to hold her cries. "I'm just sleeping in here . . . since I couldn't sleep and your father has to be up early."

"He has to be up early on a Saturday?"

"He has . . . a meeting." Her lie faded as her daughter walked into the room. Even in the dark, Grace could feel Jayde searching her eyes for the truth.

"Okay," Jayde said, though she stood in place. Almost a minute passed before she turned away. At the door, she asked, "Mommy, are you sure you're okay?."

The lump in Grace's throat swelled. "Yes, sweetheart," she squeaked. "I'm going back to my room in a little while."

Jayde paused, still waiting for the truth. Finally, she closed the door.

Grace lowered her face into the pillow hoping to hide the anguish that enveloped her. She didn't know how much time passed before she sat up, drained, with no more tears inside.

She rolled from the couch and fell to her knees. She had to go to God. As she closed her eyes, she knew that no matter what she said to the Lord, her family would never be the same again.

Chapter 13

Grace yawned as she filled Amber's bowl with Fruit Loops. When she turned to the kitchen table, she met Jayde's stare.

"Last night, Daddy said he was going to make pancakes," Amber whined.

"I told you, Dad has a meeting." Jayde spoke to her sister, but her eyes were on her mother.

"Nuh-huh. His car is still in the garage."

"Eat your cereal, honey, or you won't be able to go to the museum."

Amber looked up. "You're not going?"

"No." Grace yawned again as she sat down.

"You said you were going," Amber protested.

"I have something else to do. Mrs. Davis will take you." When Amber pouted, Grace added, "You can stay home if you want to."

Amber looked at Grace, lifted her spoon, but didn't say a word. Grace nodded, then stood.

"I told you to be quiet," Jayde hissed at her sister.

"Shut up," Amber shouted.

"Mom, can we turn the channel? I don't want to watch these stupid cartoons."

"They're not stupid," Amber objected. "You're stupid."

"What's going on?" Conner stepped into the kitchen. He kissed Amber, then Jayde. He turned to Grace, hesitated, then kissed her cheek.

Grace lowered her eyes and slipped away before they could embrace.

Conner turned to his daughters. "How're my princesses?"

"Fine, Daddy. Do you want some of my Fruit Loops?"

He chuckled. "No, thank you, sweetheart." He looked at Jayde. "How are you?"

When Jayde didn't respond, Grace looked at her.

"Fine." Jayde forced the response through her lips. Her eyes were fixed on the now-interesting antics of Scooby-Doo.

Conner took a mug from the cabinet. "What's the plan for today?" he asked all of them.

"I'm going to the museum," Amber said.

He poured coffee into his cup. "What about you, Jayde?"

She shrugged without looking at him.

Grace asked, "Don't you have tennis practice?"

Jayde turned from the television. "Yeah, but I thought I'd stay home." Her glance shifted between her parents.

Grace shook her head as she dried her hands on the dish towel. "There's no reason to do that."

"I can miss one practice."

"And what about your movie date?"

Jayde hesitated. "That's not 'til later, Mom. I want to stay with you this morning."

Grace smiled. "I have some errands to run, so go to practice." She glanced at the clock. "In fact, it's time for us to get moving. Amber, get your backpack."

As Grace passed the table, Conner reached for her hand. "Do you want me to take the girls? I don't have anything to do today."

"Mom told me you had a meeting," Jayde said.

Grace looked at Conner's hand in hers, then pulled away with as gentle a move as she could. "I'll take the girls." Her words were stiff.

"Mom, I thought you said that Dad had a meeting," Jayde repeated.

Grace let her glance move from Jayde to Conner, back to Jayde. "I was wrong about your father." She looked at Conner, then walked up the stairs.

Conner followed her.

"What was that supposed to mean?" he demanded once they were behind closed doors.

Grace moved her purse from the bed to the dresser, then looked in the mirror as she wrapped her sweater around her neck.

"I know you're hurt, Grace, but this has to stop."

"I didn't start it."

"You sound like a child."

She glared at him through the mirror before turning to face him head-on. "I guess it's more mature to be a man fathering children all over the country."

She rushed into the hallway and bumped into Amber.

"Mommy, are you mad?"

"No, honey," she said, taking her hand.

"Yes, you are," Amber said as Grace pulled her down the stairs. "You told us not to lie."

"I'm not mad, Amber. I'm a bit upset, but I'm not angry with you."

Jayde was waiting at the bottom of the stairs with her arms crossed against her chest. "Why are you mad at Daddy?"

Grace looked at her daughters' faces stretched with concern. "Come on, we're running late."

Her response satisfied Amber, but Jayde's frown remained as she picked up her bag and stomped past her mother.

They were in the Volvo when Grace realized she'd left her purse inside. Still, she started the ignition, but then turned it off. "I'll be right back."

When she stepped into the house, Conner stood, holding her bag. She took it from him and turned back to the garage.

"Grace, please."

She didn't know why she paused, but she waited, her hand gripping the doorknob. She could feel Conner edging closer. When she faced him, the tears filling the rims of his eyes matched the ones already in hers. He touched her cheek. She wanted to run, but her heart made her stay.

"I'm sorry," he whispered.

"You already said that."

"There is something I haven't said."

"There's nothing more for you to say." She turned her back to him as she opened the garage door.

"Grace . . . forgive me."

Her heart fluttered.

"Please, forgive me."

Without turning back, she walked into the garage and closed the door on his words.

Conner backed out of the driveway and weaved his SUV through the winding streets of their subdivision. At the bottom of the hill, he stopped in front of the clubhouse. But a moment later, he swung back onto the road. This was too close to home.

He drove past the guard gates and debated. Should he go north or south?

He decided to drive straight, heading east into the city. The traffic was Saturday morning light. Still, with the red lights, it took almost fifteen minutes to drive eight miles away.

Conner turned into a strip mall and parked in front of a 7-Eleven. He eyed the store, then glanced at the doughnut shop next door with a red window banner that read "$1.00 Chinese Food." He turned off the ignition and pulled his cell phone and the paper with Pilar's number from his pocket.

A moment after he pressed Talk, he heard Pilar's greeting.

"I've been waiting to hear from you. I thought you would call sometime this week."

"It took some time, but I spoke to Grace. I told her everything."

"How did it go?"

He frowned. "That's not important. This is my family, my business."

"Your family is my business. How Grace reacts is important since," a sniffle made her pause, "she is going to be Solomon's mother. I want to talk to her."

Conner closed his eyes, remembering Grace's face just twenty minutes before. He couldn't imagine that happening. He opened his eyes to the sound of giggles, and his gaze followed a man and a young boy dashing into the 7-Eleven.

"This is a lot for my family to handle," Conner said. "You're moving fast." Through the window, he watched the man help the boy fill a Slurpee cup.

"There isn't time to move slower," Pilar said.

"That's not my fault."

"It's not Solomon's fault either."

Conner watched the young boy skip out of the store. "Let me handle this, Pilar."

There was a moment of silence. "I want to talk to Grace."

That is not going to happen, he thought.

She continued. "I want to . . . explain. And thank her."

Conner wasn't sure if it was the boy he'd just watched or Pilar's plea that melted his heart. No matter what he was going through, he couldn't forget that in the end, he would be with his son and Pilar would be gone.

"I don't think . . . this is not . . . Grace needs more time."

"How many times do I have to say we don't have that? Conner, the doctors don't give me six months."

He wanted to tell her that it wasn't up to the doctors—that God would have the final word. But he said nothing.

She said, "We need to start thinking about how to tell Solomon."

Her determination to make final plans made his heart ache for this almost-stranger. "Pilar," he stopped. "I will be there for my son."

He could feel her smile through the phone. "That's all that's important."

He clicked the End button, without the formality of a good-bye. He glanced into the rearview mirror. He looked drained, his eyes heavy with sadness. But as new emotions pressed into his consciousness, a slight smile crossed his lips. There was a corner in his center that held affection he could no longer deny.

Guilt shoved the sentiment aside, but as he edged his car into the street and turned toward home, he could feel it.

At the red light, he pulled the picture that Pilar had given him from his wallet. In the photo, he saw his face. This was the boy he saw in the park. He smiled.

This was his son.

Grace stood at the door of her mother's condominium. She knocked once, then used the key Lily had given her.

"Hello," she yelled, as she entered the mirrored entryway.

"Grace?" Lily's surprised smile was wide when she came around the corner. "What are you doing here?"

Grace closed her eyes as Lily's soft arms comforted her. "I wanted to thank you for keeping the girls this week." She tried to keep the tears from her voice.

Lily pulled away. "What's wrong?" The mother tone had replaced her delight, and it made Grace hug her again.

"I need to talk."

Lily took Grace's hand, moving her through the purple-hued living room. "We'll have a nice chat." Grace stopped as soon as they entered the kitchen. "I can't remember the last time I had both of my girls here."

Grace's rounded shoulders sagged even more. "Starlight."

Her sister smiled. "Hello, Grace."

Grace sighed inside, and said, "Mom, you have company. I'll come by later."

"What are you talking about, company?" Lily scolded. "You sit down. Do you want some coffee?"

Her inner voice told her to leave. But staying wouldn't be as bad as going home, she thought. She didn't know if Conner was home, but even if he wasn't, that was not where she wanted to be.

She shrugged her sweater from her shoulders and sat across from Starlight. "Do you have any tea?"

"I have some of that chai you love."

As Lily pulled a mug from her cabinet and filled it with water, Starlight sipped her coffee. "So, Grace, I always stop by to see Mom on Saturday. What's your excuse?"

Grace's eyes narrowed. "Didn't know I needed one." When Starlight sighed, Grace said, "I needed to talk to Mom."

Lily placed the mug with water in the microwave, then set the tea's canister and a spoon in front of Grace. "What did you want to talk about, honey?"

Grace's glance moved from her mother to Starlight. "It . . . wasn't important."

Lily rested her hand on top of Grace's. "We could both help." She motioned toward Starlight.

Grace looked at her sister and shifted. "No, we can talk later."

"Okay," Lily said slowly, then got the cup from the microwave. Everyone was silent as Lily placed the hot water on the table. "Grace, your sister has some wonderful things happening in her life. Tell her, Starlight."

Though Starlight smiled, she hesitated. "I don't think Grace wants to hear this."

"Of course, she does," Lily said.

Grace took a long sip, keeping her lips to the cup.

"Well," Starlight started with her eyes lowered, "I just purchased a penthouse in the Santa Monica Towers. And I just signed a two-book deal with Forge Publishers."

Grace's eyebrows rose. Forge was one of the big three. "What are you writing about?"

"I'm not sure yet. I'm thinking about doing something on dreams."

Grace laughed. "Aren't you an insomniac?"

Starlight stared at her for a moment. "That doesn't mean that I can't dream, Grace."

"And dreams are a very popular topic right now." Lily nodded. "Her second book will probably be about psychics."

"At least that's what my editor suggested," Starlight said. "But I don't really believe in them."

This time Grace kept her laugh inside. "Oh, you have standards," she mumbled. The tea's steam seemed to be rising from Grace's lips rather than the mug she held.

"What does that mean?" Starlight frowned. They stared at each other before Starlight said, "Grace, did you know that I do about three, sometimes four, seminars a month across the country? Do you know that I'm expanding to weekend retreats and that I'll be doing a Revival in June?"

"Can't say that I knew, Starlight. I don't follow your career."

"Well, I follow yours, and as you were campaigning, saying you wanted to make your community better, I've been campaigning to help women edify their lives so we can have better communities throughout the country." She paused. "I told you that I spoke at Greater Faith."

Her internal laughter ceased. Grace placed her cup on the table. "I was surprised to hear that. What did you talk about?"

Starlight's eyes sparkled with triumph. "I should have invited you. It would be good for you to see what I do."

"I don't think so."

"You asked what I talk about."

"Just tell me."

Lily moaned.

The sisters ignored their mother.

"I talk about the same thing you do."

"There is nothing similar in what we do, Starlight."

Starlight leaned forward. "The difference between us is that you focus on children, while I work with adults who never got it as children."

"The difference between us is that I know God and I focus on Him. You don't."

"I believe in God, Grace. But I don't need Him to do what I do. My mind is open to understanding the true God and knowing that we were created in God's image, so that we could go beyond him or her."

Two beats passed before Grace said, "You've got to be kidding. *Him or her?*"

Lily pushed away from the table so fast that the chair legs screeched against the hardwood floor. "Does either of you want a refill?"

"I'm open to accepting God in any form," Starlight said, responding to Grace. "It's about understanding your god consciousness. I'm not limited the way you are. I don't just believe something because I read it in some book."

"You mean the Bible?" Grace asked.

Starlight nodded.

"But people should buy your books and believe you?"

Grace's question made Starlight pause. "Yes, because I teach the truth, which is to rely on yourself and not on some force you cannot see."

A siren sounded inside Grace. It was time to leave. But there was an itching in her bones that she'd held for days. She longed for a knockdown, drag-out brawl. Since Conner wasn't here, Starlight would have to do.

Grace leaned forward laying her hands flat on the table, but before she could begin her assault, Lily said, "We should change the subject."

It was too late for the referee.

Grace said, "I rely on myself, Starlight. But I know, just like you know, that everything I have comes from the power of God working in me."

"A power inside you?" Starlight puckered her lips, amused. "See, we do believe the same thing."

"Not even close. You're convinced that you have powers beyond God."

"We all have the same power, Grace. I know how to tap into it. God gave us the power because He doesn't play a role beyond creation. What we do after we're born is up to us."

There was a moment of silence before Grace said, "If I thought you believed that, I'd pray for you."

"I don't need your prayers."

"But I know this is all about money."

Starlight tried to hold back her smile. "I certainly don't need God for that."

"Starlight, stop it," Lily exclaimed. "You're teasing Grace."

Grace stared at her sister, though she spoke to Lily. "She's not teasing, Mom. Mabel believes what she's saying." She paused. "She doesn't need God."

Lily held up her hands. "Stop this right now. You're saying the same thing. It's just semantics."

Grace's incredulous gaze shifted to her mother.

Lily said, "Christians don't always believe the same things."

"Mom, Mabel is not a Christian."

"Grace, your sister is a Christian."

Grace turned back to Starlight.

Lily said, "I know she's a Christian because you were both raised that way."

No we weren't! Grace wanted to scream. We were just raised to get up on Sundays and go to church.

"Mom, this is one point where Grace and I agree. I don't consider myself a Christian."

"That's blasphemy, Starlight," Lily warned.

"I don't put myself in that little Christian box." Lily opened her mouth, but Starlight continued before her mother could speak. "What I believe goes beyond Christianity." Her eyes bore into Grace. "I'm inclusive rather than like people who believe their way is the only way."

Grace returned her sister's stare.

"A true Higher Power would never be exclusive," Starlight continued. "There isn't just one way to live this life. But there is only one way to have the richest existence possible. My objective is to let my light shine and show the world the way."

The ringing telephone silenced them all.

Lily looked at her daughters. "Please stop this." She picked up the cordless phone and walked into the living room.

"You know, Mabel, this wouldn't be so sad if it wasn't so serious," Grace said.

"My name is Starlight."

Grace slipped her arms into her sweater. "I know one thing for sure. You need Jesus."

Starlight reached for her purse, pulled out her wallet, and flashed a platinum American Express card. "This is the best Jesus in the world."

Grace pressed her lips together, then said, "Pick up your Bible tonight, Mabel. Read the truth. I pray it's not too late for you."

Starlight laughed.

Grace turned and her sister's laughter followed her into the living room, past her mother and through the front door.

Amber squealed as she and Nicole ran across the wide lawn.

Grace slid from the car and hugged her daughter. "Did you have a good time?"

"Yeah. We saw the dinosaurs."

"Mrs. Monroe, can Amber stay for dinner? My mom said it was okay."

Grace looked into the girls' eager eyes. If she agreed, she'd be home alone—with Conner. "Not tonight. Maybe next weekend."

As Amber continued to plead her case, Grace went into the two-story Spanish-style house to thank Linda Pogue. By the time Grace had hurried her daughter into the car, Amber was sufficiently annoyed. Grace welcomed Amber's silence. Her mind was still overwhelmed by the conversation she'd had with her sister.

When Mabel had emerged as Starlight, Grace thought her sister was passing through another fleeting phase—another network-marketing program, or some other money-making scheme. She was sure it wouldn't last.

Grace had been skeptical but encouraging when Mabel said she was writing a book. But when an actual copy was in her hand, her skepticism had turned to dismay, then to horror.

"The Higher Power is not concerned with being worshipped. He-She is the creator who has procreated perfection in you and expects you to live your life to your fullest capacity."

"He-She god is all around us. His-Her spirit is in the air we breathe, in the food we eat, in everything—because we are the gods."

What horrified Grace most was that alongside those words, Mabel spoke some truth that Grace feared would attract people.

"Thoughts are things. When you control your thoughts, you will manage your life."

"To live your fullest life, understand that *faith* is a verb, not a noun. Faith is about taking action in your belief . . . knowing that it will be."

As Grace skimmed through the pages, she realized that fifty percent of what Mabel was saying was true . . . and the other fifty percent was lethal.

Grace read her sister's book from cover to cover, then reread it twice more before she called.

"Mabel, I can't believe what you wrote. I know you don't even believe half of this."

"My name is Starlight now." She spoke in a soft, smooth cadence that reminded Grace of someone seriously high on drugs. "I call you by the moniker you choose. I would appreciate the same."

Oh, brother, Grace thought.

"I can feel your distress, Grace. You're generating negative energy. It's not good for your karma. Take a deep breath, and ask the ancestors to restore your positive power."

"Mabel, you have lost your mind."

"No, Grace. I have discovered my true mind. I am enlightened now."

Within seconds, Grace was dialing her mother's number.

"It's really bad this time, Mom." Grace spoke quickly. "I think Mabel's smoking crack."

Lily had laughed.

"Mom, she sounds like a rejected African flower child."

"There's nothing wrong, Grace. Mabel told me that she discovered her calling. But you know this won't last long."

Mabel's calling had lasted for seven flourishing years. And to Grace, the signs pointed to many more to come. In airports, Starlight's books stared back at her. On magazine covers, Starlight's image smiled back at her. On talk shows, Starlight proclaimed the self-power/faith/prosperity gospel that had turned her into a millionaire.

"Mommy, what are we having for dinner?" Amber asked, startling Grace from her thoughts.

"I'm not sure," Grace said, her mind still on her sister.

It had been a long time since Grace had sat down with Mabel, and today she realized that things had progressed too far. All this time, Grace believed it was a con job, a money-making scheme. But what Starlight revealed today was that her desires were beyond dollars. Starlight wanted her followers' minds. To have a group of disciples who sang her praises, glorified her name, exalted her above all else.

Starlight seemed to half-believe what she said, and that made her dangerous. Power was a potent intoxicant, and Grace saw it fermenting in her sister's blood. Starlight wanted to be a god.

Grace shook her head. Their unofficial truce was over. Fighting was better anyway—it kept Starlight away from her daughters. She turned into her driveway. The moment the garage door lifted and she saw Conner's SUV, thoughts of Starlight slipped away. It was time to take care of home.

Chapter 14

"Mommy, the pizza's here," Amber's voice called over the intercom.

"I'll be right down."

Grace stood from her desk and took a deep breath. She stepped into the hallway and heard Amber's and Conner's laughter. She inhaled again, trying to find energy in the air. She was about to enter a battlefield, but at least she had to face just one foe. Jayde was on her group date, so Grace wouldn't have to defend against the darting stares of her daughter. There would only be Conner. One man, one war.

She walked down the stairs and pasted a smile on her face before she stepped into the kitchen.

"Mommy, we got the Hawaiian pizza for you."

"Thanks," she said, avoiding Conner's glance. When she sat, he slid a slice onto her plate, placed a Diet Coke on the corner of her placemat, then turned to Amber.

Conner said, "You decide what movie we're going to rent."

Amber giggled. "Okay."

It surprised Grace that Conner wasn't making more of an effort with her, but she welcomed this neutral valley. It had been that way since she'd come home. Conner had accepted her mumbled explanation that she had to work. She knew he didn't believe her, but the tale enabled her to hide in their office, even though she'd filled the time shifting papers while her mind shifted between Conner, Pilar, and Solomon.

She'd tried to imagine what Solomon looked like, what it would be like to meet him, what it would be like to have him in her home.

The last thought brought her to the brink of tears. But it wasn't just for selfish reasons—she was sure the boy would be better off with his family. If anything happened to her and Conner, she would want Jayde and Amber with their family.

Just minutes before Amber had bellowed for her to join them, Grace had decided it was time to talk to Conner. They should provide financial support, Conner should develop a relationship with his son, but the boy should be with his family—Pilar's mother, father, brother, sister, cousin, niece, nephew, aunt, uncle, godmother, godfather. It didn't matter which one to her.

Now, as she chewed her pizza, Grace rehearsed her approach to Conner in her mind: *Conner, we need to talk about Solomon. I have some suggestions . . .*

"What do you suggest, Mommy?"

Grace blinked. "What?"

"Daddy asked if you had any suggestions for the movie."

"Uh, it doesn't matter." She looked at Conner, providing a hint of what was to come. "Whatever you want, I'm game."

Conner's eyes told her he understood, and she smiled.

He slid his hand across the table and paused just before his fingertips touched her. When she didn't pull away, Conner squeezed her hand. "We'll be right back, honey."

She stayed motionless until she heard the car pull from the

garage. Then she breathed. The truce had been called, both par-
ties had accepted, and it was time to negotiate the terms. She
cleaned off the table, stacked the dishes in the dishwasher, then
wiped down the table and counter. Aloud, she practiced her
words to Conner. Inside, she prayed that her heart would catch
up with what her mind told her was right.

Grace was living inside a seven-year-old's fantasy. They watched
every movie Amber called her favorite: *The Lion King, Shrek,
Monster's, Inc.*

But though Grace chuckled and sniffled where she was supposed to, inside she was on a teeter-totter. On one side, her head
told her to get over it, do the Christian thing. On the other side,
her heart ached as she thought about the living proof that her
husband had been unfaithful.

Conner pushed the Stop button on the remote. "I'm going to
get a refill." He lifted his Coke can. "Any orders?"

"No," Grace smiled.

Amber shook her head, her eyes still focused on the television, even though the tape had stopped.

Conner trotted up the four steps to the main level, as if he
were whistling inside.

Grace turned to the television, needing to focus on something. Needing to stop thinking about Conner. And Pilar. And
Solomon.

"Every boy needs his father."

Grace's eyes widened at the voice-over on the commercial. A
parade of young men marched before her, testifying about how

being with, and learning from, and loving the man who fathered them made a difference in their lives. The boys—black, white, brown, yellow—taunted her, daring her to do the right thing.

"It takes a man to be a father."

The screen darkened, filling with the Ad Council symbol.

Grace jumped from the couch.

"Mommy, what's wrong?"

Silently, she moved from the room. At the entryway, she bumped into Conner. His smile faded when he looked at her.

She brushed past him. In the foyer, she slipped on her sweater and swung her purse over her shoulder. When she turned, Conner stood in front of the door to the garage, blocking her passage to freedom.

"What's wrong?" It was a demand.

"Nothing," she said, eyeing the marble floor. It gleamed—the handiwork of Ursula. Thanks to their housekeeper, the floors were polished, their house immaculate. Twice a week, the Monroes were squeaky clean.

She looked up at Conner. "I . . . I have to go out. I'll be back." She barreled past him, rushing into the garage. She could feel Conner's eyes peering through the car's tinted windows, and she knew he was filled with the same confusion that choked her.

"Every boy needs his father."

I know that, she thought.

"It takes a man to be a father."

She reached for her cell phone, and pressed the number four. "Can you meet me somewhere?" she whispered.

"Chandler's not here," Devry said. "He's with the church basketball team in San Diego. Don't expect him until eleven or so."

Grace looked at the clock on the dashboard. It was just before nine. "Up for some company?"

"I've been waiting for you."

Grace paused. "I'll be there in ten minutes."

The front door opened the moment Grace turned off the ignition. Her sister-in-law was standing there, welcoming. She locked her car, then followed the concrete path of the driveway.

"Hey, girl." Devry stepped back, making room for Grace.

"Hey, yourself."

Grace stood in the dimly lit entryway. The rest of the house was dark except for the kitchen, where a bright light shined. Grace walked toward the light.

She dropped her sweater coat on one of the kitchen chairs, then turned back to see if Devry had followed. Her sister-in-law was leaning against the kitchen's doorway.

"Got any ice cream?"

Devry fingered a long ringlet at the side of her head. "Of course. I'm pregnant."

Grace opened the freezer door, stared at the three pints stacked inside, and wondered, *Didn't anyone eat vanilla anymore?*

She grabbed an unopened carton of Rocky Road Peanut Crunch and pulled a tablespoon from the drawer. Leaning against the center island, she pounded the spoon against the hardened mound of cream until the handle bent. Then she stuffed a spoonful of Rocky Road into her mouth.

Devry sat and pulled out the chair next to her, scraping the legs along the tiles. "You should sit and then eat yourself into oblivion."

Grace shook her head. "If I stand, I'll absorb fewer calories."

"Potato chips are better. If they're broken, they don't contain any calories."

Grace looked around the designer kitchen filled with conveniences found only in the most expensive homes. "Got a bag?"

They laughed together.

A silent minute passed as Grace stuffed two more heaping spoonfuls into her mouth. Keeping her eyes plastered on the chunks of ice cream, she said, "What has Chandler told you?"

"Enough."

Grace's head snapped back. She had expected to throw off Devry with her question. "You know?"

Devry nodded, then rushed to add, "Just a little. Chandler told me there was a problem. I was waiting for you to fill me in."

Grace tossed the half-empty container onto the granite counter and sat next to Devry. "I knew Conner would tell him. How long have you known?"

"A couple of days. You're not mad, are you?"

Grace shook her head. "Those two can't keep anything from each other."

Devry said, "I mean at me. For not saying anything."

"No." She paused. "Though I have to hand it to you. If I'd known a piece of dirt like this, I wouldn't have been able to keep my mouth shut."

"Girl, there were so many times when I wanted to say something, or run over to your house, or call you . . ."

"But you were over here on your knees."

Devry chuckled. "You got that right."

A smile peeked through Grace's lips, but it faded before it fully appeared. "It took me almost forty years to want to run away from home."

"That might work," Devry said without a smile. "Except your children may want to go with you."

Grace moaned. "Don't mention the girls. I can't imagine what will happen to them when this all comes out."

"They'll follow your lead." She paused. "So the issue is, what are you going to do?"

The question made Grace's eyes well with tears. "I don't know. There is a part of me . . ." Grace squeezed her hands into fists. "How could Conner drag us to this place?"

Devry shook her head.

Grace leaned back and relaxed her hands. "But there is another side to this," she said softly. "What happened with Conner and Pilar was so long ago. He and I are good together now."

"I know."

"Every hurdle the devil has thrown at us, we've jumped over."

"That's true."

"It's like our marriage is a two-part play. In Act One, we couldn't get our lines right, but . . ." She paused, scenes of their years fast-forwarding in her head. "The second act deserves a standing ovation." She sighed. "How can I let a long-ago sin destroy us?"

"That's a good question."

Grace stood and walked to the window. "What am I supposed to say to the girls? What am I supposed to tell the rest of the family? What am I supposed to do when this comes out to everyone?" She paused. "Our lives are ruined."

"Only if you allow it to be. "

She faced her friend. "Don't play psychologist right now. Just tell me what to do."

"Oh, no." Devry shook her head. "You're the judge and jury here, kiddo. The world revolves around you."

"Why do you say that?"

"Because Conner's decisions have to follow yours. The girls will follow you. Even Pilar's son. What will happen in his life depends on what you're going to do."

Grace closed her eyes and exhaled a long stream of air. But seconds later when she opened her eyes, the world hadn't changed. Devry was still sitting at the table, and the image of a child she'd never met still filled every space in her head.

She looked at the container she'd left on the counter. A circle of water had formed at the edge as the ice cream began its transformation. Grace stirred the loosened mound and pushed a mushy spoonful into her mouth.

"There's a little boy out there, Devry." She paused as his image flashed through her mind again. It was a face shaped like Conner's, but there were no eyes, nose, or mouth. Like the son of the invisible man. "But I have my girls to think about. How can we change our lives and have this little boy come live with us?"

"That's getting way ahead of everything, Grace. Speaking professionally, I wouldn't recommend . . ."

Grace held up her hand, stopping Devry. "Pilar has AIDS. She's dying. She wants Solomon to live with us."

"Whoa." Devry's groan was low and long.

"That's why Pilar came to Conner. Otherwise she would have carried her child's paternity to her grave." This time, Grace groaned. "I shouldn't have said that. But I think the boy would be better off with his relatives."

"I'm sure Pilar considers Conner a relative."

Grace pressed her lips together, and the pressure pushed tears to her eyes.

"Grace, I don't think Pilar would have come to Conner if she hadn't thought this through."

"Solomon."

"What?"

"The boy's name is Solomon. Pilar's son."

Devry joined her friend in front of the window. "Grace, suppose this is Pilar's final wish—to have Solomon with you and Conner."

Grace couldn't meet Devry's stare. She lifted the ice cream container, and it crumbled in her hand. The cardboard sides that a short time before held firm the immovable mound had wilted.

Grace looked at what was left inside—just a little bit of cream, absent of the ice. "I can't continue this way," she whispered as she poured the liquid into the sink and watched as it swirled down the drain. "Conner has a son. With Pilar Cruise. It is what it is." She bit her lip, before she added, "I can't expect Conner to deny his son."

Devry nodded.

"He wouldn't be the man I love if he did."

Devry smiled.

"And truth be told, I know what God expects. He'll just have to give me enough grace to handle this." Grace finally looked at her sister-in-law. A tear filled the corner of her eye. "So how much do I owe you, Doctor?"

Devry pulled Grace into her arms. When they stepped apart, more tears trickled down Grace's cheek. Using her thumb, Devry wiped her friend's pain away. "You don't have to write a check, but I want payment," Devry said. "I'm looking for a loving, compassionate woman to be my baby's godmother."

Grace wiped her eyes. "I don't think you can call me compassionate when there's a woman dying, a boy who needs his father, and I'm thinking about how sad I am."

"Grace, no woman would have cheered at this news. This is a lot for anyone to take. At least you're moving forward."

Grace sucked her lip and nodded.

"Just be patient. With yourself and Conner. Because you're holding onto the end of an emotional firecracker."

"I can feel it fizzling in my heart."

"God will make sure that you don't get burned."

Grace wiped away another tear. "I'd better get going. I have a husband I need to talk to."

Devry hooked her arm through Grace's, and they walked into the foyer. She kissed her cheek before she opened the front door. "A couple of days ago, I thought you were beginning a new ministry with your position as councilwoman. But now I suspect there's a far greater mission awaiting you." With her fingertips, Devry pushed a stray hair away from Grace's forehead. "And know that I'm always here, girl. And so is God."

Grace nodded, then walked into the night.

Grace took another breath before she opened the door. She stepped inside, and Conner stood, as if he hadn't moved since she'd left.

"Are you all right?" he asked.

Her eyes began their ascent right where his pants bent slightly at the knees. Even though he was wearing the same denim shirt and jeans as when she left, he seemed different. His shirt seemed snugger, his pants tighter. By the time her glance met his, she was smiling.

It took more will than she knew she had to resist trailing her fingers along the creases in his forehead. She wanted to kiss his concern away.

"I'm fine."

Relief accompanied his exhale.

"Conner, this has been so hard for me." She stepped closer. "I just don't know what to do."

He hesitated, then took a step toward her. "Me either. But whatever I do, I want to do it with you." He reached toward her, as if he was going to take her hand, but then stopped. "We'll make it through, Grace. I promise."

She wrapped her arms around his neck. She wondered why her heart pounded, and then realized it was his familiar beat she felt. They held each other, letting the ticks of the grandfather clock guide them through time until the lock on the front door clicked. The door opened, and Jayde took two steps inside before she stopped.

Her eyes danced between her parents. "Hi."

"Hey, sweetie." Grace squeezed Conner's hand before she walked to Jayde. "Did you have a good time?"

"It was really nice." Her voice smiled, but her eyes held uncertainty. "Is everything all right?"

"Sure, honey." Conner hugged his daughter.

Jayde grinned at her mother. "Mom, I had the best time. I met someone."

"How did that work?" Grace asked, raising a teasing eyebrow. "I thought you were out with Brittany, Charles, and Philip."

Jayde scrunched her face when her mother mentioned her boyfriend, Philip.

Conner made a "T" sign with his hands. "I'm going to leave

you ladies alone." He put his arm around Grace. "I'll be waiting for you upstairs." He brushed his lips across her cheek.

As Conner walked away, Jayde whispered, "If you want to go with Dad, we can talk tomorrow."

"Absolutely not." Grace wrapped her arm around Jayde's shoulders and led her up the stairs. "I want to hear it all now."

"But things seem better between you and Dad, and I don't want to mess up anything."

Grace stopped at the top of the stairs. "Jayde, you could never do that. Your dad and I had a disagreement, but we're fine. I don't want you worrying about us."

Jayde pulled her mother into her bedroom. "I can't help it, Mom." She flopped onto her bed, as if the weight of her family's problems kept her from standing. "It's like we have the perfect life, but something's going to mess it up."

Grace swallowed, her smile gone. Then she lifted her chin. Their life would still be perfect, just different. She sat next to her daughter. "Honey, nothing can happen to our family. Do you know why?"

Jayde sat with wide eyes, eager to hear her mother's assurance.

Grace placed her palm against Jayde's cheek. "Because we have the best insurance. Not only do we love each other, but God is here. He's our protector." Grace pushed a braid away from Jayde's eye. "So you don't have to worry. Your father and I love you too much to let anything happen. But God loves you more, and He'll take care of everything. Our family is going to be all right." She hugged her before she added, "Now tell me about this new fantastic guy."

Jayde grinned and pulled her legs under her. "Mom, he is so cute and so funny and so smart."

"Where did you meet him?"

"Philip's house. He's Philip's cousin, Donald."

Grace almost laughed.

"And we had the best time, especially when we talked while he drove me home." Grace's grin turned upside down. "Philip's mom didn't bring you?" She continued before Jayde could answer. "How old is Donald?"

"Nineteen," Jayde sang, as if it were a virtue.

Grace closed her eyes as Jayde continued. "Mom, he's the coolest. He's transferring to UCLA in the fall. That's why he's staying with Philip. His apartment won't be ready until next week." The way Jayde jumped from the bed, Grace was sure her daughter was going to dance. "He has these short reddish locks, and he had on leather pants and this matching jacket with silver studs that I know cost a fortune."

Wait until Conner hears this, Grace thought. She would never get to tell him the boy's age. Once she mentioned leather, it would be over.

"He knew that Aunt Star was my aunt."

Grace returned her attention to Jayde.

Jayde continued, "I guess Philip told him. But he's really into her. He's been to a lot of her seminars."

Nineteen, leather, and Starlight. Three strikes!

"He talked to me all night. Brittany was so jealous." Jayde grinned.

"I saw your Aunt Star today," Grace said because she wanted to get away from Donald.

Jayde returned to the bed. "Where?"

"At your grandmother's house. Starlight just bought a condo in the Santa Monica Towers."

"Oh, wow!" Jayde exclaimed, as if Grace just told her that Starlight had won the lottery. "All the movie stars live there. Aunt Starlight is always doing something totally cool." She paused. "Mom, why don't you like Auntie Star?"

Grace sighed. "It's not that I don't like her, honey. She's my sister; I love her. But you know how Pastor Ford talked about hating the sin, but loving the person?"

Jayde nodded. "That's hard to do, right?"

"It is, but that's what I try to do with your aunt."

"Donald said that Auntie Star teaches people how to use the true God."

"That's what I mean, honey. We're not here to use God. He uses us."

Jayde paused, as if she were trying to understand the difference.

Grace kissed her forehead. "It's time for bed. We're going to the eleven o'clock service tomorrow."

"Okay." Jayde hugged Grace. "Mom, you're the best."

When Grace stepped into the hallway, she leaned against Jayde's door. "Our family is always going to be all right." That's what she'd told her daughter. Now she was going to make it so.

She peeked into Amber's room, and was surprised that the covers were still over her daughter and not on the floor. Then she realized Conner must have checked on her. I really do have a wonderful husband, she thought.

Just as she turned out the light at the top of the stairs, the phone rang. She frowned. Who would be calling this late? She picked up the hallway phone, not wanting the ringing to wake Amber. But a millisecond before she said hello, she heard voices.

"Conner, this is Pilar."

"Pilar . . . is something wrong?"

"No, I'm sorry it's so late. It's just that Solomon went to bed only a little while ago."

"Is he all right?"

Grace stood in the dark, listening.

"Solomon is fine. We were just talking tonight about why he and I came to L.A."

"You told him . . . that I was his father?"

Grace trembled. Had Conner met Solomon? How many secrets did Conner and Pilar share?

"He's always known about his father, Conner. Never specifics. Never your name or where you lived. I only told him that his father loves him, but circumstances prevented us from being together. I still haven't told him anything more. But I told him that we went to L.A. so that I could start exploring the possibility of him meeting you."

Grace twisted the phone's cord around her finger.

"You know, Pilar, I would have been there if I'd known."

Grace inhaled.

"I mean, financially," Conner finished.

Grace exhaled.

"And emotionally," he said, making Grace take another deep breath. "What did he say . . . about meeting me?"

It seemed to Grace as if all three of them stopped breathing.

"He's more concerned about me and my feelings, but let's not talk about this tonight. I just wanted to thank you for your call today. I need to start setting things in motion for our son."

Grace wrapped the phone cord around her hand.

"This gives me peace, Conner," Pilar said.

"I'm glad. But Pilar, next time . . ." He paused and Grace prayed that he would tell her not to call his home, not to intrude on the time he spent with his loving family, not to upset his beautiful wife, the only woman he would ever love.

He said, "Never mind. I'll speak with you on Monday." He paused again. "I'll call you . . . from the office."

There it was, Grace thought. Her heroic husband. Who wanted to protect his wife—or keep more secrets from her.

"Good night, Conner."

"Good night, Pilar," Conner said a second before he heard two clicks. He frowned, staring at the phone in his hand. Then he heard the office door close. It took him a moment to put it together. Grace had been on the line.

He put the phone down and opened the door to their bedroom, then closed it. He couldn't go to his wife right now. Not right after he'd spoken to Pilar. He walked into their bathroom and turned on the water full blast. He needed to take a shower.

Chapter 15

"Pick up a Bible tonight, Mabel."

Grace's words had reverberated through her mind all day. Starlight had tried to block out her sister's voice on the ride home, but it was as if Grace was in the car. Even when she'd come home and seduced Lexington in the middle of the Grande Room, Grace stayed with her.

Now, as she stood on her balcony, she tried to throw Grace's words into the blackness of the night ocean. "Pick up a Bible."

She returned to her bedroom.

Lexington's soft snores mixed with the surf. He had not awakened when she got out of the bed or during the last twenty-five minutes she'd spent on the balcony. Their sexathon had left him exhausted; it had left her wound up. She couldn't sleep even though she'd taken two pills, double her prescribed dosage.

Her silk robe fluttered to the carpet as she slipped from it and into bed. Shivering in her nakedness, she turned off the light and sank into the feathered pillows. A moment later, she clicked on the light and opened the nightstand drawer. The single content stared at her: Holy Bible. She picked up the book with care, as if handling it roughly would make God angry. It felt familiar as her fingertips roamed along the uneven terrain of the leather. Her hands examined the cover for long minutes as if her touch would transmit information from inside. Finally, she opened the book.

She'd written her name in cursive on the "presented to" line the day of her Confirmation when Neil had given her the Bible. On the line with the word "from," she'd written, "My father." At thirteen, it was her proudest possession. For hours after she studied her scriptures, she would stare at the gold edges of the pages.

On the morning of her Confirmation, she'd taken the new Bible to church for the first time. While her friends gathered around admiring the gilded pages and gold lettering, Jolanda Keith had declared, "Mabel, why did you write that this Bible was from your father?" Jolanda had tossed her thick pigtails over her shoulder and stared at Mabel provocatively. "He's not your father."

Though she had never been friends with Jolanda, who walked around as if she'd been given the trust deed to the world, Mabel had still been shocked. She'd done everything within her thirteen-year-old power to hide that Neil wasn't her father.

"He is too." But though she spat the words with as much force as she could muster, she stepped back.

Jolanda had sucked her teeth. "You don't even have the same last name."

How do you know his last name? she wanted to scream. But Mabel just turned away, withering under the stares of the other seven girls who waited for her to answer Jolanda's charges.

It was then that she knew she hated them all: Neil, her mother, and Grace.

Mabel knew others who lived without their mother or father—half the kids she knew lived with their grandmothers. But it was different for her. Neil lived in her house. He just didn't want to be her father.

The first time she called him "Daddy," he'd told her to just call him Neil.

"I don't want to take anything away from your real father," he had explained.

Who is my real father? she had wanted to ask as Neil hugged her. Although his arms held her, she didn't feel loved. She just wanted to be like Grace.

Starlight stiffened as Lexington stirred. When he settled in his sleep, she breathed again. She didn't want him catching her with a Bible.

Her thoughts returned to the past. That was when it began— the drive to be better than Grace. She wasn't able to do it until she became Starlight. Until she released all the things she'd learned from this Bible.

Starlight lifted the book. It felt heavier than she remembered, as if God had inserted new words. She flipped through the pages, but as she turned from one chapter to the next, there were no familiar scriptures. No memories of a spectacular past, no promise of a future like the one she'd created.

God had nothing to do with her money in the bank, or with the penthouse she owned, or with the million books she'd sold. She was loved by women in thirteen countries. She had no proof she was loved by God.

She slammed the book shut, opened the drawer, and returned the Bible to its place. For an extra moment, she stared at the golden letters on the cover, then watched the book disappear as she closed the drawer. Finally, she turned off the light.

Chapter 16

She was awakened by lips that were as soft as the feathers inside the pillow she rested on. Starlight stretched like a Persian cat, releasing the slumber that settled inside her bones. She nestled deeper into the sheets, enjoying the sensation of Lexington teasing her bottom lip with kisses. When he tried to ease his tongue into her mouth, she nudged him away. "Let me brush my teeth," she said as she freed her legs from the comforter.

He pulled her back, pressing his naked torso into her. "No," he said, kissing her again. "I love even your stank breath."

She shook her head. Only Lexington could turn this moment into a punch line from *The Jamie Foxx Show*. That was the challenge with dating someone a decade younger, although what she had with Lexington couldn't be called dating. It was one-sided; Lexington was the giver, she was the receiver. It had been that way from the beginning.

Two weeks after they'd began their partnership, Starlight bedded Lexington, aware of the two most potent aphrodisiacs—sex and money. At that time, she didn't have money, so she used sex to capture and control. She had laid out the self-professed almost-virgin, and for seven years had sexed him until he was screaming her name in public and in private.

Lexington or Lassie—she didn't know who was more loyal. She knew Lexington would do anything for her.

Starlight closed her eyes as he rubbed his lips across her face, then blazed a trail down her neck. She moaned with the sounds of ecstasy, as she always did. She wanted him to believe that he was about to take her to heaven, although in seven years, there weren't seven times when he had. Their sexual encounters kept her right on earth—her mind filled with the day's schedule or upcoming presentation.

"How does this feel?" He sounded like a poor imitation of one of the men in the pornographic movies they often rented.

"Wha. . . ?" She almost slipped. "Oh, wonderful. Give me more, Lexi," she breathed, draping her arms around his neck.

Suddenly he pulled back. "I had a dream last night." He leaned on one elbow and smiled at her.

She pulled the cover to her chest, startled by his abrupt release.

"I've been thinking about the Women of the Earth seminar," he said. "Ways to make a lot more money. Haven't figured out the whole thing, but with two hundred and fifty women, I want to go beyond the books and tapes. I want to figure out a way to merchandise God."

"What are you thinking?"

He shrugged. "Numbers. Want to walk away with five hundred thou."

Her eyes widened. Five hundred thousand dollars for a day's work. "Make it three hundred," she said. He frowned. "Let's get three hundred women there."

His smile widened, as she knew it would. "You agree with what I'm thinking?"

"Well," she began as she slowly lowered the comforter, revealing her bare chest. "I don't know the details, but with what you've said so far, you deserve a bonus." She reached for him. "Come here, baby. Mama has something wonderful for you."

Chapter 17

At the end of the boardwalk, Grace took off her pumps. She hadn't worn stockings to church, knowing it would be warm in the sanctuary. She almost sighed when her feet met the cool sand. She trudged to the ocean's edge.

Where the water met the earth, she turned and walked along the coast, finding the peace that always awaited her here. Though the noon sun sat high, there was only a handful of beach worshippers. It was as though Los Angelinos didn't believe—it couldn't be ninety degrees. This April had been warmer than most Augusts. It was a spring that thought it was summer. Even the seasons were confused.

Her pleated dress whispered around her ankles in the sea's breeze. She crossed her arms and felt the tape inside her pocket.

She often purchased a tape of Pastor Ford's sermon so that she could study more. Today she'd purchased the tape to hear the pastor's words again, although her mind's "replay" button already had the sermon repeating itself.

"There is said faith and real faith," Pastor Ford had said. "You need to understand what it means to have a complete relationship with God. To know how to call on Him to guide you through any adversity so that you can be a living testimony.

"Are you who the Lord describes in Jeremiah 17:8 when He says, *He will be like a tree planted by the water that sends out its roots by the stream. It does not fear when heat comes, its leaves are always green.* I ask you, do you fear when heat comes, or can you stand the heat?"

Though Grace still moved along the water's edge, she closed her eyes, trying to block out all but the sound of the breaking waves.

Can you stand the heat? Pastor Ford asked inside her head.

Weeks ago, she would have body-slammed that question. Her response would have resounded through the city. *Look at all the heat I've taken. I have skid marks over my body, proving how much I can stand.*

Can you stand the heat? Pastor Ford asked in her head again.

But now her life's temperature was rising, and Grace wasn't responding with the faith she thought she had.

Grace wanted to do the right thing, and last night, she was ready. But the sound of her husband's voice mixing with Pilar's in conversation about their son had driven her to another sleepless night in their office.

This morning, there was no time for discussion as they prepared for church. When they'd returned home, Grace announced that she had to go out for awhile. Conner hadn't tried to stop her. He simply held up his hands, and turned to his daughters as if Grace would never be missed. He was annoyed, but she needed time alone.

Can you stand the heat?

She lifted her hand to wipe the ocean's moisture from her face, but it was tears that left tracks on her face. She wiped them away.

"Okay, Lord. I'm going to do this. Father, lead us all—Conner, Pilar, and me."

"Grace?"

She turned toward the voice. "Starlight."

Her sister was standing so close that Grace wondered if she'd heard her whispered prayer.

Starlight's purple caftan flapped in the beach breeze.

Grace's glance moved to the young man beside her. He stood unsmiling, as stiff as a soldier. Grace was sure the man was Lexington, Starlight's assistant, according to Lily. But as close as they stood, Grace wondered if Lily knew they were more than that.

"I haven't seen you this much in years." Starlight laughed, interrupting Grace's inspection of Lexington.

Grace turned back to Starlight. "We can't get away from each other."

"I guess you didn't make it to church today."

"I . . ." Grace stopped, wondering why she was about to explain. "Good-bye, Starlight." Grace nodded her farewell to the man.

"Wait," Starlight said before Grace could step away. "What are you doing in my neighborhood?" She motioned toward the Towers behind them.

Grace hadn't realized she had walked so far south. She stared at her sister for a moment, then turned away. "Have a nice day," she said over her shoulder.

"Why can't you be happy for me, Grace?"

Grace refused to turn around.

"You can't be happy because you always wanted to be the star of the family."

With Conner, Pilar, and Solomon demanding the energy

from every one of her brain cells, there was no room for this drama.

"I'm trying to be your sister." Starlight's words followed Grace up the coast. "You can't deny my existence because my future holds nothing but good things. Can you say the same for yours?"

Grace paused, but only for a second. She moved faster, hoping Starlight's words would soon drown in the sea. Seconds later, all that filled Grace's ears was the ocean's music.

At the Santa Monica pier, Grace looked over her shoulder. It took a moment for her to spot the colorful caftan whipping in the wind. Though they were faint forms on the sand, Starlight and her friend stood in the same place, now surrounded by a small group. Her sister was nestling in the center of fame.

Grace shivered.

My future holds nothing but good things, she remembered Starlight saying.

Grace wondered what made her quiver. Probably nothing, she thought. Anyway, she didn't have time to worry about her sister. She had to get home.

It was déjà vu. When Grace stepped inside, Conner stood in the foyer waiting, as he had the day before.

She said, "I hope you weren't worried."

"I knew you were all right." He took a step forward. "Grace, when are we going to get past this?"

"I'm ready."

He blew air through his lips, as if he had been holding his breath.

"Where're the girls?"

"I dropped Amber off at Nicole's house and Jayde went to Philip's. His mother invited her for an early dinner."

Grace chuckled as she remembered Philip's leather-clad cousin. She'd tell Conner later. He took her hand and led her into the living room, but once they sat, silence surrounded them.

Conner shifted on the couch and faced her. "You don't know how sorry I am."

Grace shook her head. "I want to get past the apologies." A silent moment passed. Then Grace said, "I do have a question." She bit the corner of her lip. "I heard you . . . and Pilar last night. You talk . . . as if . . . it's settled. As if . . . Solomon is . . . definitely . . . your son." She felt like she was speaking in Morse code. She took a deep breath. "How do you know for sure?"

Conner looked into her eyes for a moment before he stood. Her gaze followed as he walked to the table in the foyer, and then as he moved more slowly, returning with his wallet. He pulled the photo from the billfold, from the same space where he kept pictures of Jayde and Amber, and handed it to her.

She stared at the photo for a moment, then looked up at Conner. Confusion was etched on her face.

Conner frowned, matching her expression. "Pilar gave me the picture."

Grace kept the "so?" that she wanted to say inside.

"It's obvious that Solomon is my son."

Her glance fell to the image again. She wasn't sure what was obvious to him. There was a resemblance—the eyebrows, the cheekbones, even the slight cleft in his chin. Still, there was nothing that said that Conner was his father.

She inhaled. "Conner, you should have a paternity test. I'm surprised Pilar . . . or you . . . didn't suggest it." He looked at her as if she were no longer speaking English. "Just so you . . . we can be sure."

He shook his head as if he couldn't believe her request. "I know this is hard to accept, Grace, but it's not necessary. Look at the picture."

She forced herself to look again. "He looks a little like you," she said, knowing that was what he wanted to hear. Then she added, "But we have to be sure."

"I am sure, Grace."

She reared back at his tone.

"Why do you want to put us through all of that? I hate that this happened too. But Solomon is my son. I've seen him." He held up his hands, stopping her question before she could ask, and told Grace of the meeting in the park. He continued, "His mother is dying, and instead of slowing down the process, we need to be taking steps to resolve this."

Grace looked away. Conner knew the importance of this test. There was only one reason to resist. "Is it that you want a son so much that the truth doesn't matter?" Water covered her eyes.

"Oh, no, Grace."

"I always wanted to give you a son."

Conner dropped to the couch and took her into his arms. "I'm so happy with you and Jayde and Amber. I could have lived this way for the rest of my life."

"But now you don't have to."

The ringing phone startled them.

"Don't answer it," Conner said, taking Grace's hand.

"It may be one of the children."

He sighed before he rushed into the foyer to pick up the phone.

"Hello." He paused. "I told you I'd speak to you tomorrow."

The stiffness of his tone made Grace close her eyes.

"Is something wrong?" Conner paused. "Then we can talk later."

Grace stood and walked toward Conner, pausing under the living room's arch.

"I can't talk, Pilar." He stared at his wife, remembering how she looked the day they renewed their vows. He hated her expression now. His eyes asked her to forgive him. Her eyes told him she wasn't sure if she could.

"Pilar, hold on; I have another call coming in." Conner pressed the flash button. "Jayde . . . okay. Give me a few minutes." He pressed the flash button again. "Pilar, I have to go."

Grace brushed past him. "I'll pick up our daughter," she said loud enough for Pilar to hear.

"Wait . . . I . . . ," he stuttered.

She was out the door before Conner could stop her.

Chapter 18

Grace turned on the water, then glanced in the mirror above the sink. Weary eyes stared back. She hoped the makeup artist would be able to conceal the dark marks under her eyes.

"Grace, are you in here?" Zoë pushed through the bathroom door. "I have some last-minute statistics for the show."

Grace wished she could get out of this interview. How was she supposed to sit in front of a television audience and talk when she couldn't have a discussion with her husband?

"I also have a list of probable questions," Zoë said, tugging Grace from her thoughts. "You'll be questioned about your Christian platform." She moaned those words as if she were tired. "And why Jayde attends a private school." She stopped. "Why are we standing in the bathroom?"

The two walked down the narrow hall, past a wall covered with photos of the show's host, Beth Carter, with various guests. Graced paused, taking in a picture of Beth with Sara Spears. Seeing Sara usually put some fight into Grace, but not today. Nothing measured up to what she faced at home.

Last night was supposed to be filled with forgiving words. But Pilar had made sure that didn't happen. Even after she returned home with Jayde, she and Conner couldn't talk with the children present. And by the time the girls had gone to bed, she'd lost all desire to talk.

"I'm sorry we were interrupted," Conner had apologized.

"It's okay," Grace lied.

"I'd like to finish now."

"I have work to do." She had closed the office door, leaving Conner in the hallway.

Although she'd been exhausted when she climbed into bed, her eyes remained open until she rose before the sun. She wandered through the house trying to unravel the riddle: Why Conner didn't want a paternity test?

"Beth will ask about the initiative to get prayer in the schools," Zoë said when they entered the green room. "Ah, coffee." She filled one of the Styrofoam cups. "Do you want some?"

Not unless you can add something extra to that caffeine, Grace thought. "No, thank you."

"Now remember Beth's reputation," Zoë said between sips. "She can pull anything out of anyone."

Pilar and Solomon flicked through her mind.

"Beth will ask you a question you never expected, and then wham! . . . You'll be making a confession on national television." Zoë chuckled. "Thank God, we don't have anything to hide."

"Ms. Monroe?" A twenty-something red-haired woman peeked through the door. "We're ready for you in makeup."

Grace followed the woman into another room, where she was introduced to André. He barely acknowledged the introduction before he whipped a smock over Grace's St. John's pantsuit.

As André patted, then brushed foundation onto her face, she closed her eyes, trying to get some of the rest she wasn't getting at home. Twenty minutes later, Andre turned her to the mirror.

Gone were the dark circles and the slack in her cheeks. She didn't look like a woman who hadn't slept. She looked like one of the most powerful women in the city.

Yeah, right, her reflection said back to her.

Grace was escorted to Soundstage A, where Beth Carter waited. She stood when Grace stepped onto the platform.

"Councilwoman Monroe, it's a pleasure to meet you."

Grace smiled as she extended her hand.

Beth was an anomaly in Los Angeles. In the city where network anchors had to be movie-star perfect, Beth crashed that rule. With a large forehead, eyes set too far apart, and a nose that was more appropriate on a six-foot-four man rather than a five-foot-two woman, she was the picture of common.

That was the key to her success. Her appearance disarmed guests. She could be trusted.

As Grace took Beth's hand into her own, she felt her stiff shoulders soften. "Please call me Grace."

Beth motioned for Grace to sit, and Grace sank into the full chair that hugged her with its softness.

As their microphones were being fitted, the two chatted about Beth's recent trip to Singapore. A few minutes later, the stage manager gave the signal for the start of the show.

"Are you comfortable?" Beth asked.

Grace nodded as two assistants fluttered around Beth, handing her notes, filling her cup with iced coffee, and dabbing the ever-present oil from her face.

Through the slightly open side curtains, Grace saw Zoë raise her thumb into the air.

"In fifteen seconds," the stage manager yelled.

The familiar tune for *The Women's Exchange* began, and the

music transformed Beth. Her face became rigid, absent the smile that had welcomed Grace.

"Ten seconds."

Beth sat up straighter in her chair, but when Grace tried to do the same, the chair's cushions enveloped her as if she had been taken prisoner.

"Five seconds."

For the first time, Grace noticed that Beth's chair was raised slightly higher than hers.

"Four . . . three . . . two . . . one!"

"Good morning, Los Angeles. Welcome to *The Women's Exchange*. I'm Beth Carter, and in our studio today, we have the new councilwoman of the Eighteenth District. Welcome, Grace Monroe." The smile that had greeted Grace returned. "It's good to have you here, Councilwoman."

"Thank you." Grace smiled as she fought to push herself higher in her chair.

In a quick move, Beth propelled herself to the edge of her seat. "Councilwoman Monroe, during the campaign you received extraordinary coverage because your views were considered extreme for an African American."

"I don't consider my views extreme."

"But many do."

"Yes," she breathed, relieved. This was going to be the same interview. Grace relaxed and in her mind went over her standard answers.

"However, I wanted to discuss something else today," Beth continued. "Your family . . ."

Beth's words caused Grace's heart to skip.

"There are things about you that many don't know."

Grace's heart pounded. How did Beth find out? How was she supposed to respond when she and Conner hadn't even told their children?

Grace's glance darted over Beth's shoulder to Zoë. Her frown was as deep as Grace's.

"It's a secret that just came to my attention."

Grace glared at Beth as she reviewed her options. She could walk off the stage or say that her personal life could not be discussed. With print reporters or even a lesser-rated show, either option might work. But a negative response on *The Women's Exchange* would surely find its way onto every local evening news program.

"It's interesting that you and your husband haven't talked about this," Beth went on.

Maybe I should say it first, Grace thought. *If I say it, I'll control how the world finds out about Solomon.* Grace swallowed. She had to form the words quickly.

She said, "I don't think it's appropriate to talk about this . . ."

At the same time, Beth said, "I want to talk about . . . Starlight."

Grace clasped her hands together to hide their shaking. "Starlight?"

"Yes. Not many people know that Starlight is your sister."

Her blood began to flow again. Over the campaigning months, she'd been asked about Starlight once. Starlight being her sister wasn't as interesting as her side of politics. Right now, she'd never been happier to hear her sister's name.

Grace couldn't respond fast enough. "Starlight is my sister."

Beth turned to the camera. "She is known as Starlight, but was born Mabel Morgan. Starlight is the half-sister of Councilwoman Grace Monroe."

Grace heard very few of Beth's words as she tried to breathe herself back to calm.

"We'll find out more about these sisters. Stay tuned."

The stage manager yelled, "Two minutes."

Zoë rushed to Grace's side, her back to Beth. "I'm sorry," she whispered. "I thought Starlight was old news."

She's good news right now, Grace thought, reaching for her water glass. "I can handle this."

By the time the stage manager did the ten-second countdown, Grace was poised. Beth gave her return address and then turned to Grace, firing questions.

"Why wasn't your sister, Starlight, involved in your campaign? After all, she has quite a following."

"Yes, but this was a local election." Grace paused and widened her smile. "And the results are in."

Beth's laugh was a short one. "Still, Starlight could have been a major contributor, especially since so many in your family were involved. Are you ashamed of her? Is that why you keep your relationship a secret?"

"Absolutely not."

"Then what's the problem? You're a Christian politician; your sister is an inspirational speaker. It would seem her message would have been good for your campaign."

"Actually, my sister wouldn't have been able to help me. We're on very different pages."

Beth glanced at her notes. "Christian, inspirational, what's the difference?"

"Being a Christian means that a person is taking a stand for Jesus, while inspirational can mean anything."

Beth crossed one bony leg over the other. "I can't really hear the difference," she said, not letting Grace finish. She leaned forward. "Tell me, Councilwoman Monroe, are you sure there's not more to the story? Are you and your sister estranged?" It was a whisper designed to make Grace forget the cameras.

Grace shook her head. "No, I saw my sister yesterday. And Saturday as well."

The smile disappeared from Beth's eyes, and she glanced again at her notes. "Well, that's good to know." She looked into the camera. "We'll be right back."

Grace smiled, feeling victorious. Beth lost her story and returned the interview to more familiar issues: How she could be a black conservative. Didn't she believe that most Republicans were racists? And did she have aspirations for a larger piece of the pie?

Inside, Grace thanked God that she'd been able to dodge this bullet. But she knew that at any point, this gun could be aimed at her again.

"Pilar, this is Conner."

There was a pause. "Please hold on." Another pause. "Solomon."

That was all he heard. The rest of the words were muffled as if she'd placed her hand over the receiver. Still, Conner strained to hear the boy's voice.

He closed his eyes, bringing forth the image of the boy he'd seen in the park.

"Hello."

Her voice made him open his eyes, leaving behind the vision. Grace, Jayde, and Amber stared at him from the photo on his desk. He shifted his glance.

Pilar said, "I wasn't expecting your call."

"You were talking to Solomon."

"Yes. I sent him outside."

His eyes drifted back to the picture of his family. He cleared his throat. "I called so that we could begin to make plans."

"I'm glad to hear that."

"I'd like to come to New York." He heard her suck in air. "I just want to meet Solomon."

There was a pause. "Before we do that, Conner, there is something . . ."

"I agree. I want to take a paternity test." Conner couldn't decipher the meaning of her moan.

A moment later, she said, "I thought you already believed Solomon's your son."

"Is there a problem with my taking the test?" His heart pounded harder with each word of his question.

"I just don't want to slow down everything when we already know the truth."

He had said similar words to Grace.

"It just makes sense for us to do this, Pilar. So that we can all be sure."

Grace had said similar words to him.

"You mean so your wife can be sure." In his silence, she said, "I would have never come to you if you weren't Solomon's father."

"I know that, Pilar."

"I would have never come to you if I were not dying."

He massaged his eyes with his hands. "I promise this won't slow down anything. There's a DNA center in New York, one of the best in the country. We can have the results quickly." He paused. "Unless you have someplace in mind."

It took a moment for her to respond. "No."

"And then I'd like to meet Solomon." More silence. "We shouldn't introduce me as his father. We need to wait . . . until." Her silence made him continue as if he were presenting a case. "This way, Solomon and I can get to know one another . . . before we have to tell him."

Seconds ticked before Pilar said, "Maybe we should wait until after the test."

Her words felt like punishment. "If you think that's best."

"When are you coming to New York?"

"Within the next few days, but if I can't meet Solomon, we can do the test through the mail."

"Come to New York."

He didn't dare ask if those words were a change of mind.

"I'll call you when I've made the plans."

She hung up, and although that had become their way, he felt her fury.

Grace didn't know what was worse—thinking that Beth had found out about Solomon or spending thirty minutes trying to explain Christian values to someone who didn't believe.

In the car, she closed her eyes, trying to discover that calm place, but she couldn't find it. She had to talk to Conner. Convince him to take the paternity test.

The cell phone rang, and Grace looked at the Caller ID. She closed the privacy window in the car.

"How did the interview go?" Conner asked.

"You don't want to know."

"I'm sorry," he said, then paused. "I really wanted to finish what we started last night."

She wanted to make peace. "Maybe we can go out to dinner."

"I've decided to go to New York." He spoke over her words.

Her chest tightened, and she breathed to draw air into her lungs. "Why? You don't even know if Solomon is your son."

"I know that he is, Grace." He sounded as weary as she felt. "But I will take the test. We can expedite everything if we're in New York."

She exhaled, but it was just partial relief. "You can do the DNA test from anywhere, Conner."

"I know, but while we're there, we can meet Solomon."

"You're going to walk into this boy's life and then just walk away if he's not your son? That's not fair."

The crackle of dead air came through the phone. "We're not telling him anything. Pilar will introduce us as friends."

She couldn't imagine being any kind of friend to Pilar. "I think we should wait. These tests don't take long."

"Two weeks. The DNA Diagnostic Center in New York can do it. It'll cost five hundred dollars."

She closed her eyes, waiting for his next words.

"I want you to go to New York with me."

"This is not how we should do this," she said with her eyes still shut.

"I'm getting the test for you. You should go to New York with me."

She felt like one of his clients—being pressured into a settlement. "I can't do this right now." She pressed the End button before he could respond, then turned off the phone.

She glanced through the tinted windows as her car rolled past Sunset Boulevard. She was in the middle of Hollywood. But there was not a movie that could rival the drama unfolding in her life.

There was a quick knock on his door, and Chandler came in just as Conner dropped the phone into the cradle.

"You've been behind closed doors all morning." Chandler sat in front of his brother's desk. "Thought I'd check on you."

Conner shook his head. "It's not going well."

"Well, I've briefed Monica on the Jacoby case. She'll take over for you."

"I don't want to dump my work on anyone."

"Don't worry. I've got your back. Like you had mine when Devry and I spent all that time in fertility clinics." Chandler leaned across the desk. "You need to concentrate on home."

"I don't know what to do. Grace and I were making progress, but now . . ."

"Give her time. She's hurt. It's not always easy to do what you know. Sometimes it's easier to just go with what you feel."

Conner turned toward the window. "Grace wants me to have a paternity test." He shook his head as if he still couldn't believe her request.

"Of course, you should have one."

Conner turned toward his brother so fast he almost lost his balance. "I don't need a test."

"What are you talking about, bro? In today's times . . ."

"I told you, I saw him."

"I understand, but you can't turn your life upside down based on one less-than-five-minutes meeting. You need the medical evidence."

He began to speak, then stopped and slipped into his chair. "I don't need any more time, Chandler. I know in my bones that he's mine." There was a smile in his tone but not on his face.

"Then a test will prove you right. And when the proof is in, it'll be easier for Grace."

He nodded. "That's why I'm doing it." When Chandler stood, Conner said, "Solomon is my son."

Chandler smiled. "If that's what you want, bro, I hope that's what you get. But most of all, I pray that God's will is done."

Chandler turned and left the office before he saw the doubt cross his brother's face.

Chapter 19

Each of the fourteen conference room chairs was filled. Starlight stood at the round mahogany table with her arms spread as if she were about to lead a symphony. Her caftan was a shade lighter than the lavender walls, and the full sleeves fluttered as she spoke.

"Your duties are outlined in this manual."

The "Light Girls"—Starlight's assistants—flipped through the eighteen-page booklet she'd prepared.

"Each of the three hundred women must feel we are addressing their every need."

"Three hundred?" Marta, one of the Light Girls, seemed stunned. "How did you find all those people?" Her Jamaican accent was thicker with her surprise.

"L.A. is the land of self-improvement," Lexington said, oblivious to Starlight's frown. "Any seminar will draw with the right marketing."

Starlight's frown deepened. She never gave explanations. Especially not to Marta, who was too interested in the financial side of Starlight Enterprises. Starlight made a mental note. After this conference, Marta would be standing in the unemployment line.

Starlight said, "We're going to do run-throughs every day until the conference."

"Why so much practice?" The question came from a new hire.

Starlight strained to remember her name. One strike, she thought. "I'll explain . . . this time." She sat in her chair, which, with its high back, was much larger than the other seats. "People must leave this conference raving."

"Because we want to do one every quarter," Lexington offered.

Starlight could see it in their eyes—their inner calculators computing. "Any other questions?" she asked quickly. She frowned as Marta and the new hire exchanged glances, but all remained silent. She motioned for them to stand. Starlight placed her palms together and bowed. "May the light forever be with you and yours."

The women and Lexington followed. "And you as well."

The Light Girls filed from the room, although Marta lingered for a few seconds.

Once alone, Lexington said, "You seem upset. Whaz up?"

She hated when he spoke that way. It was not the language of the enlightened, and she couldn't afford him slipping at a seminar.

But she had another issue now. "Watch what you say in front of the girls."

Lexington shrugged. "They're harmless. They're stupid."

"Not Marta. In fact, get rid of her right after the conference." His eyes questioned her. "She's too curious."

"Okay. I'll catch her in something."

His words were spoken from the memory of being dragged by a former employee to the Department of Labor. They'd settled, eager to avoid government scrutiny. Since then, every employee had been terminated for cause—money missing from their stations, pornographic Web sites on their computers, anything that a suddenly unemployed person would not want on the record.

"Make sure Marta's setup is good." She opened the manila folder on her desk. "Now tell me about the rest of the conference."

"Our products could bring in another fifty thousand dollars." Starlight smiled.

"First, there's the Bless-ed Water. Sales premise: Use a dab every day to continue in the light. It will wash away negative traces of your past, freeing you from pain, disappointments, and the heartache of relationships with men that you need to cleanse from your soul."

"Are we going to buy bottled water?"

He looked at her as if she were stupid. "No. We'll fill bottles with tap water."

Starlight's eyes widened. "Where are we going to get all of those bottles, and who is going to fill them?" She shook her head. "I don't want the Light Girls involved."

He leaned across the table and rubbed her hand. "You should know that we think alike."

No, we don't, she thought, but she smiled.

He leaned back as if he were about to reveal a million-dollar plan. "The bottles will come from a recycling center. On Saturday, I'll pick up a few men outside Home Depot. I'll take them to the hotel, give them the bottles in the bathroom, and tell them, 'Fill 'er up.' " He chuckled.

Starlight laughed, imagining the sight. "Make sure the bottles are filled with water and nothing more."

He buckled with more laughter. "We'll sell close to five hundred. Some will buy two and three bottles. At twenty-five dollars a pop, that's good money."

Starlight's laughter stopped. "That's a bit pricey for water."

"It's Bless-ed Water." His smile covered his entire face. "We'll sell out. And if we don't, we'll save the bottles for the Revival." He looked down at his notes. "Next are the Anointed Cloths. The ninety-nine-cents store has packages of ten handkerchiefs. It'll cost thirty dollars for three hundred. But we can sell Anointed Cloths for fifteen, even twenty dollars apiece."

Starlight's legs began to shake as she calculated it all in her head.

Lexington continued, explaining the rest: enemas to cleanse the deep pain held within, bath salts to pull out the soul's impurities, Anointed Keys to serve as visual reminders for the future. When he finished, he clasped his hands behind his head and smiled as if he'd just presented her with that million-dollar check.

Starlight squeezed her legs together to stop their trembling and noticed another sensation. Her thoughts turned from the money. She sauntered to the door and locked it. Then she turned to Lexington.

She began with her scarf, letting it glide across his face before it wilted to the floor. Then she unzipped her top. In less than a minute, she stood naked except for her purple pumps.

Lexington's eyes consumed her.

She stood taller, proud that she was fit and looked as good as any twenty-year-old . . . almost.

"Here?" The question quivered through his lips.

Starlight tugged at his tie. "Don't you think you deserve a reward?"

"Yes." He stood, his eyes never leaving her. He unfastened his belt and dropped his pants to his ankles.

Starlight shook her head. "I want you naked, exposed, like me." She pressed into his chest, and he moaned. She stepped back. Not yet.

He stumbled out of his clothes. When he was nude, she put her hands together and bowed. "May the light forever be with you and yours."

"I'm about to give you some light." He laid her on the conference table.

It felt hard, cold, and wonderful as Starlight thought about the women outside the door. When Lexington lay on top of her, she thought about all he'd told her. When he moaned as if he'd found paradise, she asked herself if there was any difference between money, power, and sex. When she answered that question, the room filled with her own cries of ecstasy.

Minutes passed before Lexington freed her from his weight. "Was it as good for you as it was for me?"

She didn't have to hide her annoyance at his Comic View line. Today, it didn't bother her. "Lexi, baby," she said as she cupped her palm against his face. "It was as good as it gets."

Chapter 20

Grace pressed her ear against the bedroom door. She heard nothing, but she knew Conner could be reading or just laying in wait.

She paced, her steps silenced in the carpet. Her plan had worked until now. First, motherly duties kept her occupied from the moment Conner came home. She saw his frustrated frowns, but once the girls went to their bedrooms, she pretended that city council responsibilities demanded her time. She'd stayed in the office with the cordless phone in her lap in case Conner walked in.

Now she stood, ready to sleep. Not only did the clock in the foyer chime twelve times a few minutes ago, but the ache that smoked through her bones convinced her she was too tired to continue tonight's charade.

She leaned against the wall and closed her eyes. "God, please, I don't want to go into anything with Conner tonight. I promise, Lord, I will handle this . . . soon. Just make sure that Conner's asleep."

"Mom?" Her eyes snapped open as Jayde walked toward her. "What's wrong?"

"Nothing. I was . . . praying. What are you doing up?"

"I woke up and thought I heard something. When I looked in the hall, I thought you were sick."

Grace wrapped her arms around Jayde. "I'm fine," she whispered as she walked her back to her room. "Go back to bed."

Jayde's eyes remained on her mother until there was just a crack in the door.

Grace inhaled and headed back to her bedroom. In minutes, Jayde would be checking again. She turned the door knob and tiptoed inside. Only the glow from her nightstand lamp lit the room. Conner lay on his stomach, his head turned away. She stood unmoving, then breathed when she realized he was asleep.

She slipped into her closet, changed, then waited. When she heard just the rhythm of Conner's sleep breathing, she crept across the room. Grace pulled back the covers, and stared at the two envelopes, right below her pillow.

She picked up the papers, then sat on the bed's edge turning the airline tickets over in her hands.

"I want you with me." Conner's words floated over her shoulder.

She closed her eyes and wondered why God hadn't answered her prayer.

"I want you by my side when I truly meet my son."

She pulled a ticket from one envelope. "Conner." She faced him. "You want to leave on Wednesday? In just two days?"

He nodded.

"This is too fast."

He sat up. "Time's not on our side."

Her shoulders slumped. "Even if he is your son, we still have a lot to work out."

"Nothing has to stop us from meeting Solomon."

"I'm thinking about Solomon." She took Conner's hand and said a silent prayer that the Lord would soften her words. "This is overwhelming to us, Conner. How can we expect a young boy to handle it? Do we want to invade his life this way?"

Conner frowned.

She continued, "Even if you are Solomon's father, by meeting us, we may be complicating things." She looked away. "It may make it harder for . . . the people who Solomon will have to live with."

Grace was sure that minutes passed.

Conner sat up straighter. "If he's my son, he's going to live with us."

His words pulled air from Grace's lungs.

"We don't have a choice, Grace. No one in Pilar's family wants Solomon."

Grace frowned. What was wrong with the boy?

"Pilar's family doesn't want anything to do with a grandson, or a nephew, or a cousin who's black."

Surprise kept her silent.

"Grace, in a few months, Solomon won't have a home unless we give him one."

His words made her wonder. Was that why he didn't want to take the test? Was he already Solomon's father, no matter what the DNA results said?

Grace wasn't sure whether the tears that stung her eyes were for her or for Solomon. She didn't resist when Conner pulled her into his arms.

"We can do this."

Grace lay still as he held her.

"It's going to take a lot," Conner began, "but this will turn out fine. I promise."

The water that burned her eyes dripped onto Conner's arm. He turned her, making her face him and began kissing away her pain.

Sobs gave sound to her silent tears.

His gentle kisses filled with urgency and she pulled him close, trying to make herself one with him. She moved her lips to his, thrusting her tongue inside his mouth, demanding that he know her feelings.

Conner moaned; he understood.

Grace still cried.

She ripped his pajama shirt open, sending buttons flying across the room, then dug her fingers into his skin. She pressed against him, feeling his body stiffen with desire.

He wanted her.

Her tears flowed.

Conner's moans mixed with her cries filling the air with a mournful melody. With one hand, he edged Grace's T-shirt up as his other explored beneath. But when he tried to push the shirt over her head, she refused to release her lips from his, leaving the shirt bunched around her neck.

It didn't matter. It didn't stop her tears.

Conner whipped the comforter away from their bodies, then fought to break from her lips. When he freed himself, his eager tongue pleased every part of her.

Grace's eyes stung as she squeezed the lids together. She clutched the sheet beneath her. She couldn't tell the difference between the pleasure and the pain. It all fused inside and now fought to be released.

Grace rolled Conner onto his back and straddled him. He

looked up at her, and his long fingers wiped her flowing tears. She looked down at him, letting her tears drip, watering the center of his chest.

When they joined, her blood felt like a thermometer's rising mercury.

The cries that escaped from her were beyond the moment. She collapsed onto her husband. Their uneven breathing and pounding hearts were the only sounds in the room.

It was then that Grace realized her tears had finally ceased.

Chapter 21

"You should go to New York."

"Why should I when we don't even know if . . . ?" Grace gripped the telephone tighter and leaned back into her pillows. She didn't complete her sentence, tired of singing the same song.

"Because Conner asked you to," Devry said.

Grace ran her hands along Conner's side of the bed where wrinkled sheets reminded her.

Devry continued, "And because the trip to New York means nothing more than getting the paternity test done and . . . perhaps meeting Solomon. I'd go."

"That's because you're a better Christian than I am."

"That's true," she teased, but then her tone became serious. "You need to get focused, Grace. There's a very good chance that you're about to be with child. But look at it this way: you won't have the stretch marks."

"I've got stretch marks, Devry, all over my heart."

There was silence before Devry said, "Maybe God's expanded your heart. To help you make room . . ."

Devry stopped, but they both silently completed her sentence with the same words—". . . for Solomon."

Grace lifted Conner's pillow, closed her eyes, and inhaled,

swallowing his scent. The love they shared last night reminded her of their days at Yale. They would cut classes, sneak into custodial closets, even bathroom stalls. Anything to share their hearts, two, sometimes three, times a day. They explored, discovered, enjoyed, but were never able to satisfy their desire. Sixteen years ago, that kept their love on the edge. Now they didn't need that.

Not until last night.

Grace felt as if she had experienced her husband for the first time. In a way, she had. It was the first time she'd made love to him knowing that he'd been with another woman.

Devry interrupted her thoughts. "You're going with Conner."

Grace couldn't tell if it were a question or a demand.

Outside the bedroom window, she could see the outline of the city's skyline. During the campaign, she'd spent hours looking out this window, feeling victory in the view. How could you sit atop a city and not feel grand?

"I'm going to New York."

Grace wasn't sure that she'd actually uttered those words until Devry said, "See, you are a good Christian."

Her eyes remained on the window. "Maybe I just love my husband."

"That's a good thing."

"And if I love him, then I can find a way to . . ." She stopped. Find a way to do what? Love Solomon? Bring him into their home if he were Conner's son? Bring him into their home if he were not?

"My goodness, Grace, I didn't realize the time. I have a session." Devry paused. "I wish we could talk some more."

"I'll be fine." Grace hung up without saying good-bye, her thoughts beyond the phone call.

If I love him, then I can find a way to . . . She still couldn't fin-ish her sentence.

Never did she believe she would have come this far. Just days ago, she never wanted to utter another word to Conner. But last night, they had shared an intimacy that still warmed her body.

This morning, she was the one who stopped him before he got out of bed. "There's something we have to do," she had said, resting her hand on his.

He had kissed her. "You're forgetting last night."

She shook her head and scooted from her side of the bed. When she lowered herself to her knees, Conner's smile disap-peared, and he joined her.

He took her hand, and she said, "Let's pray for our children."

"Dear Heavenly Father," his voice shook as he began. "We come to you with praise and thanksgiving, raising before you the gifts you have blessed us with . . . our children. Lord, give unto Jayde, Amber, and . . ." He paused.

She said, "And Solomon."

They lifted their eyes.

"And Solomon," Conner said, keeping his gaze on Grace. With his eyes opened, he continued. "Give our children perfect hearts, to keep thy commandments, thy testimonies, and thy statutes and to do all these things, in Jesus's name."

Together they said, "Amen."

Grace shivered now as she remembered that moment. She'd been able to make a little room for Solomon.

"And if I can pray for him, I can do anything."

She hoped her words were true.

Chapter 22

The Statue of Liberty held her torch high, as the plane continued its descent. Grace wondered how many people had been welcomed into New York by Lady Liberty. Then she wondered how many people had viewed the statue the way she was seeing it today—with its back to the plane. Minutes later, the plane's tires screeched onto one of JFK's runways.

"Welcome to New York where the local time is four-forty. Please keep your seat belts fastened until the captain has turned off the sign indicating it is safe to move about the cabin."

Grace locked her eyes on the window, blocking the rest of the flight attendant's words. Her mind was filled with thoughts that had held her hostage ever since she'd agreed to come to New York.

It had been the shortest twenty-four hours of her life—from noon yesterday when she agreed to this trip, to this morning when she and Conner had taken their first-class seats in the Delta Airlines superjet. The hours had been filled with tasks that rearranged her life for this intrusion. Zoë would handle the office, and Lily was thrilled to have these unexpected days with her granddaughters.

But there were times when Grace felt as if she was living through the longest hours as each passing second tortured her with new questions. What would Pilar say? What would Pilar do? What would the tests say? Would they meet Solomon? Should they?

When she went to bed after eleven last night, she couldn't close her eyes because of the images that waited in her subconscious. She'd lain awake until she surrendered and sat in the chaise for the rest of the night staring at the half moon.

The morning's light gave her new focus when she'd awakened Amber.

"Mommy, what are you going to bring me from New York?"

Grace had laughed as she checked the suitcase for items Amber may have added or subtracted. "I don't know yet, sweetie. But I promise it will be something wonderful."

"I'm going to miss you, Mommy."

Grace hugged her. "Me too." Tears stung her eyes, but when she looked up and saw Jayde standing at Amber's door, she blinked them away.

From the moment they'd announced this trip, Grace had endured a long interrogation, proving that Jayde was her father's daughter. And from her stance, with her arms crossed and her eyes bearing down, Grace knew that the prosecution had not rested.

"Mom, who did you say you were visiting in New York?" Jayde asked.

"A business associate of your father's," she said as an image of Pilar flickered in her head.

"Who specifically?"

"I told you already, Jayde, you don't know the person." At least that was true.

"The person must have a name," Jayde insisted.

Grace slammed Amber's suitcase shut. "That's the end to the questions, Jayde. Have you finished packing?"

"Yes." But she stood in place, her stance her weapon.

"Then," Grace started, "take your bag downstairs."

Jayde held her stare for a moment longer before she turned away.

Grace wanted to be patient because she knew Jayde was treading in a pool of insecurity. In the last week, her daughter had seen a lot that didn't make sense, and this trip was another unsettling wave. But Grace didn't know how to bring peace to Jayde's heart when she had none in her own. When it was time for Conner to take the girls to Lily's, Grace had held Jayde longer than normal, hoping to fill her with assurance.

Now, as Grace focused on the other planes that crowded the runways, she wished for the reassurance that she prayed she'd given Jayde.

The seat belt sign clicked off, and Conner stood, helping Grace from her seat. He pulled her into his arms. "It's going to be all right," he said as if he'd heard her thoughts.

She smiled. She and Conner had as much of a connection as he had with his twin. The marital bed connection. That thought tore her smile away.

At baggage claim, Grace spotted the fortyish white-haired man dressed in the standard black suit holding a cardboard sign with "Monroe" printed in black marker. His smile looked as if it was part of his job as he placed their carry-ons onto the cart, then escorted them through the maze of people to the awaiting car. While Conner helped Grace inside, the driver tossed their bags into the trunk.

It had been three years since Grace had visited this city that she loved. But as they drove past various shades of gray two-story houses along the parkway, New York wasn't as inviting as she remembered. The sun that had been bright above the clouds did not shine as they edged forward on the Van Wyck Expressway.

Conner took Grace's hand, but she kept her gaze outside.

It took seventy minutes for the car to crawl from parkway to expressway and exit on the Manhattan side of the Midtown Tunnel. The sun burned on this part of the city and brought with it an energy that felt as if they'd landed on another planet.

As they moved up the Avenue of the Americas, Grace wondered if every one of New York's seven-million residents was outside. The streets pulsed; the buildings breathed. The anxiety that had been her constant companion dissipated. By the time the car cruised to a stop in front of the Plaza, she was part of New York.

"Good evening." The black doorman, dressed in the gold-trimmed navy uniform, smiled as he opened the door and helped Grace from the car. She returned his smile and wondered why he wasn't starring in a movie somewhere.

Though this was her first time at the Plaza, Grace felt acquainted with the spectacular lobby, remembering details from her favorite movie: *The Way We Were.*

Within minutes, the Plaza's staff had them inside their thirteenth-floor suite. The moment the room's door opened, they were greeted by sweeping views of Central Park that filled every floor-to-ceiling window. While Conner directed the bellman to the bedroom with their bags, Grace stood in the living room. Darkness was beginning to descend upon the never-sleeping city, but millions of lights twinkled outside.

"Would you like me to close the drapes?" the bellman asked.

"No, thank you."

Conner tipped the bellman, then joined Grace. He enveloped her in his arms as they shared the view.

"This is a beautiful place," she said.

"That's why I wanted to stay here." He turned her around so they faced each other. "These aren't the best of times, but I was praying that we could make this trip . . . pleasurable."

She pulled away from him. "So, what are the plans?" she asked, diverting her eyes.

"I thought we would have dinner. Maybe Tavern on the Green." He stopped as if it hurt to say the next words. "We can call Pilar in the morning."

She folded her arms. "We should call Pilar now, Conner. Let's handle our business."

He looked at his watch and then moved to the phone.

Grace returned to the window, watching Conner's reflection through the glass.

"Hello, Pilar," he said before turning his back, muffling his words.

But Grace could still hear it all. It was a simple conversation. The lawyer had become the defendant, answering questions with simple responses: "yes," "just now," "fine." He turned around when he said, "Yes, she's here with me."

Grace took a deep breath, but stayed in place as Conner made plans. Even when he hung up the phone, she remained still.

"Pilar said to tell you hello."

She whipped around. "What are the plans?"

"We're going to meet Pilar in the morning. She'll meet us here after Solomon goes to school. I'm sending a car for her." His words became softer with each sentence. "We'll go to the diagnostics center from here."

She nodded, then began studying the pattern in the Persian carpet.

Conner said, "Where do you want to go?" She lifted her glance. "To eat," he clarified.

She let a silent moment pass. "I'm going to bed." She brushed past him. The last thing she heard before she closed the bedroom door was her husband's sigh.

Chapter 23

"Mom," Starlight called out. She could hear the television from one of the back bedrooms.

Lily rushed into the living room. "Starlight, what are you doing here?"

Before she could respond, Jayde came into the room. "Aunt Star?"

Starlight smiled. "Come here, girl. Give your auntie a kiss."

"It's good to see you, Auntie Star."

She loosened her embrace. "My goodness, you are growing into such a beautiful young lady."

Over Jayde's shoulder, Starlight saw Amber standing with her head down. "Amber, come here so I can see you too."

Amber smiled and hugged her aunt.

"What are you girls doing here?" Starlight asked as she held them both.

"Mommy and Daddy went away," Amber said.

Starlight didn't miss the way Jayde pulled back. She watched her niece walk to the couch.

Amber continued, "We're staying with Nana."

"And I bet Nana loves every moment."

Lily smiled. "Ms. Amber, it's time for bed."

Amber set her mouth to protest, and Lily held up her hand. "No complaining, or else you won't get any ice cream."

Amber's eyes widened. "I can have a cup in bed like last time?"

Lily nodded. "Kiss your aunt good-night."

They hugged, and after Lily and Amber left, Starlight joined Jayde on the couch. She playfully poked her arm. "So how is my favorite teenage niece?"

"I'm your only teenage niece." Jayde smiled a bit.

"A technicality." Starlight cocked her head. "You're not having a good time here?"

Jayde shrugged. "It's all right."

Starlight smiled and remembered why she didn't have children. "Let's get some ice cream." Together they went into the kitchen.

When Starlight opened the freezer's door, she asked, "Where did your parents go?"

"New York." Jayde slumped at the table.

She pulled out a pint of pink bubblegum ice cream and wondered, *Didn't anyone eat vanilla anymore?* "You might want this." She held the carton in the air for Jayde to see and then searched for another package.

"What are they doing in New York?" Starlight asked as Jayde went to the cabinets for bowls.

"Mom wouldn't tell me."

Starlight's frown wasn't for the almond mocha truffle ice cream carton that she'd found. "Was it business?" she asked as they scooped spoonfuls into the dishes.

Jayde shrugged. "I don't know. But I think it was pretty bad. Mom and Dad have been acting weird."

Starlight lifted her eyebrows, but remained silent. She knew when to talk—and when to listen.

Jayde continued when they sat at the table. "I think they're mad at each other."

Starlight nodded as if she understood. "They're having problems?" It didn't make her feel good that she smiled inside.

Jayde slumped in her chair and shrugged.

Starlight knew that Jayde's information door had closed. But she had enough. "I'm sure it's okay." She paused. "How's school? Tell me about the cute boys."

Jayde's smile returned. "I met someone who knew all about you."

As Jayde told her aunt about Donald, Starlight kept her eyes on her niece, but her thoughts had wandered. So Grace and Conner were having problems. They'd been so good together that Starlight believed their past would never come back. But actually, she wasn't surprised. That old boyfriend of Grace's had probably reared his head again.

"Did you leave out this ice cream?" Lily asked.

Starlight didn't even notice her mother come into the kitchen.

"Sorry," she and Jayde said at the same time.

Lily chuckled and filled another bowl with pink bubblegum ice cream. "Do me a favor, Jayde. Take this to your sister while I talk to your aunt, please."

Jayde stood. "Aunt Star, will you let me know when you're leaving?"

"Sure, sweetie."

As soon as Jayde disappeared, Starlight said, "So give me the scoop on Grace and Conner."

"They went to New York on business."

"Jayde said Grace and Conner are having problems."

"That's not true."

Starlight stared at her mother, trying to determine if she was just protecting her sweet Grace. It didn't matter. She had enough information already. "Anyway, Mom, I wanted to remind you that I won't be by on Saturday. I have that conference."

Lily leaned forward, eager to hear the details of the Sisters of the Sun conference, and Starlight obliged. It felt good to see the gleam in her mother's eyes. Lily whooped when Starlight mentioned that Pastor Carey's wife would attend.

"I'm so proud of you," Lily exclaimed. "If I didn't have the girls, I would come."

"That's okay, Mom," Starlight said as she put her bowl into the dishwasher. "I'll fill you in next week." She hugged her mother. "I've got to go. I have an early day tomorrow."

"Don't forget to say good-bye to Jayde."

Starlight glanced toward the hall. "Give them both a kiss for me." She rushed into the hallway before Lily could protest.

As she ran down the stairs, a welter of emotions stirred inside. She couldn't say she was pleased Grace and Conner were having challenges. But if they were, it just proved what she'd been saying all along: there was really no difference between them. Maybe when Grace came home, she'd invite her to lunch. There were many lessons that she could pass on to her younger sister. This might just be what they needed to draw them closer.

She slid into the back seat of her car, and before her driver took his seat, she punched a number on her cell phone.

"Where are you?" she asked the moment the phone was answered.

"Where do you want me to be?" Lexington responded.

Good answer, she thought. "In my bed in thirty minutes." She clicked off the phone.

There was no need to spend the entire night thinking about Conner and Grace. She'd help her sister when Grace returned from New York. In the meantime, she had her own life to live.

Chapter 24

Grace and Conner stood in front of the gold letters that spelled Palm Court Café.

"Mr. Monroe, your party is waiting inside."

Grace gripped Conner's hand as they followed the mâitre d' through the restaurant to a table along the far wall. Although Grace was dressed as if she were going to a council meeting and Conner as if he were presenting a major case, Pilar wore a simple black sweater as a shawl over a white T-shirt. She sat with her back to the window; the noon light shined behind her.

Grace held her gasp inside. She couldn't remember how many days had passed since she'd seen Pilar in Encounters, but it wasn't enough time to shed ten, maybe fifteen pounds, though that's the way Pilar looked. Her makeup couldn't hide the hollowness of her cheeks or the blanched tint of her skin. Her arms were mere bones. She was being ravaged by disease.

Still, Pilar smiled as they approached. Her eyes locked with Grace's.

"Hello . . ." Pilar's voice trailed off, as if she had more to say, but couldn't find the words. When she looked at Conner, her smile widened. "Thank you for meeting me."

Conner nodded as he held the chair for Grace, then sat next to her.

In the discomforting silence, Grace smoothed the yellow tablecloth in the spot in front of her. When she allowed her glance to rise, Pilar was doing the same to her space.

"I'm glad we could all get together," Conner said. He slipped his hand across the table and held Grace's.

Pilar nodded and looked at Grace as she spoke. "I feel blessed that we're moving forward."

Grace spoke only with her eyes.

"Would you like anything to eat?" Conner asked them both.

It was almost noon, and though too many hours had passed since Grace's last meal, she couldn't fathom the concept of food. Her sole desire was to get away from this place.

"I'm not hungry," Pilar said, as if she spoke for all of them. She kept her gaze on Grace. "I've wanted to speak to you."

Something we have in common, Grace thought. She could see Conner shifting from the corner of her eye.

"I want to thank you . . . for this."

"Nothing to thank me for, Pilar. Nothing's been decided."

Pilar's glance skittered between Grace and Conner. "I'm just saying, to come this far . . ."

"New York is not far."

Pilar pressed her lips together before she said, "That's not what I meant."

Conner said, "Do either of you want coffee?"

"No," Grace and Pilar said together.

Conner cleared his throat in the silence that followed. "Then maybe we should . . ." Without finishing, he grabbed a Federal Express packet from his briefcase.

As he did, Pilar pulled an envelope from her purse.

Conner said, "This is from the diagnostics center. Everything we need is here." He turned the packet over in his hands and looked at Pilar. "I was thinking that I could get Solomon's and your samples and take the package to the center."

Pilar waited a moment. "I've decided to have the test done at the New York College Medical Center."

Grace and Conner blinked in one accord.

"I thought you didn't have a place in mind," Conner said.

"I didn't, but when I thought about it, I realized that the tests should be done where Solomon was born."

Grace's eyes narrowed.

"And it's where I'm being treated."

"Well, that makes sense," Conner said.

"And NYCMC can have the results in less than a week. Any days we can save . . ." She looked away.

Conner slipped his package back into his briefcase. "What do I have to do?"

Grace studied Pilar as she passed a plastic baggie to Conner. She examined her eyes, watched her hands, scrutinized every motion.

Conner pushed his chair from the table. "I'm going to the rest room." He lowered his voice. "Will you be okay?"

Grace's eyes never left Pilar. "Of course."

Conner had barely taken three steps away when Pilar jutted her chin forward and smiled at Grace with a different confidence. Now Pilar looked at Grace with the assurance of a woman who had shared her husband.

"I'm glad we have some time alone," Pilar said.

Grace remained silent.

"I want to thank you for coming with Conner."

"You don't have to. He's my husband."

Pilar turned somber. "I only came to Conner because of my situation."

"If Solomon is Conner's son, we should know."

"I never wanted to intrude on your life. For that, I apologize."

Grace spoke before she had a chance to think. "I thought you'd be apologizing for sleeping with my husband."

A beat passed. "What I did was wrong. My only defense is that I was helping a friend through a bad time. It turned into something more."

If she had been keeping score, Grace would have given the point to Pilar. She now knew that they'd shared more than a bed; Conner had shared details of their life.

"Look," Pilar began softly. Her tone made Grace wonder if Pilar could see the tears on her heart. "Conner never gave me a penny or a promise. There was never any doubt that he loved you." She sounded as if she harbored regret. Pilar glanced down, and when she looked up, her eyes had changed, holding more fear than sadness. "But in the middle of that sin, I received a wonderful gift, Grace. Now, Solomon is my only concern."

It was the mother's heart in Grace that said, "I understand."

"We can't be enemies. You're going to be . . ." Pilar's lips trembled. "My son has more days in front of him than behind him. You're going to be there for the best of his life. It's important that we find a way . . ."

Pilar broke her gaze as Conner returned to the table. "I did both swabs." He set the small envelope on the table as if it were precious cargo.

Pilar placed it inside her bag. "I already have Solomon's samples. I'm going to take them right over."

"We can do that for you," Grace said.

"No," Pilar's objection came quickly. "I . . . asked the driver if we could stop . . . on our way back to Queens."

Grace leaned back in her seat, crossing her arms again.

Conner said, "Well, I don't think we should hold this table. . . ."

"Yes," Pilar said, almost jumping from her seat. "I want to stop by the hospital and be home when Solomon gets there."

When Pilar stood, Conner did the same and reached across the table, helping her. "I'll walk you out."

"Thank you."

Pilar's steps were slow; she wavered as if she were marching on wooden legs. By the time they got to the lobby, Pilar staggered like a marathon runner at the finish line.

"I'll take her to the car," Conner said as he kissed Grace on her cheek.

"I'll meet you in the room."

Pilar said, "Thank you again, Grace."

Grace nodded and turned away without saying anything. She didn't have any words left.

"That went well," Conner said when he entered the hotel room.

Grace turned from the window where she'd stood. "Pilar doesn't look good."

Conner nodded and sat on the couch. He loosened his tie. "The medication has been as devastating as the disease. She's allergic to most of it." He exhaled as if he'd been holding the emotions of their meeting inside.

Grace sauntered to him. "I was surprised she didn't want to use the diagnostics center." She kept her tone as casual as she could.

"I wasn't. It makes sense that she'd want the test done at a place she could trust."

What about our trust? Grace thought.

"And the medical center costs much less than the diagnostics center. Pilar said it's only two hundred dollars. I gave her a check."

Her glance stayed on Conner for a long moment before she said, "What do we do now?"

"Well, Pilar thinks it's a good idea for us to meet Solomon." He paused, and though he looked straight ahead, Grace knew he was watching her. "Even before the results are back."

Inside, she still wanted to fight. "As long as she doesn't introduce you as the boy's father, Conner."

His eyes were weary, but he smiled. "Thank you, Grace. Pilar's going to call tomorrow. We'll probably go on Saturday."

Grace nodded. "I'm going to lie down for a little while."

She kissed Conner, reassuring him that all was well. But what she really wanted was time alone. She needed to focus, put herself inside Pilar's shoes, and figure out just how far she'd be willing to walk if she were in the same place.

Grace leaned her ear against the bedroom door again, listening. The voices from the television were only a whisper, and she prayed that Conner was either engrossed in the news or that the softness of the hotel's couch had lulled him to sleep.

She tiptoed back to the bed and pulled her cell phone from her purse. She checked the number she'd written on the pad, took a deep breath, and dialed.

"New York College Medical Center. How may I direct your call?"

She didn't know. "Uh . . . I'd like some information on a paternity test."

"Hold a moment, please."

Grace turned toward the door and tried to think of what she'd say if Conner walked in.

"Medical Genetics."

"Yes, I'd like some information on having a paternity test done."

"Well, it's six hundred and fifty dollars. That covers the mother, father, and child." Grace grabbed a pencil from the desk. "The next test is on the twenty-second of May, and the results take six to eight weeks."

Grace frowned. "Wait a minute. The test is in May? What do you mean? We have to come in?"

"Yes. There are centers that do this through the mail, but to make sure there are no errors, we do the tests in person."

"And you're sure it takes six weeks?"

The woman sighed. "Yes."

"And it costs six hundred and fifty dollars?"

Her sigh was deeper this time. "Yes."

"Thank you," Grace whispered before she hung up. She stared at the notes she'd taken and wondered why the words on the paper were so different from the ones Pilar had told them.

Chapter 25

It would have made a lot more sense if we'd stayed in Queens, Grace thought as she stared at the same houses they passed on their way to the Plaza. They were driving back toward the airport into St. Albans.

When they awakened this morning, Conner told her that a car would pick them up at nine.

"Let's rent one," she'd said. "It'll give us more options."

He nodded, and as he turned to roll from the bed, she'd stopped him. "We should pray first."

He said thank-you with his eyes, then held her hand as they prayed.

That had been over two hours ago, and they had exchanged few words since. Thoughts kept them silent. Grace tried to imagine what was in her husband's mind. And then there were her reflections. She hadn't told Conner about her call to the hospital. There could be many explanations, and when she did go to him, she would take only facts.

"There's Linden Boulevard." Conner pointed and she looked at the directions she held. They turned left, and continued down the potholed street.

When they crossed Merrick Boulevard, she said, "There's the church." Grace read the last line on the paper: "House will be two blocks down."

Her heart pounded as the vehicle slowed, and then it seemed to cease beating altogether when Conner stopped the car. They stared at the red brick two-story home. A city-abused burgundy Honda Accord sat in the driveway covered with the same urban dirt as the other cars on the street.

Grace's eyes roamed to the second floor where beige miniblinds covered two white-trimmed windows. The blinds on the right swayed, and Grace leaned forward, straining to see who was behind the window's covering. She jumped when Conner touched her hand.

"Are you okay?" His voice trembled.

She could only nod because her vocal cords felt paralyzed.

Conner opened his door and came around to her side. She kept her hand in his as they approached the house. Her legs wobbled as Conner opened the low iron gate, but she felt steadier when they moved up the cobblestone pathway. Before he could ring the bell, the door opened.

"Come in."

Grace took a deep breath and stepped inside, keeping her eyes away from Pilar's.

The entryway was small. When Pilar closed the door, the three stood with their shoulders almost touching.

"Come in," she repeated and they followed her into the living room.

Grace was reminded of 704 Hauser Street. Like Archie Bunker's house, most of the first floor was one large room. Even part of the kitchen could be seen from where she stood.

"Have a seat." Even though it was ten in the morning, Pilar clicked on a lamp.

They sat on the long brown crushed velvet couch that overwhelmed the room with its size. Pilar sat across from them in a half-moon-shaped green brocade chair.

"I'm glad you're here," she said to Conner, and then her eyes moved to Grace.

Conner asked, "Have you heard anything from the medical center?"

"No, not yet." She looked away. "They said in another day or two."

Grace crossed her legs. "I'm surprised they can get results that quickly."

Pilar's eyes met hers. "NYCMC is one of the best in the country."

Silence followed their exchange.

Conner leaned forward, his elbows rested on his legs. "Where's Solomon?"

"In his room." She motioned toward the stairs behind them. "I told him that some old friends of mine were stopping by."

Conner nodded.

Grace stared.

"Before we do this," Pilar started, "I have to make sure. I have to protect my son."

"Pilar, you're the one who keeps talking about there not being enough time," Conner said.

"That's true, but I want to know . . . when the test results show . . ."

"I will do the right thing."

Grace inhaled.

"Does that mean you're going to take responsibility?" Pilar asked.

Conner moved to stand, but Grace put her hand on his leg, keeping him in place. "Pilar, this is not a game."

"No one knows that better than me."

"What do you think my being here is all about?"

Grace said, "May I say something?" With their silence, she continued. "We shouldn't be talking about this with Solomon upstairs."

"It's fine. He's on his computer."

"Still . . ." Grace looked from Conner to Pilar.

Pilar said, "As I said, I want to be sure."

"Nothing is sure until the results come back." Conner stood and took Grace's hand. "Maybe this would be better handled through lawyers."

"No," Pilar said calmly, unaffected by Conner's display. "We don't need attorneys. I just wanted to know where you stood."

"Now you know."

She pushed herself from the chair. "I'll get Solomon." It took a moment for her to take the first step, but then she disappeared up the stairs.

Conner filled his cheeks with air, then exhaled.

"Calm down, honey," Grace said.

"I don't want to play games."

"This is not a game to her." Grace was surprised at her defense of Pilar. "She needs assurances because once she brings that boy downstairs, things are going to be different, no matter what." Her words were a warning. "This is what I was afraid of. Moving too quickly."

He stared at her. "We're just meeting him. Nothing more."

With her palm, she caressed his face. He wrapped his arms around her. They were holding each other when the first steps echoed on the stairs. Conner pulled away, but held Grace's hand.

Pilar came first, then the boy, who stood just an inch or two shorter than his mother. The two walked toward Grace and Conner. As they came closer, Grace felt Conner's fingers slip away.

Pilar placed her hands on her son's shoulders. "Solomon, these are my friends. This is Conner Monroe. The man I used to work for."

The boy smiled and a look of recognition filled his eyes. "I remember you. You were in the park in L.A."

"Yes, that was me.

He extended his hand. "It's nice to see you again, sir."

Conner hesitated, then took the boy's hand. "I am so glad to meet you, Solomon."

Grace raised her hand to her mouth to hide her trembling lips.

Pilar said, "Let's sit down."

Still holding Solomon's hand, Conner led him to the couch, and Pilar returned to the chair where she'd been sitting. It took a moment for Conner to remember Grace, still standing where he'd left her.

"Oh, I'm sorry." He turned to the boy. "Solomon, this is my wife, Grace."

He granted her the same smile that he'd blessed Conner with a moment before.

"It's nice to meet you, Solomon."

He nodded, and then turned back to Conner.

Grace looked around, and sat in a chair next to Pilar facing Conner and Solomon on the couch. A loud silence engulfed the room for seconds that felt like minutes. It was Solomon who saved them.

"Do you like baseball?"

Conner blinked, then smiled. "Yes, I do."

"I really like the Mets. My mom takes me to Shea Stadium."

"I've never been there," Conner said.

Solomon tilted his head. "Maybe you can go with me one day."

Grace clasped her shaking hands in her lap. He looked as if he would be a good baseball player—lanky, the way Conner looked as a boy.

"Solomon loves sports." Pilar picked up a photo album from the table. She moved to the couch, putting Solomon between Conner and her, and opened the book on her son's lap.

Grace watched as the three shared Solomon's pictorial biography. Within minutes, she knew that she'd made a mistake. She should have never allowed this meeting.

"Grace?" Her eyes focused on her husband. "Do you want to come over here?" Conner moved a bit on the couch, making room for her.

She shook her head. He looked at her for a moment longer, then returned to Solomon and Pilar.

Grace glanced around the living room, seeking a reprieve.

"This is Solomon's first softball championship."

Grace jumped up. "May I use your bathroom?"

"Sure, it's the first door that way." Pilar pointed, keeping her eyes on the pictures.

Grace waited to see if Conner would look up. He didn't.

She gently closed the bathroom door instead of slamming it the way she wanted to. It took minutes for her breathing to steady. She pushed the commode's cover down and sat, holding her face in her hands. This was not what she expected. The boy looked different from the picture. Today he looked like Conner's son.

Could he be? She thought of the thickness of his eyebrows and the slight cleft in his chin. What if she were meeting his son for the first time? It was as if her heart was just accepting the possibility.

She took deep breaths, trying to take herself to the place she wanted to be. She heard Devry's words. *You're a good Christian.*

She stood, looked in the mirror, straightened her suit, and turned off the light. She plastered a smile on her face, but stopped before she stepped into the living room.

"Where's Conner?"

"Upstairs with Solomon."

Grace looked toward the stairs.

"You can go up, or . . . you can stay down here. With me."

It was a challenge more than an invitation. Grace looked at the stairs, then returned to where she'd been sitting.

"I can tell that you don't think this was a good idea," Pilar said.

"I would have preferred to wait for the paternity results."

"That's not necessary. I know how they will turn out."

Grace folded her arms. "I'm sure you do."

Pilar's eyes narrowed. "I've always known that Conner was Solomon's father."

"Tell me, Pilar, why did you want the tests done at the medical center?"

She'd expected to throw Pilar off with her question, but Pilar smiled when she said, "I told you."

"Tell me again."

"That's where Solomon was born and where I'm being treated."

Solomon's giggles interrupted them.

"Pilar, your son is quite the collector." When Conner looked at Grace, it was as if he just remembered she was there. He left Solomon's side. "Are you okay?"

Grace nodded and forced a smile.

His face relaxed with relief. "I was looking at Solomon's comic books."

"He's been collecting for three years, and what he has is impressive." Pilar rolled her hand over Solomon's head. "I'm very proud of him."

Conner beamed.

Grace watched the exchange, then stood. "We should be going."

"Oh," Pilar said. "I thought you'd have lunch."

"Please stay," Solomon said.

Conner turned to Grace, and although she saw the desire in his eyes, she couldn't grant his wish. He said, "We have . . . plans this afternoon," trying to lighten the tension that tightened the room.

"But I like having you here," Solomon said. "We don't get a lot of company." He lowered his eyes. "Especially since Mom . . ."

Conner said, "We'll try to come back . . . in a couple of days."

Solomon turned ready to direct his pleas to Grace. But her stiff smile stopped him. Pilar and Solomon walked Grace and Conner to the door. The loud silence accompanied them, and this time Solomon did not rescue them.

Grace said, "Pilar, thank you for having us." She looked down at Solomon. "I'm glad I met you, Solomon."

He smiled, but his eyes continued his plea.

Grace turned away, fearing that if she didn't, she would give the boy what he needed. The noon air saluted her when she opened the door and the breeze cooled the heat that had risen inside the house.

Grace looked back and watched as Conner said, "I hope to see you again soon."

"*Si.*"

Conner chuckled. "Spanish, huh?"

"He's learning on his computer," Pilar explained as she put her arm on Solomon's shoulders. "When I told him that Spanish was Cuba's official language, he was determined to learn it."

Solomon said, "I'd like to visit Cuba someday."

"Maybe one day you'll make the trip." Conner looked at Pilar, and his eyes saddened. He wanted to apologize, but her eyes reassured him.

Grace watched Conner's hand move from Solomon's head, to his shoulder, until he took the boy's hand. It still took minutes for Conner to break away.

Finally, Conner and Grace walked to the car. By the time Conner started the ignition, Pilar had taken her son into the house. The first visit was over.

They had been silent throughout the ride back, and even when they entered the hotel, they'd exchanged only enough words to determine they would have lunch in the suite.

Now, as Grace sat across from Conner at the table that held their lunch, she waited while he put the napkin on his lap. He took her hand and bowed his head.

"Father, in the name of Jesus we thank you for this food. Father, we thank you for this day."

He paused, and Grace looked up. His head was still bowed, but when moments passed, Grace continued, "We thank you, Father, for helping us take these first steps. Help us, Father, to face the days ahead." Grace lifted her head. "And protect us, Lord. No matter what we want, let us all pray that the truth is revealed and that your will is done. In Jesus's name, Amen."

Conner opened his eyes. "Thank you."

They began eating in the silence that had become their partner. Grace twirled a jumbo shrimp in the alfredo sauce. "How do you feel?"

"Fine." He stared at the salmon on his plate, then pushed it away. "I wasn't prepared for today. Even though I'd seen him before, this was different. It was personal." He paused. "I didn't want to leave him."

"I know," she said, her apology in her tone.

"I can't explain it, but I felt so comfortable with him."

"He seems like a nice young man."

He stared at her for a moment. "He's more than that, Grace. He's my son."

Grace lowered her eyes and held her protest inside.

"But the best part," Conner continued, "was that he was comfortable with me."

Grace nodded, remembering how they were together—as if they had always been together as father and son.

He looked away when he said, "It's like I love Solomon already."

She placed her hand across her chest. "I understand. You've always wanted a son."

"I love him because I'm sure he's mine," he said quickly, turning back to her. He took her hand away from her heart and weaved his fingers with hers. "It's the same love that I have for Jayde and Amber."

She looked toward the window, staring at the blue canvas above the green carpet of Central Park. She couldn't look at him because if she did, she might say what she knew she shouldn't—that even if Solomon was his son, he was supposed to love their daughters more.

He scooted his chair closer and took both of her hands. "How did you feel?" he said, asking the same question she'd posed to him just minutes before.

In her mind, she could still hear Solomon begging them to stay. "I didn't get to talk to Solomon very much."

"But do you think . . . when we find out that Solomon is my son . . ."

He didn't have to complete the question. She knew what he needed to hear. Grace said, "Everything is going to be fine." It was all she could manage.

"Next time, I want you to spend some time with him."

She nodded as if she agreed.

"I want you to talk to him," Conner said. "Then I know you'll feel what I'm feeling."

Conner stood and pulled Grace into his arms. She could feel his heart pounding countless thank-yous. With everything in her, Grace wanted to tell Conner that they would forge forward together, slay the enemy, and be victorious. But she was the only one in this war who could uncover the truth. Her husband was falling in love with a boy who could turn out not to be his son. The image of Conner and Solomon together flashed through her mind.

The results take six to eight weeks, she heard the voice of the woman from the hospital say.

I've always known that Conner was Solomon's father, Pilar countered in her head.

She didn't know which voice spoke the truth, but if she had to place a bet, it wouldn't be on Pilar.

Chapter 26

Starlight leaned against the suede wall in the Celestial Room of the Reign Hotel. She closed her eyes. Their plan had been simple, but she was earning every dollar. It was the three hundred women. Ten groups were too many.

"Starlight, I have the last cluster."

Her eyes snapped opened. She'd been in this room for hours. A room without windows and only the soft light from the bronze-colored bulbs they'd installed. "I'm exhausted, Lexington."

His fingers grazed her cheek. "The closing is next. Two more hours, and you can sleep for a week." He kissed her nose. "And I'll be beside you. We'll be rolling in the money."

The image did little to restore her. She lumbered toward the raised platform in the room's center and positioned herself in the lotus position. Lexington opened the door.

Chimes tolled through the air as thirty women, dressed in variations of T-shirts and shorts, and leotards and tights, came in. They were escorted by six Light Girls, whose white gauze tunics fluttered to the chime's melody.

The women were directed to their places on body-size towels that were already set out.

"Join me as I bring heaven to earth," Starlight sang. Her eyes were almost closed, flitting open only enough to see. Through the dim light, Starlight watched the Light Girls give silent instructions. Her words would be the only ones heard.

This was the tenth and final session. The three hundred women were divided into ten groups and had been through four workshops. But this was the most important: the Rebirthing Zone.

She searched the room and then took a deep breath. This session would be for Pastor Carey's wife—an audition of sorts—so that she could officially break into the churches. Starlight straightened her back. Show time.

"In order to move forward, you must cleanse yourself of the past. It is time to rebirth your soul."

The chimes rang louder, and Lexington lowered the lights until the room was almost in darkness.

"Allow the earth's atmosphere to mix with your being. Allow the planet's aura to become part of you. Take a deep breath." She paused. "Deeper." Her eyelids fluttered as she peeked at the women. They lay on their backs, following her words. "Connect with the earth. Slowly roll onto your stomach, keeping your eyes closed."

Starlight waited until everyone was settled.

"The creator made us in perfect form for the earth's light to enter us. In order for your light to shine, the earth's ashes and dust must be removed from your karma. You must regress to your dawn to progress to your future."

The chimes became softer.

"Take yourself to the beginning, where you were at perfect peace in your mother's womb." With a slight nod, Starlight signaled, and one of the Light Girls moaned, just loud enough for the women to hear. "Find your space."

The women began to stretch, then coil into the fetal position. The Light Girls assisted until everyone was the way Starlight wanted.

"Now give birth to yourself. Experience life," Starlight sang, raising her voice a few decibels.

Two other Light Girls made their sounds—one giggled, the other moaned. Seconds later, a few women moaned as they stretched.

Starlight stood. "This is life," she said loudly. Suddenly her voice dropped, returning to her low singsong level. "But to truly experience it, you must first know death because life has not always been kind." Starlight maneuvered through the room. "There's been pain holding you back, killing your future." Starlight's voice trembled as if she felt each woman's sufferings. "Pain is the horror of life, and we must rid ourselves of it," she cried.

"Remember the first time you felt the horror. It came from your mother, father, sister, brother." She made a motion with her hand, and one of the Light Girls wailed.

"Release the pain and those feelings of not being loved, of not feeling good enough."

A second Light Girl began to weep.

"Remember when they called you stupid, said you were ugly, told you that you wouldn't amount to anything." Starlight closed her eyes, and her own memories poured forth, almost bringing tears with it. She was not making up this part. She'd lived it. She took a deep breath. Her pain would have to wait.

She repeated the words of tragedy, "You were never loved," and "You never fit in," and "You were never good enough," until the room filled with cries. The wailing came quicker with this group.

"There's still blockage. Misery is stopping you." She waltzed through the room. "People you trusted, you loved, you gave your heart to took everything away." She motioned with her arm, and three of the Light Girls cried softly.

"Your father should have never touched you that way. Your mother should have never beaten you. Your uncles . . . oh, the things they did to you."

The cries became so loud that Starlight motioned for the Light Girls to lower their voices. It was only then that she realized the cries were coming from the women.

Her words came faster. "What other pain is buried in the center of your soul?"

She made another motion, and a Light Girl cried out, "Please, don't hit me again."

A sudden shriek startled her, and she turned toward the sound. Pastor Carey's wife was shriveled in the corner. It made Starlight pause. Maybe there was a secret there that she could use someday.

Starlight returned to the stage. There was no need for more.

She spoke to the group. "You have moved through your past." Her words were slow and soft. "Give thanks to the ancestors. Now claim your future. You are feeling at peace."

The sobs became fainter.

"The future lies within you. It's filled with love, joy, and happiness." Her voice was soothing. "Accept your destiny."

The chimes charged the air again. Starlight remained still until the sobs ceased.

"With your eyes still closed, it is time to make decisions.

You've made an investment in yourselves, cleansing your past, polishing the path to your future. How important is it to keep what you've created today? Decide what you're willing to do to have the kind of future the creator perceived for you. To be the best, you have to be willing to pay. No price is too great for divinity.

"As you sit up, think about how you can maintain what you have gained." Starlight motioned again, and the Light Girls became nurturing assistants, aiding the women in wiping away their tears. The last woman to her place was Mrs. Carey.

Starlight motioned to Lexington. Using the dimmer, he lightened the room.

"You have accomplished what few people ever do. You have entered the light. Do all that you can to stay in this place."

Starlight raised her arms and stood using only the strength in her legs. It was a yoga move she'd practiced for weeks, and she could see how impressed the women were. Certainly only someone enlightened could lift themselves from the floor that way.

None of the women were steady as they rose to their feet, still feeling the effects of the light hypnosis that she'd used. She had to release them to the sales room while they were still shaky.

Starlight pressed her hands together and bowed. "May the light forever be with you and yours."

The Light Girls escorted the women to the room across the hall. At the beginning of the day, she'd told the women of the available products.

"I've put much thought into what is needed to help you maintain what you're going to gain," she had said. "I spent hours working with specialists who understand our mission."

Her speech worked. According to early reports, they had run out of some of the specialty products. The first to go was the Bless-ed Water.

When the last woman left, Lexington closed the door and then glided to Starlight. "Every time I watch you, I am in awe." He pulled a handkerchief from his pocket. "You're tired, but you'll feel better after I wipe your face with this Anointed Cloth."

Even through her weariness, she laughed.

"And laugh you should, my dear." Lexington stroked her. "Half of that group was pastors' wives."

"Are you serious? Who?"

He chuckled. "I'll fill you in later, but some of the most important first ladies in the city just cried their hearts out."

She smiled. "Let's wrap this up. I can't wait to get home."

"My feet still hurt," Starlight groaned. She leaned back on the couch.

Lexington glanced up, and the pencil behind his ear dropped. He walked to the couch and rested her feet on his lap.

"You're leaving your precious papers?"

He looked at the table covered with cash and other receipts. It took a moment for him to say, "Taking a little break."

She chuckled. "You won't get to me tonight, Lexington. My feet may hurt, but I feel like I'm walking on clouds. Although three hundred women were too many."

"You won't be saying that after we count the money."

She pulled away from him. "Go back to the money."

He searched her face. When she smiled, he jumped up. "Won't

be too much longer." In two steps, he was back at the table. Not even the ringing telephone broke his concentration.

"This is Starlight."

"Starlight, this is Lynnette Bonet. I hope I haven't caught you at a bad time."

Starlight paused, waiting for the familiar name to register. Then her eyes widened. "Oh, no, Senator Bonet." She waved her hand to get Lexington's attention, but he had already put down his pencil. "How can I help you?"

"It's late, so I'll get to the point. My daughter is a fan. She has all of your books and has attended several of your seminars."

With one step, Lexington leaped to the couch. He put his ear next to Starlight's with the phone in between them.

"Summer came home raving about your conference today," the senator continued.

"She was there?" Starlight pointed to the registration log, and Lexington scurried to the desk.

"Yes, and I have to admit Summer seems different. She's a senior at UCLA, but we've had challenges." The senator sighed. "She's been in college for six years and still hasn't decided what she wants to do. But today she came home with new energy; she has goals."

Starlight took a deep breath. "I'm glad."

"It's too early to know what Summer will really do, but right now, I'm pleased."

"That's my objective, Senator. To help women reenergize."

"I'm hoping you'll be able to do a bit more, Starlight." Senator Bonet paused. "Do you hold private sessions? Because I'd like you to work with Summer."

Surprise kept Starlight silent.

"I will make it financially worthwhile," the senator added, mistaking Starlight's silence for hesitation. "Perhaps we could meet to discuss this."

Starlight wanted to leap into the air. "That would be wonder . . ." She paused to steady her voice. "We can meet to see what we can work out, Senator."

Starlight paced as she checked her calendar and agreed to meet the senator in a few days.

"Thank you, Starlight. I've been watching your career, and you have a great future." She paused. "Have you ever been to Washington?"

"Yes, for book signings and other events."

"I'm talking about the Washington I know." She continued before Starlight could respond, "I'm looking forward to meeting you."

Starlight hung up, trembling with excitement. "Do you know how huge this is?"

Lexington shrugged. "We're huge already."

Starlight opened her mouth, then shut it and faced the window. Images flashed through her mind's eye of lunches with senators, speeches at congressional caucuses, weekend retreats with powerful politicians' wives. One day, she could even speak at the White House.

She shivered as the night sky slowly changed its color, becoming one with the water. With the connections that Senator Bonet had she could be as large as the Pacific Ocean and as brilliant as the North Star.

She spun around and almost bumped into Lexington.

"Take a look at the last page." His lips spread into a grin.

Starlight flipped through the lilac registration log. "Summer Bonet was the last woman to register?" she whispered.

"Number three hundred."

Starlight fell back onto the couch, laughing. "From now on, every seminar must have three hundred women. That's my new lucky number." She tossed the thirty papers into the air.

Chapter 27

Grace's Manolo Blahnik sling-back pump trembled on the tip of her stocking foot. Her eyes darted around the living room. The furniture seemed much closer today than two days before.

She slipped her foot into her shoe, then swiveled in the half-moon-shaped chair that reminded her of one that sat in her grandmother's living room thirty years ago. It was a curious piece, though it fit with the rest of the room's design. Grace wondered what was on Pilar's mind when she furnished this space. From the couch, to the gold and green brocade chairs, to the fading walnut-brown walls, the room was dark, the furniture heavy. It felt as if the house carried a burden.

She turned again, wishing that Conner would finish. She could hear him in the dining room on his cell phone. *It could be worse,* she thought. *Pilar could be sitting here with me.*

More than fifteen minutes before, Pilar had met them at the door with a sweater in one hand and keys in the other. "I'm sorry, but I got a call. My friend's car broke down."

"Oh," Conner had said. "We'll come back."

Grace had followed as Conner stepped back from the entry-way.

"No," Pilar exclaimed. Grace noticed the way Pilar lowered

her eyes when she motioned for them to come inside. "I'll be right back. It'll take fifteen minutes . . . or so."

"But . . ." Conner had started to protest, then asked, "Where's Solomon?"

"In his room doing his homework," Pilar yelled over her shoulder. Grace had never seen her move so fast. "He won't be a bother."

It's a setup, Grace wanted to scream, as Pilar backed her car away. But she pressed her lips together and waited for Conner's cue. When Conner closed the door, then motioned with his chin toward the living room, she'd followed.

Now, almost twenty minutes had passed and Pilar had been right: Solomon had not been a bother. He hadn't appeared at all. Maybe this hadn't been an arrant attempt to bind him with Conner. Still, she couldn't wait for Pilar to return, so they could have their visit and then she could leave this place.

Her eyes moved to the magazines on the end table.

"Oh, no," she whispered as she picked up a copy of *Jet*. She prayed that Solomon had more than this connecting him to his lineage.

"Do you want to go outside with me?"

The magazine slipped through Grace's fingers. Her eyes rose to the voice.

Solomon smiled at her.

Yesterday she'd watched him from afar. But now that he stood so close, she couldn't stop studying him. His eyes, nose, mouth—all were familiar to her.

He repeated his question.

"Uh, I don't know."

He placed his hand in hers. "*Por favor*. It's okay." The cleft in his chin motioned toward the back of the house.

Grace stared as he stood wearing the confidence of one much older. She glanced at the soft hand that held hers. She allowed him to lead her to the back, where they stepped through a glass doorway.

At first, Grace felt as if she was in a concrete prison. The space, no larger than the bathroom inside, was enclosed by a seven-foot-high orange-red brick wall. It would have been depressing except for the dazzling yellows, greens, reds, and blues that brightened the brick yard.

"This is my garden." Pride swelled the twelve-year-old's chest.

Grace bent over, examining the orchestra of impatiens, zinnias, and marigolds.

"I planted everything myself."

Grace looked at the smiling boy.

"I learned this in my earth science class."

Grace looked at the garden's ceiling. The sky was beaming blue; still, there was not enough light to grow this Garden of Eden.

"I know what you're thinking," Solomon said. "There's not enough light. This is how I do it." From a wicker table he lifted what looked like a television remote. He pressed a button and heated light as bold as the sun flooded the space.

Grace squinted in the glow. She hadn't noticed the lightbulbs that were fastened to the lattice affixed to the wall.

"It's not as good as natural light, but it does the job. These," he pointed to the yellow zinnias, "don't usually bloom until May. But with my lighting and the good winter, we're blessed to appreciate their beauty early."

He spoke as if he were older than Jayde.

He stared into her eyes. "Do you like?"

She held his gaze, knowing there was more to his inquiry. She looked away and noticed a photo album on the table. "What's that?" Asking her question was safer than answering his.

Solomon's smile disappeared when he turned to the book. He opened the album and gave it to her. She stared at the child's drawing, sketched with the talent of a twelve-year-old. There were three figures—a boy in the center of a man and a woman. A mother. A father. A family.

"I drew this picture a few months ago when I found out that my mother . . ." He kept the rest of his sentence inside.

Grace felt as if her heart was sinking. A boy didn't draw pictures like this. Boys drew rockets, airplanes, and racing cars.

"My mother is very sick."

Her sinking heart did a somersault. She took his hand. "I know. But you're going to be fine."

The confidence that was in his eyes was replaced with dread.

"What are you doing out here?" They turned toward Conner's voice. He was leaning against the door's frame with his hands in his pockets, wearing a smile of hope.

"I was showing . . . ," Solomon paused, "your wife my garden."

"I'd like to see it."

Grace stepped back as Solomon pointed and gave the same explanation that he'd shared with her.

She took a deep breath. All she'd been focused on were the hard parts. Solomon had just given her something easy.

From the corner of her eye, Grace saw movement. Pilar stood in the doorway. Her eyes moved from Conner and Solomon to Grace. She held Grace's gaze for a moment, her face stiff with sorrow. Then, slowly and silently, she stepped away, leaving Grace, Conner, and Solomon together in the garden.

Chapter 28

Conner kissed Grace. "Are you sure you don't want to come with me?"

She stroked his face with her fingertips. "No, I'll see you in a bit." She closed the door and listened to his footsteps as he walked to the elevator that would deliver him to the car that would take him to Pilar.

Pilar had asked for one last meeting before Conner and Grace returned to Los Angeles. Although Grace couldn't imagine what else they needed to discuss, she'd remained silent when Conner agreed.

"I'll make lunch," Pilar had told them. "Solomon will be in school."

But Grace had spent too many days in her home. Conner read her thoughts and suggested that Pilar come into the city if she were up to it. Pilar had agreed.

"Grace and I will pick you up."

But this morning, Grace suggested that Conner take the trip to Queens alone. "You and Pilar need to talk."

"There's nothing to discuss without you."

She was grateful for his words. "Pick up Pilar. I'll be waiting for you."

The moment Conner agreed, Grace had wanted to yell, *April Fool! What are you thinking?* her inside voice screamed.

Now, as she looked out the window, her internal wisdom still taunted her.

She tried to quiet the voice by taking in the Central Park view. New York wasn't enjoying the summer-like spring that heated Los Angeles, but spring was good enough for this city. Through the thick glass, Grace could almost hear the sounds of New Yorkers—who had spent the winter months prisoners in their apartments. She imagined their shrieks of joy in the air: their joy of the soft, warm air; cars honking at errant cyclists, children shrieking as they chased pigeons, Rollerbladers yelling for strollers to get out the way.

This is the worst decision you've ever made. The voice would not be denied.

"There's nothing wrong with Conner and Pilar being alone," she said aloud. "They need to finish unfinished business."

What business could they have? she continued the conversation with herself. *Anything they need to work out should be done in front of you.*

Grace shook her head to get rid of the thoughts.

Suppose they end up in bed?

"That'll never happen."

It happened before.

Grace went into the bedroom and picked up her cell phone. If she was going to have a conversation, she should at least do it with someone.

"Hey, Devry."

"Girl, I've been dying to speak to you. How're things?"

Grace lay on the bed. "Do you have an hour?"

"I have as much time as you need. Chandler just left for the office. Tell me everything."

Grace sighed. "Are you my friend or my psychologist?"

"Who do you need?"

"The shrink. I sent Conner to Pilar's house alone." Grace repeated what she'd told Conner. "So I've been sitting here having this conversation."

"With who?"

"Myself."

"Girl, you do need me." Devry chuckled. "So you've seen Pilar and met Solomon?"

"Yup, even had a private conversation with Pilar, and I didn't beat her down for sleeping with my husband."

"See, God is good."

Grace laughed, but quickly became solemn. "And I didn't slap her crazy for possibly giving Conner the one thing I never gave him."

Devry's silence told Grace that she understood. Then Devry said, "Grace, would it be different if Pilar's child had been a girl?"

"I don't know. I just feel like I'm going crazy. The uncertainty of not knowing if Conner is Solomon's father is bad enough. But then, the possibility that he is . . . I want some peace."

"Only God can give you that."

Grace sighed as the sun's shadow took a new shape in the room.

"Grace, only God's power and His glory could pull any woman through this."

"I've been praying."

"That's good. Keep doing that. He'll show you what to do."

"I hope so, Devry. I'm tired of my heart breaking."

"I know, sweetie. But if you hang in there, there's always joy at the end. Do me a favor. Look at Genesis 33:5."

"What does it say?"

"You look it up. I love you," she said before she clicked off the phone.

Grace stared at the cell phone for a moment before she pulled the Bible from her suitcase.

And he lifted up his eyes, and saw the women and the children; and said, Who are those with thee? And he said, The children which God hath graciously given thy servant.

Grace reread the verse before she closed the book.

The children which God hath graciously given.

Could it be that God had graciously given Solomon to Conner? And if He'd done that, was he a gift to her as well?

If she could believe that, then maybe she could leave the battlefield. But as much as she wanted to just lean on God's word, her human side wanted to know the truth. She just had to prove that all was not right with Pilar.

As on their previous visits, Pilar opened the door before Conner knocked.

"Hello." She looked over his shoulder. "Where's Grace?"

"She's waiting at the hotel."

Pilar raised her eyebrows and motioned for Conner to come inside.

"We decided to have lunch in the suite." He stepped in but stayed in the entryway.

Pilar said, "You can come into my home, Conner."

His eyes moved, but his feet didn't. "Are you ready?"

Pilar half-smiled. "Let me get my purse."

Conner stayed in place as Pilar tied a sweater over her shoulders, then picked up her purse. They walked silently to the car. Once inside, Conner pulled out his cell phone.

"Hey, sweetheart. Pilar and I are on our way." He started the car. "I love you." He made a U-turn, heading toward the expressway. The words from his call hung in the silence.

Finally, Pilar asked, "You're happy with Grace?"

"Very."

She stared out the window. "I often wondered," she began, "what would have happened if you had known about Solomon."

The muscle in his jaw twitched. "I would have worked it through with Grace the way we're doing now."

She looked at him. "I'm happy for you."

He stopped the car at the red light at Merrick Boulevard. "Are you?" He sounded as if he were challenging her.

"Yes, because Solomon is going to be with a mother and father. He deserves that."

It happened every time. When he became annoyed or angry, she reminded him that while he would probably be here in a year, she probably wouldn't.

The car behind him honked.

"The light is green," Pilar said. "We can go now."

They rode in silence until Conner eased onto the Belt Parkway.

"Pilar, are you afraid?" He kept his eyes on the cars in front of him.

"Only for Solomon. I want him to be well taken care of."

"I will do that."

She smiled. "I believe you. I wasn't sure at first, but you were my only hope."

"From what I've seen, you've done a wonderful job with him."

"Thank you. You gave me good genes to work with. You look so much alike on the outside I knew he would be like you on the inside."

He glanced at Pilar. "Thank you," he said, for more than the compliment.

Her smile acknowledged his gratitude, and their conversation began to flow as smoothly as the traffic around them.

"Pilar, did Solomon ever ask . . . about me? About his father?"

She nodded. "Especially once he started school. At first, I'd planned to tell him that his father died, so that knowing you would never be an issue." She sighed. "But something told me to stay close to the truth. So I told him that his father loved him, but that circumstances kept him away."

"He accepted that?"

"Yes. I think it was because I filled the story with love. He loved you without knowing you."

Conner thought about how different it could have been.

Pilar said, "I did it for Solomon. I wanted him to feel good about who he was."

Conner swallowed. "He doesn't have my name." It was a statement and a question.

"His name is Solomon Cruise." She lowered her head. "I didn't want you ever to know. By the time I found out that I was pregnant, I had put you out of my head, out of my heart, out of my life."

"I'm sorry, Pilar."

"I knew the rules."

More silent minutes sat between them before Conner said, "Thank you for telling me about my son."

He turned on the radio, letting music fill the car. His thoughts wandered to Grace. His wife had been right. He and Pilar had finished their business.

"It's beautiful up here," Pilar said.

"Grace and I've never stayed here before," Conner responded, "although I've been here on business."

Pilar moved to the window, and Conner followed.

"Ever since I moved here, I've wanted to live in Manhattan."

"I know what you mean. If I lived in New York, I'd live in the city."

"I didn't order anything." Grace held the room service menu in her hand. She had to do something to stop this lovefest. From the moment Conner and Pilar had entered the room, Grace felt as if she had walked into the middle of a movie. The two chatted like old friends, making no attempt to include her.

I guess they took care of all their unfinished business, her mind mocked her.

She handed one of the menus to Pilar and shoved the other into Conner's chest.

Conner didn't seem to notice. "Do you know what you're having, honey?"

Grace smiled. "No, sweetheart." She hoped he could read her eyes.

After turning a few pages of the menu, Conner said, "I'm going to have the oak-smoked trout."

"I'll have the same." Pilar smiled and handed the menu to Grace.

Grace took a deep breath, and turned to the phone. She placed their orders, then stood aside as Pilar and Conner continued their chat.

By the time she heard the knock from Room Service, Grace wondered if any of the windows in their suite opened and how many years she'd get if someone were to accidentally fall out of one.

The waiter rolled in the table and laid out the lunch.

When they all sat, Pilar said, "Grace, your husband is so wonderful."

Conner smiled, and Grace fingered the knife at her place setting, caressing the ragged edge.

"I know that my son will be all right," Pilar continued.

Grace's hand roamed to the knife's handle.

"Before we begin lunch . . ." Pilar lowered her eyes. "I want to show you this." She pulled an envelope from her purse.

As she handed it to Conner, Grace's fingers slipped from the knife.

Grace's heart pounded as Conner removed the contents. He flattened the paper on the table and scanned the words. The seconds lasted forever until Conner raised his eyes. He handed the document to Grace. With the way his eyes watered, Grace didn't need to read.

"He's my son."

Pilar nodded. "I told you." She turned to Grace. "But I understand your needing this. It's better that we all know."

When Conner turned to Grace, she forced herself to smile. She didn't know what to say. She was relieved when Conner wrapped his arms around her, expecting no words. She closed her eyes as she held him, hoping her pounding heart didn't give her away.

When she opened her eyes, she saw Pilar's smile. Her eyes spoke, "I told you."

"Well," Conner began as he leaned away. "We can start planning."

Pilar nodded. "I spoke with a child psychologist about our next steps." Her tone had changed. She sounded as if she were leading a board meeting.

Grace frowned. "How long have you had the test results?"

"Since this morning. But I spoke to the psychologist when I returned from Los Angeles." She paused. "I didn't have to wait for something I already knew."

Conner nodded, as if he understood her. Grace stared as if she didn't believe her.

Pilar handed a business card to Grace. "It may be good for you to talk to the doctor. Dr. Jordan met with me and Solomon. He doesn't think there is going to be any challenge acclimating Solomon into your life because he has always wanted to know his father." She paused. "Dr. Jordan says one advantage is that Solomon is a male. It would have been a bit different with a daughter."

Grace wondered if Pilar stomped on her heart on purpose.

"The most difficult part for Solomon," Pilar paused as she looked out the window, her eyes raised as if she were looking to heaven, "will be losing me."

A lump formed in Grace's throat that threatened to choke her. "He asked me if I knew you were sick."

Pilar nodded. "I've been honest with him. Solomon is older than his years, and I knew he could handle the truth. He's been such a comfort. We pray together every day."

Grace nodded and squeezed Conner's hand.

Pilar continued, "It's been a difficult journey, but the last part will be bearable . . . because of you." She wiped a solitary tear that hung at the corner of her eye.

Grace kept her eyes on Pilar. She didn't dare look at Conner.

"Grace, I cannot thank you enough for your graciousness throughout all of this."

They sounded like words of peace, but Grace's war hadn't ended.

Pilar wiped her eyes. "Enough of this. Our food is getting cold. Let's eat."

Conner blessed the food, and as they ate, Pilar asked questions about Grace's position as councilwoman and about their daughters. Grace knew this was Pilar's attempt to glean as much as she could about what she thought would be her son's new family.

Then she took her turn, telling them about Solomon's accomplishments.

"We have special children," Pilar said. She reached across the table and covered Grace's hand.

Grace looked down at the fingers so thin she could almost see the bones. She smiled but said nothing.

"Anyone want to celebrate with dessert?" Conner stood and retrieved the dessert menus the waiter had left on the table.

Pilar nodded. "Sounds terrific."

Grace took the menu from Conner. She wasn't ready for any celebration. Not until she knew for sure. But she'd go along with Conner . . . for now.

She lifted her head. "I'll have the . . ."

At the same moment, Pilar said with her, "pumpkin cheese-cake."

For the first time since she'd been in New York, Grace laughed.

Pilar laughed too. "Do you want to share a slice?"

Grace allowed a beat to pass. "I don't share."

Pilar looked away. When she returned her gaze to Grace, her eyes were glazed with tears. "There is one last thing I have to tell you." She paused. "I'd like to move to Los Angeles . . . to get Solomon used to everything . . . with me there."

Conner took Grace's hand. "That's fine. We'll work out the details."

Pilar's eyes moved from Conner to Grace. "I'd like to move . . . in a week or so."

Grace felt her hands begin to tremble.

Conner said, "It might be better if we let Solomon finish the school year."

"It would be," she agreed. "Except for the report I got this morning when I received the paternity results." She took a breath, then spoke as if she were reading a newspaper. "I'm not responding to the new medication."

Grace's heart pounded as Pilar told them the rest of the news.

Chapter 29

Conner sat on the edge of the bed, his hands folded beneath his chin. Grace took a deep breath before she sat next to him.

"There's nothing to worry about," she said as she rubbed his back.

"I just want to do this right." He stood. "I hate that I have to tell Solomon that I'm his father and then get on a plane to L.A."

Grace inhaled. "You could stay if you wanted to. For a day or two."

He stared at the floor considering her words. "No, we have to get home to the girls. Especially Jayde. She didn't sound good when I spoke to her last night."

Grace breathed, but hesitated before she said, "Conner, I'm going to meet you in Queens at Pilar's." When he frowned, she continued, "Zoë asked if I would check on her aunt."

"Oh." He looked relieved. "Well, I'll go with you."

"No," she said quickly, then smiled. "This is something I want to do." She paused. "And we both could use some time alone before we talk to Solomon."

He nodded and pulled her into his arms. "Thank you, sweetheart, for staying by my side. And for being with me when I tell Solomon that I'm his father."

He leaned over to kiss her, but she backed away before their lips could meet. "Of course, I would be with you, Conner," she said with as much cheer as she could gather. "If we're going to do this, we're going to do it together."

His frown asked why she'd said *if.* But he remained quiet while she put on her jacket. "I called for a car this morning," she said, picking up her pocketbook. "It should be here."

"Okay." Conner looked around the hotel room as if he didn't know what he was going to do. "You'll meet me at Pilar's?"

She nodded. "I'll probably be there before you." She kissed him and then rushed into the hallway. Grace wished that she could stay to hold his hand, to assure him that all would be well. But right now all she was concerned about was protecting him.

Grace paid the driver, waited until the car pulled away, then walked up the walkway and knocked on the door.

"Grace?" Pilar tightened the belt on her bathrobe. It looked as if it could have wrapped around her twice. She stepped aside so that Grace could enter. "I didn't expect you for another hour." She peeked outside. "Where's Conner?"

"He'll be here." Grace walked into the living room leaving Pilar at the door. "Is Solomon home?"

Pilar closed the door and rubbed her palms on her robe. "No, I didn't plan to call the school until you and Conner got here." She paused. "What are you doing here now?"

"We need to talk."

She looked as if she wanted to deny Grace's request, but she sat and motioned for Grace to do the same.

Grace placed her purse on the table. "We don't have a lot of time, so I'll get to the point." She looked into Pilar's eyes. "I don't believe the paternity results."

Her statement pushed Pilar back in her chair. "I don't understand."

"I called New York College Medical Center. I know how much the tests cost, how long it takes, and even that they only do the tests in person."

Pilar lowered her eyes. "Oh." When Grace said nothing, Pilar added, "The tests told the truth, Grace."

"It takes six to eight weeks to get results. Not five days." Grace stood. "I'm not going to allow my husband and my entire family to be dragged into something . . ."

"My doctor had the tests done for me."

Grace's stare told Pilar that she knew she was a liar.

Pilar continued, "Dr. Austin understood my position. He knew I was being forced into the tests."

"I would have thought you'd want the tests as much as I did."

"I didn't need them." She paused. "But you did. So Dr. Austin rushed the procedure for me because he knows how critical time is."

"How do you explain not having the tests done in person?"

Pilar frowned. "I don't know what you mean."

"The center told me they only do the tests in person."

"I didn't know that," Pilar said. "I only spoke to Dr. Austin, and he gave me the package for Conner."

It's a good story, Grace thought.

Pilar stood and walked to the phone. She lifted the receiver and dialed. Grace could hear the telephone ringing on the other end when Pilar said, "You should talk to Dr. Austin."

Grace swallowed. "You're calling your doctor?"

"Yes. He can tell you everything." Pilar brought the receiver to her ear. "Hi, Anita. This is Pilar. Is Dr. Austin available?"

Grace stared, wide-eyed.

"Yes, please tell him I called." Pilar looked at Grace. "Tell him I have some questions about the paternity test. There is someone I want him to speak to."

Grace's silence continued.

Pilar dropped the phone back into its place. "Grace, I wouldn't have disrupted your life if this wasn't true. Can't you look at my son and see? It's obvious that Solomon is Conner's son."

Grace closed her eyes. Those sounded like Conner's words. It was obvious to everyone—except her.

"You need to talk to my doctor, Grace, because I need to know where you stand. If you don't want your husband to be his son's father, that's fine. Just let me know because I need to die knowing whether my son has a home. I need to die in peace."

Grace pressed her lips together at Pilar's words. Peace. They were two mothers searching for the same thing.

"I have to get dressed, but when I come downstairs, I hope you'll give me an answer." Pilar scribbled on a notepad and handed the paper to Grace. "Here's Dr. Austin's number. He's with a patient, but you can call in a few minutes. He'll verify the results. You should call before Conner gets here."

It seemed to take more effort than normal for Pilar to turn and walk up the stairs.

Grace waited until she heard Pilar's bedroom door close before she covered her face with her hands. Uncertainty was much easier than the truth. But the truth was here. The war was over. Solomon was Conner's son.

*   *   *

Grace didn't know where she should be. Should she stand and let Pilar and Conner tell Solomon? Or should she sit next to her husband? When Conner reached for her, the decision was made. She took his hand and sat on the couch, perched on the edge as he was.

"Solomon should be here any minute," Pilar said as she came from the kitchen. "The school van will bring him."

"What did you tell them?" Conner asked as he stroked Grace's hand.

"I told them it was a family emergency, but to make sure that Solomon didn't think I was sick." Pilar peeked through the curtains.

Conner nodded. "I've presented some big cases, but none was ever like this." He chuckled, although there was no humor in the sound.

Grace jumped at the sound of a car door slamming.

Pilar looked through the curtains. "He's here."

Conner squeezed Grace's hand and she tried to smile. It was the best she could do. While Conner had had weeks to process this, Grace felt as if she was just getting the news. She'd talked herself out of believing it. Ever since she'd demanded a paternity test, she'd convinced herself that this was not Conner's son.

Conner and Grace stood when Pilar opened the door.

"Mom, what happened?"

They watched as Solomon ran through the front door.

"Nothing, sweetie. I'm fine."

"When they said I had to come home, I was scared . . ." He stopped when he stepped into the living room. "Oh, hello." He stared at Grace and Conner, then turned to his mother. "Is everything okay?"

"Yes, honey. Mr. and Mrs. Monroe wanted to see you again."

Today, Grace saw it. The boy screamed that he carried Conner's DNA.

"Hello, Solomon." Conner stepped toward him. "It's good to see you again."

By the way he held his mother's hand, Grace knew that he was aware this was not the same as their other visits.

"I didn't know you were coming." He paused. "Mom, is this why you called me home?"

Pilar nodded. "Come and sit over here." Solomon continued to hold her hand as they moved to the couch.

When Conner joined them, Grace found herself in the same chair she'd sat in on Saturday—across from father, mother, and son.

"There's something wrong. I can tell," Solomon said.

"Nothing's wrong," his mother assured him. "But there is something we have to tell you."

He sat in the middle but kept his eyes on his mother.

"Solomon, remember the talks we had about your father?"

He nodded.

"I told you it might be possible for you to meet him."

Grace held her breath as Solomon turned to Conner. "You're my father."

Conner nodded.

Solomon tilted his head. "I'm not surprised," he said, astonishing them all. "The first time I saw you, I noticed you looked like me."

There was silence before they all laughed.

"I thought about asking my mom the other day, but I figured she'd tell me when it was best."

Grace shook her head. Wise words from a child.

Conner lifted Solomon's hand. "So how do you feel?"

Solomon shrugged. "It's good, right? Now I'll get to see you."

"Yes." Conner looked over Solomon's shoulder to Pilar.

She nodded, confirming that would be all they would tell Solomon today.

Conner continued, "You'll get to see me a lot."

Solomon smiled.

"Do you have any questions, sweetheart?" Pilar asked.

He was silent for a moment, then said, "I missed nutrition. Do you think I could have something to eat?"

They laughed again.

"I think that can be arranged," Conner said. "Let's go out. What's your favorite restaurant?"

"Anna's. I love the lasagna." Solomon took his mother's hand and then turned to Conner. When he took Conner's hand, Grace blinked to hold back the tears. Then when Solomon turned to her and smiled, her first tear fell.

Chapter 30

"Mommy, Daddy," Amber squealed. She ran toward them, with Jayde a few steps behind.

Grace hugged Amber, then she held Jayde. "How's my girl doing?" Grace whispered.

"I'm fine, Mommy. Glad that you're home."

Jayde hugged Conner, but held Grace's hand as they weaved through the baggage claim crowd. Lily stood on at the edge, waiting and smiling.

Grace embraced her mother. "I thought you were going to meet us at the house."

"Your children changed that." Lily laughed and pulled one of Amber's pigtails.

"Let me find our driver," Conner said. "I'll tell him we got a better offer."

By the time they got into the Suburban, Amber had filled her parents in on every minute with her grandmother. In the car, Amber switched from reporter to inquisitor, wanting to know all about New York. While Amber chattered, Jayde stayed silent.

Even after they got home and Grace pulled the children's gifts from her suitcase, Jayde remained subdued. When Amber went to bed and Conner took their suitcases upstairs, Grace walked Jayde to her bedroom.

"So, anything happen while we were away?" Grace sat on the bed while Jayde hung her denim jacket with the "I Love New York" emblem on the back.

"No."

"What about Philip and his cousin?"

Jayde sighed and sat next to Grace, resting her head on her mother's shoulder. "I didn't see him. I just stayed with Nana."

"You didn't even go to the movies?" Grace asked, trying to remember the last time her teenager volunteered to stay home.

Jayde shook her head. "I was worried when you and Daddy went away."

Grace put her arms around Jayde. "Why? We've traveled lots of times."

She felt her daughter shrug against her. "This time seemed different. Like something was wrong."

Grace cleared her throat. "Everything is fine."

Jayde lifted her head. "Are you sure?"

She looked into her daughter's eyes and wondered what her child saw. "I promise." She kissed Jayde's forehead. "It's getting late." As she turned away, Jayde hugged her.

Grace closed her eyes. "Good night, sweetheart." She stepped into the hall, closed Jayde's door, then rushed to her bedroom. "Conner, we have a problem."

He came out of his closet already dressed for bed. "More teenage drama?" He chuckled.

She shook her head, and his smile disappeared.

"She knows something." Grace repeated her conversation with Jayde. "She's scared."

Conner sank onto the bed. "We've got to tell Jayde and Amber."

Grace sat next to him. "They're not ready."

"We have to get them ready. Pilar and Solomon will be here in a few weeks. Plus, I want them to know before we tell anyone else."

"What are you planning to do, Conner?" She stood. "Take out a newspaper ad?"

"Grace, we have to say something. People are going to ask questions once Solomon moves in."

She pressed her lips together. "What are you going to say?"

"I don't know yet. But it should be easy if we tell the truth."

"Conner, nothing about this has been easy. So why should it be easy for two children who thought they were the center of your life?"

Conner pushed himself from the bed. "They are and always will be. That hasn't changed, and you know it."

"I'm talking about the way the girls are going to feel. You're mistaken if you think it's going to be as simple as when you walked into Solomon's life. There, you were giving that boy something he's always wanted. With your daughters, they're going to feel as if they're losing something." She paused. "Just like I felt."

His chin jutted forward. "Grace, no one is losing anything."

She turned away from him.

He asked, "So what are we going to do when Solomon is staring at Jayde and Amber across the dinner table?"

"I said we're not going to tell them now." Grace stood and stomped toward the door.

"Where are you going?"

"To the office."

He sighed. "We can't do this again, honey." Conner took her hand.

"I'm just going to call Zoë to let her know I'm home."

Conner let his fingers slip from Grace's.

"This situation has taken over everything," Grace continued. "I need to take back my life."

"What does that mean?"

"Just what I said." She went into their office. For weeks, their life had consisted of what Conner and Pilar and Solomon needed.

Well, she was putting herself and her daughters higher on the priority list. And she would make sure that Conner did not reveal any of this to Jayde or Amber. Not yet. Not until she said so.

Chapter 31

Conner tapped on the conference room door, then stepped inside.

Chandler dropped the stirrer into his cup. "You're back."

"Seems that way," Conner said. He nodded at Albert, one of the new associates. "I need a moment with Chandler."

"The Jacobys will be here in ten minutes," Albert said before he stepped from the room.

Conner and Chandler hugged.

"How was New York? You could've called a brother."

"Sorry." Conner took a seat. "The days were filled." He pressed his fingertips together as the days' images rewound through his mind. How could he express all that he thought, saw, felt, experienced? "You have no idea what it was like to meet Solomon. And what it was like to tell him that I was his father."

Chandler whistled. "You did that?"

Conner nodded. "The results are in. I'm his father." He pulled a photo from his wallet and grinned as he slid it across the cherry wood table. "The first picture of father and son."

Chandler chuckled. "So, what's the plan?"

Conner's smile slipped away. "We're flying Pilar and Solomon out." He took a deep breath. "They're moving here."

"Moving in with you?"

"Solomon will, but we haven't set any dates. We're taking this slow. Although . . ." He paused and lowered his eyes. "Pilar doesn't look good, man."

Chandler shook his head.

"But we're all still praying. There's a lot more, but right now, I want to get to work. Marilyn gave me the notes. Looks like we've got a case with the Jacobys."

"Yeah, but if you need more time . . ."

Conner pictured Stefan Jacoby in his mind. "I've got this one." He leaned across the conference table. "Nothing's more important than taking care of that boy."

Chandler wasn't sure which boy his brother was talking about. But Albert's knock on the door didn't give him time to ask.

"The Jacobys are here," Albert announced. "I'll get Monica."

Conner stood and buttoned his jacket. He was ready for the battle.

"It is good to have you back," Zoë said.

Grace looked up from the calendar Zoë had prepared. "You already said that."

"I'm talking about really having you back." She paused. "After the election, you seemed distracted, and I was worried. But New York was good for you. It's like it changed you."

You have no idea, Grace thought. She said, "I'm ready to take on the Eighteenth District."

Zoë's eyes twinkled with the excitement she'd had as campaign manager. "As soon as you tell me how to schedule things, I'll get moving." She stood. "We still have several weeks before you officially take office, but we should sure up the staff. I'll be in my office when you're ready."

When Zoë closed the door, Grace leaned back in the chair, recalling her conversation with Conner last night.

She couldn't believe that he wanted to tell their girls about Solomon, even after she told him how Jayde had been feeling. Jayde was too unsettled, and Grace didn't know what this news would do to her. She knew they couldn't wait long. But making Jayde feel secure came first.

Second was her business. Her meeting with the mayor to declare her committee interests was scheduled for Friday. She already knew where she wanted to be—on Education. She had only days to prepare.

She shifted her chair to the computer. Pressing one button, she opened the Education Proposal file and sat back as the Word document filled the screen. Yes, New York had changed her. At home and in her office, she was determined to be in control.

Chapter 32

Starlight sauntered into the Bel Air Hotel as if she'd been there before. Her eyes scanned the capacious space. Spotting the silver letters for the Bel Air Club, she glided across the vestibule past women in designer dresses and men in thousand-dollar suits. She kept her face stiff, as if she were totally unimpressed. But her skin tingled with the excitement of being in the midst of Los Angeles's elite.

Her heart hadn't stopped pounding since she received the call from Senator Bonet. For days, she imagined where the senator could take her career.

Even though it was early evening, the light in the bar was dim, providing added privacy to the movers who shook the city. It took a moment for Starlight and the senator to spot each other. Starlight walked slowly. *No need to be anxious,* she thought as she took in the senator's red Chanel suit. Her hair was fastened into a tight bun.

Starlight held out her hand as the senator stood. She wanted to gush but held back her words, letting the senator speak first.

"Starlight, it is a pleasure."

"The pleasure is mine," she said in the tone she'd been practicing all morning. The senator had to know immediately that she was fit for Washington.

Starlight sat first, and the senator followed.

"I hope I didn't keep you waiting."

"Not at all."

Starlight smiled as the senator closed a folder in front of her. Indeed she'd kept her waiting. Ten minutes—just long enough.

A waiter approached. "May I take your order?"

Starlight looked at the cup and saucer in front of Senator Bonet. "I'll have chai tea, please."

The waiter nodded and left them alone.

"Thank you, Starlight, for meeting me. I know you're quite busy."

"As are you, Senator." Starlight rested her arms on the table, making sure her back was straight.

The senator leaned forward, mirroring Starlight's stance. "Then let's get to the point. I want you to work with my daughter."

Starlight's eyes asked the senator to continue.

"I don't want to go into much detail, but Summer has had a difficult time." Senator Bonet sighed. "You would think that with my position and her father and brothers being doctors, it would be easy for her. But she's a wanderer. We don't understand the problem."

You're her problem, Starlight wanted to say, thinking how familiar the disappointed expression that the senator wore was. "How old is Summer?"

"Twenty-four." Senator Bonet stated the number as if her daughter didn't have much time left.

Starlight wanted to scream, hearing her mother's voice.

"Anyway," the senator continued, "the only time Summer says anything positive is when she talks about you. And when she came home from the conference the other day . . ." Senator Bonet paused, trying to finish the sentence with her hands. "There's hope."

"Of course, Senator Bonet. We all have to find our passion." Starlight pulled the words from her heart. "Sometimes a person has to begin a number of paths to find the right journey. But each step has to be taken."

"I like your passion, Starlight. Can you help my daughter?"

"I know I can."

Senator Bonet pulled a yellow pad from her briefcase. "Let's make some plans."

They developed a schedule. When Starlight told the senator what she could accomplish with Summer within weeks, the senator was pleased. "I appreciate this, Starlight."

"This is why I believe . . ." Starlight paused. She didn't know if Senator Bonet was a Christian. Should she say God? "This is why I believe I was put here." As she spoke, she made a mental note. Lexington would have to find out the senator's beliefs so that she could sprinkle her sessions with the right words.

Senator Bonet leaned forward. "Starlight, I promise that when this works, you'll have the keys to any doors you want opened."

Starlight reached across the table, and shook the senator's hand. She smiled as she wondered if the keys would fit the door to the White House. There was no stopping her now.

Chapter 33

One day twisted into the next as the Monroes returned to their schedule of school, work, tennis practice, dance practice, homework, dinner, and all the other tasks that filled their days. Conner and Grace embraced their work, working late into the night—together in their home office.

Pilar and Solomon were covered through simple sentences.

"Did you speak to Solomon today?" Grace asked every evening.

"Yes."

"How is he?"

"Fine."

That was all she wanted to know.

A week after they returned, as they ate Chinese take-out, Grace felt as if their lives were almost back to normal. Grace watched Jayde as she chatted with Conner about her boyfriend's cousin.

"Donald plays Ping-Pong, Dad, so I was wondering if we could put the Ping-Pong table back in the family room."

Grace tried not to smile. She could tell Conner was considering the request.

"And, Dad, do you think I could get a job this summer?"

Grace shook her head. She didn't want any part of that discussion.

"Mommy, are you listening to me?"

She turned to Amber. "Of course, sweetheart. You said next year you want to play the clarinet."

Amber nodded as she popped half an egg roll into her mouth.

Grace basked in the chatter and laughter that just a week ago she feared she would never hear again.

"So what do you think of the clarinet, Mommy?"

"That's great, Amber."

Her daughter grinned. "That's what I'm gonna do. I won't play the flute like Jayde. I'm gonna be my own woman."

Grace laughed, letting her cheer join the giggles that already filled the room.

After dinner, Grace cleaned the kitchen, while Conner checked homework. When Grace finished her Bible study with Amber, she was surprised to find Conner in their bed, already settled with papers covering his lap.

"You're working," she said.

"I can go into the office so the light won't bother you."

She kissed him. "No, this is perfect. I want to review my proposal for the mayor." She sat and leaned against Conner.

He lifted his hands to her shoulders and began to loosen the tightness that rested there. She moaned under his touch.

"Maybe neither of us should work." His lips grazed her ear.

She smiled at his invitation. "I wish. But we have too much to do."

He tapped her behind as she stood and went into her closet. When she came out, she posed at the door, wearing one of his pajama tops, a black and white checkered shirt that brushed the top of her thighs. With her hands on her hips, she sauntered toward the bed.

"How am I supposed to work now?"

She laughed and leaned over, but a second before their lips met, the phone rang. They stared at the telephone before Conner grabbed it.

Grace looked at the clock. It was after ten. Not too late if the call was from California. But if it were from New York, it was late enough for bad news.

Conner spoke succinctly, answering, then questioning.

Her stomach twisted as she paced. She resisted the urge to run to the extension in the hall. She stood still when Conner began taking notes.

Conner blew air through his cheeks when he finally hung up. "Pilar's in Jamaica Hospital."

Fear would not allow Grace to move.

"Solomon is with neighbors. That was his friend Benji's mother."

Grace swallowed. She didn't need to ask what was wrong. Symptoms didn't matter. "What are the doctors saying?"

He shook his head. "Mrs. Downs didn't know anything, but she gave me the doctor's name. I'll call in the morning."

The boulder that held Grace in place lifted, allowing her to take steps back to the bed. She let the silence settle as she sat. She wasn't going to say it first.

"Grace." Before Conner said another word, tears burned her eyes. He continued, "I don't know . . . when . . . but Solomon . . . I think . . ."

"There's no more time." The words creaked past her lips.

"We have to tell everyone. And the girls have to be told first."

Her chin fell to her chest. "They're not ready." But the conviction she'd spoken with days before was gone.

He knelt beside her and lifted her chin. "I promise the girls will be all right."

She nodded, needing to believe him, knowing she didn't.

He pulled her from the bed, and they held each other. When Grace looked at the clock, it was almost eleven, and she wondered who had stolen their time. She broke their embrace, and Conner helped her into bed, covering her, settling her like she was his child. When he slipped into bed, he put his arms around her, holding her like she was his wife.

She could feel the tears on his heart; he wiped the tears on her face.

"Conner," she said, through her sobs. "I think we need to pray for the children . . . tonight."

Still lying down, they held hands and he prayed. Then together they said a prayer for Pilar.

Chapter 34

Grace entered the mayor's outer office and was surprised that Marie, the mayor's assistant, was not at her desk, although the opened folders and coffee mug with steam still rising told Grace she would be back.

She took a seat in one of the burgundy-cushioned wingback chairs and eased her briefcase onto the table while she balanced her Styrofoam cup in one hand. Settled, she took a sip and frowned as the hot liquid slid over her tongue. She'd asked for extra espresso in her cappuccino, but now she hoped she could swallow the drink.

She closed her eyes. How was she supposed to make it through this day when there was no sleep behind her and she dreaded the hours ahead?

This morning, she was ready to draw back on her agreement with Conner, wanting to wait to speak with the girls until they knew more about Pilar. But she changed her mind when she saw his expression when he came down the stairs.

"The doctors didn't say much," he had whispered as they stood at the door to the garage. He kissed her. "I'll call you."

She had nodded and kept her doubts about their girls inside.

When she turned back to the kitchen, Jayde was standing there watching, and Grace wondered what she'd heard.

"You're the early bird."

Grace didn't open her eyes. Even when she whispered, Sara Spears's voice was as grating as fingernails scraping a trail against a chalkboard.

"How're you, Councilwoman?"

Grace opened her eyes and stared at the leader of the Anti-Christian Coalition. "What do you want, Sara?"

She sat on the edge of the chair next to Grace. "I want an interview."

Grace smirked.

"For *City Talk,* my new cable show."

Grace shook her head. She opened her mouth to give an explanation, then simply said, "No."

"Come on, Ms. Monroe. Surely you wouldn't mind defending your views."

"Sara," she said, drawing out her name as if it had four syllables. "No."

Sara shrugged and stood.

"Besides bugging me, what are you doing here?" Grace wasn't sure why she asked the question. With her column in the *Times* and now her cable show, Grace was sure that Sara was always sniffing the halls for a story.

"I'm here to watch you, Grace. Make sure that you're not appointed to any important committees."

Grace rolled her eyes as Sara laughed, then disappeared into the hallway. She waited until she could no longer hear Sara's chuckles, then pulled her proposal from her briefcase. She didn't know why Sara thought she had that much power. She was nothing more than a horse's behind. No one took her too seriously.

Still, Sara's words made Grace want to review her proposal. Sara did have a few allies and Grace wanted to be prepared in case the mayor was one of them.

Ambivalent was the way to describe Grace's feelings toward Mayor Haley. The second-term mayor supported some of her views—he had a major commitment to public education—but he opposed many of the issues she believed in, like affirmative action and prayer in schools.

"Grace, how nice to see you again." The silver-haired, six-foot-five ex–college basketball star gave her a two-palm handshake. Mayor Haley reminded her of Rhett Butler. But unlike Butler, Haley had more style than substance. "Have a seat."

City Hall may have been sixty years old, but the mayor's office appeared as if it had been decorated last week with designers hired straight from *Architectural Digest*. Grace wondered who paid for the mayor's taste.

"Been looking forward to this meeting, Councilwoman. You're a great addition to our city's government."

Grace smiled. "I'm glad you feel that way, Mayor. I'd like you to look over this." She slid the plastic-covered folder across the oversized desk.

He stared at the papers, but only for a moment before he looked up. She was surprised by the puzzled frown he wore.

"Mayor, I'm sure you're aware that I want to be appointed to the Education Committee, and with my experience, as well as my commitment to public education, I believe I can help make a difference in the public schools."

The mayor leaned back in his chair and tapped the tips of his fingers together, squinting his eyes as if he were deep in thought.

"Grace, I didn't know you were interested in the Education Committee."

Liar! She widened her smile. "That was the major issue of my campaign."

"Still, your older child attends a private school. I didn't think your interest in public education was . . . well, I'll just say it. Real."

She wondered how the media would spin the story if she just reached across the desk and punched him. "Mayor, during my campaign, I explained that the only reason my older daughter is in private school is that the high school in our district hasn't ranked well in the national standings. My younger child is in public school, and it is my intention to keep her there—by making sure she receives the same level of education and support that she would receive if she were in private school."

The mayor nodded. "I understand, but, Grace, I'm not sure the people of Los Angeles will."

"They understood enough to vote for me."

"In your district. But I represent the entire city, and I have to make decisions that will benefit all."

"I'm looking to improve the school system for every child, Mayor. No one in this city is more committed to our school system than I am." She paused. "And anyone who has studied my record—without prejudice—knows that."

She stared at him, daring him to say that he wasn't biased when it came to her. He stared back, challenging her to bring up the real issue: school prayer. It was no secret that Mayor Haley was trying to block the school prayer public hearings led by U.S. Senator Sanford, one of the most powerful Republican figures in the country, from coming to Los Angeles. He had often said that this issue was the quintessential example of how the church should be separated from the state.

Finally, he said, "I've given a lot of thought to where each of the new council members would do the most good. With this being my last term, I want to make a positive impact."

"We have the same objective."

He nodded. "Then we agree. With your background and expertise, you'll do much better on the Budget Committee." He spoke as if she'd just been given a prize.

"With respect, Mayor, I don't see how I bring anything to the Budget Committee when I served ten years on the school board. During that time . . ."

He held up his hand. "I know your record, Grace, and that's why I'm pleased that you're part of my team." He paused long enough to toss her a Hollywood smile. "But the committees have been set up."

"It doesn't make sense."

"I'll review the appointments next year, and maybe then . . ." He waved his hand as if the motion finished his thought.

The intercom buzzed.

"Excuse me." He lifted the handset, and Grace allowed her eyes to roam the walls of the large room, lined with photos of mayors emeritus. She'd studied most of them, knowing their politics and what they'd done for the city. She wondered if there was even one who chose the people before politics.

A few seconds later, Mayor Haley hung up and stood. "Grace, I apologize. My next appointment is waiting."

She raised her wrist and took a long glance at her watch.

"I know we didn't have much time," the mayor said as he walked around his desk, moving to within inches of her. "But we're finished, aren't we?"

She looked up at him, straining her neck to take in his full height. She stood. "Thank you for your time, Mayor Haley." She shook his hand.

His smile showed all of his teeth, and he pressed her hand between both of his. "My pleasure, Grace. And, let's revisit this next year."

Grace turned and took one final look around. At least on the Budget Committee, she'd find out who paid for this furniture. He might regret his decision.

The mayor opened the door, and Grace almost bumped into Sara as she stepped into the mayor's office.

"Grace, good to see you," Sara said, as if they hadn't spoken minutes before.

Grace turned to the mayor. "Thank you, again." She nodded, then stomped past Sara, keeping her head high. It was going to take more than Rhett Butler and a horse's behind to stop her from putting her plans into action.

Conner tapped his fingers on the desk as he waited for the hospital operator to connect him. A few minutes later, he was taken off hold.

"Hello."

"Pilar?" He stood. "I was calling your doctor. Why are you answering?"

"My doctor just left, but I've been awake most of the morning."

"I wanted to talk to your doctor."

"There's not much for him to tell. Last night, I kept throwing up, and I didn't want to be home alone with Solomon."

"So what did your doctor say?"

She was quiet for a moment. "It's what's expected, Conner. There are no surprises." The message was inside her words. "Conner, Solomon and I need to move as soon as I'm able to travel."

Conner closed his eyes. Those were the words he wanted to hear. But his heart ached because his son came tagged with a high price.

"I'll handle everything." He tried to keep the sadness from his voice. "I'll need information from your doctors."

"That won't be a problem." She stopped. "I've put you down as . . . the one to be contacted when . . ."

Conner swallowed. "Don't worry, Pilar. I'll take care of you and Solomon."

Conner and Pilar reviewed all that she'd need: plane tickets, a real estate agent to sell her home, a nurse so that Solomon would never be alone if she got sick at home. Before she said good-bye, she promised to call if she thought of anything else. He agreed to do the same.

Conner stared at the telephone and tried to count the days since the first call had come from Pilar. He couldn't remember, but it didn't matter. There were too many plans to make, and it all began with his family.

Chapter 35

"Here they come."

The headlights of Lily's Camry flooded the living room.

Grace stood and pressed her hands together as if she were about to pray. Conner pulled her into his arms, and they held each other until they heard the front door open. Amber ran in with Lily, with Jayde lumbering behind.

"Hi, Mommy," Amber said, tossing her backpack at the foot of the stairs.

Grace rushed into the foyer and hugged her children. "Thanks for picking them up, Mom."

Grace had called Lily and had asked her not to bring the girls home until seven. But even if Lily didn't bring them until morning, she wouldn't be ready for this.

Lily's eyes wandered from Grace to Conner. "What's wrong?"

They exchanged glances.

It had been Grace's idea to include Lily, hoping that her mother's presence would soften the news. But now she wondered if she should have kept this a private moment.

When Jayde started up the stairs, Grace said, "Honey, stay here for a moment, please."

"Mom, I have homework."

Grace took her daughter's hand and led her into the kitchen. "You have the whole weekend, sweetheart," she said lightly, although her heart was heavy. "Your father and I want to talk to you and Amber." She paused. "You too, Mom."

Lily stared at her for a moment, then took Amber's hand. She sat Amber next to her, and Grace pulled out a chair for Jayde. Grace had planned it all—from where each sat, to deciding to do this in the kitchen where they'd be shoulder to shoulder.

Jayde asked, "Can I go to the movies tomorrow?"

It was a natural request at an unnatural time. "I think so," Conner said. "We'll talk about it."

"Is this a family meeting, Daddy?" Amber asked with her eyes wide.

He nodded.

"Nicole said they have family meetings because her brothers are always in trouble." Amber paused. "Are we in trouble, Daddy?"

Grace wanted to reach for her husband as she watched his Adam's apple jump.

"No, baby," he reassured Amber and placed his hand over Jayde's. "I just have to tell you something." He inhaled, then continued. "First, I want you to know that your mother and I love you. Nothing will ever change that."

Jayde leaned forward. "Are you and Mom getting a divorce?" Her glance raced between her parents.

"No," Conner exclaimed.

Grace rubbed her daughter's back. The air was charged with the same excruciating waves that had filled the living room when she sat waiting for Conner to give her this news. The torture wasn't any less harrowing now, especially as she watched Jayde. "Conner, just tell them," she pleaded.

He looked at his hands, folding, then unfolding his fingers.

For the last weeks, Grace had visited the gamut of emotions with Conner. But now she felt only love as she watched him struggle to find words for their daughters.

Conner began, "There's a boy who lives in New York." He paused when Lily gasped. Her mother's eyes told Grace that she guessed at least part of the story.

"And I'm his father." The four words hung by themselves for seconds. "Jayde and Amber, you have a brother."

Amber frowned, but it was a wide-eyed Jayde who said, "You and Mommy gave a baby up for adoption?"

That was a brilliant solution, Grace thought. Jayde's explanation would have saved them. Though in the end, they would not lie. Solomon deserved the truth.

"No," was Conner's only response.

Lily, who understood, said nothing.

Jayde moved her eyes between her parents. "I don't understand. How can you guys have another child?"

"Jayde, I have a son."

Conner had no more words. But with the way Jayde's eyes darkened, no other words were needed.

"You have a baby?" She spat the words.

"He's not a baby. He's twelve years old."

Jayde shoved her chair from the table, but Grace stopped her. "Stay. We need to finish."

"There's nothing else to talk about. I already know too much."

"Wait a minute," Grace said, matching Jayde's tone. "Don't ever talk to your father that way, and you'll stay until we say we're finished."

Jayde folded her arms and slid down in her chair.

Conner continued, "He lives in New York, and I didn't know about him until recently."

The legs of Jayde's chair squeaked against the kitchen floor as she pushed herself farther from the table.

Conner looked at Amber and Jayde. "It's a surprise, but it's good because you have a brother."

"I don't want a brother," Jayde growled.

"Look at him as a blessing from God," Lily said, wrapping her arms around Amber.

Grace wanted to hug her mother.

Amber tilted her head. "I don't get it."

"Are you going to go over this for her?" Jayde motioned toward her sister with her chin. "Because if you are, can I go to my room? I understand everything."

"You can go, Jayde," Conner said.

He had barely finished before Jayde tore up the stairs. They remained quiet until Amber asked, "Daddy, you have a little boy?"

Conner nodded.

"Did you find him when you went to New York?"

"Something like that."

"Amber, would you ride with me to Baskin-Robbins?" Lily asked. "I need to get ice cream since you cleaned me out."

Amber giggled. "Okay." She jumped from her grandmother's lap as if she'd forgotten this conversation already.

With her eyes, Grace thanked her mother, and they hugged before Lily led Amber away. They watched Lily's car roll down the driveway, and Conner said, "That didn't go well. I didn't say it right."

"It wouldn't have mattered how you said it."

"I'm going to talk to Jayde."

"Let me go."

"But she's mad at me."

"She's mad at everything, Conner. But there are some things I want to discuss with her before we go into any more about Solomon."

He looked as if he wasn't sure but nodded anyway.

Grace took deep breaths as she climbed the stairs, knocked on Jayde's door, then stepped into the darkened room. She turned on the light.

Jayde lay on her stomach with her face turned away. Grace sat beside her daughter and let the silence soothe them as she rubbed Jayde's back. Minutes later, Jayde sat up and put her arms around her mother.

"Mommy, I'm sorry," she cried.

"There's nothing for you to be sorry about." Grace wiped Jayde's tears.

"That's true. Daddy should be sorry," she sniffed.

"Your father is sorry that you feel bad. But he can't be sorry for Solomon."

Jayde looked into her mother's eyes. "Is that his name?" she whispered.

Grace nodded.

"How could Daddy do this to you?" She hugged Grace again. "Don't worry. I'm going to stay with you after the divorce."

Grace hugged Jayde tighter. "That's not going to happen, sweetheart. Your father and I are working this out."

Jayde broke their embrace. "You're going to stay with him?"

"Yes."

"I can't believe you." Jayde scooted away from her mother. "After what he did to us. . . ."

"Jayde, this has nothing to do with you. This is between me and your father."

"But he cheated on you."

Grace pointed her finger at Jayde. "I told you not to raise your voice." She paused as Jayde looked away. "Jayde, you're fifteen. You don't even know what you don't know." She was silent for a moment. "Honey, I know this is hard, but as long as you're in this house, I will not allow you to disrespect me or your father."

When Jayde remained still, Grace stood. She leaned over and pulled Jayde into her arms. Although Jayde sat on her bed like one of the rag dolls on her bookcase, Grace held her for a minute.

"I'm going to grill some hamburgers."

"I'm not hungry."

Grace let her arms slip from Jayde. "Okay, but if you change your mind, come downstairs." She waited for a response, but when there was none, Grace walked out.

Conner was standing in the hallway. "How is she?"

Grace pressed her finger to her lips and motioned toward their bedroom. The moment he closed the door, Grace said, "She's still upset."

"I want to talk to her."

"I don't know, Conner. I think we should give her some space. I don't want Jayde saying things she'll regret later," Grace said, remembering some of the words she'd uttered. "And I don't know what else you can add. I explained this isn't about her."

"But she doesn't see it that way." Conner shook his head as if it was heavy. "She thinks I betrayed her."

Grace wanted to tell him that he had betrayed them all. But she held back, knowing that only God's grace kept her from bearing Conner's burden. Just as easily, she could have brought home a child. She shuddered.

She pulled Conner into her arms, consoling him without words and declaring that one day their life would again be normal. But she had a feeling that in between now and normal, there were some tough times ahead.

Chapter 36

A stream of sunlight washed over Grace's face. She squeezed her eyes shut, wishing she could stay in bed for the rest of the day—or the rest of the week. She rolled over, reaching for Conner, but felt cool sheets instead. She bounced from the bed. It was only six-thirty, an hour before Conner got up on Saturdays.

Silence greeted her when she stepped into the hallway. She opened Amber's door; she was still asleep. She knocked on Jayde's door, then opened it. Only crumbled sheets covered her bed.

At the top of the stairs, Grace heard muffled voices from downstairs. At the bottom of the stairs, she paused.

"Jayde, it's never going to work if we don't talk," she heard Conner say.

"I don't want to talk. Anyway, Mom said this was none of my business."

"She didn't say that."

"How do you know? You weren't there."

Jayde's words made Grace want to slap her; the grief in her tone made Grace want to hold her.

"I'm sorry, Jayde, but you've got to talk to me."

Grace listened to the silence.

"We can't pretend that my son doesn't exist."

Grace closed her eyes, knowing how Jayde felt. These were the same words he'd spoken to her.

"He's your son, Dad. And you can't make me like him." Jayde ran from the kitchen, bumping past Grace and then up the stairs.

Conner sat at the table, staring at his hands. He didn't look up when Grace walked in. "I tried to talk to Jayde."

Wordlessly, Grace sat next to him.

"I have one daughter who doesn't understand and the other who understands too well."

"Conner, you're trying to force Jayde. Remember, it was difficult for me." She lowered her eyes. "And, I'm still . . ."

He took her hands and brought them to his lips. "Grace, if there was any way . . ."

"You can't take it back, and I'm tired of the sorrys."

He raised his arms to hold her, but a voice stopped them.

"Mommy, I'm hungry."

They looked at Amber, standing in her wrinkled pink nightgown, rubbing her eyes.

They laughed.

The rest of the family could wallow in sorrow all they wanted. But Amber knew the truth. No matter what, life moved on.

Grace knocked on Jayde's bedroom door. "Are you ready?"

Jayde zipped her bag, then put her tennis racket inside its cover. "Yes, but Philip's mom is taking me and Philip to practice."

"Okay," Grace said, tucking her hands into her jeans. She watched Jayde close the racket's cover. She had wanted to take Jayde to practice, as she did every Saturday. Especially today, wanting the time alone with her. "Well, I'll pick you up, and then we can go to Magic's Fridays or to Houston's for a piece of that apple walnut pie."

Jayde shook her head. "I'm going to the movies, remember? Brittany's mom is going to pick us up, and I'm going to change at her house."

Grace sighed. Her daughter had wiped her family from her Saturday slate.

A car horn blew, and Jayde scrambled to her window. "That's Philip." Jayde picked up her bag and racket and rushed by Grace.

"Remember your curfew," Grace said, catching up with Jayde at the front door. She adjusted Jayde's collar.

Jayde held her head low, not meeting her mother's eyes.

With a single finger, Grace lifted Jayde's chin. "We love you." She hugged her, then waved to Philip and his mother as Jayde climbed into the Lexus.

With Conner dropping Amber at Nicole's house for their Girl Scout meeting and then going to the office, Grace had a day of freedom. A few weeks ago, she would have paid for this day, but now she just felt alone. She picked up the phone. She hadn't spoken to Lily, even though she knew her mother had a million questions. But after Lily and Amber had returned from Baskin and Robbins last night, she had quickly left with just a kiss on Grace's cheek. "Call me if you need me," was all she said.

Now as she dialed the number, this seemed as needy a moment as any.

"Hey, Mom."

"Grace. Are you all right?"

"I'm fine. Do you want some company?"

"I would love that, sweetheart."

Grace smiled.

"Starlight's here."

Her smile vanished. "Thanks for the warning," she whispered as if her sister could hear.

"I do want to speak to you," Lily whispered back.

"Maybe tomorrow."

Lily's silence told her that she wanted to do it sooner, but she said, "I'm here if you need me."

"Thanks, Mom. Do me a favor?"

"I won't say anything," Lily answered before Grace could ask. "I love you," she said before she hung up.

Though Lily spoke those words often, today it felt as if she had reached through the phone and wrapped her arms around Grace.

Now Grace embraced her day's freedom. In her mind, she checked off what she could do: look over the council manual, review the résumés of potential staff members, plan a new strategy to get her education programs implemented, even read her Bible, which she had not done enough lately.

But she smiled when she stepped into the family room. She lay on the couch, clicked on the television, and turned to the Lifetime Channel. Surely there was a movie that would make her life seem like heaven. Right now, that was what she needed.

Chapter 37

Conner looked at the clock. "What time is Jayde supposed to be home?"

Grace's eyes rose from the manual on her lap. "At ten." Her eyes moved to the clock. "Time for bed, sweetie," she said to Amber, who sat cross-legged on the floor.

"Mommy, why does Jayde get to go to bed later than me?"

"Amber, we're not going to have this discussion." She swung her legs from Conner's lap. "I'll be right back."

Amber hugged Conner. But as she got to the door, she turned back. "Daddy, am I going to meet Solomon?"

Grace kept her eyes away from Conner. All evening, Amber had been asking questions—an inquiry every hour or so. Just enough to make sure that neither she nor Conner could ignore the cloud above them.

"Yes, Amber," Conner responded.

Satisfied, Amber trotted up the stairs.

But before Grace could follow, Conner said, "I have a call to make, and then I'll check on her."

Grace returned to the couch and watched him, his shoulders slumped with the burden he carried. He was the hub of this family and was doing what he could to keep the wheels turning so they wouldn't crash.

Grace lay back on the couch as she had done much of the afternoon. She flicked the remote, settling on the Home and Garden Channel. Not that she was interested in the intricacies of decorating a small space, but she didn't have to commit to this program. She could watch with her eyes closed, pretend that she was sleeping. As the announcer outlined the details of the evening's show, Grace settled into the couch's leather. By the time the music took the show to the first commercial, Grace had fallen asleep.

"Grace, Grace."

Her eyes slowly fanned open, and first she noticed the clock. It was after eleven.

"I didn't realize I'd fallen asleep." She stretched.

"Jayde isn't home."

His words made her bolt up.

"I just called Philip's, and his mother said Jayde left two hours ago."

"I thought they were bringing her home."

"Philip's mother said her nephew gave Jayde a ride. Apparently he's brought her home before."

Grace jumped from the couch and picked up the phone.

"Who are you calling?"

"The police."

"Grace, wait. Philip's mom is sure that Jayde is with their nephew. Let's check him first."

"What's his number?"

"He doesn't have a cell phone." Conner thrust his arms through his sweatshirt sleeves. "Philip's mother said that Jayde asked Donald to drive her home early because she wasn't feeling well."

"Then she should have driven Jayde home or called us." She paused. "Do you think he's taken her somewhere? Kidnapped her?" she sobbed.

"No." Conner grabbed her shoulders. "Calm down, honey. Amber's upstairs." She nodded. "I'm going to Donald's apartment. Philip's father is meeting me. In the meantime, call your mother and Devry and Chandler. Maybe Jayde's with them."

She nodded again and followed him to the garage. "Conner, please find her."

He hugged her before he got into his car and sped into the night.

Grace closed the door and rushed to the phone. Before she dialed, she prayed. Jayde had to be at her mother's or Devry's, because if she wasn't, Grace didn't know what she would do.

Grace paced in front of the window and willed herself not to call Conner again. In between the waiting minutes, she'd spoken to her mother and Devry. Chandler had joined in the search, but there was no sign of Donald or Jayde. Now they were all searching the streets. Grace looked at her watch. She'd told Conner she would call the police at midnight. He had five minutes.

The shrill of the telephone made Grace jump. She looked at the Caller ID and rolled her eyes.

"Starlight," she began the moment she picked up the phone, "I can't talk right now."

"Jayde is with me, Grace."

It took a moment for the words to settle and smother her with relief. "Thank, God." She fell onto the couch. "Is she all right?"

"She's fine."

Grace stood. "Thank you, Starlight. Are you bringing her home, or do you want me to come there?"

"She can spend the night here with me."

Starlight's words were barely out before Grace said, "Absolutely not. I'll be right there." She had on her jacket before she finished, then remembered Amber. "I'll have to wait for Conner. I'll call him, and we'll be right over."

"That's not a good idea. Jayde's upset."

Grace wasn't sure what made her fume more—that her daughter had run to her sister or that her sister spoke as if she knew what was best. "Starlight, thank you, but I'll take care of my daughter."

She clicked off the phone before Starlight could respond, then dialed Conner's cell.

"Honey, Jayde's okay," she breathed. "She's with Starlight."

"Thank God."

"I want to go get her."

"I'll be right there."

Grace hung up and leaned back on the couch. She knew she should call Devry and her mother, but although Jayde was safe, she couldn't get the visions of what she had imagined from her mind.

She raised her eyes to the ceiling. "Thank you, Lord," she whispered and wiped tears that seeped from the corner of her eyes. She prayed that this was the end. That this would be the last thing her family would have to endure.

* * *

Conner clicked on his cell phone.

"Conner?"

He frowned when he heard her voice. "Yes, Starlight. Grace already called me. Thank you."

"No problem. I would do anything for my niece. That's why I'm calling. Please let her spend the night with me."

His frown deepened. Grace would never agree, and he wanted Jayde home too. "Starlight, we're having some . . . family challenges that we need to work out."

"I know." Her pause made him wonder what Jayde had told her. "Conner, Jayde needs some time. If you and Grace rush in here and force Jayde home, I guarantee she'll be back out tomorrow or the next day."

"That's why Grace and I need to handle this with Jayde . . . ourselves . . . tonight."

"But what difference does it make if it's tonight or in the morning?"

Conner hesitated. "I don't know . . ."

"Conner," Starlight sighed as if she was struggling with the fact that he didn't agree. "I can help Jayde. I've calmed her down." She paused. "And she did come to me."

Conner shook his head as he pulled into the driveway. The front door opened the moment he turned off the ignition, and Grace stood in the doorway. The light from the foyer glowed behind her as if she was standing in the middle of a sunrise.

Starlight continued, "Jayde said she's not going home. If you drag her out of here, the next time she runs away, you won't find her."

Conner closed his eyes. His daughter was a runaway. Because of him.

Maybe Starlight was right. He couldn't chance Jayde's leaving home again. And Grace had said that Jayde needed space.

"Conner, let's do what's best for Jayde."

He opened his eyes as Grace moved toward him and the light behind her faded. He could read the question on her face as she got closer. Who was he talking to?

"Let me talk to Grace. I'll call you back."

"Just remember Jayde is most important here."

He wanted to scream. Who was she to say that to him? He would give his life for his children. Only Grace's tap on the window stopped him from telling her so.

"Starlight, I'll call you back." He clicked off his phone and stepped from the car. In the quiet of Saturday's midnight, Conner drew Grace into his arms. He could feel her pounding heart.

"I was so scared," Grace said.

Conner held her tighter.

"We should both go to her." Grace pulled from their embrace. "I can call Mom, or we can drop Amber over there. But Jayde needs to see us together."

"Grace, no."

She continued, as if he'd said nothing. "When Jayde sees us, she'll know that even though we're upset, we're both here for her."

Conner stopped walking and hugged Grace again.

"Don't worry, honey," Grace responded, mistaking his affection for uncertainty. "We'll all be fine."

He squeezed her hand. "Let's go inside."

As soon as they stepped into the house, she said, "I'll get Amber."

"Grace," he called before she could touch the first stair.

She turned and his expression told her what his words had not. "No, Conner."

With his arms around her shoulders, he led her into the living room. "Grace, I don't want Jayde to run away again."

"Run away?" she said as if he'd stuttered. "Jayde didn't run away."

He remained silent for a moment, giving her time to question her own words. "Grace, it doesn't matter what we call it, but we know where she is tonight. If we force her home, next time . . ."

Grace pressed her fingers against her lips.

"You said yourself that Jayde needs time," Conner reasoned. "Maybe this is it."

"Okay, but she can stay with Mom or Devry and Chandler. Just not there." She lifted her purse from the table and looked at Conner. "Are you coming with me?"

He shook his head. "Don't do this."

The quivering of her lips pumped tears into her eyes. "Are you coming with me?"

"We can't go anywhere. Amber's upstairs."

"I'll get her," she said, although she didn't move.

Conner shook his head. "Starlight won't hurt Jayde."

"Please come with me."

His arms encircled her before the first sob escaped. He held her until her tears had ended. When she stepped away from him, she wiped her face with the back of her hand. "I'm going to get her first thing in the morning," she said as if it was a threat.

"We'll both go."

Grace's eyes burned with words that blazed in her mind. She had told him that their children weren't ready. She had wanted to wait another week, even another day. Any amount of time would have made a difference. But instead of screaming what she thought, she turned and went upstairs to their bedroom, leaving Conner alone to sink in the situation that he had created.

Starlight stood under the archway in the Grande Room and watched Jayde on the balcony. She stood straight, stiff, her black jeans and jacket blending with the night.

Starlight's lips spread, though her smile wasn't one of triumph. She was pleased that Jayde felt safe with her, but she hated to see her niece hurting. From the moment Jayde entered her apartment, her pain permeated the air.

Starlight slid the balcony door open. "It's chilly. Come inside." Jayde shook her head.

"Carletta made some hot chocolate."

"Do you have marshmallows?"

Starlight smiled again. The fifteen-year-old faded, and in her place the six-year-old whom Starlight remembered appeared. "Lots of the little ones that you like." She put her arms around Jayde and led her inside.

Steam floated from matching lavender mugs that Carletta had put on the dinette table. She hovered at the edge of the kitchen.

"You can go back to bed," Starlight told her housekeeper as she pulled out a chair for Jayde.

Carletta tightened her robe's belt. "Good night," she said before she scurried away.

Jayde wrapped her hands around the warmth of the cup. Quiet minutes passed as they sipped. And as Starlight planned, Jayde finally spoke.

"Did you tell them that I am not going back?" Jayde forced her words through clenched teeth.

Starlight nodded. "Your father agreed that you should spend the night."

Jayde's eyes lifted quickly. "I'm never going back," she quivered. "Auntie Star, can't I stay with you? I can go to school from here. The van will pick me up, and I won't be any trouble."

Though Starlight kept her smile, she swallowed the lump that Jayde's plea planted in her. "Jayde, we're going to do what's best." She laid her hands on top of her niece's.

Jayde shook her head. "They're going to make me go home."

Starlight took her hand. "Come over here." Starlight motioned toward the pillows. "Sit on this." She tossed one of the cushions to Jayde.

Starlight lowered herself into the lotus position in a motion that made Jayde stare.

"Wow." Jayde tried to follow her aunt's example, but lost her balance. She giggled, then dropped onto the floor. But her laughter was gone a moment later. "Auntie Star, I could never live with my parents again."

"Why not?"

Jayde searched Starlight's face as if she wasn't sure what she should say. "My dad told us that he has a son." She paused. "And he's not Mom's."

Starlight didn't know why Jayde's words made her heart pound. "I didn't know."

"No one knew," Jayde said shaking her head. "Dad just found

out. His name is Solomon." Jayde lowered her eyes. "That's why they went to New York."

When Starlight was sure that Jayde wasn't going to add more, she said, "That is a lot to handle."

"I'm really mad at Dad."

"I can understand that."

"And I'm mad at Mom because she's not getting a divorce."

"That's a good thing."

Jayde made a sound that Starlight couldn't decipher. "I wouldn't let anyone treat me like that."

"Just live a little longer." Starlight moved her pillow next to Jayde and rested her niece's head on her shoulder. "You're all up in business that you've got no right sticking your nose in." Starlight chuckled inside. Gone was the decorum of the spiritual motivational speaker. She had reverted to auntspeak.

"I have a right, Aunt Star. They're my parents."

"That's my point, sweetheart. They're the parents; you're the child. And children don't belong in grown folks' business." She paused and kissed the top of Jayde's head. "No matter how mature and wonderful and beautiful that child might be."

"I just feel bad for my mother."

"Your mother can handle this."

"Why isn't she mad?"

"I'm sure she is. But Jayde, if you feel bad for her, why don't you help?"

"I want to."

"Are you helping by having her in the streets at night searching for you?"

Jayde lifted her head. "Was she doing that?"

"You know your mother."

"Maybe I should have called her." She paused. "So what should I do?"

Starlight smiled. "Go to bed. We'll handle this in the morning." Starlight stood and helped Jayde to her feet.

Chapter 38

"My name is Grace Monroe. I'm here to see Starlight." She spoke with the authority of a councilwoman, the passion of a mother.

The concierge punched buttons on his console.

Grace tapped her fingers atop the desk. Her eyes roamed through the lobby filled with the standard amenities: marble floors, gold chandeliers, mirrored walls.

"I'm sorry, Ms. Monroe." The concierge interrupted her inspection. "There's no answer."

"What do you mean," she lowered her voice when Conner placed his hand on her shoulder, "there's no answer?"

The concierge's eyes darted around the lobby.

"Try. Again."

His fingers sped along the numerical keys on the console.

Conner edged Grace from the desk. "Be calm, sweetheart."

"How can I be?" she asked through lips that barely moved. "My sister is playing games."

When they turned around, the concierge diverted his eyes and dialed again.

Grace pulled her cell phone from her purse. She dialed

Starlight's number. After more than ten rings, a voice filled with sleep answered.

"Starlight, this is Grace. We're downstairs. Tell your doorman to let us up." She didn't wait for her sister's response. She handed the phone to the man.

After a few seconds of "yes," "no," "yes, ma'am," the concierge opened the elevator to the penthouse.

Grace shook with anxiety, and only Conner's arm steadied her. But her strength returned the moment the elevator opened. She rushed to Starlight's door.

A Hispanic woman, clothed in a bathrobe, opened the door. *"Entre, por favor."*

They stepped into the massive space, and even from the long entryway, Grace could see the floor-to-ceiling living room windows that framed the ocean view.

"I get Ms. Starlight for you."

"Wow," Conner whispered when the woman disappeared.

Through her anger, Grace was impressed. Not just by the size of the apartment, but with the decor. The lavender enveloped her, soothing, calming, almost extracting the displeasure from her.

Then Starlight sauntered into the entryway.

"Good morning," she whispered. "I didn't expect you this early." She yawned. "What time is it?"

"Time for us to get Jayde." Grace looked over Starlight's shoulder. "She's still asleep."

Grace glared at her sister. "Wake her up."

"That's not a good idea."

"It's a wonderful idea," Grace uttered through lips that were as unmoving as her eyes.

They stared, a war of wills. Grace took a step toward Starlight, and Conner moved between them.

"Starlight," he began. "Please, wake up Jayde."

She held her stare for a moment longer; then her lips spread into a smile. "I'll get her, although I'll probably wake her from the first good night's sleep she's had in days."

She turned, then said over her shoulder, "Have a seat. That is, if you want to give Jayde a chance to dress."

When Starlight moved down the hall, Grace growled.

"Let's go inside." Conner motioned with his chin.

Grace lumbered through the carpet's thickness. She stood at the balcony. The morning's waves crashed heavily, and again Grace felt herself drawn into the surroundings, easing in the lake of lavender. She wondered if there was something in the paint or in the air that hypnotized Starlight's guests.

Grace felt them before she heard them, and turned around. Jayde stood with Starlight's arms around her.

She rushed to her daughter. "I was so worried," Grace said as she held her tight. When she pulled away, she said, "What were you thinking?"

Conner kissed Jayde's cheek, then whispered to Grace, "Let's go home."

Grace read his eyes and nodded. She took Jayde's hand and turned to her sister. "Thank you, Starlight."

"Not a problem, Grace." She paused. "I want to help."

Jayde hugged her aunt.

"Remember what we talked about." Starlight pushed back Jayde's braids.

Grace sighed and wondered how much debriefing she'd have to do.

They were silent as they rode in the elevator and then got into the car. Silence kept them company as Conner maneuvered through the streets. Grace glanced into the back seat a few times, but Jayde kept her eyes on the window. The moment Conner turned into their garage, Jayde opened her door, jumped out, and ran into the house.

"Should we talk to her now?" Grace asked as they followed her.

"I don't know."

Grace sighed. "Teenagers should come with a manual."

"This isn't about teenagers. This is about me." He paused. "Let's talk to her."

Jayde was waiting, sitting on the edge of her bed. "All I want to know is—what is my punishment?" she demanded.

Just minutes before, Grace had been glad to see her daughter. Now she could have wrapped her fingers around Jayde's neck.

Neither Grace nor Conner responded. Grace sat in the chair at the desk and Conner stood, not far from the door.

"Don't worry, Jayde. You'll get your punishment," Grace said. "I can't wait to give it to you. But first I want to know. What did you think you were doing?"

Jayde said nothing.

Conner said, "Do you know how worried we were?"

Silence was Jayde's response.

"I'm very disappointed in you, Jayde," Conner said.

She raised her eyes, filled with tears. "And I'm disappointed in you, Daddy."

Grace held her breath as Conner moved toward the bed. He stood, towering over his daughter. When he sat down, Grace breathed.

"I know you're disappointed, but this is what life is about. The good times and the bad." He hesitated for a moment, then took her hand. "I'm sorry you feel I've let you down, but I can't make Solomon disappear, and I don't want to.

"You can sulk. You can walk around making everyone wish you didn't live here. But the truth is, you have to figure out how you're going to deal with this."

Conner wrapped his arms around Jayde, though she sat limp. He kissed her cheek, then left the room.

Grace waited a minute before she said, "Jayde, what happened?"

She looked at her mother and shrugged. "When I left yesterday, I was mad. And when I got to Philip's house, I thought about what my friends were going to say when they found out, and I got angrier."

Grace sat next to Jayde. "I understand, but running away didn't make any of those concerns disappear, did it?"

"No."

"And your father and I were worried."

"I'm really sorry about that, Mom."

"I know you are." She paused. "You'll be on punishment for two weeks: no phone calls, no movies . . ."

Jayde's mouth opened into a wide O. "Next week is Brittany's birthday party."

She shook her head. "I'm sorry."

"But you said you understood," Jayde whined.

"I do. But it doesn't change what you did." Grace kissed her daughter's forehead.

Jayde flopped back onto the bed and stared at the ceiling, dismissing Grace.

When Grace walked into their bedroom, Conner lay across the middle of their bed. "I told her she was on punishment for two weeks."

"That was pretty easy."

"It'll be tough. Brittany's party is next Saturday."

Conner lay still.

Grace put her arms around her husband and closed her eyes. At least Jayde's punishment would be over in two weeks. She had no idea when theirs was going to end.

Chapter 39

Grace leaned over and kissed Conner just as he turned off the ignition. "This was a treat."

"We should do this every morning."

"Wouldn't that be wonderful," Grace said as she thought about how Conner had readied the girls for school this morning while she slept. When her eyes finally eased open, she jumped from the bed. "I overslept," she said when Conner walked into the bedroom.

"No problem. The girls are already gone. And I'm taking you out to breakfast." He chuckled.

She grinned. "What about work?"

"I'm going to work from home today." He lost his smile. "I have to take care of some things for Pilar, and I'd rather do it from here."

She nodded, wondering how the mention of Pilar's name could still dampen their mood. "We don't have to go to breakfast. It was a nice thought, but you're busy, and my calendar is full too," she said, filling the air with excuses. "I've got to work on my alternative educational plan."

"We're going, Grace. I want to spend an hour with you." He nudged her toward the bathroom. "Just you and me. No children, no Pilar." His smile returned. "So get dressed, woman."

For the next two hours, the world consisted of just three: the two of them and the waitress who brought them the best chicken and waffles in the city.

"It's time to get to work, Ms. Councilwoman."

They held hands as he walked her to the front door of her office.

"Have I told you I love you?" he asked as he put his arms around her.

"Not in the last few minutes."

"You've been wonderful, Grace, with all that you have on your plate."

She cupped her hand against his face. "We share this plate."

As he kissed her, the front door opened.

"Grace, the tabloids are going to love this story!" Zoë said, her face stretched with seriousness.

Grace froze.

"I can see the headlines. "Councilwoman Monroe Makes Out with Her Legal Eagle Hubby." Zoë laughed.

"Oh," Grace breathed and glanced at Conner. His eyes told her that he shared her thoughts—that their secret had somehow been uncovered.

He kissed her cheek, waved to Zoë, and trotted to his car.

"How was your weekend?" Zoë asked when they stepped into the office.

Grace paused. She'd found out the mother of her husband's son was coming to L.A. sooner than expected, she'd told her children they had a brother, and she had found her runaway child. "My weekend was fine," she said. "You know, regular stuff."

"Sounds as boring as mine." Zoë sighed. "But I've made up for it. I've been finding information on the complete city budget. Here's what I've printed out."

Grace flipped through the stapled pages as she walked behind her desk. "This is good, Zoë. Also, I want to talk about our staff . . ."

The front door opened, stopping her words. Sara Spears, dressed in a navy suit complete with red tie, entered.

"Good morning, ladies."

"What do you want, Ms. Spears?" Zoë asked crisply.

Grace raised her eyebrows at her chief of staff's tone. "Zoë, I don't think we should speak to guests that way."

Sara smirked.

"What do you want, Ms. Spears?" Grace asked, matching Zoë's tone.

Sara half-smiled and sat in one of the chairs in front of Grace's desk. "May I sit down?"

Grace chuckled and motioned for Zoë to sit next to Sara, but before she did, Sara said, "Grace, we need to talk alone."

Zoë planted her feet and crossed her arms.

Grace almost laughed out loud. Her five-foot-two, one-hundred-ten pound chief of staff had lost all signs of political decorum. Zoë stared at Sara with a glare that would have made Evander Holyfield proud.

"Zoë, would you mind leaving me alone with . . . Ms. Spears?"

She nodded, though her boxer's stare remained as she swaggered toward the door.

Sara shook her head. "My goodness, Grace. I would think you would surround yourself with Christian workers. You'd better tell that girl to read her Bible."

I should tell her to beat you down, Grace thought. The image made her smile. "What can I do for you?"

"It's really about what I can do for you." Sara leaned back. "You got turned down for the Education Committee."

"Sara, don't you have anything else to do? Like shopping for a new broom to whip around town on?"

Sara laughed. "I'll chalk that up to your disappointment with not getting on the Education Committee." She paused. "I know how much you wanted that, Grace, so I have a proposition for you."

"What can you possibly do for me?"

Sara leaned forward, resting her hands on Grace's desk. "I can get you on that committee."

Grace stiffened and pressed the tips of her fingers together. Her silence permitted Sara to continue.

"We think you could have a positive impact on the Education Committee . . ."

Who's we? Grace wanted to ask.

". . . with the experience that you bring."

This is politics, Grace thought.

"But there are certain things we cannot tolerate."

There was that *we* again. Grace shuddered as she wondered who was behind Sara's coalition.

"Here's the deal. You drop your crusade for prayer in the schools, help us to block the public hearings on school prayer, and we'll let you have your campaign against drugs because, after all, that is good for everyone." She paused. "So agree to our terms, and you'll get a call from the mayor."

Grace blinked rapidly. "Would you mind repeating that?"

She could almost see Sara's tonsils with her wide smile. "You heard me."

Slowly, Grace's lips spread, matching Sara's smile. "You can leave now."

Sara lifted her purse from the floor. "I'll take that as a, you'll think about it."

"You can take it whatever way you want and do with it whatever you wish."

Sara laughed as she stood. "We'll give you a few days." She put her hand on the door knob, but before she opened it, she turned back. "Grace, you should reconsider that interview I requested."

"I don't think so."

"Let me give you a scenario. Suppose there's a story floating around that within the next few days will break."

Outside, Grace was cool. Inside, every organ in her body was on fire.

"Now, many entertainers, athletes, and even politicians find themselves in this position," Sara continued in a singsong tone, sounding like she was reciting a fairy tale. "What the smart ones do is bring the story forth themselves so they can spin it their way."

Grace licked her suddenly dry lips. "What are you talking about?"

"Just the story I want to do about you, Grace. What do you think I'm talking about?"

Grace's heart pounded. There was no way that Sara could know about Solomon. There were no records she could have found, no hospital personnel she could have bribed. Still, her heart hammered to a beat that was well beyond normal.

"Have a good day, Grace."

Sara opened the door, and Zoë stood as if she'd been waiting the entire time. Sara slithered past Zoë, then out the front door.

"What did she want?"

Grace motioned for Zoë to sit down. She didn't think she'd believe it until she said the words herself. "I've just been propositioned, and I'm not sure what to do."

Conner and Grace whispered in the darkness of their bedroom, having turned out the lights long ago.

"I don't know which is worse—the conspiracy to keep me off the Education Committee or Sara knowing something that she can use against me."

Conner's arms tightened around her. "There's no way she could know about Solomon." His statement didn't carry much confidence.

"I agree, but . . ." Her hands roamed over his bare chest. "Now that the girls know, I need to make this public before someone else does."

"Do you think our personal business will really matter to anyone?"

"Conner, there is a string of politicians whose personal business is lying in the streets because journalists believe that private means public if more than three people know your name."

"But you're a local politician, sweetheart."

"And Sara's a local sleazebag who's looking to put her name on the local news. Think about the number of people in L.A., the number of council people who've had their personal situations exposed on KCAL's breaking news."

He blew a puff of air through his lips.

"I don't want to do this." She combed her fingers through the hairs on his chest. "But you're the one who said that we had to move toward the truth."

She didn't think that he could hold her any tighter. But he did. "I support whatever you want to do." He paused, and she could almost hear his thoughts. "Maybe we should get together with our team. If we strike, we want to be in the best position."

She nodded and tried to lean deeper into him. They tried to sleep. But rest eluded them, and they waited, holding each other until the night gave birth to morning.

Chapter 40

Jayde followed her mother into the living room and laid the platter with glazed prawns and spring rolls on the table next to the tomato cheese tart. "Are you finished with me?" she asked.

Completely, Grace thought. Jayde was the one on punishment, but it had been a tough time for them all. From the moment Jayde awakened to when she lay on her pillow at night, everyone was aware that she was an unfairly punished prisoner.

Grace had endured an endless stream of comments: "I'll probably be kicked off the tennis team," and "My grades will drop from all of this stress," and every complaint that Jayde could muster in between.

"You can go upstairs now, Jayde."

Jayde breathed as if she'd been held under water.

"I want you to come down when everyone gets here."

Jayde moaned as if that act was too painful to think about. As she passed her father on the stairs, Grace watched Jayde slip pass without a word.

"How's everything?" Conner asked as he picked up a spring roll.

She slapped his hand playfully. "I'm ready." Then she lowered her voice. "Jayde's still not speaking?"

"Not for two days."

Grace waved her hand in the air, dismissing Jayde's actions. "Where's Amber?"

"In her room watching TV."

The doorbell rang, and Grace glanced at her watch. Seven exactly. "Showtime."

Together, Conner and Grace greeted their guests. This was more than family; this was their team of confidants and advisers. Grace's own Christian coalition.

Chandler and Devry were first, and before Conner could close the door, Zoë drove up. As they began moving to the living room, Lily used her key to come inside.

Grace lingered behind while her mother took off her sweater. Then Lily wrapped her arm through her daughter's. "So how've you been?" she whispered.

Grace patted her mother's hand. "Really good, Mom." She led her mother into the living room with the rest, and she smiled, watching the group as they stood conversing and laughing, as if they were celebrating. Even though Grace was surrounded by people she loved, her nerves were porcupine quills poking through her skin.

Conner cleared his throat. "Guys, let's sit down."

It was as if a breeze flowed through the room, changing the atmosphere from festive to somber in seconds. Grace sat in front of the wide window, and Conner stood beside her, resting his hand on her shoulder.

He cleared his throat once again, and Grace suspected that his words were stuck inside. Finally, he said, "Thank you for coming. I don't want to draw this out, so I'll begin. Grace had a run-in with Sara Spears." The somber air became filled with groans. "I'll let Grace take it from here."

Grace stayed in her chair as she repeated her conversation with Sara—about the Education Committee and breaking story.

Zoë's frown deepened as she realized she hadn't been told all that had happened in that meeting. "What story is Sara talking about?" Zoë asked. "What is she threatening?"

This time it was Lily who cleared her throat. When Grace looked at her mother, Lily lowered her eyes.

Conner said, "That's what this meeting is about, Zoë." He took a breath. "A few weeks ago, we found out that I have a son. A child I didn't know about."

Zoë's expression was as if Conner had just given a weather forecast. The practiced stare of a politician's assistant. She said, "Sara knows about this?"

Conner said, "I don't think Sara knows. She's a professional leech who knows how to coax information from people. And she does it through innuendoes and threats."

"I agree," Grace said. "But if Sara is snooping, it's not going to take her long to find out. Especially since Pilar and Solomon will be here the day after tomorrow."

A collective gasp was the response to the news Conner was supposed to tell. But the words had slipped out.

"Well, we know what this is about," Devry said, as if she was stating the obvious. When no one responded, she continued. "You're being attacked because of your beliefs. You weren't supposed to be elected, and you're a threat. Sara is just a front, but whoever she's working for fears what you might do." Devry sat back as if she had made her case.

Zoë said, "So what's our plan? How badly do we want the Education Committee, and what do we do about Conner's son?"

It was strange hearing those words—*Conner's son*—spoken from outside the family. Soon the world would be saying that.

"Well, I won't cower," Grace said, her mind set. "I'm staying with my agenda."

Lily said, "But if you give up the fight for prayer in the schools, you can get some of your other programs implemented."

Grace stood and paced in front of where'd she'd been sitting. "But if I give in, I won't be standing for anything."

"Make sure you're not being stubborn," Lily said, leaving Grace feeling as if she were being scolded. "Decide if it's better to be on the committee and accomplish a little."

Grace was silent. Was it better to compromise, get on the committee, and make changes from the inside?

She glanced at Conner, then Chandler, looking for some indication of their thoughts. But the twins remained stolid, informing her with their expressions that she was supported, but the decision was hers.

"Let me think about it."

Everyone nodded.

"Now, point number two," Zoë said, as if moving through a preplanned agenda. "Conner's son. Any suggestions?"

"Make the announcement." These were Chandler's first words, but spoken as if absolute, no room for discussion.

"Just like that?" Conner asked his brother.

Chandler nodded. "Bro, we should do what we do in court. Get the ball first. He who wins the coin toss wins the game."

"But Sara doesn't know anything," Lily said.

"It doesn't matter. Solomon is going to be here in a few days. Someone is going to ask a question." He faced Grace. "With the platform and the issues you ran on, people are watching, ready to judge every move. You need to stand in the center of the truth."

They all pondered Chandler's words.

After a few moments, Zoë nodded. "This is not the way I would've gone at first, but you make a lot of sense, Chandler. This is a test, and we have to pass before anyone even knows we're being tested." She paused. "So if we're going to vote, my vote is let's tell the world about Solomon. I'll think about the best way to do it, but let's stand up."

With their nods, they all agreed.

"Zoë and I will write my statement, but I would like your input," Grace addressed the group.

"That's a good idea," Conner said. "And I have a suggestion." All eyes focused on him. "These are some tough issues," he began solemnly. "And we have to do our best to address them. But first . . ." He paused, and their anticipation made the others slide to the edge of their seats. "Let's get some good food into our stomachs."

The air's tension deflated like a punctured balloon, and they laughed. The family stood and Grace smiled, pushed her shoulders back, and followed Conner into the kitchen. She was grateful for this diversion, even if it was for only a few minutes. By the time she and Conner returned to the living room with plates filled with food, the strain had dissipated, the laughter had returned. For a few minutes, they could pretend that all was normal before the storm.

Chapter 41

Starlight kicked off her silver mules, letting them fly across the room. She flopped onto the couch.

It had been longer than a long day. What was supposed to be lunch with Summer Bonet had turned into a marathon wailing session where Summer complained of the massive conspiracy holding her back from personal achievement.

At first, Starlight had sat in awe at the young woman's imagination, as Summer blamed everyone, including her third-grade teacher. By the fourth hour, Starlight was sure that she would have found more joy if she had just leaned forward and banged her head on the table.

As Summer rambled, Starlight added the dollars, convinced she hadn't charged Senator Bonet enough. But at two hundred fifty dollars an hour, she was earning what many top therapists were paid. And Summer was the key to more important doors.

She pushed thoughts of Summer aside and glanced at the clock. She wasn't sure if it was too late to make her call, but she picked up the phone anyway.

"Grace, this is Starlight. How're you?"

Starlight heard her sister's sigh.

"I'm fine." Grace paused. "What can I do for you?"

Starlight shook her head. Grace would never consider that she was just checking on her sister and her family. "I'm calling to see how everything is going . . . with Jayde."

"Jayde's fine." Grace stopped. "Thanks for asking."

Starlight smiled. A thank you—a grand gesture on her sister's part. "Is Jayde home?"

There was a moment of silence. "Yes."

Starlight waited for Grace to say more, but when the silence continued, she realized she had to beg. "May I speak to her?"

Again, silence, before Grace said, "I'll get her." She sounded as if those words were hard to say.

Starlight sat with the phone's dead silence, and minutes later wondered if Grace had forgotten her. But she grinned when she heard her niece's voice.

"Jayde, honey. It's Aunt Star."

"Hi!"

"How're you?"

"Fine."

By the way she lowered her volume and changed her tone, Starlight could tell that Jayde's smile had disappeared. She imagined Grace hovering nearby, studying every word her daughter uttered.

"How would you like to have dinner with me tomorrow?"

"That would be great," Jayde exclaimed, then followed with a sigh. "But I'm on punishment." She spoke as if it were a death sentence. "Can I see you when my punishment is over?"

"Sure, honey. I can't wait to see you. Call me when we can get together."

"Okay," Jayde dragged the word out. "I wish I could see you now. Maybe Mom would let you come over here . . ."

Beep!

Starlight said, "Sweetie, I have another call. I'll speak to you soon, okay?"

She hung up before she heard Jayde's good-bye and clicked over. "Hello."

"May I speak to Starlight, please?"

She sat up. "Pastor Carey, how nice to hear from you."

"You recognized my voice."

Starlight laughed, a chortle from her throat. "Of course. Why wouldn't I recognize my favorite pastor?"

"Your favorite, huh?" He paused and lowered his voice. "One day we'll get together and . . . talk about that."

Starlight raised her eyebrows. Pastor Carey had been married for thirty-five years, had more salt than pepper atop his head, and was never seen without his minister's collar. In this city, he was a revered man of the cloth. But Starlight was beginning to see that there was more man in him than cloth on him. She filed his comment away. You never knew when you'd need a prominent pastor on your side.

"I'm always available to you, Pastor," she said, knowing he heard what she hadn't said. "But what can I do for you now?"

He cleared his throat. "I have some news. Pastor Walsh wants you to call him. He wants you at his church. I told him you could do for him what you did for me." The pastor chuckled. "Though don't give him everything. I want you to keep a few special things for me."

Starlight rolled her eyes, but he only heard her smile when she said, "Of course, Pastor Carey. You were my first," she continued the flirtation.

She'd granted him the words he wanted. Then he passed on what she needed—Pastor Walsh's telephone number. "He's out of town until Friday. Call him then."

"I will." She paused. "And thank you, Pastor Carey," she said raising the words from her throat.

He coughed. "So when are you coming back to my place?"

"You set the date; I'll be there."

"We could get together to . . . discuss it."

She held back the gag she felt rising. "That would be nice, Pastor. I'll look at my calendar and get back to you."

"Do that, little lady."

She could imagine his smile even after they hung up. She could handle Pastor Carey's flirtations. His introducing her to Pastor Walsh proved that Pastor Carey belonged on the positive side of the balance sheet. Pastor Walsh was second only to Pastor Carey in his influence. A speaking engagement at his church was a coup.

She leaned back onto the couch and put her feet up. Pastor Carey, Senator Bonet, and now Pastor Walsh. Her assets were certainly growing.

Chapter 42

Grace barely breathed as they waited at the bottom of the escalator. From the moment she and Conner had been driven through the LAX gateway, she had planted a smile on her face. Her lips were still spread wide, even though her cheeks were beginning to ache.

Conner squeezed Grace's hand, but she didn't look his way. Her eyes were waiting for Pilar and Solomon. Finally, she saw them at the top of the moving stairs.

Solomon spotted them, said quick words to his mother, then ran down the escalator into Conner's arms. As she watched her husband with his son, the pain eased from Grace's cheeks.

"How're you, buddy?" Conner laughed.

"Fine. I loved the airplane." Solomon beamed, then turned to Pilar who had just made her way over to them.

She seemed to have shrunk, although Grace could tell that it was really the way Pilar slumped over the cane that she now walked with.

"We requested a wheelchair," Conner said.

Pilar waved the cane. "I didn't need it. I feel much stronger." She turned to Grace. "How are you?" Pilar smiled as if she weren't balancing herself on a walking stick or dying from AIDS. She took Grace's hand, and Grace noticed the strength of her handshake.

After a moment, Grace pulled Pilar into her arms, feeling more bones than flesh in their hug. There were tears in Pilar's eyes when she pulled away.

"I'm so happy to be in California again," Solomon said.

Grace looked at the boy, his eyes wide. But she saw more than excitement inside the windows to his soul. A sense that his words were needed to crack the sadness that threatened to conquer them in the middle of the Delta terminal.

Grace smiled. "We're happy that you're here, Solomon."

He nodded, then entwined his fingers with hers.

Grace glanced at his hand, small and strong. When she looked up, her eyes met Pilar's as Solomon took his mother's hand. He walked between them, a bridge uniting.

Conner led them to baggage claim and a bench where Pilar sat while Conner turned to the luggage carousel.

"Honey, I'll call the driver," Grace said.

He hugged her before she stepped outside. "I love you," he said.

After Grace called, she waited at the curb, ready to direct their driver. Her head filled with the events of the past weeks, running forward like a silent movie. At the center of each frame, Pilar stood, making Grace shake her head. She wanted to rid her mind of the composite of sentiments that accompanied every thought of Solomon's mother.

She signaled the driver and watched him ease the Town Car to the curb. Minutes later, Conner helped the hired driver load the car. Then he returned to the terminal for Pilar and Solomon. A minute later, they were maneuvering out of the airport.

"Those trees are much taller than the ones in New York," Solomon said.

"They're palm trees."

Conner pointed to the hotels on Century and then other sights from the freeway. "Are you hungry?" Conner asked his son.

"Yes, sir," Solomon exclaimed.

Pilar said, "I'm a bit tired. But you can take Solomon somewhere."

"Let's just pick up something," Grace suggested and Conner agreed.

"I want to see the beach," Solomon said.

"You'll be able to see the beach from your apartment. Your bedroom window faces the ocean."

"Wow."

Grace looked at Solomon and he grinned. She returned his smile, but stared at him, wondering what was inside this young man. From the beginning, she sensed something. In the timing of his actions, in the words he spoke, it was as if he was aware of things they didn't know. He was wiser than all of them. She guessed disease did that to children—robbed dreams but granted wisdom.

This time, Grace took Solomon's hand, and his smile widened. They held onto each other until the car stopped in front of the Greenwich Apartments. Grace had suggested a month-to-month furnished executive suite complete with appliances, linen, cookware, dishes, and silverware. Conner had agreed because the apartments were only five minutes down the hill from their home.

Conner unlocked the front door of apartment G105, and Solomon ran to the windows, drawn by the lure of the beach that could be seen the moment they stepped inside.

"Wow," Solomon exclaimed, running from room to room.

Grace could tell from Pilar's smile that she shared her son's sentiments. But she had only enough strength to sit on the couch and enjoy the view from there.

"Conner, Grace, this is beautiful."

Grace sat next to her. "We want you to be comfortable."

Conner slid the balcony door open, and the breeze escorted in the ocean's fragrance.

"Wow," Solomon said, joining Conner on the terrace.

Grace and Pilar watched father and son. And Grace was surprised by the joy that filled her.

"Can we go to the beach?" Solomon asked.

Conner glanced back into the living room, and Grace gave him a slight nod. "Okay, but not for too long. We want to get you and your mother settled in. We can pick up some hamburgers or something down there."

Solomon kissed Pilar, then ran to the door with Conner following behind.

The moment the door was closed, Pilar said, "Grace, I appreciate everything that you're doing."

"You're welcome."

Pilar smiled and then looked away. "I don't want to be too much trouble."

"You're not."

"I can imagine what this has done to your family."

"You can't."

Pilar looked up. Surprise stretched her face.

Grace said, "There is no doubt, Pilar, this has been difficult. But Conner and I have a good marriage, and with God, we'll make it through."

Pilar nodded.

Grace continued, "I want you to know that we're going to help you. And we're going to take care of Solomon."

She nodded again. "That's all I want." She paused. "This is a lot to put on a young boy."

Grace touched Pilar's hand. "I know, but Pilar, Solomon has you." She paused. "And he has me."

Pilar lifted arms that looked as if they were sure to break and hugged Grace. Then she frowned when the doorbell rang.

Grace looked at her watch. "That could be the nurse."

When Grace opened the door, all three stood outside.

"We ran into Virginia," Conner said, his hands filled with bags.

Grace motioned for the nurse to come inside. "Good to see you again." She introduced Virginia to Pilar, then stood back as the nurse sat down with Pilar.

While they spoke, Conner took Solomon into his bedroom, and Grace went onto the balcony. But though her eyes enjoyed the ocean's waves, her ears stayed focused on the conversation inside. As she listened, she knew she and Conner had made the right choice. Virginia was experienced and knowledgeable, and her interaction with Pilar made Grace feel comfortable. Almost thirty minutes passed before Grace heard Solomon and Conner, and she stepped back into the apartment.

"It would be good for Ms. Cruise to lie down," Virginia said. "It's already been a long day."

Grace turned to Conner. They hadn't made plans for what was next. When he was silent, Grace asked, "Pilar, would you like Solomon to come with us?"

Solomon answered before Pilar could. "I want to stay with my mom."

"That's a good idea, buddy." Conner hunched down and hugged his son. "We'll see you later."

Grace smiled at Solomon and curved her fingers into a wave. But when she turned to the door, he ran to her. His arms circled her waist and she bent over, holding him.

"I'll see you later too," he said once he pulled away.

He poured new emotions into her heart. Grace didn't need to look at Conner to know that similar affections tugged at his center. They held hands as they walked through the hallway into the street, both silent with their thoughts. They'd been spinning in this storm for weeks, but now their feelings didn't seem as important as what awaited the two people they'd left in the apartment.

As they approached the Suburban they'd parked near the apartment earlier, Grace's steps slowed.

"What's wrong?" Conner asked, then followed her gaze.

Across the street, a woman dressed in a navy man-tailored suit with a red tie leaned against a black convertible BMW.

Conner said, "That's Sara Spears."

Grace kept moving, but even as Conner held the car door for her, she kept her eyes on Sara.

"Do you think she followed us?" Conner asked when he got into the car. Before Grace could answer, he said, "I'm going to find out." He started the ignition and twisted the steering wheel to make a U-turn, but Grace stopped him.

"She wants a confrontation. We just need to go home."

The tightness in his jaw told her he didn't agree, but he acquiesced.

Sara waved as they drove away, and Conner watched through the rear mirror until she was no longer in sight.

"Maybe we should warn Pilar," Conner said.

"What would we say? Sara can haunt any corner she wants."

"What is her problem?"

"I'm a Christian holding a public office. That's all she needs."

"There are lots of Christians . . ."

"Yes, but someone in a higher office might crush her. Sara knows what she's doing." Grace paused. "She thinks she's picking on someone her own size."

But thinking is her first mistake, Grace said to herself.

Grace walked back into the bedroom just as Conner put down the phone.

"Are the girls in bed?" he asked.

She nodded. "Amber is. She's excited about meeting Solomon tomorrow, so she'll be awake for awhile. Now Jayde . . ." She didn't need to finish. "Did you speak to Solomon?"

He shook his head. "Solomon was taking a bath."

Grace looked at the clock. "I'm sorry you didn't get to say good night to him, even though you've spoken to him at least five times since we got home." She chuckled.

"Do you think it's too much?" he asked seriously.

She caressed his face. "No. It's what Solomon needs."

The telephone rang, and they stared at each other for a moment before they laughed. "Solomon," they said together.

"Let me say good-night first," Grace said picking up the phone. "Hi." She was still chuckling.

"Grace?"

Her face stiffened. "How did you get my number?"

Conner's smile dropped when he saw her frown.

"I'm a reporter."

"Sara, do not call my home. You know where I work." She slammed the phone back into the receiver. "Can you believe that?"

The phone rang again before Conner could respond. "I'll get it," he growled.

Grace shook her head and answered the phone without saying hello.

"Fair enough; I won't call your house again," Sara said, as if their conversation had not been interrupted. "But since I have you on the phone, we need to know if you've made a decision about the Education Committee."

Grace pressed her lips together, hoping that would bridle what flared inside. "Sara, take your offer and . . ." She left the sentence for Sara to finish. "And if I ever see you following me or anyone else in my family, you'll regret it."

"That sounds like a threat from a Christian. Can I quote you, Grace?"

"Do whatever you want, Sara. But you don't want me as an enemy."

Sara chuckled. "I'll give you a few more days to make a decision about the interview I requested."

Grace hung up the telephone.

Chapter 43

Grace had wondered all day if they should have this dinner at Pilar's apartment. Now as she leaned against the front door and watched Conner help Pilar, she doubted their decision to bring Pilar to their home. Pilar struggled to stand, then took cautious steps across the walkway. She was too weak for this trip. But Grace knew that Pilar's beyond-valiant effort was to be by her son's side when he first came into the house that would become his home.

"Mommy, is that them?"

"Yes, sweetie," she said without turning.

Grace put her arm around Amber's shoulders and glanced at the stairs. She didn't expect to see Jayde. Her oldest child would have to be dragged down.

"Welcome to our home," Grace said, stepping aside so that Pilar could enter. They hugged.

"Hello," Amber said, swinging her pigtails and reminding everyone that she was there.

"Is this beautiful young lady Amber?"

Amber tilted her head. "How did you know my name?"

Pilar said, "I know a lot about you. Your mom and dad told me you were pretty, but they didn't tell me just how pretty you were."

"Thank you," Amber said, but she was already looking beyond Pilar.

Conner had one arm around Solomon, and Amber walked toward them. She extended her hand. "Hi, my name is Amber." She held a solemn smile.

"My name is Solomon." They shook hands, and the adults chuckled.

"Let's sit down," Grace said.

Amber said, "Do you want to see my room, Solomon?"

His eyes were big as he looked at Conner. But Grace said, "Amber, let's do that after dinner."

Amber nodded. Anything would work for her. "Okay. Can we go into the family room so I can show Solomon our big-screen TV?"

Conner laughed. "Yes."

Grace breathed, relieved as she followed Conner and Pilar, then Amber and Solomon down the steps to the family room. She wanted to keep everyone, especially Solomon, away from Jayde, at least for the moment.

"You have a beautiful home, Grace." Pilar smiled as she lowered herself onto the couch while Amber showed Solomon the remote for the nine hundred channel television.

"Thank you." Grace's eyes roamed to the stairs.

Pilar asked, "Where's Jayde?"

Conner and Grace exchanged glances.

After a pause, Grace said, "I'll get her."

She dreaded every step as she moved toward Jayde's room. She knocked on the door once, and then went inside. Jayde was at her computer, flipping solitaire cards. "They're here, honey."

Jayde clicked off her computer and faced her mother. "I don't want to go down there, Mom."

Grace folded her arms. "We don't have time for this. You're going to come downstairs and act like the polite young lady you were raised to be."

Her eyes filled with tears. "Mommy, why are you mad at me, and you're not mad at Daddy?"

Grace sighed. There were not enough words to explain this to a teenager—and especially not to a daughter whose hero had betrayed them both. She put her arms around Jayde. "Being disappointed with people you love is a part of life. So I understand how you feel."

"You do?"

Grace nodded. "When your father first told me about Solomon, I was upset. But I realized I couldn't stay angry forever. So I started thinking about the best way to get over it."

Jayde looked at Grace, eager for her wisdom.

"So I just asked God."

"And what did He say?" Jayde looked at Grace as if God had given her a written personal message.

"He said not to sin."

She twisted on the bed to face her mother. "I'm not sinning," she said, defending herself. Then she added in a weaker tone, "Am I?"

Grace shrugged. "You have to decide that, but . . ." She paused. "God told us to forgive. If God can forgive your father, then we sure can."

"That's so hard."

"How difficult do you think it is for God when He has to forgive you all day long?" Jayde looked at her, and Grace smiled. "And me too. God spends a lot of time forgiving me."

Jayde closed her eyes as if she was mulling over her mother's words.

"Solomon is a very nice boy. You'll like him."

Jayde twisted the ring on her finger. "Is his mother here?"

Grace nodded.

"Aren't you mad at her?"

Grace couldn't begin to utter the thoughts she'd had about Pilar. "I'm not anymore" was as honest as she could be.

Grace stood and held out her hand. "So, whaddaya say? Let's go downstairs and show these people a couple of special Monroe women."

Jayde took her mother's hand and they went down into the den together.

No matter how hard they tried to pretend, this wasn't a normal family gathering.

Conner sat at one end of the table, while Grace sat at the other. In between, Pilar sat next to Jayde, with Amber across next to Solomon.

Tension thickened the air, although Amber and Solomon didn't notice. While the new fast friends chatted through dinner, sharing stories about school and their hobbies, the rest of the conversation did not flow. It wasn't just Jayde's obvious displeasure that strained their dialogue; it was Grace's own unsettled feelings. One moment, Pilar was the harlot who had tried to steal her husband. But seconds later, she was the dying mother in need of sympathy.

"So, Jayde, you're fifteen," Pilar said, reducing the dinner chat to information gathering. That was all that was left.

"Yes."

Grace sighed as she looked at Pilar. For the moment, she was the mother again.

"I understand you're doing well in school."

Jayde shrugged.

Conner said, "Jayde's a straight A student and a star tennis player."

Jayde glared at her father, and Grace knew the talk she'd had with her daughter an hour before was long gone from her thoughts.

The dinner talk continued with devised questions and strained answers until Conner mercifully asked Pilar if she would like to see the rest of the house.

Grace almost jumped from her seat. "That's a good idea, honey. You and Amber can show Pilar and Solomon. Jayde and I will clean up."

Jayde rolled her eyes.

"I'll help you," Solomon said eagerly.

"We don't need your help." Jayde cringed under the stare of the three pairs of adult eyes and added, "I can help my mother by myself." Though her words were softer, her tone was not.

She deserves a slap for that one, Grace thought, as she glanced at Solomon. His permanent smile disappeared, but only for a moment. Amber took his hand and led him from the room. Conner and Pilar followed.

When they were alone, Grace whipped toward Jayde. "I don't care how angry you are," she hissed. "If you ever talk to anyone like that again, you're going to have to call the police on me."

Before Jayde could protest, Grace picked up her plate and stomped into the kitchen. In silence, Grace and Jayde scrapped the cream gold-trimmed china, placing the pieces in the dishwasher. When Jayde stacked the last of the catering trays on the counter, she asked, "May I go to my room now?"

Grace stood at the sink with her back to Jayde. "Please do."

Jayde began to walk away, then stopped. "I'm sorry."

Grace didn't respond. She didn't move until she heard her daughter's steps fade on the stairs. Then she sank into a chair.

Jayde had been a terror, but she was more upset with herself. The dinner should have been smoother, but no one knew how to handle this. The only hope was that next time would be better.

Grace went into the foyer just as Conner was helping Pilar down the stairs.

"Would you like some coffee?" Grace asked.

Pilar smiled but shook her head. "I can't believe how tired I've been getting," she said. "I don't want to end such a wonderful evening, but would you mind?"

"Of course not," Grace said, then paused, hoping she hadn't responded too quickly. "Where are Solomon and Amber?"

"Upstairs," Conner said.

"I'll get them."

As Conner led Pilar into the living room, Grace paused in front of Jayde's closed door, then continued to Amber's. But the conversation inside the room made her stop.

"I'm glad I have a brother."

"I'm glad to have a sister." Grace heard Solomon's smile. He added softly, "I have two sisters."

"I don't think Jayde likes you," Amber said.

Grace wanted to rush into the room, hold Solomon, and assure him that he was loved. But she held her place, pressed against the hallway wall.

"She doesn't know me, so she can't not like me." Grace smiled. "I think it's just the circumstances."

Grace pushed toward the door.

Amber asked, "What does that mean?"

"Jayde was surprised to find out about me."

Grace frowned, wondering if Pilar had told him that, but suspecting Solomon had come up with this on his own.

"I thought you were a good surprise."

"Jayde might not like surprises." He paused. "And she's a teenager too. My friend Benji told me that teenagers are crazy."

Grace wanted to laugh at Solomon's seriousness.

"Really?" Amber asked as if Solomon had spoken a scientific truism. "How does he know?"

"He has a sister who's a teenager."

"Oh." Amber's exclamation gave Solomon's friend the status of an expert. "Sometimes Jayde acts kind of crazy But she's really okay."

There was silence for a moment.

Amber said, "I'll tell her how nice you are."

"You can, but she'll find out for herself."

Grace stepped into the room. "Solomon, it's time for you to go home."

Amber and Solomon were kneeling at her bed, shoulder to shoulder, friends sharing secrets. It was so simple to them.

Amber said, "I wish you could stay longer." Then she asked, "When are you coming to live with us?"

Solomon looked at Grace, and she put her arm around his shoulders.

"We don't know yet, Amber." Grace took her daughter's hand. "Let's go so you can say good-night to Ms. Pilar."

As they passed Jayde's room, Amber said, "We should tell Jayde you're leaving."

"I don't think so," Grace said, and tightened her arm around Solomon. "Let's leave her alone. You know how crazy teenagers can be."

They giggled as they went down the stairs, but Grace's laughter stopped halfway down. Conner and Pilar stood under the living room's arch, side by side, the way she and Conner had the day they renewed their vows.

Grace's eyes narrowed. The harlot had returned.

"Well," Grace began when she got to the bottom of the stairs, keeping her eyes away from the arch. "I'm glad you came over tonight."

Pilar stepped closer. "Thank you." Pilar took her hand. "For everything."

The mother replaced the harlot, and Grace squeezed Pilar's hand. "We'll see you tomorrow."

Conner kissed Grace. "I'll be right back."

Solomon walked toward the door, but before he stepped outside, he turned around and hugged Amber. "It was nice meeting you."

Amber giggled.

Solomon turned to Grace, and when she opened her arms, he fell into her embrace. Like he belonged inside her arms. Grace kissed the top of his head. Then he followed Conner and Pilar.

With Amber by her side, Grace watched until her husband's car disappeared into the night with Pilar and their child.

Chapter 44

The children had been gone for thirty minutes before Conner pulled out of the garage. The moment the door closed behind him, Grace grabbed the kitchen phone. She dialed, and when it was answered, Grace said, "Devry, can you meet me for breakfast?"

"Good morning to you, too."

"I'm sorry, but I need to talk to my best friend." Grace paced the length of the kitchen.

"And who would that be?"

"You."

"Of course. You don't have any other friends."

Grace laughed, knowing that had probably been Devry's objective from the moment she'd heard Grace's voice.

"So what's the emergency?" Devry asked.

"I can't do it over the phone. I'll treat you to a fabulous breakfast."

"No."

Grace frowned.

"And get that grimace off your face," Devry said, as if she could see her friend. "I'm not saying no officially. I'm going for a walk, so if you want to talk, you'll have to use some muscles."

Grace's shoulders slumped even more. "You want me to work out?" She sighed, thinking it would be much better to go somewhere and order butter-soaked grits and fried catfish. "You're weeks away from having a baby."

"That's why I'm working out. And I'm only going to wait for twenty minutes."

Grace measured her choices—food or friend. "I'll be there in fifteen."

A foot-tapping Devry was waiting at her door when Grace parked, and she was at Grace's car before Grace could even get out. "Let's go." Devry took Grace's hand.

One block later, Devry was swinging her arms and breathing like she was training for a triathlon. Her swollen belly was hidden under the oversized T-shirt that reached her knees.

"So what did you want to talk about?" Devry asked, granting permission for them to speak.

"I missed you in church yesterday."

Devry looked at Grace though she kept her pace. "That's not what you want to talk about. How was dinner on Saturday?"

"How'd you know?"

Devry chuckled, making her take a stutter-step. "Maybe it was the ninety thousand messages you left or the fact that you're beating the pavement with me now instead of scarfing down chicken and waffles."

Grace laughed, though her chuckles faded quickly. "Girl, if you had been at that dinner, you would have had me committed. It was a disaster. Jayde acted like Blair Witch from the projects."

"Sounds awful."

"It was worse than that. I didn't know if I should reach out to Pilar or squeeze the life out of that white woman."

Devry frowned. "Why do you have to call her that?"

"What? White woman? That's what she is."

"Why do you have to put a label on her at all?"

"Well, to me, she's a woman who's not black. So that makes her white."

Devry hesitated before she said, "You know that's messed up." She kept her eyes straight ahead and pumped her arms higher and harder.

Grace had to trot to keep up with her pregnant friend. "Okay, what I said wasn't Godly. I know it," she said through heavy breaths.

"I'm not even talking about God. He'll deal with you." She stopped and put her hands on her hips. "Grace, you're a council-woman in the most diverse city in the country. How can you talk like that?"

Grace matched Devry's stance. "I'm not talking about people who live in my district. I'm talking about the woman who slept with Conner, knowing he was married. I can do my job and hate the fact that my husband had sex with a white woman."

Devry rested her arms on her belly. "So this would be accept-able if Conner had bedded a black woman?"

Grace glared at Devry and swallowed the curse she wanted to spit at her friend. She turned away, swinging her arms, propelling herself forward, faster than she'd been walking before. But she could hold the pace for only a few minutes. She stopped, resting her hands on her knees.

"Are you okay?" Devry asked, breathing as if she'd been strolling.

It took a moment for Grace to look up. Perspiration poured from her hairline like slow rain, dripping into tear-shaped puddles on the sidewalk. "It hurts, Devry. Every time I think I'm over it, my heart aches again."

Devry pulled Grace into her arms. "I know, sweetie."

"And I feel like I don't have a right to hurt because of all the pain I caused Conner with my affair and . . ." She stopped, not knowing if it was her tears or that she was still breathing hard that made her pause.

"Of course you hurt, sweetie. But I'm scared of the hate that is resting in your heart," Devry said. "The woman who slept with your husband was Pilar Cruise, all those years ago." She paused. "The Pilar Cruise who was at your home is the dying mother who trusts you with her most precious possession." Devry took Grace's hands and rested them on her stomach. "She trusts you with her child. Nothing else should matter."

Grace smiled through her tears. "Every time I see Solomon, it gets easier. He's a joy. And quite the psychiatrist. He told Amber not to worry about Jayde because teenagers are crazy."

Devry laughed and squeezed Grace's hand. "Come on, let's go back. I'll scrape up some frozen waffles for you before you go to serve the city."

They walked several blocks, hand in hand, before Devry interrupted their silence. "That observation that Solomon made was a good one. Maybe one day, he and I can go into practice together."

Grace laughed and hoped that in the days ahead, she'd find a way to keep laughing.

It was almost noon when Grace stepped into her office, still smiling from her morning with Devry.

"The press conference is scheduled for tomorrow." Zoë's announcement made the smile fade from Grace's lips. "But I have a better idea," Zoë said. "My contact at Channel 2 wants an exclusive. You wouldn't have to do the conference, and Channel 2 would feed the other channels after they air the interview."

"Why would they want an exclusive? What did you tell them?"

"Just that you had a personal announcement."

Grace shook her head as if she doubted Zoë's words.

"Grace, you're not just a councilwoman. You're a Christian councilwoman. For now, everything you say is news."

"Yeah, so they can attack me," Grace said, seeing Sara in her mind. She sat behind her desk. An interview would be better than facing reporters who would be eager to put their own spin on the story. It was tempting.

"The interview is the better way to go," Zoë encouraged.

Grace remained silent.

"You and Conner could do it together, like Bill and Hillary's *Sixty Minutes* interview in ninety-two."

Grace imagined Conner and her sitting shoulder to shoulder, mighty in their offense against her assailants. "Can I review the questions ahead of time?"

Zoë shook her head. "Channel 2 doesn't do that."

"So my choices are a full interview . . ."

"Under friendly fire," Zoë interjected.

"Or a three-minute statement where I speak and then walk away. No questions."

"But the reporters won't make it easy. They'll be shouting questions. It'll be difficult not to address some of them."

Grace debated the options. "I'll keep it my way."

Zoë twisted her lips. "I don't agree, Grace. With an interview, the audience will be more sympathetic. They'll feel as if they know you, and they'll be able to relate to your pain. Then after the interview, I'll really be able to work it. And," Zoë paused as if she were about to make a major declaration, "it would keep Sara Spears away."

More temptation. Grace wasn't excited about facing her adversary, who would be slithering somewhere around the front row. "You make a good case, but the thing is, I'm not looking for sympathy. I don't want to do this at all because no one belongs in my business. I'm going to make it clear that I'm being forced into this by the media."

"You could do that in an interview."

Grace shook her head. "I'm going to make this statement alone. Not with Conner, not with the kids. Just me facing the people who voted for me." She paused. "And I want to look like the reluctant participant being bullied by the big bad media."

With a final nod, Zoë said, "Okay. The press conference stands. I'll prepare the statement. Do you want to give it to anyone ahead of time?"

Grace shook her head.

"It's scheduled for two."

Grace nodded as she thought about what awaited her. She wished she could do the conference earlier; she didn't want Sara preempting her, leaking whatever she knew. But she'd just have to leave this in God's hands.

Grace pulled a folder from her briefcase. "Here's the education plan."

"I'll summarize it and include a bit in the statement."

"Good. That'll show people where the focus should be: on the public schools and not in my home."

"Now I have something for you. Here are some résumés." Zoë slipped the bios one by one across the desk. As Zoë reviewed the names, Grace tried to concentrate on her chief of staff's words. But her mind raced with images of Pilar, Solomon, and Sara. It was going to be a long afternoon.

Chapter 45

There were times when Lexington's leer annoyed her, but tonight Starlight loved his gaze. She stretched her naked body, making it longer.

"You really are beautiful, Starlight." His words came from deep inside his throat.

"Get naked with me."

It took seconds for him to dispose of the starched shirt and navy suit. And with the smoothness of a sixteen-year-old, he lay atop of her. Starlight didn't direct him the way she usually did. Tonight, it wasn't his sophomoric moves that were going to please her. She lay moaning, wanting to edge him toward his peak. She wanted his quickness. She just hoped she could hold on.

She reached for the telephone. It took a moment for Lexington to notice.

The grimace on his face was between a frown and simper of arousal. "What are you doing?" His hands continued to fondle her.

"I have to make a call."

"Now?"

"Now," she said pushing his head so his lips would meet her chest.

He paused for only a moment before he returned his attention to her body. He moved with new urgency, excited about this twist Starlight brought to their union.

The telephone number was programmed into her phone in anticipation of this moment. She pressed the button, and as Lexington traced his tongue along her neck, she muttered an awkward prayer that her call would be answered.

She closed her eyes when she heard, "Hello."

"May I speak to Pastor Walsh?" she breathed.

"Speaking."

His voice was deep and rich, and she pulled an image of his face into her consciousness. "Pastor Walsh, this is Starlight," she said positioning Lexington on top of her. She wanted to be ready. "Pastor Carey asked me to call you."

"Ah, Starlight. How are you feeling this evening?"

She placed two fingers into Lexington's mouth, sighing as he sucked. "Just fine, Pastor."

"Starlight, I understand you had quite a successful program with Pastor Carey, and I wanted to discuss what you could do for me."

She closed her eyes as Lexington's tongue traced the curve of her waist.

Pastor Walsh said, "When would be good for you, Starlight?"

She opened her mouth. *Now,* she mouthed to Lexington. *Now.* She rolled over and straddled him, looking into his eyes as she said, "Pastor, any time would be good." She wondered if he could hear the quivering in her voice. She moved slowly, closing her eyes with her motion.

Sweat trickled from Lexington's forehead, and he moaned.

Pastor Walsh said, "I have some time tomorrow. Can you come to the church?"

She moved faster and almost laughed at his words. "I certainly can come . . . to your church, Pastor." She folded her bottom lip under her teeth trying to hold back the utterances fighting to break from inside.

"Starlight, are you all right?"

"Oh, yes, Pastor."

Lexington moaned louder.

"Not yet," she slipped.

"Excuse me?"

"I mean, we haven't set a time yet. What time tomorrow . . . do you want me to come?" she squeaked.

She could tell by the pastor's pause that he was trying to figure out what was happening on her end of the phone. She wondered what he would think. Would it turn him on?

"Ah, Starlight, why don't we try two?"

"I'll be there." She put her hand over Lexington's mouth as his eyes rolled back. "Good night, Pastor Walsh."

She clicked off the phone, and tossed it behind her. Moments later, the room echoed with sounds of their ecstasy. When she collapsed onto Lexington's chest, she wondered what she would do when she ran out of ideas. *Maybe I'll try a pastor,* she thought.

She sat up and looked down at Lexington. And before he could open his mouth, Starlight said, "I hope it was as good for you as it was for me."

Lexington balanced two mugs on a tray and closed the door with his foot.

"I think we scared Carletta this time." He chuckled. "You should have seen her. She was hovering at her door, doing her best not to peek into the hall."

Starlight waved her hand as she took her cup of tea. "She's heard us before."

He sat on the bed and let his robe slip from his arms. "She might have heard sex before, but tonight we made love."

She moved the cup to her lips and gazed at him over the rim.

"Don't you feel it, Starlight?" His fingertips traced a line along her face. "We're great together."

Outside she smiled. Inside she groaned and prayed that he wasn't going to start talking about marriage again.

"We're soulmates, Starlight. How much better could we be . . . really together?"

Why did he want to get married? But she let her smile convince him that her desires were the same.

"We shouldn't put our focus on too many projects," she said. His smile turned down, and she placed her mug on the night stand. "Let's get through the Revival." She put her arms around his neck and pressed her naked torso against his. "I wouldn't want anything to interfere with our wedding plans," she said before she kissed him.

His smile returned. "After the Revival."

She lounged back on the bed, picked up her cup, and wondered how much longer he was going to accept her excuses.

"Speaking of the Revival, I have some information." His tone was light and Starlight sighed, relieved. "We won't be able to get ten thousand into the arena. It only holds eight."

"Do you really think we can sell ten thousand tickets?"

He nodded. "We've sold six thousand tickets in the first week, and we still have four weeks to go."

She clasped her hands trying to hold her excitement within. "So we need to find a way to get two thousand more people in there."

"I don't know how."

She stood and paced in front of him. "There's got to be a way."

He stared at her nakedness.

She stopped moving. "Lexington. Look at me."

He cleared his throat before he lifted his eyes, meeting hers. "I don't know how we can get more in there unless we put chairs in the aisles on the balcony. But the city inspectors . . ."

She held up her finger, stopping him. "There's room for extra chairs?"

He closed his eyes as if the memory of the space was behind his eyelids. "On the balcony. But the inspectors won't allow it."

"How many extra chairs? What does it look like? What about downstairs?"

"I'll do some more work on this."

"Find a way to get another two thousand people in there." Before he could protest, she straddled his lap. "Come on, Lexi." She planted short kisses over his face. "You can make anything happen." She moved her lips to his. "After the Revival's a success, it's all about us."

"I love you, Starlight."

She smiled. When his eyes told her he wanted to hear the same, she kissed him.

Lexington's fingers teased her skin, and goose bumps rose all over her. But the excitement she felt had nothing to do with him. It was about the biggest event of her life. The Revival was sure to change her forever.

Chapter 46

Grace moved in front of the window, though she kept her eyes outside on the steps leading into city hall. She didn't expect to see any reporters. Most would park underground, then take the elevators to the press room.

She wondered if it would have been better to have the conference outside on Sixth Street. The city sounds of passing buses and honking cars would have been allies, drowning out her reluctant words.

There was a quick knock on the door, and Zoë walked in with a cup in her hand. "I thought you'd want some coffee." Grace nodded and took the mug. "We have five minutes."

"How many people are there?"

Zoë shrugged. "The room was half-full. But Sara Spears is there. Camping in her front-row seat."

Grace's sigh wasn't one of surprise. What was surprising was that when she'd searched the newspapers this morning, there was nothing about her pending announcement. Still, over coffee, she and Conner had pondered just what Sara knew. It had been four days since she'd called, and her silence was more ominous than when she was prancing in public.

Her cell phone rang, and she took it from her purse.

"Sweetheart, it's me. How're you?"

She inhaled. "Okay. It starts in a few minutes."

"I wish I was there. I could have waited out of sight."

"With reporters, there is no such thing." Grace chuckled. "If I'm asking them to keep my family out of the news, we can't give them a picture of us leaving this place."

Zoë tapped her finger against her watch.

"Conner, I have to go."

"I'll be praying. Call me." A short pause. "I love you."

He hung up before she could respond, and Grace took a final sip of her coffee. Zoë took her hand. They bowed their heads and prayed. When they finished, Zoë said, "You're going to be terrific, like always."

Grace smiled her appreciation, then walked through the connecting door to the press room. The murmurs silenced when she entered.

Zoë took a front-row seat as Grace positioned the microphone. She raised her head and looked into the crowd that eyed her with curious expectation.

She recognized many of the reporters—most had followed her campaign. Several of her fellow council members filled the last row, though she knew it was curiosity rather than support that had brought them.

Grace glanced at the front row. On her right, Zoë sat, sitting straight and filled with confidence. Then her eyes moved to the left and met Sara Spears's.

Grace cleared her throat. "Thank you for joining me. There are two issues I want to cover. One is on a personal level, and the other is professional. I will begin with the professional."

After much discussion, Grace and Zoë had decided to make

the announcement about Conner and Solomon last, making it easier to escape uninvited questions.

"As you know, my major goal during my freshman term is to work on our schools. There are many programs that I want to implement, including developing an initiative for the governor focusing on bringing prayer back into the classroom and special abstinence and drug education programs.

"However, due to the fact that I am newly elected, I will not be able to sit on the Education Committee." She paused and looked at Sara. Though a smile spread across her face, Sara folded her arms. "Still, I will forge forward with the programs that are important to me. To that end, I have established the Education Improvement Foundation."

Grace explained the foundation, which was yet to be formed but would implement her ideas—away from the political arena. When she glanced up, Grace noticed that some of the reporters' pens moved across their pads, keeping up with her words. But most were leaning back in the fold-up chairs, waiting for the second part of this conference—the part that was clearly more newsworthy.

"I will keep you abreast of the foundation's activities."

She paused and shifted the papers she held in her hand—her segue to the dreaded part two of this conference.

"Before I make my second announcement, I'd like to say that I am speaking reluctantly. I believe that my personal life should be private. However, due to pressure from various media . . ." She paused again, and stared, holding Sara hostage.

This time, Sara shifted in her seat. Grace wanted to cheer. Her adversary was squirming, and she wanted to hold onto the moment.

Grace continued, "I am coming forward so that the truth is told. I ask that after I make my statement, my family be left alone."

When she looked up again, the reporters were moving to the edges of their seats.

She took a deep breath. "Recently my husband and I were informed that he is the father of another child—a son, who until this point has lived in New York." She spoke as if the sentence were one word. She continued through the surprised sighs.

"His son is part of our family, and we will provide for him in every way: emotionally, spiritually, and financially."

The murmurings became louder.

"Of course, this will in no way affect my position as councilwoman. Professionally, I serve. Privately, please allow my family to work through this away from the public eye. Thank you very much."

With her final word, a gentle roar began, growing louder with each second until the shouting was full blast. Reporters' words rolled over each other as they hurled questions at her.

Zoë rushed to her side, eager to escort her away from the reporters. Over the rumbling, one voice waxed above the others.

"Councilwoman Monroe, do you believe it would be right for you to maintain your position, especially as a Christian, when it is obvious there is a lack of morals in your home?" Grace stopped at the sound of the scratchy voice. "And is it true that you've had a number of extramarital affairs yet you ran under a Christian platform?"

Grace turned around and glared at Sara.

"Come on," Zoë whispered.

The rumbles had died to scattered whispers, and the intense stares burned through her as the reporters waited for her response.

"Let's get out of here," Zoë said. Her voice had deepened two octaves.

Grace shook her head. She couldn't leave now and allow Sara's questions to hang in the air.

"If you answer one question, you'll be open to others," Zoë warned.

Grace took a deep breath and followed Zoë from the room. But before they closed the door, one last question made its way to her ears. "Is this the reason you and your husband are getting a divorce?"

Grace leaned against the closed door. She looked at Zoë, who stood, shaking her head. But her chief of staff would never say I told you so.

Grace said it for her. "Channel 2 would have been better." She paused. "Do you think we can fix this?"

Her smile was as fake as the Persian rugs sold on street corners. "Of course."

But Grace didn't miss the way Zoë lowered her eyes before she turned away.

Grace's cell phone rang the moment Frank scooped her into the car and screeched away from city hall.

"It's over?" Conner asked without saying hello.

More than you know, Grace thought. "Yes, and it was bad."

Conner moaned.

"I don't want to talk now." She shook her head, as if the action would rid Sara's words from her mind.

"Grace . . ." He stopped before he apologized, and Grace was relieved. She didn't want to hear his regrets right now. "Where are you going?"

"I had planned to go to the office, but I'm sure we'll be inundated with calls. I'm going home to regroup and thank God that I don't carry a gun."

"Sara Spears?"

Was it Sara, or was it you, Conner? her mind asked. "I'll see you later," she said without answering his question.

"Grace, I would come home now, but the Jacoby case . . ."

"That's fine."

It wasn't anger that made her click off the phone without saying good-bye. She just couldn't stand to hear his sorrow.

Grace leaned back and closed her eyes, replaying the press conference's end. Sara had scored first, but the game wasn't over. The ball was in Grace's court now, and when she emerged from this time-out, she would run all over Sara. By the time the final bell rang, Sara Spears would never mess with one of God's children again.

The shrill of the telephone startled Grace. She blinked at the bedside clock. It was three-thirty; she didn't realize she'd fallen asleep. Before she could say hello, she heard Solomon's cry.

Grace sat straight up. "Solomon," she called him calmly. "Honey, what's wrong?"

"My mother is sick," he sobbed. "She's on the floor."

"Where's Virginia?"

"She went to the store," he cried.

Grace was already sliding into her shoes. "I'm on my way. I'll be there in five minutes."

"Okay."

"When I get to the car, I'm going to call you from my cell, so answer the phone."

"Okay."

"And, Solomon, sweetheart," she said steadily to soothe him. "You're mom's going to be fine."

"Okay."

She barely hung up before she dialed nine-one-one. "This is Councilwoman Monroe," she said, then gave the operator Pilar's information. "Please, hurry. There's a little boy alone with his mother." Grace gathered her sweater, purse, and keys in one motion.

In the car, she called Conner. Marilyn answered with more cheer than usual.

"Marilyn, is Conner there?"

"No, Grace, but how are you?"

Grace rolled her eyes. "Fine. Where is he?"

"Well," she began so slowly that Grace wanted to scream, "he's at a deposition for the Jacoby case. He'll be back around six."

She moaned. "Please do me a favor." She paused, hoping that Marilyn heard her urgency. "Leave a message on Conner's cell for him to call me right away."

"Grace, what's wrong?" Her cheer was gone.

"Just call Conner. Leave a message the first time, and then keep calling until he answers. I'm on my cell."

"Okay, Grace. Call me if you need anything."

She waited at the red light ready to call Solomon. But as she looked at the numbers on the keypad, she stopped. What was Pilar's number? Oh, God, she thought. She closed her eyes. Please, Lord, what is the number? The car behind her honked, making her jump at the same time she opened her eyes. She turned the corner. What was the number? Well, she'd be there in five minutes.

But I promised, she thought, as her car swerved down the hill. She said a quick prayer and began dialing. When Solomon answered, she thanked God. "Solomon, I'm on my way. How's your mom?"

"She's still sick, but she's awake now. Do you want to talk to her?"

"No, sweetheart. I don't want her to move. But tell her I'm on my way, and so are the doctors."

Grace waited as he yelled those words to Pilar.

"You're doing great, Solomon. Thank you for being so grown-up right now."

"Okay."

She turned onto Pacific Coast Highway and double-parked in front of the apartment.

"Solomon, I'm outside."

"Okay." Then he hung up.

The moment she jumped from the car, Virginia came strolling around the corner with a shopping bag in each hand.

"Virginia!"

"Oh, my," Virginia shrieked when Grace told her the news. Together they ran through the hallway.

As Virginia put her key in the door, Grace yelled, "Solomon, I'm here."

He rushed to the door the moment Virginia pushed it open and squeezed his arms around Grace.

She hunched down, and held his face in her hands. "You and your mom are going to be all right." She wiped the tears that poured from his eyes.

"I'm scared."

"I know." She glanced over his shoulder as Virginia whispered to Pilar. A knock on the door tore her gaze away and she let the paramedics inside. Then she pulled Solomon onto the balcony, not wanting him to overhear anything he wasn't prepared for.

"Do you think my mother is going to be all right?" he asked, stretching his neck to watch.

Grace hugged him. "I think so, sweetie. But there is something that you and I can do."

His wide eyes asked, *What?*

"We can pray." She ran her hand over his head.

He nodded. "Okay. I pray all the time with my mom."

Grace smiled. "I would like to pray with you for your mom."

He held her hand, bowed his head, and closed his eyes. She followed. "Father, in the name of Jesus, we come to you with praise and thanksgiving because you are our wonderful God. Lord, our hearts are heavy now, because we are concerned about Solomon's mother. But we know, Lord, that you are a gracious and merciful God, and you will take care of her. And you will take care of Solomon. We know, Lord, that you are going to protect us all and help us through anything we have to face. Thank you, Father, for loving us. We love you. In Jesus's name we pray."

Together, they said, "Amen."

Solomon tried to bend his lips into a smile. Then he hugged Grace as if he never planned to let go.

"Mom," Grace yelled as she entered the house.

Lily rushed from the kitchen with a dish towel around her arm. "Hi, sweetheart." Lily kissed Grace, then looked down at Solomon. "I've been looking forward to meeting you." She hugged him.

"Solomon, this is my mother."

"Call me Nana. Just like Amber and Jayde."

Solomon nodded. The smile that he always wore had been missing for hours.

"Hi, Solomon." Amber stood at the bottom of the stairs.

"Hi."

Solomon's wide smile made Grace want to kiss her daughter.

Amber walked to Solomon and hugged him like she'd always known he was her brother. "I'm sorry that your mother is sick."

"She's going to be all right now." Solomon looked up at Grace, and she nodded.

"Do you want to watch TV with me?" Amber asked.

"Sweetheart, it's almost bedtime." Grace glanced at her watch. Then she added, "You can watch for a little while. I'll come in there in a few minutes."

Amber led Solomon away, while Grace followed her mother into the kitchen.

"Honey, you look tired."

Grace massaged her eyes. "It's been the longest day."

Lily put down the dish towel. "You need to rest."

"So everything is fine here?"

"Of course. The girls have eaten. Amber was getting ready for bed and Jayde . . ." She paused. "She's in her room. Been there since after dinner."

"Still in her mood?"

Lily nodded. "How's Pilar?" she asked as she joined Grace at the table.

"The doctors haven't said much. Conner's there making sure she gets settled." She sighed. "But, Mom, I don't need the doctors to tell me anything. Pilar's getting worse . . . fast."

Lily tsked.

"It's as if she's worsened since Conner and I agreed to take Solomon."

"That makes sense." Lily continued when Grace frowned. "Pilar knows that her son is going to be fine now. She doesn't have to try so hard to live anymore."

"I'm not ready for this."

Lily laid her hand on top of her daughter's. "You've known this was going to happen. This is God's will."

Grace pulled her hand away. *This isn't God's will!* she wanted to scream. *God doesn't take mothers from their children.* But she didn't have the strength to debate.

She stood. "I'm going to get the kids to bed."

"Do you want me to stay until Conner comes home?"

"No, Mom." She hugged Lily. "You could use some rest too, and I'm going to need you tomorrow."

Lily smiled. "I'll be here first thing."

They went into the family room, and Lily kissed Amber and Solomon. After she watched her mother drive away, Grace retrieved the bag that she and Solomon had packed.

"Come on, you guys," she said to the two who had settled in front of the television. "Time to turn in."

Amber clicked the remote, and she and Solomon followed Grace up the stairs.

"Where's Solomon going to sleep?" Amber asked.

"In your room, and you're going to camp out with Jayde."

"Okay." Amber turned to Solomon. "You're going to like my bed. I got it for my birthday."

"I saw your room the other day," he reminded her.

When Grace stepped into Amber's room, it was as if this was

the first time she saw the candy-pink walls and the lacy curtains that hung from the canopy bed. She laid Solomon's suitcase on the dresser.

"Amber, get your pajamas. We'll get your school clothes in the morning."

Solomon edged onto the bed and folded his hands. Grace watched his sadness slump his shoulders.

"The bathroom is right through there." Grace pointed, wanting to rescue him from his thoughts.

"But lock the door if you use it, or else Jayde will burst in," Amber nodded, giving advice from her experience.

Solomon frowned.

"Jayde's bedroom is on the other side," Grace explained. She cupped his chin in her hand. "Let me get Amber settled in, and I'll come back. Okay?"

He nodded, but said, "I go to bed by myself."

"I know." Grace smiled. "I just want to say good-night."

He tried to smile back.

"Good night, Solomon." Amber waved.

He tried to wave back.

Grace closed the door, wishing she could fill him with peace.

Amber knocked on Jayde's door. "Jayde, let me in."

"Sweetie, you don't have to scream." Grace knocked on the door and then opened it.

Jayde was sprawled across her bed with headphones covering her ears. Her head hung over one side and her feet swung from the other.

"Took the shackles off my feet so I could dance," Jayde sang off-key. It wasn't the first time that Grace was glad Jayde played the flute.

Grace tapped Jayde's shoulder. She jumped, jerking the headphones from her ears. Grace could still hear Mary, Mary blasting from the earpiece.

"Amber is going to sleep with you tonight," Grace said handing Amber her nightgown.

Jayde's mouth opened as wide as her eyes. "Why?"

"Because Solomon is staying in my room," Amber said before Grace could respond. She made a face, then went into the bathroom.

Jayde tore the earphones from around her neck and threw them onto the bed. "Solomon is staying in our house?"

Her daughter's question made her think back to the way her day had begun. She had to take crap from Sara Spears. She didn't have to take it from Jayde.

Grace folded her arms. "Yes."

"Why can't he sleep in your office, like you did?"

Grace grinded her teeth, took a breath, and held up her hand. "Unless you've started paying some of the bills around here, I don't want to hear another word."

Jayde scooted back on the bed. "I guess you only care about homeless orphans."

In less than a second, Grace grabbed Jayde's arm and dragged her from the bed.

"Mom," Jayde screamed.

Grace lifted her other hand.

"Mommy!"

She turned toward the voice. Amber was standing in the bathroom's doorway, her eyes filled with terror.

Grace's hand shook above her head, then she lowered it. It still took a moment for her to release Jayde's arm.

Jayde scampered away, her eyes wide with fear. She massaged her arm where Grace had held her with a death grip.

"I want the two of you to go to bed." Grace's voice was low and steady. "I don't expect to hear a sound from this room. Do you understand?"

Only their heads moved as they nodded. Their eyes were plastered on their mother, afraid that she might make a sudden move.

Grace backed out of the room, closed the door, and then leaned against it. She closed her eyes, praying that would hold back her sobs.

"Grace?"

She opened her eyes, and Conner was staring at her. She didn't know where the trembling began, but by the time it got to her lips, she ran into his arms.

"Sweetheart." He held her tight.

"Jayde said . . . then Solomon cried . . . and, Pilar's sick . . . and then Sara did . . ."

Conner squeezed her tighter, pumping the tears from her. And in her husband's arms, she released her pain from the day.

Chapter 47

It was the first time that Grace had seen Sara Spears's column so far front in the newspaper. Page three was a coup for the ACC leader.

Conner came out of the bathroom with a towel wrapped around his waist and another in his hand. He paused when he saw the newspaper.

"The headline alone will make you scream," she said before he could ask. "Councilwoman's Husband's Hidden Love Child."

Conner moaned.

"She's calling for my constituents to question whether I can truly represent them since I am not the moralistic, righteous, upstanding Christian that I claimed to be." Grace looked down at the paper and read, "Councilwoman Monroe is not an example that anyone can hold up—especially not the children that she claims to care so much about."

Conner settled onto the bed.

Grace continued, "She ends with, 'If Monroe wants to impart her Christian values on the people of this city, we suggest that she begin at home. When she can pull her family together, then maybe Angelinos will be willing to listen to her holy message. Until then, we hope that Monroe will do the righteous deed and place her letter of resignation on the mayor's desk by noon." Grace closed the newspaper.

Conner sighed.

Grace moved to the window. Outside, the air was gray, broken only by the weary palette of the homes planted in the Palos Verdes hillside: steel-blue, earthen-tan, dried-grass green. It seemed the city was in mourning.

Maybe the air's sorrow was a sign. Since she'd been elected, the challenges had been mounting, piling high on her family's emotional shoulders. Anything more was bound to break them.

Conner stood. "This is not about you, sweetheart. This is an attack on your faith."

Her examination of the view beyond her window continued. "But now the war's being waged against my family. It's not worth it anymore."

He spun her around so fast she rocked on her heels. "This is definitely worth it, Grace. People have been and will be touched by what you're doing and what you stand for. If you back away now, what will you be saying?"

She let a few silent moments pass. "I should keep on fighting."

"Fight the good fight."

She smiled. "Well, if I'm going to wage a war, I'd better get dressed."

"That's my warrior!"

In the bathroom, she turned on the shower, then looked in the mirror. She would fight for herself and for her family. She really didn't have to worry about her family's emotional burdens. With all they'd been through, they were definitely in the basement. It was time to start taking the elevator back to the top.

*   *   *

Conner waved to Amber as Lily drove around the driveway. He closed the door and smiled as he looked up to the second level. Solomon had been asleep when he checked on him earlier, but he was sure to be awake now.

He knocked on the door and stepped into the bedroom. His smile evaporated. Solomon was sitting in the middle of the pink bed with his knees pulled into his chest.

"Hey, buddy. How're you?"

Solomon's eyes were dry but full of sadness.

"Fine."

Conner sat on the edge of the bed. "Are you sure?"

He nodded, but then with quickness rocked to his knees and hurled his arms around Conner. "I'm scared."

"I know you are." Conner held his son as if there were no missing years. "But the doctors are working hard to make your mother well."

"Mom said there's nothing the doctors can do."

Conner swallowed the reassuring lies he wanted to offer and squeezed Solomon's hands. "Your mother is very sick, but the doctors are doing their best to keep her with us as long as they can."

Solomon's brown eyes became clearer. "Mom is going to die soon." He stated the words so calmly that Conner wondered if he understood what he'd uttered. He added, "Maybe we should pray so that God knows how we feel."

Conner nodded and held his son's hands. "That's a great idea."

"I'll do it," Solomon exclaimed. He closed his eyes. "Father, God, I'm scared. But I know that you don't want me to be. My mom told me that if I ever got scared, I should talk to you, and then I wouldn't be scared anymore. I want my mom to get well. Please help her, God." He paused. "And if she can't get well, please don't let her be scared and don't let her hurt. I don't want to see my mother cry. Amen."

Conner kept his head bowed a bit longer, blinking to soften the burning in his eyes. Then he pulled his son into his arms, holding him for the moment and all the days, months, and years that he'd missed with him.

"Can I see my mom today?"

"After you finish with your tutor, I'll take you."

It was the first time Solomon smiled. "Thank you . . . Dad." The statement shook from his lips as if he was unsure how his words would be received.

It took a moment for Conner to move, but his trembling matched Solomon's when he held his son once again.

The phones hadn't stopped ringing, and Grace was pleased that Zoë had called Claudia and two other staffers in. She didn't think she'd need an administrative assistant until she officially took office, but after yesterday's conference, Zoë decided they needed Claudia now.

Grace's fingers whished across the computer keyboard, and then she paused, reading the paragraph she'd written.

This was supposed to be her response to Sara's article. Zoë had the newspaper executives itching for her retort. But Grace hadn't decided if she was going to submit this. Her theory remained the same: the way to manage Sara was to pretend that she had leprosy.

Zoë knocked once and walked into Grace's office.

"I just got off the phone with Channel 2. They would still love to have you." There was hope in her voice.

Grace smiled at her chief of staff, who had reverted to her campaign manager's stance. The pencil was propped behind her ear, and her hands were filled with media contact sheets. Zoë was spinning this story.

"I'm sure Channel 2 does want me. Then this can be blown into a full-size scandal." She held up her hand, stopping Zoë's protest. "I know they wouldn't do that. I just don't understand the interest."

"Maybe it's a slow news month. But we need to find a way to control this."

Claudia tapped on the opened door. "Grace, your sister is on the line."

Grace sighed but said, "I'll take it."

Zoë pressed her lips together and shook her head as if she couldn't believe Grace would take a call over a discussion about a prime-time interview. "Think about Channel 2," she said, tapping her fingernail on the desk to emphasize each word.

Grace waved her out of the room, then picked up the phone.

"Good morning, Starlight."

"Grace, how're you?" she asked, then continued without giving Grace a chance to respond. "I saw the article, and I'm very upset. Is there anything I can do?"

Grace half-smiled. "No, but thanks for asking."

"I can't believe how they've gone after you." She paused. "You know, I have some important contacts. I'm personal friends with Senator Bonet."

Grace's eyebrows rose. Her sister's star was certainly rising.

Starlight continued, "She might be able to do something about Sara Spears."

"Short of pulling out her tongue, there's nothing anyone can do. And I support free speech."

"Well, let me know if you change your mind."

The bold knock on the door startled Grace.

"Starlight, hold a second." Grace covered the mouthpiece and called for Claudia to come in.

"There's a call from the principal at Jayde's school."

Grace nodded. "Starlight, I've got another call."

"Grace, if you need anything . . ."

"Thanks." Grace hung up and her hand shook as she pressed the button for the other line. "Mr. Thomas." Grace spoke without breathing. "Is Jayde all right?"

"Yes, Ms. Monroe. But she's been suspended, and someone has to pick her up."

"I'll be right there." She hung up without asking questions, though all kinds of queries sped through her mind.

Grace grabbed her purse and waved at Claudia before she barreled through the door. "I'll call you" was all she said.

She rushed to the car, grateful that she'd driven this morning. She trembled as she drove, imagining what kind of trouble had found Jayde. This morning, Grace had been sure that their lives couldn't get worse. But this was proof that she'd been wrong: they were still sinking toward what seemed to be a never-ending bottom.

"You're on top now," Lexington exclaimed as he burst into Starlight's office just as she was hanging up the phone.

She shook her head, her thoughts still with her sister.

"What's on your mind?"

"Nothing." She stared at the phone.

"I come here, ready to sing your praises and you're not interested." He settled into a chair.

She fingered the telephone cord. "I talked to my sister."

"Yeah, I heard about that article," he sneered.

"It's not fair."

He reclined. "You're feeling sorry for her?"

"No."

"Good," he said with narrowed eyes. "Because there's no need to focus on falling stars when yours is rising."

For the first time, she met his eyes.

He shifted under her stare. "I'm just saying that after the Revival, you're going to have everything that you deserve." He grinned. "There's no doubt about it with what I just learned."

Starlight rested her chin on her folded hands. "Let's hear it."

"Pastor Carey is on board. He's going to promote the Revival on his radio show. The announcements will begin this week."

"You're kidding." She dropped her hands. "That's major." But then she frowned. "How much does he want?"

Lexington sat up straight. "Nothing," he sang. "He said he's doing this for you, and the two of you would work out something later."

Starlight imagined what the pastor would accept as payment. She couldn't begin to conceive of the blessings that would flow if she bedded one of the most influential men in the city. She squeezed her legs together. "So how is everything else coming?"

He opened a folder that he'd laid on the desk. "We can get twenty-five hundred, maybe three thousand more people in there." His excitement had faded. "There's a bit of room on the first level, but the balcony has a lot of space. Still, that's a lot of people to put in that arena."

She brushed her hand through the air. "Others have stuffed more bodies in there than the law allows. Think of those rock concerts in the seventies and eighties."

"What about the Coliseum or the Forum?"

She sighed. "How many times do we have to go over this? The arena is less than half the price, and you're the one who said that by paying less, we'd have our chance at our first million-dollar event."

"I know."

"And with the Revival so close, it's too late to change."

"True, but still . . ."

Starlight held up her hand. "So what do we have to do?"

He sighed, his signal of surrender. "We won't be able to get permits for ten thousand."

Starlight shook her head as if he didn't get it. "Get the permits for whatever is allowed."

"We may have to pay off a few people. The promoter will know that we sold ten thousand tickets."

She stared at him for a moment. "Lexington, do whatever you have to. Just do it in cash."

He shook his head, stood, and slipped a paper across the desk. "The contract says that we must have security."

"It's a ploy to get more money."

"Can't get around it."

She sauntered toward him and perched on the edge of the desk. "Lexi, you'll find a way," she crossed her legs, letting the split in her dress expose her thigh, "to make this Revival the best."

He licked his lips.

She laughed. "Not now, Lexington. We have too much to do. We have to get through this Revival because you know what's waiting on the other side."

He nodded like a boy about to be rewarded with candy. "Our wedding," he breathed.

She smiled. "So meet me at my place tonight with the final details, okay?" She clutched his jacket lapels and pulled him toward her, letting her lips graze his. "I'll see you tonight."

She released him, and he backed out of the room. When he closed the door, she blew air from her cheeks. She smoothed her dress and turned to the window. The sun was finally bursting through the cloud cover, spreading its rays on the Hollywood sign and shining on everything around it, especially her.

Chapter 48

"Ms. Monroe, I'm sorry." Mr. Thomas, the headmaster of Wentworth Preparatory School opened his desk drawer. "This fell out of Jayde's backpack."

Grace frowned at the plastic bag, then noticed the tiniest white pill.

"It's Ecstasy," he explained.

Grace was sure she was about to faint, and she breathed deeply to force oxygen into her lungs. "Drugs?"

Mr. Thomas nodded. His eyes and cheeks drooped as if he felt sorry for her.

"Where did Jayde get drugs?"

Mr. Thomas's eyes pierced her. "I was hoping you could tell me, Ms. Monroe. Outside of one or two incidents over the past five years, we haven't had a problem with drugs in this school."

"We've talked to Jayde about drugs." Grace stared at the bag. "That was one of the issues in my campaign."

"I know," he murmured.

With his tone, Grace expected Mr. Thomas to add "you hypocrite!"

"We cannot tolerate this, Ms. Monroe."

From that point, Grace heard pieces of Mr. Thomas's lecture:

suspended for five days, must enroll in a drug awareness program. Grace barely breathed through her shock.

When Mr. Thomas stood, she did the same. He reached across the desk and shook her hand, dismissing her and her troubled daughter.

Grace walked on unsteady legs into the outer office where Jayde waited. With photographs of past presidents of the prestigious school staring down at them, Grace eyed her daughter. She turned and rushed into the hall. Jayde grabbed her backpack and ran after her mother.

The tapping of their heels along the polished floors was the only sound that filled the hallway. Grace moved as if speed would keep her anger at bay. Even when they got into the car, she remained silent.

She punched the number 1 to speed-dial to Conner's cell, but there was no answer. She thought about calling the office, but she didn't have the patience for Marilyn. Instead, she sped home, driving as she'd been walking. When she approached the hill that led to their home, Grace accelerated. She maneuvered the curves as if she were a NASCAR pro.

Jayde's breathing filled with fear, and Grace didn't know if it was her driving or that they were closer to home that made her daughter quiver. It didn't matter. She wanted terror implanted inside her child.

She slowed as she turned into their driveway, pulled into the garage, then closed the door, leaving them in the dimly lit garage.

Even after she turned off the ignition, Grace stared straight ahead. The shelves held remnants of normalcy: Conner's garden tools, the girl's Rollerblades, her old sewing machine.

"Go to your room." Her tone bore an ominous threat, and before she uttered the last word, Jayde scooted from the car.

Grace tried Conner's cell phone again, but there was still no answer. She slammed the phone back into her purse, then tapped her fingers on the steering wheel. When Grace finally got to the door, Lily was waiting.

"What are you doing home?" Lily sighed when she saw Grace's expression. "What's wrong?"

Grace shook her head, unable to find words. "Where's Solomon?"

"In the family room with the tutor." The frown remained on Lily's face.

Grace walked up the stairs. "Do me two favors, Mom. If Conner calls, please come and get me."

"Sure," Lily said as she watched Grace. "And what's the second one?"

Grace stopped at the top. "If you hear Jayde screaming, come up here and stop me from going to jail."

Lily stared at Grace for a long moment, then hurried into the kitchen.

Grace took a breath and opened Jayde's door. She was on her bed, waiting with her hands folded. It was becoming too familiar a sight.

Grace stood, allowing a lifetime of memories to travel through her.

From birth, Grace believed Jayde was destined to be a star. And Jayde had fulfilled her mother's vision, excelling at every milestone. When she entered school at four, she was able to read and write better than any first grader. She had maintained her overachieving ways, exceeding expectations in academics, shining in every sport she played. Grace was so proud.

"I don't understand," Grace said, speaking to herself as much as Jayde.

Jayde scurried farther back on the bed. She flinched when Grace sat next to her.

"I could be arrested for the thoughts I have right now."

Jayde sobbed.

"I'm going to ask you some questions," Grace continued calmly, "and I want each one answered truthfully." She left her demand suspended in the air before she said, "How long have you been taking drugs?"

Jayde looked up with tears welling in her eyes. "I'm not, Mommy." Gone was the mature confidence of her fifteen-year-old, replaced by the squeal of a toddler.

It took little effort for Grace to believe Jayde. From the moment Mr. Thomas shoved the plastic bag containing the pill in her face, Grace knew there was no way her child was taking Ecstasy. She couldn't explain the situation; she just knew her daughter.

But during their ride home, doubts had attacked her like darts as she wondered how many mothers were absolutely sure that their dope-smoking, crack-taking, heroin-injecting children were not strung out.

She turned to Jayde and lifted her chin.

Jayde's eyes overflowed with tears. "I know I'm not supposed to swear, Mommy, but I swear I'm not taking drugs."

Grace took a deeper breath. With the same tone and her hand still cupping Jayde's face, she asked, "Where did you get the Ecstasy?"

Jayde's lips quivered. "I don't want to get anybody in trouble."

She squeezed Jayde's chin—just a little—and stared into her eyes.

"I got it from Donald, Philip's cousin," she sang faster than a snitch on Death Row.

Grace lowered her hand. She wasn't sure if it was Jayde's words or the way she ground her teeth that made her head hurt. In the fleeting moment, millions of thoughts paraded through her. She wondered who she needed to tell about this. She wondered if she could have Donald arrested. She wondered if a jury would convict her for what she really wanted to do.

"Donald said that since I was feeling so bad, the pill might help," Jayde continued her confession. "I told him that I didn't do drugs, but he said that this time it was free."

Grace breathed so that her words would remain calm. "When did you see Donald?" Jayde lowered her eyes and remained silent through the tears that dripped onto her lap. "I'm only asking my questions once."

"I . . . I met him after school. I didn't go to tennis last week."

Grace swallowed. "And what did you and Donald do while you were lying to your father and me?"

"I didn't do anything, I promise. And I didn't think I was lying," she cried. "I just wanted to have some fun because I didn't think it was fair that I was on punishment and . . ."

Grace held up her hand. She stood because the thoughts of the capital offense that she entertained before returned. "I need to talk to your father. Until then, you are not to talk on the telephone. Don't turn on the TV or the computer."

"I have homework."

Grace glared at her. "You have five days to do your homework." She paused. "I don't want you to leave this room. Even if you have to use the bathroom, you'd better ask."

When Grace turned toward the door, Jayde said, "I'm so sorry, Mommy. I was feeling bad, and I didn't know what to do."

Grace could feel the blood squeezing from her heart as she watched Jayde trembling on the bed. There was really no difference between the two of them. She hadn't handled the news of Solomon well either.

Grace walked out of the room. It was a long journey to her bedroom, where she tried to reach Conner again.

"Grace?"

"Mom, I'm in my bedroom."

A moment later, Lily stood in her doorway. "Zoë needs you to call the office right away." Grace nodded. "And Solomon's finished with his tutor. I'm going to pick up Amber. Do you want me to take Solomon with me?"

Grace wanted to tell her mother to take all the kids. And to take Zoë and Sara and Conner and everyone else in the city.

"I think Solomon would like to ride with you."

"I already started dinner, so don't worry about that."

Grace flopped back onto her bed the moment her mother was gone. She didn't care about dinner. That was the very last of her troubles.

Conner leaned over the rail and lifted the pillow behind Pilar's head. "Is that better?"

"Yes." Her lips spread into a grimace of pain that was meant to be a smile.

Conner sat in the chair at the side of the bed. "I wanted to bring Solomon, but when I called, he was still with his tutor."

Pilar's grimace widened. "When I spoke to him last night, he sounded fine. But how is he really?"

"He misses you. And he's scared. But we prayed this morning. He has a lot of faith."

"And that's only one of the great things about your son."

Conner grinned. "It's still hard to believe."

"You've stepped into the role well."

His smile weakened. "I've always wanted a son."

Pilar frowned and tried to push herself up. "You feel guilty?" When Conner met her eyes, she forced her hand into the air. "Don't say that you're not. I hear it."

It took him a moment to respond. "It's not like Solomon was conceived under the best circumstances."

"But he was conceived and born, and has grown into quite a young man. That's the part you should be pleased about."

He nodded.

"I know I made a mistake not telling you." She paused. "I was afraid that you would hate Solomon." She shifted her eyes from his gaze. "And I knew you would never leave Grace." When she glanced back at him, tears filled her eyes.

"I understand," he said softly.

"And now you'll be with Solomon for the best years of his life."

He didn't trust himself to speak. He folded his hands under his chin.

"Don't be sad. I've had wonderful years with him," Pilar said, mustering cheer. "He was a beautiful baby."

"Spoken like a mother." Conner chuckled, grateful for the shifting mood. "Why'd you name him Solomon?"

Pilar tried to laugh but coughed instead. She said, "That is such a heavy name for a little boy, right?"

"Our son carries it well. I'm curious. I want to know as much as I can . . ." He bit his lip, stopping the next words—"before you die"—from pressing into the air.

"Solomon was my grandfather's name," Pilar said, rescuing both of them from returning to despair.

"I didn't know that."

"And I loved that name from the Bible. I was thinking about King Solomon and his beginnings. I guess that was a way to push my hopes, dreams, and desires onto him. One day my son would be king."

Conner chuckled.

Pilar lowered her voice. "And the situation in the Bible between David and Bathsheba wasn't very different from ours."

He nodded.

"Conner, there are some things I want to talk to you about." This time, her tone was the one that carried "before I die."

"Whatever you need, Pilar."

She was still for a moment. "I won't be going back to the apartment."

Conner sat up straight. "The doctors said that you'd be released in a day or two."

"But not because I'm getting better." She paused again. "I don't think I should go back. With Solomon, it's too risky. I need . . . a hospice." The request seemed to choke her. "I know there are waiting lists, but maybe Grace can do something."

Conner swallowed and prayed that she wasn't giving up. He wasn't ready. Solomon wasn't ready. "We don't need to talk about this now."

"Decisions have to be made."

"Well, maybe you can stay with us."

"Conner, please." Pilar smiled wanly. "Don't even think about asking Grace to move me into your house. She doesn't need to become my caregiver."

He paused. "I'll look into the hospice for you."

She nodded. "You should have all the papers you need." They sat in the sadness of the silence. Pilar pressed her lips together, making her already bloodless-looking lips paler. She said, "I want Solomon's name changed. I want him to be a Monroe."

Conner nodded. He couldn't speak.

"Maybe he could keep Cruise as his middle name," she said, as if she hadn't thought of that before.

"Yes."

More saddening stillness surrounded them.

"I didn't know what to expect when I came to Los Angeles all those weeks ago, but you've made this easy."

Conner thought about how the time had been for him. He remembered when he wondered if he would lose his wife. And how, even now, they struggled with Jayde. But in the end, he knew that Grace and their children would be alive to celebrate.

Conner took Pilar's hand. They sat together, allowing the past to converge with the present and understanding that no hope would allow them to share a future.

Conner frowned when he entered the silent house. Only the glow of the foyer chandelier lit the downstairs. He glanced at his watch, wondering how the time had slipped away. But it was only eight, though the house felt more like it was after midnight.

He peered into the kitchen. No signs of dinner. If it weren't for Grace's car in the garage, he would have thought no one was home.

He loosened his tie and climbed the stairs, struggling with each step. But he smiled the moment he opened the bedroom door and saw Grace sitting on the bed, with her legs stretched in front of her and her Bible resting on her lap.

"Hey, you." He leaned against the door frame.

"You sound tired."

He nodded, not noticing her tone. "It's been a long day." He moved toward the closet. "I'm sorry I didn't make it home earlier. I know you wanted to talk about the press conference."

"The press conference . . . was that today?"

He stopped, hearing her strain. "What's wrong?"

"I've been calling you for hours."

He patted his jacket and pulled out his cell phone. "I forgot to turn it back on. I was at the hospital."

Grace placed the Bible on the bed and folded her arms. "You were there all day?"

He nodded. "From about two. Pilar needed to talk."

Grace waited for him to go into the closet. Then she stood. "While you and Pilar were talking, Jayde was suspended from school for possession of drugs."

Silent seconds slipped by before Conner walked out, shirtless and surprised.

"What did you say?"

She repeated her words, a bit louder this time.

His eyes widened. "Jayde's taking drugs?"

"She said she's not, but there's still a problem, Conner, because she got the drugs from a nineteen-year-old she's been hanging out with instead of going to tennis practice."

Those words were the knockout punch, dropping Conner onto the bed in a daze.

"And then," Grace continued, not allowing a ten-count, "I had to handle your son because he thought he was going to see his mother today."

Conner massaged his eyes. "Was he upset?"

"That's one word to describe it. When I couldn't find you, Solomon was sure something had happened to his mother."

"Oh, no."

"I would've taken him to the hospital myself, but my mother and Devry had other plans. And with all that's going on with Jayde, I didn't want to leave the girls alone."

Conner sighed and stood. "I'd better talk to Solomon."

"Conner!" Grace took deep breaths to hold back her rising rage. "I just told you that your daughter was suspended, had drugs in her possession, and is seeing an older boy, and you don't want to talk to her?"

His forehead crinkled with confusion. "Didn't you already do that?"

"Yes," Grace exclaimed, losing her battle to keep her voice steady. "And I talked to Solomon too. Both of your children need you."

"Grace, Solomon is losing his mother."

"And Jayde thinks she's losing her father."

His shock filled the silence that followed her words.

Grace sighed. "I spoke to Devry this afternoon, and she said that Jayde's trying to get your attention." They sat together on the bed. "Jayde is sure she's losing your love."

"That would never happen."

Grace continued as if Conner had not spoken. "At the very

least, she thinks she'll start coming in second." She paused. "And with how you're handling this, she's right."

Conner held his head. "I thought Jayde could handle this. Amber's fine."

"Amber's seven. Jayde's a teenager experiencing emotions that she doesn't even understand. We throw this at her and expect her to handle it like an adult."

When Conner looked up, tears trimmed his eyes. "I want to do right by all of them."

"Oh, honey," she said, her anger fading, and she pulled him into her arms. "You're a great father. We just have to remember all of our children." She kissed him. "I'm sure Jayde's still awake."

Conner stood, and Grace followed him to the bedroom door where she waited while he walked down the hallway. He stopped at Jayde's room and knocked. When Jayde opened the door, he beckoned her into the hall.

Grace watched as Jayde took halting steps toward her father. Even thirty feet away, she could see the alarm in her daughter's eyes.

Conner and Jayde stood, staring for seconds before Conner embraced his teenager. Grace stepped into her bedroom as Jayde sobbed in her father's arms.

Chapter 49

"I told Conner what you said." Grace tried to wipe the weariness from her eyes. "But I'm still having difficulty wrapping my brain around all that Jayde's done."

"Jayde's traumatized. Once she understands that she's loved anyway, she'll get back to normal."

"I'd love to have that moody teenager back."

Devry laughed. "I'm going to remind you that you said that."

Grace chewed on the corner of her lip. "You really think that Jayde'll be all right?"

"As all right as any teenager can be. She'll get used to looking up and seeing Solomon. And she'll get used to sharing her room with Amber. She'll come around."

Grace sat up straight in her chair. She replayed Devry's words in her mind. "I've got to go. Speak to you later."

Minutes after their good-byes, Grace was still staring at the phone. How did she and Conner miss that?

She picked up the phone and dialed. "What time will you be home?"

"Is that an invitation?"

"I wish, but I'm exhausted."

Conner agreed with his laughter. It had been a full week filled beyond the normal school activities and lessons. There was the added pressure of making sure Solomon was comfortable while working with his tutor. And with Conner and Solomon's daily visits to Pilar and the preparations to have her moved to a hospice, the schedule had drained them all.

"So, if this isn't an invitation, what are you asking?" Conner was still chuckling.

"We need to talk about Jayde."

His sigh told Grace that his smile was gone.

"What's she done now?"

Grace frowned. "Conner, we can't think that every time Jayde's name is mentioned, something's wrong. This time, she's fine. We're the ones who messed up." She paused. "Why are Jayde and Amber sharing a room?"

His silence told her he didn't understand her question. She continued, "We're the ones changing Amber and Jayde's lives, but our daughters are the ones doing all the adapting."

"And Jayde had to give up her room, her private space," Conner said, then blew a loud breath. "What should we do?"

"I discovered the problem, Counselor. You find the solution." She hung up smiling, knowing that Conner was probably sitting with his mouth open. Maybe their lives would shift now to some semblance of normalcy.

Grace punched the intercom. "Claudia, could you come in here?" She was ready to get to work. It looked like home was finally going to be able to take care of itself.

Chapter 50

Starlight smiled as she sat across from the senator. Since that first time more than four weeks before, Starlight and Senator Bonet had met in the Bel Air lobby a dozen times.

"Starlight, Summer is already a new woman. Not only is she in school, but she got a part-time job at Ultimate Records." She paused. "I bet you had something to do with that."

Starlight lowered her eyes, then spoke to the senator through her downcast lashes. "Senator, Summer is doing this herself. I'm just bringing out what's already inside." Though her voice was soft and steady, her legs were shaking under the table. She knew rewards were waiting.

The senator laid her hand on top of Starlight's. "I owe you."

Yes, you do, Starlight's mind screamed. But she sat, cool as an ice block. She kept her breathing even, anticipating what was coming.

"You have delivered," the senator continued. "Now it's my turn." She pulled a folder from her briefcase and slid it across the table.

Starlight waited a moment before she opened it.

"If you can get these kinds of results with Summer, we need you in Washington."

Starlight's eyes scanned the first page of the proposal, searching for the financials. She turned the page and stared at the budget.

"I've discussed this with some of my associates, and this is our proposal. For the first session, with members of the Senate, senator's wives, and other influential women in Washington, we will raise enough to pay you fifty thousand dollars."

The senator continued, but her explanation met deaf ears. Starlight nodded, as if she was listening, but the last words she heard were "fifty thousand dollars."

For the last year, Starlight had received almost ten thousand dollars for each engagement. Her hope had been to reach fifteen, even twenty. But this . . . she was approaching the levels of some celebrities.

"I know that you need time to peruse this."

No, I don't, Starlight thought.

"There are probably items you want to add."

What else could I need?

"Of course, the fee is negotiable."

Starlight stared at the senator. The first thing she was going to do was train these politicians how to negotiate. She closed the folder. "I'll look over this."

Senator Bonet reached for her briefcase. "By the way, I really wish I could attend your Revival, but Summer will be there. And she's bringing a few friends."

"I believe the Revival will take Summer to where you really want her to be."

"She's already taking the right steps." The senator looked at her watch. "I have to go, but let's meet after the Revival. I want to hear all about it." She paused. "In fact, I'll have you over for dinner."

Starlight stood with the senator.

"After we've done the workshops in D.C., we may want to put together an East Coast Revival."

Starlight shook Senator Bonet's hand.

"Are you walking out now?" the senator asked.

"No, I'm going to finish my tea."

"Give me a call next week."

When the senator was out of sight, Starlight stared at the proposal once again. Then she signaled for the waiter.

"Yes, Ms. Starlight."

Her eyes roamed over the young man. He was twenty, maybe twenty-two or twenty-three, slightly built, probably a surfer from the way his blond waves curved over his head. She crossed her legs. "I'd like an apple martini."

"Coming right up."

She watched him saunter away, his black pants hugging his backside like a pair of new leather gloves. "Hmmm."

When the waiter returned with her drink, she smiled her thank-you. "Put this on Senator Bonet's tab."

He nodded and turned away, and as she watched him, Starlight leaned back, licked her lips, took a sip of the green liquid, and began her celebration.

Chapter 51

Grace's heels clicked along the antiseptic white tiles of the fourth floor intensive care unit. Although Pilar had been admitted three weeks before, this was the first time she'd visited. She felt these trips were for Conner and Solomon. She wouldn't be here now if it hadn't been for Pilar's call.

She stopped at the nurses' station and was directed to Room 407 across from the desk. Grace took a breath before opening the door. Though the window's shades were drawn, the room was still bright in its whiteness. She squinted before she stepped inside.

Although she had requested a private room for Pilar, there were no amenities. The room was institutionally bare, with just a single bed, a box-styled nightstand, and two plastic chairs in front of the window.

Every night, Conner reported Pilar's deterioration. The doctors said these were the final stages. There was nothing medication could do. But even with their prayers and that knowledge, she was worse than Grace had imagined.

Pilar lay still, on her back, eyes closed.

Grace took a few steps forward and stopped. She held her breath until she saw the thin sheet rise, then fall against Pilar's chest. She waited a few seconds, then turned back toward the door. But she'd taken only two steps when Pilar called her.

Grace forced a smile and faced her. "I thought you were asleep."

"I was, but I'm glad I heard you." She pushed a button on the remote wrapped around the bed's rail and raised the top half of the mattress. Still, she was reclining more than sitting up. "Thank you for coming."

Grace stood in place, wishing that she had questioned Pilar when she phoned. But she'd been so surprised by the call that she had agreed to Pilar's request.

"Please sit down." Pilar motioned toward a chair with the ease of a woman inviting a guest into her home.

Grace pulled the chair closer to the bed, sat down, crossed her ankles, and lowered her eyes because she didn't want to stare at the thin-skinned skeleton before her.

"You don't like being here."

Her words forced Grace to meet her gaze. "I'm glad to see you, Pilar. I'm just sorry you're here."

Pilar coughed, a long dry hack that emerged from her center. "I won't keep you." She gestured toward the water pitcher on the table.

Grace filled a small paper cup and handed it to Pilar. It took her a minute to finish the water, and then she crushed the paper in her hand. "I'm looking death in her eye. I thought I'd be ready, but it's very hard."

Grace opened her mouth to protest but changed her mind.

"I'll make this short, Grace." She coughed again. "There are two things I need to tell you." She paused. "First, you need to know that you were right about me."

"About what?"

"The DNA test."

Pilar coughed, and Grace's heart beat as if it were coming through her chest.

"There was a reason that I wanted the test done at NYCMC."

Pilar waited for Grace to speak, but when she said nothing, she licked her lips and continued, "I wasn't sure. I didn't know if Conner was Solomon's father."

Her relief did not stop her heart from pounding. She hadn't been crazy. But what would this news do to Conner? And Solomon?

"I had the tests done with my doctor because I wanted to get the results before they went to you and Conner. If they weren't the way I wanted . . ." She stopped. "But by the grace of God, Solomon is with his father."

Grace blinked, not sure she understood. "The results are . . ."

Pilar tried to nod. "Conner is Solomon's father. I don't want you ever to have any doubts. And if you do, please call my doctor. You'll know for sure that I'm telling the truth." She paused. "I had to tell you this because there is something I must ask of you."

In less than a minute, she'd gone from believing Conner was Solomon's father, to knowing he wasn't, and back again. Grace didn't know what to feel. Still, she said, "What is it, Pilar?"

Pilar pushed herself up further and twisted so that she faced Grace. "Please take care of my son."

Grace swallowed, needing to moisten her dry throat. "Conner and I have already . . ."

"I'm not talking about his father," Pilar interrupted.

Grace pressed her lips together.

Pilar continued, "I'm glad that Conner is in Solomon's life." She paused. "But to be whole, my son will need his mother, and I won't be here."

This time she couldn't hold her protest. "Pilar, you don't know that. The doctors don't have the final say. We have to trust God. We have to . . ."

"Grace, please." She held up hand. "I can't fill my time with hopeful words. I'm dying. I need to take care of my business."

Grace had no words to match Pilar's blunt ones.

"I am grateful to Conner but more to you, Grace. You have opened your home to my son." She paused. "Now I'm praying that you will open your heart."

Grace nodded and blinked back tears.

"Solomon will always have my love," Pilar said.

"He knows that."

"But I want to give him more than memories." She paused. "I want to give him a mother's love. I want to give him you."

Grace took Pilar's hand and waited for her lips to stop quivering. "Pilar, I don't want to replace you."

She nodded. "I know that. But I wanted to give you my permission . . . and my blessing. I don't want Solomon to have a stepmother. I pray that you can find a way to give him the same love you give your daughters."

Grace lost her battle with her tears as drops trickled down her face.

Pilar squeezed Grace's hand. "That's my final wish."

Grace nodded because a mass in her throat constricted her words.

Pilar exhaled and relaxed her grip on Grace's hand.

"I promise you, Pilar, I will take care of Solomon. I love him already." She paused. "And I will always remind him how much you loved him."

Pilar released Grace's hand. She pressed a button on the remote and lowered the bed's mattress. "Thank you," she said. Then she closed her eyes.

Grace sat staring at the woman who had given her husband his son. She stood, not sure if Pilar was sleeping. Grace held onto the bed's railing, leaned over, and kissed Pilar's cheek.

Pilar remained still, eyes closed, her breathing steady as if she didn't feel Grace's touch.

Grace stepped away, took a final look back, and walked from the room.

Through the hospital's halls, on the elevator, and then as she rushed through the lobby, Grace held her sobs. Once inside her car, she released the agony that had filled her chest from the moment Pilar uttered, "That's my final wish." Grace knew that she would never see Pilar alive again.

Chapter 52

Grace inhaled as she stirred the spaghetti sauce. She sprinkled oregano onto the top, then replaced the cover on the oversized pot.

"That smells good, Mom," Jayde said as she peered over her mother's shoulder.

Grace smiled as she watched her daughter sit next to Amber at the kitchen table. Jayde opened her history book and a moment later was engrossed in homework.

It was hard for Grace to believe that almost four weeks had passed since she'd been called to Jayde's school. But time was medicinal. As the days advanced, the anger that had wedged itself inside Jayde was fading, and in its place were glimpses of a teenager playfully teasing her younger sister, poring over magazines, and falling to her knees in gratitude when Grace told her that she could listen to her CDs once again.

Grace leaned against the center island taking in the view. Jayde, Amber, and Solomon sat, focused on their assignments. Usually it was only Amber and Solomon who did their homework in the kitchen. But when Jayde joined them tonight, Grace knew it was another one of her daughter's peace efforts. Jayde had been offering small treaties over the past weeks, beginning when she and Conner announced that Jayde and Amber would no longer be sharing a bedroom.

"Your mother and I have decided to give up our office so that you can all have your own room."

The three children had sat in silence at the news.

"Amber, we thought you'd like the new room," Conner said.

But it was Jayde who spoke up. "I'll take it."

Grace and Conner had exchanged surprised glances at Jayde's exclamation, but asked no questions.

"I need a change," was her explanation.

Grace thought it was Jayde's attempt to relocate her living quarters as far from Solomon as possible. But on the day the family joined together to paint the office-turned-Jayde's-bedroom from beige to sunshine yellow, Jayde had taken her first step toward peace.

"It's much easier with the brush, Solomon," Jayde had said when she noticed Solomon struggling with a roller on the baseboards. "Here. Use mine."

Grace had tried not to stare at her daughter, though she was sure she was witnessing a first. She had never before heard Jayde speak directly to Solomon.

As was his way, Solomon took the brush from Jayde with a smile that covered half his face. "Thank you," he had said as if he and Jayde had had many conversations.

The next day, it was Solomon who approached Jayde.

"I'm having some problems with math," he had said softly, standing in the doorway of Jayde's new bedroom, still smelling of fresh paint. "Can you help me?"

Grace eavesdropped from her bedroom, and when it took Jayde just minutes to explain the algebra problem to Solomon, Grace suspected that he was assisting the peace process.

Since then, Jayde and Solomon had maintained an affable relationship, though they often still looked like strangers when they passed in the hall. But Jayde's efforts were slowly lessening the tension that had become a sixth member of their household.

Although there had been moments when Grace doubted, their lives were working out. Solomon was part of the Monroe household, just as his mother wished.

The telephone interrupted her family reverie.

"Hello."

"This is Dr. Brotman from Cedar Sinai. Is Conner Monroe available?"

No more words were necessary. She turned her back to the children as she took the information that Pilar Cruise had passed away less than an hour before. She fought tears that wanted to fall for the woman who had first delivered heartache and then helped turn her family's cries to joy.

"Mom, are you okay?" Amber asked.

"I'm fine." Grace glanced at Amber, then Jayde, keeping her focus from Solomon.

Jayde closed her book. "Mom, do you want us to go upstairs and get ready for dinner?"

Grace nodded and turned away as tears burned her eyelids. It took a minute for the children to gather their notebooks, and when Grace heard their footsteps on the stairs, she collapsed on the counter.

Although it was expected, sadness still engulfed her—grief for the passing of a woman who would forever be a part of their lives. But what overwhelmed her most was Solomon.

"Excuse me."

She took a deep breath before she turned to the soft voice. Grace forced a smile when she faced Pilar's son. "Yes, honey."

"Was that telephone call about my mother?"

Her heart was falling. "The call was for your father."

His eyes told her that she hadn't answered his question. But he nodded and returned upstairs.

Grace didn't exhale until she was sure Solomon was in his bedroom. She reached for the telephone and dialed Conner's cell.

"Hey, babe, I'm on my way," he said. Without a breath, he added, "We settled the Jacoby case, and you're not going to believe for how much."

"Conner, Dr. Brotman called."

"Oh, no," he moaned, knowing the truth before she spoke it. "How's Solomon?"

"I haven't told him. I think you should."

"I'll be home in about ten minutes."

She put the phone down, turned around, and jumped. "Solomon, you startled me."

"I'm sorry." He took a step toward her. "You were talking to my father."

She nodded and turned away. "He'll be home soon. And then . . . we'll eat, okay?" She couldn't face him. When silence filled the air, she turned. Solomon was gone.

She allowed her tears, then wiped them away. She needed strength for Solomon and the girls.

Conner pulled Grace into his arms the moment he walked through the door.

"Are the children upstairs?"

She nodded. "They know something's wrong. Solomon asked if the call was about his mother, but I couldn't tell him."

Conner held her hand as they climbed the stairs and then knocked on Solomon's door.

When they stepped into the room, only Solomon's silhouette could be seen. He was staring into the darkness.

Wordlessly, he stood and bolted to his father.

Conner held him, letting love and comfort flow from his arms. "I'm so sorry, son," he whispered repeatedly as Solomon released his grief into his father's chest.

Grace turned on the nightstand light, then stood to the side. When Solomon turned to her, she knelt and gathered him into her arms, holding him until his tears began to subside.

"Solomon, your mother loved you very much," Grace said, still kneeling and barely noticing that her knees ached. She cupped his face in her hands. "You know she's with God now."

He nodded. *"For the godly who die will rest in peace."*

Grace's head jerked back as Solomon quoted Isaiah 57:2.

"My mother told me to remember that scripture when this time came."

With burden-heavy legs, he dragged to his bed.

Conner took Grace's hand and lifted her from the floor. "I want to tell the girls," she whispered.

They hugged before she turned to Solomon.

"We love you." She kissed the top of his head.

She glanced at Conner, and his smile delivered a million thank-yous that Grace knew were for much more than this night.

Grace stepped into the hallway, leaned against the wall, and closed her eyes, thanking God for harnessing her emotions in front of Solomon.

"Mom, did Solomon's mother die?"

Grace opened her eyes and looked into Jayde's. "Yes, sweetheart."

Her tears flowed, and Grace opened her arms, welcoming her daughter into her embrace.

"I feel so sorry for him. It must be awful to lose your mother."

"Yes, it is, sweetie." Grace stroked Jayde's braids.

Jayde sniffed and stepped back. "But we'll take care of him."

Grace grazed her fingertips across her daughter's cheek.

"You think I don't like Solomon, Mom, but I do. It was just hard at first."

Grace kissed her daughter. "Come on. We have to tell Amber."

Jayde nodded, but her eyes focused on Solomon's bedroom door. "Is he all right?"

"Yes, your dad's with him."

Jayde stared at the door for a moment longer. "After we tell Amber, I think we should go in there."

"Good idea."

"He needs to know that his sisters love him too."

Grace covered her heart with her hand. In the middle of this pain, Jayde was bringing her joy. She was sure now that her family would survive and thrive.

Chapter 53

Grace twisted, opened her eyes, and glanced at the clock. It was almost eight, but instead of the normal morning noises, silence surrounded her. Amber lay next to her, in the center of the king-size bed, and Jayde rested near the edge on the side where Grace normally slept.

Grace raised herself carefully, not wanting to disturb the girls. Jayde stretched as the mattress shifted; when her daughter settled back, Grace stood.

Still drunk from fatigue, Grace stretched and looked at her mirror's reflection. Her hair was flat against her scalp, all signs of her visit to her hairdresser forty-eight hours before gone. Her white shirt held wrinkles, evidence of her restless sleep.

She turned back to her bed and covered Amber with the comforter that she'd kicked to the floor along with her red socks. They'd all slept in their clothes after her daughters announced they were going to stay with her.

"We don't think you should be alone, Mommy," Amber had declared when Conner had fallen asleep holding Solomon.

Grace agreed. "Why don't you two sleep with me?"

The question had barely departed from her lips before Jayde

and Amber bounced onto her bed. It was after eleven when they lay down, but questions kept them awake.

"Is Solomon's mother in heaven?" Amber had asked.

"I believe so."

Amber was the first to fall asleep just after midnight. Grace had stayed awake with Jayde until morning threatened to reveal the first light.

"Dying scares me, Mommy."

Grace had tightened her arms around Jayde. "I know, sweetheart. But when you know the Lord, you don't have to be afraid."

"That's what Mrs. Watson said in Sunday school when we memorized 2 Corinthians 5:8." She paused. "Is it true that when we die, we are with God?"

"Is that what the Bible says?"

Jayde nodded. "If you're a Christian."

"Then it's true. You can believe everything God's Word tells you. That's why when you've accepted Jesus into your heart, there's nothing to fear."

"I know I don't have to be scared," Jayde said. "I remember when I was little and would get stomachaches. You told me to put my hand on my stomach and say, 'In the name of Jesus, my tummy doesn't hurt.' And it always worked."

Grace smiled. Many years had passed since she remembered those times—when Jayde pretended to be sick to get her mother's attention away from the new baby.

"I should just say," Jayde began, interrupting her mother's memories, "In the name of Jesus, I'm not afraid."

Grace held her tighter.

It was after five the last time Grace glanced at the clock and then drifted to sleep.

Now she took a final glance at the girls before she stepped into the hallway—and almost collided with Conner.

"Good morning," he said, pulling her into his arms.

"How's Solomon?"

"Still asleep." He glanced behind him. "He woke up in the middle of the night, and we talked. He cried a lot, but Pilar prepared him and he's strong. Sometimes I forget he's only twelve." He paused. "I checked on you and saw that my daughters were taking care of their mother." He smiled. "We have three special children."

She returned his smile and held him, thinking of Pilar, grateful to have her husband so near.

"I need to go to the hospital and make arrangements." Conner hesitated. "I hope Solomon is going to be all right without a funeral. But I want to do what Pilar wanted."

"I'm sure she talked to him about that."

He nodded. "Are you going to be all right here?"

She nodded. "The children will sleep for a few more hours, and I called Zoë last night."

Conner looked down at his sweat suit. "I'll sneak into the bathroom and clean up." He kissed her before he tiptoed into their bedroom.

Grace walked down the hall and opened Solomon's door. He was asleep, his eyes shut tight. Grace tiptoed inside and eased onto the bed.

Her eyes stung with old tears as she stared at Conner's son.

She was still staring when Solomon stirred. He smiled when he opened his eyes.

"Good morning." She smiled and rubbed his head gently.

"Where's my dad?"

Her smile faded a bit. Conner's son. "He had to take care of some things, but he'll be right back. How are you feeling?"

This time, it was his smile that dimmed. "I'm sad."

"So am I." She paused. "Are you hungry? You didn't eat last night."

He shook his head. "I'm tired. Can I go back to sleep?"

She nodded in understanding. Even children grasped the perfect escape of unconsciousness.

She stood and turned toward the door, but before she put her hand on the knob, he said, "Would you stay with me, please?"

Her smile was restored, wider than before. She took Solomon into her arms. In just minutes, his breathing returned to the steady tempo of slumber.

As he slept, she filled her head with memories that she didn't have of his childhood and drew mental pictures of his future. With each moment that passed, Grace held the boy tighter. Pilar's son. Conner's son. Her son now.

Chapter 54

"Starlight! Starlight! Starlight!"

She smiled into the darkened half-moon-shaped arena. Starlight held her arms wide to the thousands, receiving their adoration.

It had been this way from the beginning, when more than an hour before she had walked onstage. The audience had been told to be silent as she glided onto the platform in her white silk wide-legged jumpsuit trimmed in gold. She'd stood in the middle of the stage, pressed her hands together, bowed, and said, "May the light forever be with you and yours."

The ten thousand were supposed to return her greeting in the same manner, but instead, a deafening roar filled the arena.

Since then, it had been difficult for Starlight to speak through the continous screams and ceaseless stomping. She loved this passion.

"What we're going to do today is celebrate life," she said at the beginning. "Celebrate that you are part of the universe."

When she held her hands to the stage's ceiling, the crowd followed.

"Celebrate!" she shrieked into the microphones. "You are a star, and I am your light."

The applause roared like thunder.

"This is about energy that you need to grasp now, take into the world, and be the god that you were designed to be. Stand and receive your measure."

Howls mixed with their applause.

"Dance! Dance to celebrate life!"

The multitudes began to jump, twist, and turn.

Since that point, Starlight had been able to speak only a few sentences at a time.

"I am here today to teach you what has taken me to the highest level that the One meant for all of us to achieve. You too can have millions in the bank. You can live anywhere you want. You can drive any luxury car you desire. First, you must recognize that you are god. Recognize your supremeness."

The cheering that followed kept Starlight silent for almost ten minutes.

"The key is to believe in yourself. Believe that you can accomplish every dream because you are a god. The Higher Being gave you the capacity to become greater than the creator. Yes, yes, yes!" She clapped her hands.

The crowd followed.

"*For all the promises of God . . . are yea,*" she said quoting part of 2 Corinthians 1:20. It had been Lexington's idea to include scripture. "God says yes to your being great. God says yes to your having all that you desire. Yes, yes, yes," she yelled, working the crowd into a greater frenzy.

She smiled. One more scripture for good measure. She looked at her notes—the cheat sheet that Lexington had created with Bible verses that might fit her message.

"The Higher Being says, *What things soever ye desire, when ye pray, believe that ye receive and ye shall have.*"

It worked. The roar was louder than before.

"You can have whatever you desire. If you believe, you will receive!"

Through the cheers, Starlight glanced at her watch. This was supposed to be five hours, but after ninety minutes, the crowd's cries told her it wouldn't last that long.

"Believe and achieve!" Starlight yelled because she was too exhausted to say more. The fever that she raised with that exclamation would give her time to rest and enjoy these moments.

The crowd's roar created a rumbling that made the entire arena tremble. Starlight closed her eyes. This was where she belonged, in the center of the light. This was why she did this: to bask in the affection. And it didn't hurt that in the end, Lexington said they would clear a million dollars.

The screams were much louder. It was wonderful to be in the midst. The arena quaked. She was adored.

"Starlight!" She squeezed her eyes tighter. They were worshipping her.

It was the tug at her hand that made her open her eyes. She blinked, then squinted when a wave of dust and debris accosted her.

The dark powder, inches thick, billowed in front of her, filling the air with a dense mixture of concrete chunks and ash. She snapped her eyes shut as Lexington dragged her backstage.

"We have to get out of here," Lexington screamed above the others.

"What's going on?" She coughed into her hand, trying to clear her lungs.

"The building—it's falling," he cried, pulling Starlight through the screaming bodies that packed the staircase.

Starlight's heart pounded as she bumped through the crowd, tripping as Lexington dragged her faster than she could move.

It had taken minutes to get from the limousine into her waiting room when they arrived. But now as Lexington crushed past others running toward safety, the minutes were much longer.

When the day's light finally greeted them, Starlight jerked her hand away from Lexington, bent over and coughed, releasing the grit that was floating inside her chest. But Lexington gave her only seconds. He grabbed her hand and pulled her through the maze of screamers.

Moments later, Lexington shoved Starlight into the car. "Go," he yelled to her driver.

She coughed, trying to clear the dust from her lungs and the thick ash from her tongue. "What happened?" she asked hoping that what he'd said before was not true.

Lexington's breathing was labored as he looked through the back window. "Part of the building collapsed."

"Oh, my God." She didn't dare follow Lexington's gaze. His wide eyes told her all she needed.

"Maybe we should go back," she said, through the fear that rose from her toes and filled her completely.

He shook his head.

"But suppose someone is hurt?"

He looked at her for only a second, before he turned his eyes and his body away. "I'll make some calls." He pulled his cell phone from his pocket and dialed.

Starlight closed her eyes and listened to the succinct communication. She heard only words that defined disaster: *collapsed, injured, ambulances.* It was when he said *police* that she opened her eyes and stared at the back of his head.

Her mind couldn't comprehend this. She remembered that she was speaking and that people were screaming. She told them to dance—they were dancing in their seats. She told them to believe and achieve—they chanted. After that, only confusion.

Lexington hung up the phone. "It doesn't look good."

"Tell me." When he didn't answer, she peered in his eyes. "Lexington?"

He shook his head. "The balcony collapsed, Starlight." He grimaced. "Too. Many. People."

She tried to clear the thick knot expanding in her throat. "You don't know that for sure."

His thoughts came through his eyes. Then he turned toward the window.

"Where are we going now?" she croaked.

"My place." He remained turned away. "Don't want to be tracked down at the penthouse."

She nodded, even though he wouldn't look at her. He believed they needed to hide, but what were they running from? She trembled at the answers that whirled through her mind.

"Too many people." His words replayed in her head.

She closed her eyes, and for the first time in a long time, she wished that she could pray.

Starlight paced the narrow space that formed the living room and dining room as Lexington held his cell to one ear and his land phone to the other. His words, quick and short, made her shudder.

She stopped in front of the balcony, a square concrete box that overlooked one of the ponds scattered throughout the apartment complex. These ponds, with water cascading over the rocks, were the only reason she enjoyed Lexington's apartment. She melted to the sound of tranquility in the middle of Culver City.

But today the pond's waters were still. Just like the leaves on the trees. Not even the air moved.

"Okay, keep me posted," she heard Lexington say. He clicked off his cell phone. "I'll get back to you," he said into the other phone.

He sank into one of the plastic-covered chairs that surrounded the octagon-shaped dinette table.

Starlight took slow steps to him and waited until he raised his head.

"It's bad." The fire that Lexington carried in his eyes was gone, extinguished by the words he'd just heard. He dropped his head again in defeat.

Starlight sat next to him. "Tell me everything." She tried to sound strong, but she managed only a whisper.

When he looked up, the tears that clouded his eyes made Starlight change her mind. She didn't want to hear what he'd heard.

Lexington's lips quivered. "People may be dead."

She shook her head.

"The balcony collapsed. No one knows if everyone got out."

She stood and rubbed her hands along her arms, trying to warm against the chill that streaked through her. She began to pace.

"Starlight." She could feel Lexington behind her. "It was the balcony. Where we added the chairs. Where we put the extra people."

His words poured guilt into her soul. She covered her ears, unwilling to hear more.

"We put too many people in there," he yelled, breaking through her barrier. "Twenty-five hundred more than capacity."

She whipped around, almost striking him, he stood so close. "Why are you telling me this?" she hissed.

He leaned away. "You asked." He reminded her as if it pleased him.

Her chin fell to her chest.

"It won't take long for the investigators to realize what happened."

She raised her head, stared at him, then grabbed her cape from the couch and stomped toward the door.

"Starlight, we have to talk about this."

She opened the door and rushed into the hallway, but his words followed her. "The police will be coming."

She pressed the button for the elevator.

"I'm not going to take the fall alone."

She turned toward the Exit sign.

"I will tell them what I know."

She stopped her steps but didn't look back. A moment later, she ran down the stairs.

Outside, her eyes wandered up and then down Green Valley Circle, finally spotting her driver. She was standing in the middle of the street when the limousine slowed in front of her.

"Take me home," she said. She closed her eyes as the car rolled toward the freeway. But her mind wouldn't close to Lexington's words: "I'm not taking this fall alone. I will tell them what I know."

She shivered, his threatening tone settling in her mind. Surely she couldn't be held responsible.

It wasn't my fault.

The arena was over twenty years old. It must have been an earthquake or something else that made the building fall.

It wasn't my fault.

"Dance! Believe and achieve. Dance!"

Her own words taunted her—the last ones she remembered before the gigantic plume of dust ensconced her.

It wasn't my fault.

The more she silently recited the mantra, the more she thought about Lexington and the fear in his eyes and the threat in his voice.

A husband cannot testify against his wife.

Her eyes snapped open at that thought. *Where did that come from?* But as she closed her eyes again and settled back into the seat, she began to wonder if Lexington had been right. Maybe they should have been married.

Chapter 55

"Mom, I can't believe we're not going to have a funeral for Ms. Pilar," Jayde said as if a major crime had been committed. "We have to . . . for Solomon."

"We're honoring Pilar's wishes. Funerals can be sad, and maybe she didn't want Solomon to remember her that way."

Jayde sighed, then slinked into her bedroom. Minutes later, she raced across the hall, interrupting Grace as she sat at the desk they'd moved from their office into their bedroom. "I have an idea."

As Jayde explained, Grace listened and marveled at the metamorphosis—how the wrathful child had transformed into the compassionate one.

Now Grace recalled that conversation she and Jayde had had two days before as they all made their way toward the ocean. It hadn't taken much to implement Jayde's plan: a few phone calls, a talk with Conner, and then she and Conner taking the idea to Solomon. Their son had sat silently at first. Then he rushed into Jayde's room and hugged her.

As the group strolled down the boardwalk, no one noticed the seven who moved past southern Californians zipping by on skateboards, moseying by with hands filled with snacks from the

Santa Monica eateries, or just sitting on the weatherworn benches revering the sun, sand, and surf.

They stopped at the edge of the promenade, and though no one said a word, they formed a small circle.

Pastor Ford spoke first. "Solomon." She smiled as she said his name. "We're here today to celebrate your mom's life. I know you're sad because you'll miss her. But you can be glad because your mother knew God, and now she's resting with Him."

Conner put his arm around his son.

"Is there anything you want to say, Solomon?" Pastor Ford asked.

He shook his head, but then began to speak as if a thought suddenly came to him. "My mother was a good mom because she taught me about God, and she loved me."

Everyone in the circle nodded.

Pastor Ford looked at the rest of them. "Does anyone else want to speak?

For seconds, no one moved. Then Amber stepped to the center of the circle. "I want to tell Ms. Pilar that we will take care of Solomon."

"I agree," Jayde said, though she kept her place.

Pastor Ford nodded as the ocean breeze blew her shoulder-length hair away from her face. When almost a minute of silence had passed, Pastor Ford opened her Bible. "I want to read a scripture." As she flipped through the pages of her book, she asked, "Solomon, do you know what it means to mourn?"

He nodded. "It means to be sad."

"Yes," the pastor agreed. "Let's see what God says about that. Matthew 5:4 says, *Blessed are they that mourn: for they shall be comforted.* Solomon, when you tell God that you're sad and that you're mourning, He will put his arms around you and comfort you, making you feel better, just like your mom did when you were feeling bad."

It was the first time Solomon smiled since they'd begun this trip after the second church service this afternoon.

Solomon looked up at Conner. "Is it time?"

"Yes, son."

"I want to go first."

Solomon kissed the pink balloon, then allowed the string to slip through his fingers. When he said, "Good-bye, Mommy," and then waved as the balloon drifted over the blue brine, Grace blinked.

She looked up, shielding her eyes with her hand from the sun's light, and watched the balloon glide toward heaven. With the others, she stayed still until Solomon's salute was just a sliver in the sky. One by one, the others released their tributes to Pilar Cruise, whispering their own farewells.

They stood until the seven balloons became one with the sky. Then without words, they turned away—first Conner with his arm around Solomon, next Grace, holding a daughter's hand in each of hers. Behind, Pastor Ford followed with Lily.

As they made their way to the parking lot, Grace's cell phone rang.

Before she could say hello, Chandler said, "We're on our way to the hospital." He spoke so loud that Grace had to hold the phone away from her ear. "The doctor said it will still be a few hours, but another Monroe is on its way."

Grace made the announcement to the others. The sorrow that

had circled the group just moments before was replaced with excited expectation.

"I'm going to have a new cousin," Amber chirped.

"Me too," Solomon said, and took Amber's hand.

Grace slowed her steps, letting the group move ahead. She turned back to see if she could find any signs of the balloons they'd just released. She saw nothing. The symbols of death were gone. This day had become about life.

Grace filled her mother's coffee cup and then sat at the table and wrapped her hands around the warmth of her mug. Although June burned its sun's rays through the kitchen window, Grace relished the heat her cup radiated, taking away the chill that still filled her from this morning's boardwalk ceremony.

Behind them, the television played on the counter, though the sound was only one notch above mute. Grace made no moves to turn up the TV's volume. She and Lily sipped their drinks, savoring the quiet. Conner had taken Amber and Solomon with him to the office to pick up the final Jacoby documents that had to be delivered to the courts in the morning, and Jayde had been furloughed for the first time in a month. This was precious downtime.

The sun was sinking, shifting the kitchen's shadows when Lily said, "Solomon did well today. He's really adjusting, isn't he?"

Grace nodded. Although surprise was in her mother's tone, Grace held no amazement. For the few months that Solomon had been in their lives, Grace knew there was something special about the boy—something different that allowed him to see, hear, feel, know, and understand better than those around him. Whatever grew inside him would get Solomon through and beyond his mother's death.

"Have you spoken to Starlight?"

The ends of Grace's lips turned up slightly at her mother's question. Weeks ago, she would have cringed. But the challenges her family had borne through the spring led to a renewed mind this summer. What was important two months ago wasn't so now. And, the reverse was true too. She was going to make some kind of peace with Starlight.

Grace shook her head. "It's been about a month since I've spoken to her. With all that's been going on . . ."

Lily held up her hand. "I understand. I had planned to attend her Revival and didn't even get the chance to call and tell her that I wouldn't make it." Lily's eyes fixed on the television. "Grace, honey, turn that up," she said.

Grace followed her mother's glance as a photo of Lexington Jackson flashed across the TV screen.

"The Police Commissioner has announced that the District Attorney will be involved in the investigation as criminal charges may be brought in the collapse of the arena. As reported, the arena collapsed yesterday during a motivational seminar given by Starlight, a national speaker who is a resident of Los Angeles. There are unconfirmed reports that fifteen people are still missing. Now, here's Victor Blume with a look at today's weather."

"Oh, my God. The arena collapsed?" Lily pushed back her chair, scraping the legs across the tiles and rushed to the telephone. As she dialed, Lily walked toward the foyer.

Grace pressed the remote, turning from channel to channel

for more news. But when there was nothing, she lifted the Sunday newspaper from the table where it had stayed since it'd been delivered that morning.

Her eyes widened at the headlines—a double-column front-page story on the arena's collapse. Her face stretched longer with surprise as she read. It was the final lines of one article that made her shudder: investigators suspected that illegal permits had been issued to fill the arena beyond capacity. "'It makes me sick to think that people may have lost their lives due to greed,' the District Attorney stated. 'If this is the case, those involved will be prosecuted to the full extent of the law.' "

Illegal permits? There had to be a mistake. She and Starlight had many disagreements, but there was no way Starlight would put money ahead of safety.

"Was there anything in the paper?" Lily asked, returning to the kitchen.

Grace tucked the front page between the folds of the Calendar and Lifestyle sections. "Nothing much. What did Starlight say?"

Lily shrugged, her face bunched in a frown. "She said that everything was all right. That part of the arena collapsed, but that she's fine and everyone got out."

Grace's eyes narrowed, but she kept what she'd read to herself.

Lily returned to the table and sipped the last of her coffee. She smiled, but a smile that was full of doubt and concern.

"Why don't you go over there, Mom? I'll drive you if you want."

She shook her head. "Starlight doesn't want me there. She's resting from all of the calls she's had to take." Lily paused. "I can understand that." But her tone said that she didn't understand at all. "There's nothing to worry about." The creases in Lily's forehead deepened. "Starlight said everything was fine." Lily lifted the empty coffee cup to her lips and sipped as if she were swallowing liquid.

Grace took a deep breath, sat next to her mother, and covered Lily's hands with hers. She prayed that there was nothing more to the story than what her mother said. But the twisting in her stomach told her that was not so.

Chapter 56

Starlight jumped from the couch when she heard the pounding on her door.

"Carletta," she yelled, before she remembered that she had tucked her maid away with relatives two days ago. She didn't want Carletta around in case the media began snooping or the police came questioning.

But as the pounding continued, she wished that her maid was here. Fear tied her to the couch as the violent knocking matched her heartbeat. Was this the manifestation of her nightmare? The one she'd dreamed for two nights where the police arrived in the blackness of the night and towed her away.

It wasn't my fault.

No one could get up to her apartment without being announced—except the police. She turned toward the window, and the morning sun cast its rays into the room, making her squint. In her nightmare, it was always dark. Right now, she was sitting in the middle of light.

The light freed her, allowing her to take slow steps toward the door. She peered through the peephole and sighed with relief.

"I've been trying to reach you for two days, Lexington," she said the moment she opened the door. But her words faded and she frowned, following his movements as he lunged past her. Though he was dressed in his trademark suit, there was nothing familiar about him. It was apparent that he'd slept in his clothes. And from the stubble on his face to the odor of his body, she could tell that he hadn't spent any of the last forty-eight hours caring for himself.

But that didn't minimize her anger. "Why haven't you returned my calls?"

He stared but didn't answer.

"Lexington, I'm still in charge. You work for me."

He grunted, a combination of a moan and a laugh. "So you're the boss, huh, Starlight? The boss of what?"

She swallowed. "I've been calling to find out if you have any more news."

He slumped onto the couch. "You haven't been watching television?"

She shook her head, although she'd seen every breaking report and had read every front-page article. But she wanted to hear his words.

He glanced at the dining table where two days of newspapers were spread. "I don't have anything to add. Nothing but bad news. I'm surprised you haven't been contacted yet."

She lowered herself next to him. "Contacted by . . ."

"The police," he finished before she could ask.

"Why would the police contact me?"

He looked at her for a long moment, then released a laugh as if she was one of the queens of comedy.

She ignored his snickering. "Have they contacted you?"

His laughter stopped. "Are you worried?"

She shook her head.

"Then you're dumber than I thought."

Her eyes and mouth opened wide at his words. All reverence was gone. Now his glances and his words were filled with contempt.

He stood. "I just came over to see if you were worried yet."

She stood with him. "Lexington, talk to me. What's going on?"

He moved to the table, picked up the *Los Angeles Times,* and held the front page across his chest like a banner. She'd read the paper several times, but now the headline screamed at her: "Arena Collapse Under Investigation."

"It's all here," he said, waving the paper in the air. "People are still missing, probably dead. It's nothing but chaos—except for one thing: the cause has been determined." He paused. "Too many people in the balcony. And we know how they got there."

"Lexington, none of that is our fault. We had permits."

"That we paid a lot of money for."

She wanted to tell him that there was no "we." He was the one who had paid for the permits.

"And I paid for everything with your money," he said, stepping on her thoughts. Then his eyes added his threat—the words that he'd uttered once but that had echoed a million times in her mind—"I'm not going to take the fall alone."

Although her heart pumped faster, she forced a smile. With unsteady legs, she sauntered toward him. "Why are we fighting, Lexi?" she purred as she wrapped her shaking arms around his neck. "We're in this together."

He chuckled. "You got that right."

She resisted turning away from his reeking breath. Instead, she tightened her arms and leaned in. But before she could meet his lips, he jerked away.

"I have to go."

"Why?" She hoped she didn't sound as desperate as she felt. "I thought we'd spend some time together. We haven't done that in a while."

He laughed. "Now you want to be with me? The other day you wouldn't even talk to me."

"Why are you acting this way?"

He glared. "I just came by to make sure you understood my position." He paused. "When they come to me, Starlight, I'm telling the truth."

Her eyes flared. "You speak as if I have something to fear."

His stare was as intense as hers. "You do."

She squeezed her hands into fists. "When it comes down to it, Lexington," she paused, her tone now one of steel, "who do you think they'll believe?"

Her words chipped his armor. The smirk he'd worn since he arrived dissipated.

She softened. "I don't want to fight, Lexi. We're on the same side."

"There are no sides," he said sadly. "There's only what's right." He waited a moment before he turned toward the door and walked from her sight.

She stared at the paneled double doors, still smelling his presence. When minutes passed and she hadn't willed his return, she turned away. No matter how much she wanted him to, he didn't come back and pull her into his arms, reassuring her that they would be all right, helping her to plan the strategy that would keep them safe.

She walked slowly to the door and locked it. She didn't need

Lexington Jackson. There were many others who would help her. She picked up the phone and dialed. Senator Bonet would be the first.

"I'm sorry. As I told you before, Senator Bonet is unavailable."

Starlight sighed. Since she had met the senator, she couldn't recall one time when she wasn't available. Either Senator Bonet was in her office, or Starlight was dispatched to her cell phone.

But today she'd been told the same words for two hours.

"This is an emergency, Carole," she pleaded with the assistant, who had always gushed over her.

"When the senator is available, she will call you."

Starlight hung up and tried to harness her runaway thoughts. She breathed deeply, wanting to return her heart's pace to normal.

She picked up the phone again and dialed Summer Bonet's apartment, allowing the phone to ring twenty times as she'd done fifteen minutes before.

"No," she said aloud. "I am not going to think this."

But as she'd done after she called Summer's number before, she rushed to the table. Her heart pounded as she searched the paper, even though she knew the names of the injured and missing had not been released. But it didn't matter because Summer couldn't possibly be among them. She'd given the senator's daughter VIP seats, only rows from the stage. All of the damage was in the back.

There was nothing to worry about, her mind told her, although her heart debated the other side.

She glanced at the clock. It was after noon, and she was still in her robe. She hadn't even had her morning coffee. Nothing was as important as forming her protective alliance.

She looked at the phone. It was too soon to call the senator again, but maybe it was time to strengthen the hedge around her.

For the first time in days, she smiled as she picked up the phone. With the people she knew, there was no way the police would come knocking.

She dialed the private number and was surprised when a woman's voice answered.

"May I speak with Pastor Carey."

"Who may I tell him is calling?"

"Starlight."

"I'll see if he's available."

She heard muffled words, and Starlight strained to understand.

"I'm sorry, the pastor is not available."

Starlight's heart fluttered. "May . . . may I leave a message."

There was a pause. "If you want."

"Please tell him that I need to speak with him immediately."

Before she hung up, Starlight knew that either her message would not be delivered or worse—it already had been. And Pastor Carey's message had been delivered to her, as loud as Senator Bonet's.

She was a pariah.

Her friends were fading, while her enemies circled.

Chapter 57

It had been exactly twenty-four hours since Grace had received the call. And now she beamed at her sister-in-law as Devry held her two-hour-old son.

Grace and Conner had stayed in touch all night, expecting a baby by morning. But when Conner had called before the sun even shone and there was no new Monroe, he had paced their bedroom as if he were in the delivery room.

"Don't you remember?" Grace had chuckled. "First babies take their time."

Two hours after noon, Chandler Anthony Monroe II screamed at the world.

Now Grace cooed when the baby's pinkish-brown toes peeked, then wiggled from under the birthing blanket that swaddled the rest of him. In an instant, she was transformed to another space—when she had held her babies for the first time. She'd loved Jayde so much she worried whether there was enough room in her heart for another child. But the moment Amber had been placed in her arms, her heart expanded. It was then that she first yearned for a third—a boy.

"You have a son, Grace."

She took her eyes from the baby and looked at Devry. She wasn't sure if she'd imagined the words or if her sister-in-law had read her mind. But when Devry smiled, Grace decided it didn't matter. Whatever voice spoke, it told the truth: Solomon was Conner's and her son.

"He's beautiful," Grace said, returning to her nephew.

"I know."

They laughed together.

"I'd better go so that Conner can see him. He's dying to see this Monroe child."

Devry nodded. "Chandler is probably telling Conner tall tales about how his son has already spoken his first words."

"And Conner would believe him." She kissed Devry on her forehead and turned to the door.

Before she stepped from the room, Devry said, "Grace, we both did good."

Grace smiled at her friend.

"We had a tough labor, but God was working. We have beautiful sons."

She did read my mind, Grace thought. She smiled and walked from the room. The moment she stepped into the hall, she could hear Chandler's laughter as he waited with Conner at the other end of the hall.

Grace smiled. Yes, they'd all been through quite a labor. She began to tick off the challenges in her mind, but then decided against it. No need to look backward. But she did pause. And looked up. And said, "Thank you."

*   *   *

Grace moseyed into their bedroom. "All of our children are accounted for. Amber and Solomon are almost asleep and Jayde," she paused for a second, "well, she didn't feel like talking." Grace smiled. "I am glad to have that teenager back." When Grace turned to Conner, his eyes were still buried inside the newspaper. She frowned. "Starlight?"

He nodded. "It's getting serious. There's a full-fledged criminal investigation, and the district attorney's throwing around charges that could carry prison sentences."

Grace rested her head on his shoulder. "Starlight hasn't returned my calls. Mom keeps saying everything is fine. She must not be watching the news."

Conner laid the newspaper aside. "Did you hear anything at the office?"

Grace shook her head. "Zoë tried to contact her sources, but she couldn't squeeze out any information. That's what scares me."

Conner nodded in agreement. "Only the most serious investigations are so secretive."

"Starlight is not guilty."

"No one has accused her of anything."

"The implications are there. They keep talking about her organization and the illegal payoffs. If there were any payoffs, I would bet her assistant had something to do with it." She paused. "Hopefully, I'll find out something tomorrow at city hall."

"Well, all we can do is let Starlight know that we're here."

"And we can pray."

Conner turned off the light and laid back. As she lay in his arms, Grace squeezed her eyes, thinking of those who tonight were praying for the safe return of loved ones who were missing or injured in the arena collapse. She gave thanks to the Lord that with everything they had been through, the five of them rested under the same roof tonight.

Conner's arms tightened around her, and Grace knew that her husband was praying and giving thanks for the same blessings.

Chapter 58

"It's been more than forty-eight hours since the collapse of the arena, a major disaster for the city," the Channel 2 anchor droned.

Starlight flipped to Channel 5: "Because of the high profile of this tragedy, Commissioner Roby is moving to wrap up the investigation as soon as possible. He has been speaking with everyone involved."

"He hasn't spoken to me," Starlight muttered. Although she feared the police coming to her door, what scared her more was the eerie quiet. No one came by, and her telephone rang only when her mother or sister called. The silence ignited her fear, making it impossible for Starlight to function beyond rising from bed for more than going to the bathroom.

She pressed the mute button on the remote before she turned to Channel 9. But not even silence provided relief. Underneath the Halle Berry look alike anchor, a banner sputtered across the screen, updating viewers on the latest: "Fifteen still missing."

Starlight shuddered. She clicked off the television, but less than a second later, turned it back on, flipping to CNN. There the news had nothing to do with her. But within ten seconds, her picture flashed on the screen. Then a camera panned the site of the collapsed arena.

"What is this?" she yelled, wondering why CNN would be covering the story. Starlight crawled to the bottom of her bed and rested on her knees. Moments later, she covered her mouth with her fist.

"Senator Lynnette Bonet viewed the site where her daughter attended the religious Revival two days ago. Though the senator refused comment, a spokesperson said that the Bonet family is positive and still praying that Summer Bonet will be home safely."

The camera zoomed in on the senator as she was rushed by assistants past the screaming media. The senator's eyes and much of her nose were covered by oversized dark glasses. But Starlight didn't need to see the senator's face to feel her pain. It was clear in the slump of her shoulders and the stagger in her steps.

"The senator is determined to assist in any way she can. Whoever is responsible will be brought to justice." It was one of the assistants who spoke before he jumped into the car that whisked the senator from the scene.

With shaky fingers, Starlight clicked off the television, then threw the remote against the balcony door. She didn't look toward the noise; her eyes were fixed on the black television screen.

It took effort for her to inhale, then exhale. The knot in her throat threatened to keep life's air from her lungs. She couldn't move, even though she'd been resting on her knees for long minutes.

You're in the right position, a voice whispered. *Pray.* She frowned at the foreign words coming from inside. Why should she pray? And what would she say anyway? Could she pray for Summer? If there was a God, He would answer that prayer. She closed her eyes and began. "Dear God . . ." She paused, trying to remember words from long-ago Sunday school lessons. But though she pressed, nothing came to mind. She collapsed onto the bed, releasing her anguish and wishing that she'd never met Dr. Carr.

Chapter 59

Grace twirled in a slow circle, her eyes absorbing the blank walls of the ten-by-ten office. She'd been told she would inherit whatever Samuel Douglas left behind. Her legacy was the ecru-colored blinds that covered the two poster-size windows.

She smiled. She'd be more effective with her personal belongings surrounding her. It was better this way, since she planned on holding this position for the two terms the law allowed.

A knock at her door, and her quick glance snatched her smile away.

"How are you, Grace?"

"What are you doing here, Sara?"

"Nice office."

Grace folded her arms and waited as Sara strolled around the room, eyeing the blank walls as if she were perusing a museum. She pursed her lips and revisited all the plans she'd had for Sara Spears. Plans that included Sara losing her job, being disgraced in public, and ending up at the head of a soup line on Skid Row. But those thoughts had evaporated from her heart. Pilar's death had delivered a different perspective.

Love your enemies, bless them that curse you, do good to them that hate you, and pray for them which despitefully use you, and persecute you.

Grace thought about Matthew 5:44, a scripture she'd learned as a child. But while the verse was much easier to memorize than live by, she had decided to leave the hate to Sara. There were greater challenges for her to overcome. The challenge now was to get Sara out of the office.

"I know you're here to harass me, Sara, but why? You won. I'm not on your Education Committee. I made my statement about my husband. What's left?"

"News flash, Grace. The world doesn't revolve around you."

"I thought your world did."

Sara chuckled. "I want a statement about your sister. About her arrest."

Her heart skipped, even though she was sure Sara was lying. "Your information is wrong this time, Ms. Spears."

Sara looked at her with the confidence of a psychic. "Sources tell me Starlight will be picked up within the next few hours."

Grace's heart beat faster, but she refused to give Sara joy by letting her see her building anguish.

"Well, you've delivered your news, so you can leave. I have work to do."

Sara swung her purse over her shoulder. "Just wanted to give you a heads-up."

Sara disappeared as quickly as she'd come. Grace waited until she could no longer hear her footsteps before she pulled her cell from her purse. By the time she pressed the number for Conner and Marilyn put her through, she was rushing down the long hall of the city building.

"Conner, Sara Spears told me that Starlight is going to be arrested."

"For what?"

"I don't know." Grace rushed into the sunlight. "I'm on my way over there."

"Did you call her?"

"No. If she's home, she won't answer. But I've got to find out what's going on."

"Okay, I'll make some calls. Tell Starlight I'm here for anything she needs."

"Thanks, sweetheart." She slid into her car. "Can you call Mom? I don't want the girls or Solomon to watch TV until we know what's going on."

Grace hung up. Her head pounded with the belief that Sara was a liar, but every beat of her heart told her that Sara spoke the truth. How could her sister be responsible for the collapse? Starlight would never put anyone's life at risk. An image of Starlight's assistant flashed through her mind.

By the time Grace turned onto the Santa Monica Freeway, she was convinced that Sara had lied. Yes, the police probably did want to talk to Starlight, but only to find who was responsible. This would be over before the day ended.

"Yes," she said aloud.

But the twisting in her stomach delivered a different message. And when she could no longer ignore the churning, she prayed.

Chapter 60

"Hello," Starlight answered.

"The deed is done."

"Who is this?" The Caller ID showed the call was from Lexington's cell.

"Come on, Starlight. You know me . . . very well."

She swallowed. "Lexington, I've been trying to reach you."

"I've gotten all your messages. The deed is done," he slurred.

She could almost smell the liquor through the phone.

"I've talked to the police," he said before she could ask. "I told them all about you, the illegal permits, the extra people, everything."

She was surprised that her heart was still beating.

"They're coming for you. Coming to take you away," he sang.

She remained silent. There was nothing to say.

"We shouldn't have done that." His slurring was replaced by sobs. "People could die." He paused. As suddenly as his cries came, they left. "But you were greedy," he spat into the phone.

"And you are weak, Lexington Jackson." She slammed the phone down.

She leaned back onto the couch, lifted the paper cup she'd filled before the phone rang, and swallowed the liquid that was as clear as water. It burned her throat, but she relished the feeling. It reminded her that she was alive.

She piled the empty cup on top of the others. There were at least twenty now. She stared at the paper monument before she flicked her finger against it, toppling the tower to the ground.

Lexington Jackson was spineless; she'd always known that. But she'd never bet that his weakness would take away everything she had accomplished. She could very well be going to jail.

Jail. Jail. Jail. The word rolled through her mind. How ridiculous that she could be sent to prison. She wanted to laugh at the absurdity. She wanted to cry at the reality. She leaned back on the couch, closed her eyes, and did both.

Chapter 61

"You can go up, Ms. Monroe."

Grace had held her breath while the concierge called Starlight's apartment. She rushed to the elevator, not exhaling until she pressed the button for the penthouse.

But a minute later, when the elevator doors opened to Starlight's apartment and she rang the doorbell, she held her breath again.

Starlight opened the door, then turned away, leaving Grace standing in the hall. Grace followed her into the living room.

The sun should have been shining its light, but the massive windows were hidden by purple silk sheets that covered the glass and were stapled to the walls.

Newspapers were spread across the floor, the pages opened to pictures of the arena. Paper cups were scattered everywhere. Grace glanced through the room, looking into the kitchen and the hallway, searching for signs of other life. She realized her sister was alone.

She settled onto the couch at the opposite end from where Starlight sat. She wanted to reach across the blanket between them and pull her sister into her arms' safety.

But Starlight leaned away, pushing herself into the depths of the couch's cushions. She pulled the belt on her robe tighter around her waist.

"I guess you've heard." Starlight wiggled her fingers through her short curls that lay flattened on the right side of her head.

"Some of it. I've called you quite a few times."

"I know." Starlight's gaze dropped to the cordless phone.

"Tell me what's going on."

Starlight shrugged. "You've seen the news."

"I don't believe them."

For the first time, Starlight met her sister's gaze. "Thank you."

Grace edged closer. When Starlight didn't move, she placed her hand on top of her sister's.

Instant tears filled Starlight's eyes. "I'm in trouble, Grace."

The soft squeeze of her hand told Starlight to continue.

"I don't know what happened. The Revival was supposed to help." Her sobs began. "One of the missing is Senator Bonet's daughter."

"Have you spoken to Senator Bonet?"

Starlight shook her head. "No one will speak to me. Not even the police have called."

Grace exhaled. Sara had been lying.

Starlight said, "Lexington called this morning. He gave the police his statement."

More relief rushed through Grace's veins. This would be cleared up now.

"Lexington told how I paid for the illegal permits."

Every muscle in Grace's body twitched with her sister's words.

"I guess he made a deal." Starlight glanced at the clock. "I should be getting dressed." She spoke as if friends were coming for lunch.

Millions of thoughts collided in Grace's mind. People hurt, some missing, a senator involved. The charges could be serious. Could her sister be charged, convicted, and sentenced to time in a concrete-walled, barbed-wire-trimmed prison with murderers and thieves? She closed her eyes, needing to block the image of a small gray cell with bars so thick, the steel hid Starlight's face from view.

Her eyes snapped open. "Starlight, Conner and I will help you. He's already making calls."

"Thank you, Grace." She paused. "I've had days to think this through. You've always tried to tell me . . ."

Grace raised her hand, halting Starlight's words. With gentle fingers, she wiped a tear from Starlight's cheek. "None of that matters. Just remember you have family who love you."

"I'm scared."

Grace fought her own tears. "You're going to get through this."

The ends of Starlight's lips turned upward into a grimace filled with fear. "That sounds like a guarantee."

"It is."

Starlight stared at her sister for a moment, then turned away. "Don't talk to me about God right now, Grace."

"That's the guarantee you need."

Starlight lowered her head, remembering that when she tried to pray and when she asked God for help, nothing came. "God can't do anything for me." Starlight thought of the scriptures she'd used in her messages. And at the Revival, it was after she quoted the last scripture that the arena collapsed. God's wrath. "He won't listen to anything I say."

"You're wrong. He wants to hear from all of us, especially those who are hurting. And He has given us an open line to Him to use at any time. We have that right. We can get through any storm because He is a God of grace."

Starlight chuckled, though there was no joy in her sound. "God of grace. Sounds like He belongs to you."

"To me and you."

Starlight paused for a moment. "You always sound so sure when you talk about God, Grace. How do you know? How do you know for sure that everything you believe is real?"

Grace waited, wondering if her sister could feel the answer in the silence between them. "It's what's called faith. I just believe." She paused again. "I know what I know. But even if I'm wrong, isn't this a better way to live, Starlight?"

The ringing telephone startled them, and Grace was surprised when Starlight reached for it.

Her sister was silent for a moment before she asked, "They're on their way?"

Grace trembled for both of them.

Starlight dropped the cordless phone. "I know he wasn't supposed to call," she said as if a welcomed guest had been announced by the concierge. "But Rick has always liked me. It pays to have someone on your side."

"Jesus is on your side," Grace said as if time was moving too fast. "All you have to do is ask Him to forgive you and ask Him into your heart. He'll take it from there."

Starlight stared at Grace, her dark pupils a laser beam to Grace's heart. "Will He keep me out of jail?"

Grace nodded. "He will . . ." Her lips shook as she prepared to utter the next words. "If you're not supposed to be there. But whatever, He will help you survive." Starlight blinked as if she was trying to believe her sister's words. Grace continued, "But I'm talking about the broader picture—making sure that you're saved and have a better life, no matter what happens. Talk to God. Take hold of your rights . . . Mabel."

Starlight's head jerked back at the sound of her birth name, but then three swift knocks on the door captured their attention.

They stayed still until the knocks came again, stronger this time.

Starlight stood first.

Grace said, "I'll get the door if you want to get dressed."

Starlight nodded and walked from the room. Grace waited until she heard the bedroom door close before she opened the front door.

Two detectives stood, dressed in what could have been matching blue K-Mart suits.

One squinted as if he recognized her. "Ms. Monroe?"

She stepped aside, motioning for the detectives to enter. "My sister is getting dressed. She'll be out shortly."

"Your sister? Starlight?"

Grace nodded.

The other detective looked down the long hallway. "There's no other way out of this apartment?" His words were a demand to know.

Grace wanted to scream. She was a councilwoman. Her sister was a well-known speaker. Neither was a criminal. She pressed her lips together before she said, "No. My sister wasn't dressed. She'll be out in ten minutes." She motioned toward the living room, giving an invitation to the uninvited guests. "Would you like to wait in here?"

The detectives exchanged glances, and then the one who recognized her nodded.

"We'll give her five minutes," the one who didn't believe said.

Grace crossed her arms and led the detectives inside. The friendlier one sat; the other stood. Both stared at the sheets that covered the windows. Grace leaned against the wall and watched them. And all three eyed the clock over the fireplace, counting the minutes, waiting for Starlight to appear.

Starlight clasped her hands behind her back and cringed as the cold metal of the handcuffs embraced her wrists.

"You have the right to remain silent."

There's nothing I have to say, she thought. *What words can I give them to free me?*

"Anything you say can and will be used against you in a court of law."

Lexington had given the police what they needed to use against her, though she wasn't sure what he'd said. Whatever, it was enough to gift her with the metal bracelets that clasped her hands together.

"You have the right to an attorney. If you cannot afford one, one will be appointed to you."

Starlight almost smiled. There were few things she couldn't afford. She twisted and then squealed inside when the metal cuffs cut into her wrists.

"Do you understand these rights as they have been read to you?"

For the first time, Starlight looked up and into her sister's eyes. Grace had said that she had a right. She had a right to God.

As she looked at her sister, Starlight noticed the way her palms met inside the handcuffs, similar to the manner in which she greeted her followers.

May the light forever be with you and yours.

If she bowed now, the handcuffs might break her wrists.

"Do you understand these rights?"

It took Starlight a moment to understand the detectives were waiting for a response. She understood her rights—all of them.

She nodded and took a final look at Grace.

I love you, Grace mouthed.

Starlight stumbled, almost falling. She wanted to reach out and grasp those words. But her hands were not free.

The detectives helped Starlight regain her stance. As they moved her forward, she closed her eyes. Although her lips didn't move, her heart did, and she remembered the words from long ago. "Dear God, I know that I am a sinner in need of a Savior. Please come into my heart." She wondered if she was ready to say that prayer.

They moved into the hall, away from the apartment that she cherished and into the elevator that opened only on her floor. As she was led through the crystal-adorned lobby and finally into the day's light, she heard her sister again: "He is a God of grace."

When the detective eased her into the back seat of the unmarked car, Starlight took one last glance at the sky and knew then that God had enough grace for her.

Truth Be Told

1. In the beginning of the novel, Grace and Conner seem like the perfect married couple. But as the story unfolds, it becomes clear that Conner has not been completely truthful with his wife. If Pilar had not brought her son forward, would Conner have ever told Grace about his affair? Knowing the history of Grace and Conner's relationship, what is Conner's bigger betrayal: having the affair or failing to reveal it? Conner has his reasons for not telling Grace about Pilar. Do you think they are valid? Should a married couple be truthful about everything?

2. Grace's sister, Starlight, longs for Grace's approval and acceptance. Nevertheless, Grace remains very critical and judgmental of her sister. Discuss the sibling rivalry between Grace and Starlight. How did it begin? Is Grace jealous of Starlight's success? In what ways are Grace and Starlight alike?

3. Lily, Grace's mother, chides Grace for not inviting Starlight to her city council win celebration. She stresses that "Family is the most important thing"(page 10). How is the importance of family handled throughout the novel? Discuss how Grace and her family must redefine their notions about family.

4. Starlight is a motivational speaker who coaxes women "to rely on our power within"(page 74). Do you believe Starlight's motivations are sincere?

5. Lexington, Starlight's business partner, seems to be truly in love with Starlight. At the end of the novel, however, as Starlight's luck takes a turn for the worse, we see Lexington's genuine feelings. Describe the nature of their relationship.

6. Religion and Christianity are prominent themes in *Truth Be Told*. At one point in the novel, the narrator explains that Grace "wasn't religious, although she'd tell anyone who'd listen that she was a Christian, serious in her love for Jesus"(page 41). Explain the difference between being Christian and being religious.

7. One of Grace's primary goals as a city councilwoman is to get a seat on the education committee so that she can lobby for school prayer. She believes this will be a way to return "morals and ethics" to young people. How do you feel about prayer in schools?

8. Sara Spears, Grace's nemesis from the Anti-Christian Coalition, remains hot on Grace's trail in search of any dirt. Grace decides that she must go public with the news of Conner's affair and his son, Solomon. Do you think her strategy is wise? How much does the public need to know about a politician's private life? Where should the line be drawn?

9. In Chapter 44, Grace tells her sister-in-law, Devry, that she hates "the fact that my husband had sex with a white woman"(page 348). How is the issue of race handled in the book?

10. In talking about Pilar's worsening condition, Lily says, "This is God's will"(page 368). What, if anything, does this suggest about Lily's attitude toward illness in general or AIDS in particular? What about the other characters? Does anyone in the novel extend real sympathy to Pilar and her condition?

11. Both Grace and her teenage daughter, Jayde, feel betrayed by Conner's hidden relationship with Pilar Cruise and the news of his having a son. How do you think you would have handled the situation? What keeps the family together in the end?

12. Betrayal and forgiveness are two themes that resonate throughout the novel. Discuss.